Abdullah al Asmari, grandson of the Emir of Rahsmani, the richest Arab oil-producing country, has been charged by the Emir with investing his country's superabundance of money. That task is to take him to the United States where he is to buy a few banks, and the first stop is California...
Nothing before in his experience has prepared him for this trip and the high life opened up to him by his friend Ali Hassan, the famous Egyptian movie star – the glamorous and willing starlets, parties where champagne flows and brawls follow, the carefree existence of the beautiful and the rich...

Also by Maggie Davis

ROMMEL'S GOLD

Maggie Davis

The Sheik

MAYFLOWER
GRANADA PUBLISHING
London Toronto Sydney New York

Published by Granada Publishing Limited in
Mayflower Books 1979

ISBN 0 583 12974 9

First published in Great Britain by
Hart-Davis, MacGibbon Ltd 1977
Copyright © Maggie Davis 1977

Granada Publishing Limited
Frogmore, St Albans, Herts AL2 2NF
and
3 Upper James Street, London W1R 4BP
1221 Avenue of the Americas, New York, NY 10020, USA
117 York Street, Sydney, NSW 2000, Australia
100 Skyway Avenue, Toronto, Ontario, Canada M9W 3A6
110 Northpark Centre, 2193 Johannesburg, South Africa
CML Centre, Queen & Wyndham, Auckland 1, New Zealand

Made and printed in Great Britain by
Richard Clay (The Chaucer Press) Ltd
Bungay, Suffolk
Set in Linotype Pilgrim

What's it like
to be *twenty-three* years old and
the richest man in the world?

The author gratefully acknowledges
the assistance of Richard Gary Davis
for his help with
military and aviation details.

ONE

At five o'clock, which was dawn, he drove his motorcycle down through the city and out the north highway to the tennis courts behind the Section A field of the abu Deis refinery. In every way now, as far as Abdullah was concerned, these first hours of the day were the best part of his life, filled with the solitude and freedom that had, since his return, been hard to find. With the throttle of the Harley-Davidson opened up and the concrete road unfolding like a pale string in front of him, he was at last completely alone in the most solitary place of all, the desert. And for a change he could do just about anything he wanted. When he was on his Harley there was no way even that his body-guard could follow him. At one particular stretch in the road he always zigzagged the bike from side to side, cutting the machine in great arcs just to savour the sense of release. The roadbed was hard to see at that speed and in that uncertain light and he knew if he hit a film of drifted sand he could go into a spin and perhaps crack up. But lately he had taken to thinking, not very seriously, that if he were going to die this would be a good place to do it, alone and in control of his life, and while he was feeling so good.

The desert at dawn was cold. The wind honed in the strings of the tennis racket strapped behind him and cut across his bare knees like a knife. By nine o'clock the desert heat would lie like a burning blanket over everything, stifling the desire to breathe, but now the air was clear and frigid and a glitter of frost edged the limestone rocks that dotted the sand flats. Behind him the sky was still black with a few dying stars; overhead it was chocolate brown paling to shades of mauve and umber, and straight ahead as the road swung east wide bands of sapphire shot with peacock blue and neon pink lined the horizon, showing the first reflections of a metallic sun. The whole sky as he rode into it was changing with the dawn. The lights of the refinery blazed blue-white like some Martian landscape. But in all this vastness there was not a sound. The noise of the Harley was like an invading army.

Dallman, the assistant engineer of Light Distillates was a good tennis player, not much older than he was, which was twenty-three, and about the same size and strength. Dallman had been especially recommended as a tennis partner by Sam Crossland, the director of Rahsmani Petrochemicals, one of the first oilmen in the Arabian Gulf, and longtime adviser to Abdullah's grandfather. The suggestion to Dallman by the director of the refinery division that Dallman might want to play tennis in the early mornings with the Emir's grandson was, as they all knew, about equal to a diplomatic appointment. What Abdullah liked was that it made no difference. In the eight months they had been playing since Abdullah had got back from college he had given the matches everything he had, and still the young American engineer had won about two-thirds of the games. Since they met to play good hard tennis and hardly ever talked, it could not be said that they were really friends. Which was just as well. Anything more in this part of the world was bound to be unnecessarily complicated. Especially with oil people.

Now, Dallman gave him a casual wave of the hand and they chose up for the serve.

Under the spheres and the ten-storey-high cylinders of the crackers the pot-pot of the tennis ball echoed flatly, lost in the silver surfaces, repeating in the backs like some ghostly tapping fingernail. On the high catwalk above them a couple of Asmari workers in red-checkered *kaffiyeh* headcloths watched them running about on the tennis courts, as small as ants to their eyes in the artificial moon-brilliance of the refinery floodlights. The game always stopped when the sun was up. Of the three sets that morning, Abdullah took two.

It was good that he had won. Losing always put him off in some vague way, accompanied by the feeling that he had not yet learned, in spite of four years at college, to take these things in the proper spirit.

Two hours later, bathed and shaved and dressed in a flowing white *disdasha*, and his own *kaffiyeh* held with the red and black silk rope that signified a sheik of the al Asmari, Abdullah sat in a canvas sling chair in the middle upper courtyard of his grandfather's house. He had been summoned for a meeting of the Emir's smaller council that was to begin at nine. Or nine-thirty. Or perhaps ten. Or as soon as his grandfather was through with the daily reading of the Qur'an that always headed up his schedule.

Abdullah picked away in a desultory fashion at a new pocket calculator with, as the literature assured him, a power supply guaranteed to last two years. It had been sent as an introductory gift by the manufacturer to his business offices in the city. He had had time to try out the memory function and a system of programmes that, by the insertion of a metal key, would put each into operation. It was a nice machine, very compact and uncomplicated. He had also had plenty of time to read all the booklets that had come with it, including the manufacturer's guarantee and the user's handbook, not once but twice while he had been sitting there, and he was growing restless. He was out of the habit completely of sitting, endlessly waiting, giving himself over to that blankness of mind with which, he told himself, one got through the damned dead spots of Arab life. There were many times when he had wished that he had his grandfather's talent for dropping into instant meditation, that sort of withdrawal into himself where – if there was nothing really going on – the old man could shut out boring talk and silently recite the *surahs* of the Qur'an to himself and be perfectly content and occupied. His grandfather had memorized the Holy Book as a result of his old-fashioned classical training, and it was amazing that he

13

could drag up a saying of the Prophet from memory and still find anything new and interesting in any of it. Abdullah seldom read anything but *Newsweek* and *Al Ahram* from Cairo, and as for his memory, he had a tendency to forget a subject unless there was something in it that he liked. Which had been a big problem at college; the things he liked often had little to do with what he was supposed to study.

It was said of Abdullah's father that he had had something of the same sort of mind, fickle and restless, and that he could not concentrate on anything much except for a few strange, erratic bursts – and then he was like a super-charged dynamo. At one time Prince Tewfik had decided to become a famous aviator and had rushed wildly through the books to the point where he could take and even pass the written examinations for his licence. There had been a terrible time keeping him out of airplanes. He had gone berserk on the Rahsmani airstrip and had tried to climb into the cockpit of one of the oil company airplanes and had stabbed two security guards before he was subdued. After which he had taken off to Switzerland for the usual prolonged rest and treatment. This had been just a few months before Abdullah was born.

The sad history of Abdullah's father was fairly well known; it would have been hard to keep secret the long string of incidents that had taken place, many of them before the eyes of the world. There was the time the Prince had stood stark naked in a window of the Dorchester Hotel in London prophesying the end of the world through fire and pestilence while the hotel staff struggled to break down the doors of the suite. All of which had been well covered in the London press. And the attack upon the zebras in the Monte Carlo zoo with the glass from a broken bottle, which had so horrified the French. But since his father's death his grandfather had forbidden anyone to speak of him or even refer in passing to those unhappy times. The Emir had spent too much time and money and agony on his son; it had been hard to arrange a marriage and even more difficult to see it consummated, and he wanted to take every care that this long-desired heir of the al Asmaris was not damaged in any way by the tales of his father, Prince Tewfik. Who had been called, when he was alive, simply The Lunatic.

The precaution had done little good. Abdullah knew all the stories of his crazy father backward and forward, his relatives had seen to that. One of the facts of life in the coastal emirates of the Arabian Gulf was to recognize that, family rivalries being what they were, cousins and uncles were natural enemies. There were more reasons than one for his grandfather's solicitude.

Naturally, since Abdullah had come back he frequently had to fight off the feeling that he was smothering. What else could one do, he asked himself, held down as he was in the lap of his family? *The lap of one's family*. He liked the expression, an American one, because it described just the way it was. At home, one was always in the lap of the family, the ample, all-encompassing crotch of Arab kinship. There was nothing like it in the world. He pictured it as about the size of one of the beds in the *hareem*, sinking a person down into its yielding, down-pillow softness, seeking to wipe out all desire for separation. Mother, brother, sister, grandfather – in the lap of the family they were all over you, constantly. The idea, he supposed, was to reinforce blood ties, to keep you from growing up, ever, and breaking away. For eight months he had not mentioned going out to the abu Deis refinery each morning to play tennis, although he was pretty sure his grandfather knew about it. Wadiyeh al Qasim, the bodyguard, knew where the ultimate loyalty lay and undoubtedly reported everything. Abdullah dreaded the inevitable conversation with his grandfather, which could come up at any time, about the reasons why he should stop. A conversation that would be, as always, couched in his grandfather's usual oblique terms but that would be a command nevertheless. His grandfather had only to look at a person and that was enough.

Abdullah punched up some current per-barrel figures from the abu Deis field on the calculator, watching the red lighted numbers silently march across the display. From time to time he went down to his offices in the tower of the Rahsmani Overseas Investment Corporation and read the reports that were always neatly laid out on his desk. He had been surrounded with oil production data or the talk of it since he had been able to walk, and he tried to keep up to date on the condition of Rahsmani oil. Which was, he told himself, the condition of Rahsmani and the condition of the al Asmaris from his grandfather the Emir down to the lowest labourer with a discarded rusting Volvo automobile in the yard of his government-provided modern concrete bungalow.

According to this year's figures, which were virtually the same as last year's figures, the Middle East provided some 60 per cent of total oil reserves in the world, and in the Middle East the emirate of Rahsmani ranked fifth after Kuwait, Saudi Arabia, Abu Dhabi, and Iran. To be fifth represented a big leap out of nowhere, for Rahsmani had come late into the oil picture. English and American drillers of forty years ago had found nothing in the Rahsmani desert in spite of years of prospecting and millions of dollars spent putting down dry wells. The south end of the country, which bordered the Trucial States, was still full of abandoned rigs around which the Bedouin now pastured their sheep. One oil company after another had come and gone in the southern desert, paying good prices for oil exploration rights and losing fortunes when luck and money ran out. The last combine of Texas independents had spent more than forty million dollars before pulling out. As it happened, the oil was not on the edge of the vast pool in the south but north, in the direction of Saudi Arabia and Kuwait. There was no telling about oil, as the oilmen said; sometimes it was where it ought to be and sometimes it was where all the geological surveys said it hadn't ought to be. Now in the north at Ras Deir the fields were pumping seventeen million tons of low sulphur crude under the administration of a number of companies who had chanced that the oil would be where it hadn't ought to be. Only a consortium of Royal Dutch Shell, British Petroleum, and two large American companies had had the financial strength to gamble on a strike in Rahsmani where so many others had gone broke, and their gamble had paid off in the billions. Production figures for the new fields could only be estimated. When Abdullah punched them up on the pocket calculator the figures ran off the red lighted display.

Estimating how many tons of oil there were under the desert in Rahsmani was like trying to count all the stars in the sky.

His grandfather, who had come from a long line of gulf brigands and pearl-fishing sheiks had a natural talent for money, even the tidal waves of dollars that had suddenly swept down on his country. Also, he had the examples of the other gulf states to study during the long, arid years. Two whole floors of the black-glass skyscraper in the city of Rahsmani that housed the Oil Directorate were devoted to a watchdog operation of oil income. The Accounting Department, a pet project of his grandfather's, was staffed by Lebanese and Iranian accountants who reported only to the Emir on the divisions of Asmari holdings. The arrangement was one of long standing. Even as far back as the nineteen thirties, when the fees from the drilling rights were about all of Rahsmani's income, his grandfather had kept the bookkeepers in an old pearl-factoring building outside the city, patrolled twenty-four hours a day by Bedouin guards. The buildings in those years weren't air conditioned and the clerks who had spent their time there said that with the heat, the isolation, and the ever-present Bedouin guards it was just like being in prison. His grandfather had even had a small restaurant installed, run by Pakistanis, so that it was not necessary for the employees to go home in the middle of the day to take lunch and the usual three-hour siesta. The rigours had been such that, if there had been any other way of making a living in Rahsmani, most of his employees would have quit.

But it had paid off. The Emir soon got a reputation as a tough man, a pretty good student of oil leases, and a fanatical Moslem with an almost religious dedication to accumulating and hanging on to his wealth. When the strikes had come in the north the Emir was ready with a royalty arrangement higher than any of his neighbours'. He had no intention of being as backward as the old Sheik of Bedida down the coast who would not spend a penny of his oil royalties on his starving, medieval little country but kept Maria Theresa gold pieces and millions in pound sterling notes in a side room of his palace until the rats had eaten through much of the paper money and a good part of the gold had fallen down the sluices between the walls and into the Arabian Gulf. Or the Saudis who with millions flowing into Riyadh had still managed to get deeply into debt in the fifties.

The head of the al Asmari tribe of Rahsmani considered himself an intelligent and educated man in the traditional Moslem fashion; he had nothing but contempt for the ragged, ignorant sheiks of the gulf who had struck it rich and could not begin to grasp the enormity of their sudden wealth. The al Asmari family had been pirates and robbers in their time, it was true, but they were also well connected through marriage with the Hashemi, the rulers of Mecca, who had led the struggle for independence against the Turks in the First World War. The Emir's first wife was a distant cousin of the Mufti of Jerusalem. Although it was said that the taint of schizophrenia that showed itself in his firstborn, Prince Tewfik, had come from that side of the family and not from the Asmaris, the Emir had never expressed any regret. Such things were in the hands of Allah, and unforeseeable.

Abdullah put the calculator on a table nearby and settled back in his chair. The waiting really put his nerves on edge. The courtyard was open to the sun and growing hot. He had chosen to sit outside by himself rather than be cooped up in one of the reception rooms, but the courtyard was not as comfortable as he had hoped. The roar of the window air conditioners was at his back, spurting hot blasts into the air. Added to that noise was the blare of his sister's television set tuned to the station in Kuwait. Even the splash of the fountain got on his nerves as it burbled endless gallons of precious desalinated water into the tile basin. His grandfather loved water with the passion of a true desert Arab, it was one of his great extravagances. Most of the highways in Rahsmani had been planted with oleanders, lavishly irrigated. Every turning in the fort seemed to have a fountain installed. There were sunken tubs in the family bathrooms big enough to swim in. And below the fort on the desert plain more than twenty acres had been irrigated to fix a garden the size of a municipal park with date palms, rose beds, banana trees, pomegranates, mangoes, and towering daturas. In the evenings the Emir would take his unfailing stroll in the oasis accompanied by his first wife and sometimes his second, a dozen Bedouin guards, assorted relatives including a flock of their children, the *ulemi* of the city mosques, a clutch of Burmese cats, and anyone else who cared to tag along. Irrigation ditches ran through the whole place in deep channels but his grandfather would plod in and out of the mud with magnificent indifference, picking fruit and handing it to anyone in the crowd who wished to eat.

The Emir had rejected the idea of moving out of the fort, which the Asmaris had held since the Portuguese left three hundred years ago, to build himself a modern palace in the style of his relatives, whose homes lined the highway like luxury hotels. Instead, the Emir had renovated the old fort piecemeal and at great expense, installing French and Italian bathrooms that were gorgeous but full of broken fixtures, partitioning old storerooms and breaking out walls to make courtyards and terraces. All of it had been furnished with expensive junk from department stores in Beirut and Cairo. Most of the rooms, although dazzlingly whitewashed and covered with Persian carpets, were cramped and kept the air of old barracks, which they once had been. The corridors of the fort were like tunnels in spots, hardly wide enough for two people to pass. Into every corner were crowded chandeliers and Italian sofas with gilt legs and damask coverings in Dayglo reds and blues.

In his own room Abdullah had piled most of the stuff into a corner. If he had wanted to buy his own furniture from New York or London, there would have been plenty of money, he had only to ask. But he had not been interested enough to bother. Most nights he slept out on the terrace with the stars over his head. During the day he didn't spend much time there except to change his clothes.

The Bedouin, Subah al Said, came into the courtyard with the child, Karim, in his arms. The boy was sucking, of all, half a hard-boiled egg, which had almost disintegrated in his hand. The yellow wet paste of the yolk was smeared down the front of his robe.

'Put the boy on his feet,' Abdullah snapped. It was something he said nearly every time he saw his son, but without much effect. 'If you continue to carry him about, as I have told you more than once, he will never learn to walk properly. Is this not a matter of truth?' Before the Bedouin could answer he went on, with mounting irritation, 'And what is that in his mouth? Who gives him things to chew on, like a rat, with the dribble hanging down his front?'

'Oh lord, the Lady Fawzia has given him thus, because he cried for it,' the Bedouin said, keeping his eyes cast down respectfully. But he oozed an air of great indifference. This, too, was something he had heard many times, nearly every time he brought the child to see his father, and the continuing conflicts between the young sheik and the child's mother were not any of his concern. Except, occasionally, as he got caught in between and had a shoe or a portable radio hurled at his head by one or the other. His responsibility was to the boy. He had taken his life's oath on it, this was the only son he would ever have. As part of this thought, he gave him an affectionate squeeze and the child grunted.

'God Almighty,' Abdullah said in English. He made an impatient gesture and the Bedouin put the child down, setting him on his feet with tender care.

Karim started toward him obediently. He really was, as Abdullah could see, unsteady on his feet. He hasn't had enough damned practice walking, he thought savagely, and he's too fat. Remembering American children the same age it seemed to him that by comparison his son was alarmingly backward.

'Papa,' the child said to him, trying to climb upon his leg.

'No, hell, stay away from me with all that crap on you,' Abdullah said, hastily fending him off. But then he caught the boy by the arm and drew him to one side so that he could look into his face.

The eyes were soft and brown and beautifully luminous. Just as, he remembered, his father's had been. Once he had woken in the middle of the night to find his father bending over him, that same shallow unfocused beauty like a light in the gloom. His father's eyes had been enormous, they dominated his face; they gave false witness to an intelligence that wasn't there except to niggle away at small thoughts like setting fire to the bedclothes or trying to throw somebody out the window. They had lived in a state of siege.

There wasn't much intelligence either that he could see reflected in his own child's face. But the eyes were round and open, the lips curling with a slow happiness. He loved the tall, explosive young man who was his father. 'Papa, read,' he said. He looked over his shoulder at the body-guard, wanting him to fetch a book.

'Le, le, there's no time to read to him from the picture-books now,' Abdullah said. 'I will go attend my grandfather in the council shortly.' But he felt like cursing. Was there no one to read to this kid besides himself? Fawzia barely knew enough to make her way through the newspaper, even if she had the inclination, which she didn't. His grandfather, like most of the men in the house, passed Karim from hand to hand and tickled and rumpled him like some sort of pet monkey, made to enjoy, but appeared to give little thought to any sort of education. Four was too young to educate, they told him.

He knew that wasn't true. At four American children went to nursery school or kindergarten. Subah, who would be with his son until one or the other of them died, was illiterate.

'Papa, read,' his son repeated, pushing him on the arm.

'Say, "O father, read to *me*," ' he corrected. Four years old and his kid couldn't even speak in sentences. He motioned for Subah to come and get him. 'Walk,' he snarled, and the Bedouin obediently took the child by the hand.

His son seemed willing enough to walk if you gave him a chance, he observed, watching them go. He got out of the chair and started toward the door leading to the women's quarters. It was the matter of stuffing his face with food every time you looked at him that had to be settled.

His sister came out of her room as he was going down the corridor. She was wearing blue jeans and a skimpy French knitted top and boutique jewellery and sandals, and he knew she had spent all morning getting herself together. She might have just stepped out into the streets of St Tropez, so pretty did she look. When actually she was seldom allowed out of the fort and even then only when heavily veiled and accompanied by a flock of bodyguards and women relations.

'Bibi, come in a minute, I want to talk to you,' she said urgently.

He gave her a wave of his hand. He knew what she wanted to talk about; they had been talking about it for six months and he had given her plenty of sympathy and encouragement and had even gone to see his grandmother about it, but there still wasn't much that he could do.

'Later, later,' he told her.

The corridor dropped to a flight of stairs in what had once been part of the magazine of the fort, now tastefully turned into a suite of ten rooms for Fawzia and Karim and her servants and her girlfriends and all the other people he always found collected there.

The television was turned on to the station in Kuwait here, also. The Kuwaitis had just recently started offering a daytime programme of soap operas produced in Cairo and the women of the household seldom missed a moment of them. Fawzia was lying on the floor with a couple of her girlfriends beside her, eating dates and American pretzels from the oil company commissary and drinking Coca-Cola. They didn't move when he came in, just lay there, their stares unwavering and insolent, their backsides turned up in generous curves like so many pigs. They wore the long traditional women's robe, hiked up at the hips, and their legs were unshaved.

'Out, out!' Abdullah shouted. He started swinging his arms in circles, sweeping all of them out, servants, girl-friends, the whole lot. 'Out – out –'

The maids rushed out. The girls got up slowly from the floor and sauntered off to an adjoining room, where he could hear them giggling and whispering as they pressed against the door.

He had been married to Fawzia at fourteen. It was a good enough age, as was customary, and the idea was to marry the young and keep them busy with sex, if this was what they wanted. Otherwise to deny it would make of the thing an obsession. And at fourteen he had been easy enough to please; at fourteen he was a grinning idiot led by his rela-tives to the sacrificial bed filled by Fawzia, who was nearly illiterate and hardly spoke to him at all during the first year. But like a decently brought up Asmari girl she had been rehearsed in a whole repertory of sexual nuances that she proceeded to exhaust him with, much as she now over-whelmed his son by cramming his mouth full of anything which he expressed the slightest desire to eat. Only unlike Karim, he had got sick of it. The first child, born when he was sixteen, had died of the usual summer diarrhoea and he could hardly bring himself to go back to her and conceive another. But his grandfather had been adamant. His grand-father had even bought him a concubine, an Armenian girl, very young and pretty, but that had been a disaster. He couldn't explain to his grandfather that he had had enough of these female animals, more of the same thing wasn't going to revive his interest, he wanted to forget about the whole thing. Yes, he was normal. He was not a pig, that was all. Fawzia was a pig.

He simply started yelling at her. There was no need to try to be reasonable. Once or twice in the past he had punched her and had given her a kick in the ribs while she was lying on the floor but she had only squealed like a trapped rabbit, her eyes hard, storing up resentment against some other day. God, this scene had been repeating itself in *hareems* for hundreds of years! Was it impossible for Arabs to ever learn?

'He's hungry!' she screamed at him. 'I give him food to eat because he's hungry!'

Now he swung at her with his foot because he was infuriated with her beyond all control and she caught it and held it and pulled it down against her breast. Her eyes were malevolent, like someone contemplating a goat about to be slaughtered for a feast. The top of the robe was falling open; her large moon-shaped breasts slung against the cloth while his foot, encased in its tennis shoe, was jammed into the cleft between them. 'My lord, look!' she mooed. She tried to move her legs wide apart so that the robe would fall open there. He sought a glimpse of the large fat globe of her pudenda, neatly hairless and kept that way by depilatories, and a roll of heavy thighs. It seemed to him that she had gained fifty pounds since he had last been to bed with her.

But all this was for the benefit of her girlfriends listening behind the door, and the maids, who had gone to hide somewhere, probably the roof where they could hear quite clearly all that was going on inside.

'By Allah,' he howled, beside himself. 'I'm going to kill you! Give me back my foot!'

The girls behind the door were in hysterics. He bent down to grab her hands and break her grip on his ankle and she seized him neatly, throwing his leg and foot up while he was off balance, up-ending him. He fell sprawling on the cushions. There were whoops and screams from the roof.

'Goddamn you!' He got on top of her body and got his hands into her hair and began methodically slamming her head into the tiles. She offered no resistance. He moved her head slightly to get it off the cushions and all the way on to the floor for greater impact. Somehow her nose had got hit; it began to bleed.

'Bibi – oh, name of God!' It was his sister behind him at the door. 'Bibi – Grandfather wants you! Bibi, let her go!'

His sister was on his back like a cat in an instant, her hands under his chin, pulling back his head to break his grip.

'Bibi – stop! She's only making a fool of you!'

His sister fell to screaming 'Bibi!' 'Bibi!' again and again and finally, with his head pulled back like that, he had to let Fawzia go. He knew what she meant. If he fractured Fawzia's skull it would only mean the doctor, explanations to his grandfather, some sort of large family explanation to Fawzia's family, who ran part of Rahsmani shipping and were not without consequence. And an indefinite, perhaps permanent loss of face in any part of the women's quarter. Everyone would know who had won. Even if Fawzia were dead by his own hand everyone would know who had won.

'You lump of grease,' he choked. He was almost blinded by his rage, he could hardly see. He got to his feet without his sister's help, pushing her aside. On the floor Fawzia lay panting, her eyes half closed, but deadly serious now. She pushed back the robe with both hands and lay there, legs spread apart, her nose and lip a bloody smear. If he got on top of her now, she would have an orgasm.

'She wants me to beat her, can't you see?' he shouted. 'If she can't get me to pay attention to her any other way, she'll do this. Look at her!'

'I don't want to look at her,' his sister said. 'Hush! Come away, Grandfather will be furious.'

'He can afford to be furious. He isn't married to her!'

But before his sister pulled him away he turned and spat accurately between Fawzia's sprawling legs.

'Are you mad?' his sister hissed. 'What a thing to do!'

'It was heartfelt,' he told her.

She dragged him out of the door, pushed him down the corridor, her hands in the small of his back.

'They are waiting for you. Grandfather sent for you a long time ago. Pray they don't find out you've been beating Fawzia's head on the floor in the *hareem*.' She switched to English as they came out into the courtyard. 'You act like such a child, really!'

She was sixteen, seven years younger than he was, and yet she frequently took this attitude. He was the child, she was the adult.

'Don't talk to me like that. I'm not a child. And don't say I'm crazy, either. That's a dirty word around here.'

There was blood all down the side of his robe from Fawzia's nose-bleed.

'Stop pushing me,' he told her. 'I can't go in there like this.'

But Subah appeared from one of the doors with a clean robe in his hand.

Every wall in this house has ears, Abdullah told himself, as the Bedouin pulled him out of the *disdasha*. He stood in his jockey shorts, still shivering with anger, while the body-guard slipped the other robe over his head. In about three minutes, he thought, Subah knows everything that's going on and has brought clean clothes. Just like that.

His sister had put a clean *kaffiyeh* on his head and was trying to adjust the folds.

'Smile on me, dear brother,' she said in Arabic. 'Bless me with one smile from fortune's lips!'

But he was not yet in the mood to be cajoled. Not even by his kid sister, who was probably his only friend in the whole world.

'Thanks a lot,' he said in English, and stalked off.

TWO

When Abdullah got there they were all in their usual places: the American in his khaki suit, the Englishman, his uncle Hakim, the concubine's son Ameen Said, and Sheik Fuad ibn Khas'al. This was the smaller council of the Emir Ibrahim al Sullakh al Said of the al Asmari of Rahsmani, the group the oil people referred to wittily as the Closet Cabinet. The council sat on several layers of Persian carpets, close under the low-hanging banks of fluorescent lights illuminating the central hall. Abdullah's grandfather liked lots of bright lights so that he could see what was going on, a precaution taken since the time when, several years ago, a would-be assassin had come lunging out of the shadows of a dimly lit mosque. Before each guest was a serving of Turkish coffee on a low wooden tambour. At intervals dates and hard candy were passed by silent servants. The Emir, being a strict Moslem, did not allow smoking in his presence.

The American, Sam Crossland, was a geologist from the University of Texas who had stayed on after the first wave of drilling companies had gone broke in the thirties, to act as technical adviser to the Emir. Since his advice back in those hardscrabble days had been to keep on issuing drilling permits to anybody who could pay for them, the Emir had found in him a man of great common sense. When the drilling paid off a decade or so later and the rich oil strikes had come in, Crossland was given most of the credit. Abdullah's grandfather liked anyone whom he considered lucky. The American was now head of the Rahsmani Petrochemical Division, a job with a title that told little of his real power.

Sitting in a heap of billowing traditional robes and looking, Abdullah always thought, as though his ulcers were kicking up again, was his half uncle the Sheik Hakim ibn Ibrahim al Asmari, son of the Emir's Sudanese second wife and OPEC delegate from Rahsmani, chairman of the board of the Rahsmani Oil Directorate, former Rahsmani Delegate to the United Nations (a job now held in rotation by two of his sons) and president of the Rahsmani Drilling Company where the rest of his sons and other relatives had been installed in high places.

The Englishman in a canvas bush jacket looking properly detached and agreeable was James Brooke-Cullingham, a very smart cookie, financial adviser to the Emir and last remaining unofficial representative of the departed British Protectorate.

On the other side of Brooke-Cullingham was Ameen Said, head of the Ministry of Education and Public Works, a graduate of the University of California at Berkeley and holder of a degree from the London School of Economics. Said was a product of the Emir's later years: although a half uncle, he was only five years older than Abdullah. He had considerable contact with the Palestinian refugees who made up a sizeable part of the country's population.

On the far right Sheik Fuad ibn Khas'al rose up like a grizzled mountain. The Sheik was a half brother of the Emir, had fought with him in the old days of feudal politicking and was head of the northern branch of the al Asmaris and sometime overlord to the wandering Bedouin who crossed back and forth over the Rahsmani–Saudi Arabian boundaries with their sheep. Sheik Fuad carried the title of Minister of Information although it was rumoured that he had never bothered to find out where the Ministry was located.

The Emir sat in an outsized gilt armchair the size of a throne, with special Reclino-rest construction so that he could elevate his legs during attacks of the gout. Behind him, as always, stood two Bedouin guards. To the rear and to one side of the throne there was a filigree wooden screen lined with red silk from which there drifted the scent of Joy perfume.

'Lord,' Abdullah muttered as he dropped to his knees in front of his grandfather. The Emir did not demand that his grandson kiss the hem of his robe but he was strict about the other formalities. Abdullah launched into the long formal greeting in Arabic and invocations of the blessings of God, and his grandfather responded in an offhand manner, although Abdullah could feel his eyes on him. He hoped he looked sufficiently neat and tidy and that his grandfather would overlook the fact that, in a rush, he had had only time to throw on a clean robe and a *kaffiyeh* without checking it out in a mirror. He was still sort of out of breath. Out of the corner of his eye he saw his grandfather's foot move slightly, impatiently. *And no mumbling.* Abdullah raised his voice. The business of a formal Arab greeting took so long and there were so many parts of it; he always felt self-conscious in front of Crossland and Brooke-Cullingham. The others, being Arabs, knew how it went.

Right in the middle of one of the flowery inquiries his grandfather leaned forward suddenly and put his hand on top of Abdullah's head. Abdullah stopped right where he was, the words frozen, and could not proceed. It was totally unexpected, the most unlikely thing for his grandfather to do in front of the others, and it took him completely off guard. When he looked up his grandfather was regarding him with a rather strange expression. It should have been a simple thing to look his grandfather in the eyes, but it wasn't. In front of the old man the years stripped away, leaving him feeling about five years old. Being down on his knees didn't help any.

But his grandfather said nothing. The hawklike nose that was the Emir's distinguishing feature was bent down now with age toward his upper lip; the prominent eyes with the half-dropped lids made him seem tranquil and inattentive, but they could also open wide and bulge with rage; the Emir had gained a lot of weight in recent years and it showed in his jowls and small, protruding mouth. The light beard was shaped to a point and stiffened with wax. Looking into that face it was easy to remember that the Emir had deposed his own father with the help of his half brother Fuad, and that his father's father had taken the sheikdom from his own brother, a coup that had seen the brother go off the wall of the fort and into the sea.

Hardly anyone was ever late to his grandfather's councils, either the Closet Cabinet or the fifty-man Council of State. But if anyone was to be, it was usually Abdullah. If his grandfather had meant to hit him on top of the head for it, he would have used a riding crop or the brass tray that stood on a stand by his side.

Instead, 'All things pass,' his grandfather said. His voice sounded tired. 'The man who has applied himself to learning must soon come to apply learning to knowledge of the world.'

Abdullah had to stop and think. He hadn't got his thoughts together properly, he had been in too much of a rush and he did not, in a manner of speaking, know where they were. Had they finished the business of greeting? He couldn't remember. With his grandfather things were alway the same, nothing out of the ordinary unless there was a reason for it. The Emir had said something about wisdom and learning, but Abdullah was not sure if there was supposed to be a response. He felt streams of nervous perspiration trickle down his back. Was it poetry? If so, he didn't have the frame of reference. Perhaps it was a philosophical observation. The Qur'an was full of them. But he was as incapable of this kind of classic Arabic quotation-stringing as someone born and raised in Chicago.

Maybe he's trying to trip me up, Abdullah thought. It was some test of manners and cultivation his grandfather had aimed at him, probably to needle him for being so late.

Abdullah set his jaw. Life in the lap of the family was one hurdle after another. You couldn't even breathe without somebody prodding you to see if you were paying attention. Usually his grandfather didn't single him out like this, a chewing out in his private apartments was more the Emir's style. On the other hand, he could be greatly angered. Especially if he had already heard about the row in the *hareem*.

In spite of everything Abdullah felt a sudden surge of obstinacy rising up in him. I can't be expected to cope with every damned thing, he told himself. For one thing, his education hadn't been like his grandfather's; he, Abdullah, had been raised with two languages, English as well as Arabic, he had been tutored by Englishmen, had two years of prep school in America and had gone to Yale. He had studied things his grandfather had never even thought of. Now he was expected to seize, identify, and return some proverb or some damned thing his grandfather had lobbed at him. Just, he supposed, to show that he had the best of two worlds.

The Emir sat, the folds of a white and gold *kaffiyeh* falling forward over sagging cheeks, the great beak of a nose sticking out between. I wish, Abdullah thought suddenly, I knew what in the hell my family wanted for me. I'm getting sick and tired of being shot down.

Not this time.

'Fortunate,' Abdullah said loudly, 'is he who is the master of a silent tongue. And wise are they who apply themselves to learning but yet know the true wisdom of the heart.' It sounded okay, he was just crazy enough to pull it off. 'But humble are the young in their ignorance, for theirs is not yet the learning and wisdom of the years.' He didn't dare to look his grandfather in the face to see how he was taking it. 'Wise are they who honour such spirit in youth, but even more fortunate are they who still seek after learning. Blessed are the humble. Twice blessed are the wise, and good are they in the eyes of the learned who are ignorant.'

He could have gone on, but something told him he should stop right there. When he sneaked a look it seemed that his grandfather appeared baffled.

There was a long, deep pause and he heard Crossland or Brooke-Cullingham cough behind him.

The Emir said, 'Well enough, well enough,' and continued to stare at him.

'Humble are they who have wisdom,' Abdullah added.

'Ummm.' His grandfather touched his lower lip with his finger. 'Truly, more humble than it would appear.' But the lip quirked upward, finally. 'Go and sit down.'

His knees were shaking as he backed away. Something had got into him, and his grandfather had let him get away with it. Abdullah kept his face smooth and unconcerned as he sat down next to Crossland. Brooke-Cullingham, whose Arabic was as good as the Emir's looked faintly amused. Abdullah saw Ameen Said lean forward and say something to his uncle Hakim, who responded without turning his head. Well, those two had it figured out, anyway; it would give them something to think about.

At some sort of signal that could not be seen or heard from where the council sat, one of the Bedouin guards was called to the filigree screen. The Bedouin came back with a folded piece of paper that he handed to the Emir. The old man held it up to the light and read it, taking his time, then crumpled it up and tossed it on to the brass tray at his side. There were already four or five crumpled pieces of paper there.

'Now, with due permission,' Brooke-Cullingham said. The Englishman had been making a report on the possibility of the United States government reopening antitrust hearings on major American oil companies, to take place before the elections. The subject under discussion was how many senators on the antitrust committee had been passed sizeable contributions for their campaign funds by the oil companies, and how many of them would keep this in mind when the congressional investigations started. Brooke-Cullingham didn't know. The oil companies, especially those who made up the Gulf Arabian Oil consortium in Rahsmani, kept this sort of negotiating to themselves. Since there were no Rahsmani representatives within Gulf Arabian or on the executive board of the consortium, there was no way of knowing without being told by Gulf Arabian itself. And GAROC wasn't saying.

It was their usual guessing game again, since the oil company always kept them in the dark about such things. Brooke-Cullingham's opinion was that there were at least two senators on the committee who could be counted on to keep the oil people out of trouble. One, Alf Hurt from Oklahoma, was the traditional standby, a senator from an old oil-producing state, as good as gold where oil interests were concerned. The rest of the names proposed by Brooke-Cullingham were greeted with blank stares or, in Hakim al Asmari's case, a shrug. In an election year things were difficult to predict. Not to have any more say than they did was exasperating.

'It's insanity,' Ameen Said spoke out suddenly, 'to be subject to the whims of these foreign governments! Our profits should not be decided by the acts of these stupid politicians in the United States Congress! What do they know of us? Nothing! It has been shown time and time again that American senators do not know how to identify the Arab oil-producing nations even when given a map! To such ignorance, now, do we depend for our prosperity!'

'Gerhardt of New Jersey is a possibility,' Brooke-Cullingham said. 'He's the one who took the oil tour here last year. The fat one, who wanted to ride a camel.'

'It was a highly select camel,' Fuad rumbled. 'It could not be known it would spit.' Sheik Fuad had supplied the camels for the congressional junket. It was still a touchy subject.

'But then,' Ameen Said continued bitterly, 'we must realize that Arabs are not members of this private club, this Western conspiracy of imperialist international oil companies and capitalist manipulators who seek to drain us dry of our oil with enormous profit to themselves! The oil monopolies and capitalist governments care nothing for the rights of oil-producing nations – they pump our oil at extravagant rates, bringing in more revenue than our country

33

needs! They have exploited us shamefully! They pay us royalties for our oil like money thrown to lackeys, and we are supposed to take it and know our place! They will never admit it is *our* oil, not theirs! But Arab oil belongs to the Arab people!'

No one said anything. The argument of participation by the oil-producing nations in the international oil companies operating inside their borders was something that went from meeting to meeting, just as it did in the Organization of Petroleum Exporting Countries and the other governments of the gulf states, but without much resolution. Mostly the Arab oil companies had long pressed for more control over their oil, preferably by admittance to the boards and decision-making offices of the oil companies. And always the big oil companies had shut their doors to them. The year before, when faced with a standoff in Abu Dhabi, the oil company there had been forced to raise oil royalty payments to the Abu Dhabians enormously; but in everything else the oil company hadn't given an inch. No Arabs inside, was the rule.

The alternative to some sort of representation within the oil companies themselves was the outright seizure of the oil fields by the Arab governments, and this was promoted by radicals everywhere within the Arab world. The militants wanted to see Arab oil companies pump and sell their own oil on the world market, from well head to refinery to tanker. How to do this without Western technicians and marketing agreements was the big problem.

Sam Crossland kept his silence. They hadn't had this sort of talk ten years ago when the Emir and his family had been willing to take their money and keep busy spending it. But it was becoming very fashionable these days to talk participation or seizure. It was all over the Arab world, even in states like Rahsmani that really didn't have much of an axe to grind, when you came right down to it. The old Emir was satisfied enough. But then he wasn't the generation of Third World politicians like his offspring from the left-hand side.

Crossland took off his glasses and wiped them with his handkerchief and held them up to the light to see if they were clean. In the old days when the Emir and his tribe supported themselves as desert brigands with a little piracy on the side, Sam Crossland had prospected the desert in a Ford truck. Out there, as he well remembered, a man's blood would literally boil in his veins if he stayed in the sun too long. Crossland had been shot at by desert tribes, run out of water and food, had come down with forty kinds of unknown fevers, and had been harassed and threatened by the very sheiks of Rahsmani who now owed their wealth to men like himself. As an old hand he couldn't say he was exactly bowled over with enthusiasm for the idea of having Arabs participate in the actual running of big operations like Gulf Arabian. As far as he was concerned these people – and he counted some friends among them – had a long way to go before they could handle that. As for nationalization – well it was hard not to give a big horselaugh to that one. After the first family fight over who was going to do what, their oil production would go haywire. These people, he thought, just never could remember that one well shut down could affect a whole field. And it was easy to spoil one well if you didn't know what you were doing.

Still, Crossland allowed, the big oil companies just couldn't be made to see that they were between the devil and the deep blue sea as far as the future was concerned. Some sort of change was coming in the Middle East, participation or nationalization, and there was no way that Crossland could see that anyone was going to stop it. The Saudis were already putting pressure on ARAMCO and it looked as though the U.S. State Department was backing the Saudis. There had been too much talk, too much political pressure from all over the Middle East for things not to change. And the fat little Arabian Gulf oil countries were as unstable as a plate full of jelly, too much money in too few hands, the power mostly held by a bunch of crumbling old men like the Emir of Rahsmani.

Ameen Said had just reminded them of Qaddafi in Libya, the Arab house revolutionary.

'Qaddafi is an idiot,' Sheik Hakim murmured with distaste. The Libyan president was not his idea of an Arab world statesman.

'He's not an idiot, he's a *bedu*!' old Fuad put in with a guffaw. The wandering men of the desert were notoriously simple-minded.

'Arab oil belongs to the Arabs!' Ameen Said cried. He leaned into the circle to yell at them. 'The oil belongs to Arab nations to produce and sell on the world market and not only this, but to use as a political weapon in the balance of world power! Not as it is now – taken away from us to be disposed of in Europe and Japan as these international monopolies see fit! When the oil is completely out of Western imperialist hands and into the hands of the Arabs where it belongs, then only will we see justice for our people!'

'Oh well,' Brooke-Cullingham murmured. These meetings of the small council were informal affairs, held mainly to update the Emir on what they had been doing and permit him to ask questions on one thing and another, which he could not do in the Council of State, where his remarks were prepared beforehand. Also, the smaller council was a good way for the Emir to keep the strings of power out of the way of the National Police and the governors of the districts and others who might want to make a bid for them. Although this was not much of a danger; in Rahsmani, as in most other gulf oil countries, most of the junior and middle-rank officials were reluctant to take much responsibility and were not notably energetic, either. Still, with Sheik Hakim's protégé carrying the banner for Third World militancy at the expense of everybody's patience, it had got out of hand.

It's possible, Brooke-Cullingham thought, we're coming into our own shifting of the balance of power right here, and sooner than we had thought. Since the Emir doesn't seem inclined to put a stop to what's going on, or can't, we might see Uncle Hakim – who's been promoting himself abroad with OPEC and OAPEC and the Arab League – in charge here soon with the upstart from the *hareem* as junior partner. Ameen Said is hand in glove with the radical factions and the Palestinians, and that's the coming fashion. All that remains is to get the family darling, Abdullah, out of the way. And slipping a dose of something into the old man's morning orange juice.

For Brooke-Cullingham it was all a matter of familiar patterns. It was really too bad, he told himself, that the British Protectorate was gone; the English had a way of handling tight spots that the Americans could never master. If the CIA was operating at all in Rahsmani they had precious little to show for it.

The Bedouin guard went to the screen behind the throne once more, came back with yet another note, which the Emir read as before, then crumpled up and tossed on the tray.

Abdullah had been watching these trips, too. Now he thought, My grandmother's at him again, but he's just ignoring her. I wonder what she's trying to get through.

His grandmother always sat behind the wooden screen at council meetings. Her presence was well known, but it was a gross impropriety to mention it. At the larger Council of State she merely looked out from a hole in the red silk and took note of what was going on. She was a pretty good politician and his grandfather had, generally, considerable respect for her opinions. But in the Closet Cabinet she sent out notes to him and sometimes this got on the Emir's nerves.

The Council had heard Ameen Said's views on the Western imperialist conspiracy before and said nothing. Hakim al Asmari sat motionless behind his customary dark eyeglasses, playing out his unknowable game. The Emir fingered his beard and looked remote, obviously having withdrawn into one of his meditations. Abdullah put his hands behind his head and gave a long stretch. It looked as though no one was going to come out and propose government seizure of Rahsmani's oil wells at this time.

But Ameen Said was not ready to give up.

'They will have to account for their attitudes, these capitalist exploiters and ignorant Western politicians,' he shouted. 'We know their contempt for us! Just because they are stuffing us with money, they feel they can dismiss us as totally corrupted, dependent clients!'

Brooke-Cullingham lifted his hand to his nose quickly to hide a smile. Corruption was hardly the word. With the oil revenues running thousands of millions of pounds sterling a year the Arab oil states were a Disneyland of riches. In fifteen years Rahsmani had grown from a poverty-stricken slice of desert coast into a nation of highways, the city filled with modern hotels and fantastic palaces to house the al Asmari family. The world's largest desalinization plant made the desert bloom, there was an international airport with a fleet of customized jet liners for the Emir and his relatives. The shops were stuffed with expensive imported clothes, food, watches, perfumes, and jewellery. Enough hospitals to provide a bed for every ten Rahsmanis had been rushed into construction, and there were over two hundred schools at the primary level alone. The Emir was thinking of building a university as soon as there were enough educated Rahsmani youth to make up a student body. One in three Rahsmanis now owned an automobile and this number included women and children – and women were not allowed to drive. On the desert highways large imported cars rusted in the sand, wrecked at high speeds or with the engines seized up because the owners had forgot to put in any oil, or even abandoned because of a flat tyre. A few of the Emir's relatives who had managed to slip out from under his control had racked up millions of dollars in gambling losses at the casinos in Monte Carlo. A few more, deep into government corruption, were providently storing their money away in Swiss banks.

Not even the Arabian nights could compete with the reality.

All was not smooth sailing, even so. There had been a few

minor riots and disturbances down in the city the year before, mainly by Palestinians and other Arab nationals who were excluded from Rahsmani citizenship. The protests had called for representation in the Rahsmani government, greater controls on the National Police, and the encouragement of political parties, including lifting the ban on communists. None of which had been granted.

'There is much to consider,' the Emir said, coming back from his contemplations. He inclined his head toward Brooke-Cullingham. 'We must address ourselves to the money.'

The Englishman picked up a stack of papers from the cushion beside him. 'I think,' he said, 'we're still looking at the need to take action on a large supply of uninvested capital.' With a deliberate gesture he passed the papers over to Abdullah.

'I've read them,' Abdullah said shortly.

It was true. The business of handing him the papers was only a gesture to acknowledge Abdullah's position as chairman of Rahsmani National Industries and the Rahsmani Overseas Investment Corporation, organizations that did little or nothing without orders from his grandfather. They had made the same gesture, passed the same papers six months ago when the latest projection of investment possibilities was first issued, without having the Emir take any action. What it all meant was, the oil money was backing up again.

There was a story among the oil companies that when the Emir of Rahsmani knelt down to pray five times a day he invariably ended up by pleading, 'Allah, tell me and my people, what are we to do with all our money?'

It was just as simple as that. They were already flying any Rahsmani who needed medical attention to any hospital in London or New York cost-free. Every man, woman, and child had a television set, a house, and two of anything else. The city was overcrowded with construction, some of it put up so quickly it was already falling down. There wasn't much more they could do at home except perhaps supply

39

every Rahsmani family with its very own moon rocket.

'Perhaps,' the Emir said gently, 'we should consider some banks outside of Rahsmani, ones with large vaults to put the money.'

There was an appreciative silence. They all knew the Emir's views on the Moslem prohibition against lending money at interest. For several years the old man had been consulting his religious advisers about the Rahsmani Insurance Company and whether insurance premiums violated religious laws. With the result that the first policy had yet to be written. The government and business firms struggled to work around the obstacle. Rahsmani shipping was insured by Lloyd's of London through a branch office in Bombay. However, there were indications that the Emir was considering some sort of compromise.

'There are some small banks in California that look rather interesting,' Brooke-Cullingham said. The descriptions, compiled by Roehart and Simpson, their agents in New York, had been looked at before.

'We must not overlook the list of allocations,' Hakim put in smoothly.

'We would consider increasing it by ten per cent,' the Emir said. He appeared to have already thought it over. 'And the Palestinians by seventeen per cent.'

That would cause a ripple in the city. The Palestinians had a permanent mission and an office building of their own, donated by the government.

Nice work, Brooke-Cullingham thought. Perfect timing. All the handouts had been neatly sandwiched in. Subventions to Egypt and Jordan were already running in the neighbourhood of $140,000,000 a year; even he didn't know the breakdown of the list of the others.

'It would be necessary to have descriptions of these banks,' the Emir cautioned, 'and also to take a look at them and see how large the storage places for money would be. How many banks would be suitable?'

'Honoured Presence, the descriptions are available,' Brooke-Cullingham told him. The old boy had forgot they had them in hand six months ago. 'To look at one or two would be proper, as American banks are not yet a glut on the market.'

'These are sound banks?'

'Rather small, sound banks, yes. Well run, and in a prosperous part of the country.'

Abdullah watched his grandfather closely. The Emir was well aware of the effect he was having, and enjoyed it. To choose a few banks to buy, as casually as one would choose a few oranges in the market. It was his way of amusing himself and at the same time making a point for all of them to note. Particularly Hakim. The power was still in his hands.

And it was. The decisions made in the Closet Cabinet were often passed out immediately, without waiting for the Council of State. A supply of messengers was always kept waiting outside the hall for fast contact with the whole structure of Rahsmani operations, the Rahsmani Oil Tanker Company, the Petrochemical Company, the Rahsmani Chemical Fertilizer Company, and Abdullah's own domain, the Rahsmani Overseas Investment Corporation and Rahsmani National Industries.

The Emir leaned back in his chair and made a small noise in the back of his throat. It was the signal for adjournment. If there was other business, it would have to be put over to the next council. The Emir's secretary would advise them of the exact date. But as the members got to their feet the Emir singled out Abdullah with a pointed finger.

It meant his grandfather would see him in his apartments in about fifteen minutes.

The discussion was coming, and Abdullah was going to catch hell, he was sure of it.

He was at his grandfather's private living quarters in fifteen minutes but he was kept waiting, standing outside the door some fifteen or twenty minutes more. When the Emir's bodyservant finally let him in Abdullah went through the small antechamber built in the old style with vaulted ceiling and painted columns, and then into the bedroom.

Adbullah saw his grandfather lying in the super king-sized bed custom-made in Paris, a cloth dipped in cologne over his eyes, stripped down to the old-fashioned pantaloons he wore under his robe and an embroidered vest. The air conditioners were off, his grandmother sat beyond the open doors to the terrace, leafing through a magazine.

The cloth over the eyes puzzled Abdullah. When his grandfather sat up and took it away, he saw lines of strain around the lids. Another headache.

'Permit me, lord, I hope you are not unwell?'

His grandfather shot him a look of irritation.

'I am always well. Allah has seen fit to make me strong and grant me many years,' he snapped.

'It is so. I only wondered –'

'Bibi!' his grandmother called.

He went out on the terrace and she rose from her chair to grab him by both arms and look searchingly into his face.

'My little lion,' she crooned. 'My black gazelle of the desert, how beautiful you are! You sat like a king, an emperor, with those others! Look, Ibrahim, is he not magnificent today?'

His grandfather, who had got up and was now wiping his face with the perfumed cloth, only grunted.

'You are lovely as ever, lady,' Abdullah said awkwardly. It was hard to deal with his grandmother's effusions, even though he ought to be used to them by now.

What he had told her was perfectly true. She was still lovely. She was now over sixty years old but she had an erect and well-proportioned figure and had not run to fat as was so common in Rahsmani women. Her hair was copper-coloured and swept high in elaborate puffs and curls, the colour and the style kept that way by her French hair-dresser, and her skin, the luscious fair skin so prized by upper-class Arabs was a testimonial to the roomful of creams, machines, cosmetics, and treatments she was constantly buying to keep it that way. There was still a great deal of tension between his grandmother and the second wife, the Sudanese woman, and it hadn't relaxed as they grew older. In the middle of the day his grandfather went to the second wife's apartments off the women's quarter and from there he often visited the two women in the *hareem*, one of them Ameen Said's mother, and took some time to talk to a couple of teenage daughters of whom he was especially fond. His grandmother still took these visits poorly, although there were no longer the hysterical scenes he remembered from his childhood.

His grandmother had managed to keep her position as first wife all these years, however, in spite of formidable odds. But then, she had been a beauty, an educated woman, and she was a cousin of the cousin of the former Mufti of Jerusalem. Her father had been a prominent merchant in Jaffa and a judge in the Moslem courts, and she had gone, for about six months, to the American school in Beirut. This must have been back in the twenties. The other women of the Emir's household were nothing, she always maintained, merely the usual assortment of her husband's passing fancies. Except for the dark Sudanese. That one had been as clever a woman as herself and had managed to challenge her power successfully, not the least by giving the Emir several sons. When his grandmother had given birth to only one child, and that with difficulty.

What her life had been like since her marriage Abdullah knew all too well. The confinement of the strict Arab society of the gulf states, the constant intriguing both inside the *hareem* and in the Emir's government, the power she held over his grandfather, shot through with bitter, screaming arguments, and finally the tragedy of her only son, Prince Tewfik. A few years ago she had managed a trip to Paris, escorted by guards and heavily veiled women friends, but that was about all. She subscribed to every magazine out of the Arab capitals, was a member of several English and American book clubs, and kept up a correspondence with friends in Cairo and Amman. She was still a delightful companion, fiery-eyed and a bit strident at times, but with a great talent for wit; she could make his grand-

43

father dissolve into wheezes of laughter as no one else could. The effort at her age was tremendous: the elaborate coiffures, the diamonds and ropes of precious stones, the makeup, the highly coloured Paris gowns of chiffon trails and metallic splendour, but the overall effect was as invincible as a great, glittering, fantastical dragon bird out of the tales of the *djinns*. Only when you got up close did you see the heavy layer of Estée Lauder crème foundation, the wrinkles at the corners of the eyes and the crepey flesh of her throat.

Abdullah rested his hands lightly on his grandmother's shoulders and kissed her on the mouth. She was remarkably tall for a woman of her generation, even against his own height, which was over six feet.

'Yes, he is magnificent,' his grandfather said, coming to the door. 'Also a discoverer of unknown poets, as has been revealed.'

So his grandfather knew, after all. 'Lord, forgive –' Abdullah began. He might as well try to make some explanation and get it over with. He was even now regretting his attack of the smarts.

His grandfather put up his hand. 'Please do not concern yourself. It was very clever. However, I am thinking that I am at a loss to understand what was the inspiration for it all.'

'I thought you wanted –' Abdullah said, and found that the words died in his mouth. Another misunderstanding all around. He had gone off half-cocked and had made a fool of himself. Again.

His grandfather must have sensed what he was thinking. The corners of his mouth lifted in the usual ironic quirk. 'An effort all unexpected, surely, but not unappreciated,' was all he said.

'It was very naughty,' his grandmother said under her breath. But she winked.

Well, at least he gives me credit, Abdullah thought, relieved. That was something.

'You should try to eat more, darling,' his grandmother

44

murmured. She pinched the flesh of his ribs. 'Bibi, you are so thin!'

'I eat like a horse, Grandmother,' he assured her. It had got so she mentioned this every time. He was thin, but hardly skinny.

'Stop, stop,' his grandfather said, dismissing all this with a wave of his hands. He motioned them to sit down in the wicker chairs on the terrace. The rooms of the Emir's private apartment were high up in the fort and overlooked the harbour. Beyond them the sea was burning sapphire and the sky white hot. The servant brought in a tray of coffee and *loukhoum* candy but his grandfather dismissed that, too, shooing him out.

When they were at last alone his grandfather said, lifting his chin imperiously and half closing his eyes, 'The man who has applied himself to learning must soon come to apply that learning to the knowledge of the world. Of all things there comes a time of fruition.' It was the statement with which he had greeted his grandson at the council meeting. 'I have been thinking on it, it has been much on my mind. Tell me,' he said abruptly, 'are you now this man?'

Abdullah hesitated a moment before he could think of an answer.

'I am that man if you wish me to be, Grandfather.'

The Emir sat back in the wicker chair and regarded him with an approving look.

'Good, good, this is what I had hoped to hear. Abdullah ibn Tewfik al Asmari, I wish you to go to the United States and buy these banks.'

'Yes, Grandfather.' It was good form to conceal his surprise.

'The Englishman will go with you accompanied by the assistant who does most of his work –' he inclined his head towards his wife, who supplied the name. 'Yes, Adam Russell. Also the secretaries and stenographers, as many as may be needed. I wish also for you to have with you at all times Wadiyeh al Qasim, whom I have seen you take pains

45

to avoid these past months, much against my desires. He has been rebuked.'

'Grandfather —'

'Rebuked only, not punished.'

Abdullah was relieved. He didn't want his personal body-guard flogged, as was customary, for something that was his own fault. Since Wadiyeh belonged to him, he was supposed to have full control, but that wasn't always the case. It was a good sign that his grandfather had respected his wishes.

His grandmother reached over and patted his hand with her own diamond-covered one.

'Darling, this is a great responsibility. I am so happy for you.'

His grandfather made an impatient noise. 'Enough, enough, we have not come to that yet; leave him alone.' The Emir lowered his heavy eyelids until his eyes seemed almost completely closed, like a hawk in evening. 'You will go to New York and meet with our agents there and then you will go on to the place where the banks are located, to study and assess this possible purchase. While this is going on, Crossland will go to New York and make sufficient preparations – *which I wish only to be done at this time* – for you to meet with the presidents and directors of the Gulf Arabian Oil Company. Some of them you have met before, some of them you have not.'

Gulf Arabian was the international consortium that operated the fields in the north of Rahsmani. Abdullah was stunned, unable to move, feeling his grandfather's hooded eyes on him.

'If this can be done, Grandfather.' He was thinking that Crossland, flying into New York alone to set up a meeting that would have to include Gulf Arabian's British and Dutch members, as well as American, would have little time to get it all together. But his grandfather wanted it done while he was still in California. So there was to be no advance notice.

It was a lot to absorb all at once. Negotiations with the

oil combine were normally his uncle Hakim's area. After all, Hakim was the OPEC delegate, he had the data, the current demands, including the new Saudi proposals for ARAMCO, the history of past negotiations for participation – such as they were – at his fingertips. But Hakim was not to know about any of this, apparently, until the meeting with GAROC was over with. A whole new ball game, then, cutting out or bypassing his uncle's carefully gained power structure, including most of the sycophants in the Rahsmani Oil Directorate, and last but not least ignoring their spokesman for the Third World, Ameen Said. Down inside himself Abdullah allowed himself the equivalent of a small, amazed whistle. Right off the wall! he thought. He saw his grandfather in a sudden new light. The old man sitting in front of him in a vest that barely covered his flabby stomach, legs in pantaloons crossed European-style, still had the cunning for which he was famous. His grandfather was not sinking into the sunset quite yet. He'd known what the story was all along.

'In this meeting with the directors and so forth of the Gulf Arabian Oil Company,' his grandfather went on, 'I wish you to present my feelings on the present situation of Rahsmani oil operations. That is, I wish you to talk most earnestly and with the help of the information which I will give you, concerning participation of Rahsmani nationals in this company's production and marketing. We wish to be represented.'

Abdullah fixed his eyes on the upper right-hand side of his grandfather's vest and let his face show nothing. But he was thinking, I'm to present the case again for Rahsmani participation in GAROC at high levels, and *I'm* to do it. I'm going to New York with Crossland and the secretaries and briefcases full of arguments but when we come right down to it, there's only me. GAROC can only come to one conclusion when I make my speech, that I'm the candidate, their new vice president, if we can make them see their way clear to such a step.

In quick succession he thought:

47

My grandfather, of all the gulf rulers, is going to push this first. It's going to reverberate through the oil companies like a bomb blast.

It's going to be me, for some reason, and nobody else. Not Hakim, who is going to cut somebody's throat when he hears of it.

It's not going to work.

'Yes, Grandfather,' he said finally. There was nothing else for him to say.

'In presenting my desire for Rahsmani participation in Gulf Arabian Oil to these presidents and directors, I wish you to emphasize that, if they and other oil companies do not finally allow participation now, they will be faced with a more serious threat of nationalization or seizure than they have faced before.' His grandfather held up his hand, not to be interrupted. 'Not only in this country, but in the other nations of the Arabian Gulf in the not too distant future. I believe the situation has now become critical. There is continuing interference and pressure by the Palestinians and other radical factions to bring about the seizure of the oil companies as a political measure. That is, not only to consolidate power in the Middle East and relieve us of Western domination, but in the more conservative states such as our own – where they think we love our money too much – to assure this power by' – his grandfather paused with distaste – 'this so-called people's revolution. It is my desire that you understand this.'

Abdullah nodded, unable to speak. His grandfather was saying that they no longer could afford to stall around with GAROC, in the hope of maintaining the status quo. Any Arab government that resisted the pressures to nationalize the foreign oil companies was open to some radical-inspired change in that government. His grandfather was saying that this could happen in the sheikdoms of the gulf if participation were not brought about, fast. Even their neighbours the Saudis had had their problems in the past.

'Surely GAROC and some of the other companies have considered some part of this,' Abdullah said carefully.

48

'They have means of gathering information. It is said they work closely with the CIA.'

'They have means of gathering information, yes,' the Emir said. 'But it is the nature of all large and powerful bodies, whether they are industries or governments, to avoid the thought of possible change. It is written – wealth and power dull the imagination. Eventually all powerful bodies such as oil companies come to believe only what they wish to believe. And especially these Western corporations find it difficult to give up their idea that we are so ignorant and backward in the gulf states that we will be passive and happy with our riches for yet another generation. By that time, as they see it, the oil will have run out and they will no longer be involved. It is to be hoped that you will find some of the presidents and directors with their faculties still alert and responsive to what you will say. Change, whether they wish to acknowledge it or not, appears to be close at hand.' The Emir motioned to his wife, who went to the bedroom and returned with a small, folded piece of paper. 'Read this and after you have read it I wish you to burn it. Yes, I wish you to burn it here, after you have read it.'

His grandfather still did not trust him completely. It was a small hedge against his well-known carelessness.

There were only two paragraphs. The Emir's tiny, neat Arabic script detailed the workings of Rahsmani's sizeable Palestinian population in conjunction with several underground revolutionary groups in Rahsmani that he, Abdullah, didn't even know existed. From the million-dollar donations granted by the Rahsmani government each year to the various Palestinian groups, there was a figure on how much was sent abroad to finance guerrilla operations. And there were ties to Egyptian and Iraqi leftist groups. Several names in Syria, who were the receivers.

His grandfather put his hands together and assumed a judicious expression.

'Naturally when one considers all this, there is a danger that we insist on the obvious. For above all things we do not wish to appear to cry for help. On the contrary, of all the small states in the gulf we can contain an uprising of foreign nationals well enough. But this subversion is most dangerous. If such a threat can become apparent here it can happen elsewhere. It is sad that with one successful revolutionary attempt there would be others, to make all the gulf oil nations fall at once.'

It was a lot to consider. 'To make one big state,' Abdullah said. There had been mention of something of the sort before.

'That is one of their dreams, doubtless. And one can consider that these things work in the opposite way, also. If the Saudis or the Kuwaitis become uneasy again, they may think of annexation of the small states before this can happen. As always, the big fish are sure to be hungry to eat the small ones.'

'Yes, Grandfather,' Abdullah said.

'Therefore,' the Emir said, fingers tapping together pensively, 'it is past time for these oil companies to think constructively of participation rather than to be adamant, ignoring the threat of revolution and seizure. A threat that, if it should come about, would bring about a shifting of world political balance. Perhaps not to Western advantage.'

'You expect me to say this.'

'I expect you to say it, and well.'

As his grandfather was pointing out, the argument was not exactly new. The obstinacy of the oil companies in the face of radical pressures in the Arabian Gulf was hard to understand. They certainly couldn't be ignorant of the fact that in the past ten years the influx of Arab nationals like the Palestinians had altered gulf oil state populations drastically. In Rahsmani the foreigners were in the majority, and only the government's refusal to grant them citizenship kept them politically powerless. But none of the gulf oil states had done much to prevent the takeover of most of the government jobs by the hard-working foreigners. His grandfather maintained a strong National Police force that was practically an army, and a secret police arm that reported directly to the Emir. But they were all well aware of how many refugee Arabs actually ran much of the country.

'You may ask why I have chosen you to do this,' his grandfather said softly.

Abdullah hadn't wondered about it. On the contrary, he was just surprised that it had come up so suddenly. He knew his grandfather's reluctance full well. It had dragged on for years.

'Grandfather,' he said, 'there just isn't anybody else.'

It wasn't that he was the most talented or best qualified – his grandfather had made himself clear on that point many times – but everything else was pretty obvious. The old man has got to trust me to do it right, he thought. God knows it must have cost him nights of agony to come to this decision. He still regards me, deep in his heart, as a half-assed kid, one who will do well enough in this life just not setting fire to the house like his lunatic father.

It's putting a lot on me, he thought. His stomach knotted painfully. I haven't prepared myself – my grandfather hasn't prepared me, either because he's been too stubborn to face the fact that I am, after all, the legitimate heir, whatever else I may lack. And hell, I don't know that anybody could be ready for this, this sudden assumption of responsibility for the welfare of nations, the fate of gulf politics, possible revolutionary takeovers – you name it!

'I will do anything you want me to do,' Abdullah said, feeling for once genuinely humble. He read the paper over again, hoping that he would not forget anything, that the tiny cramped handwriting would remain forever burned in his memory. Then he did as his grandfather wished, he set fire to the paper with a match and dropped the remains on the tiles to let them burn.

For once his grandmother did not reach out to touch him, pat him, or even try to speak. Her eyes were soft with worry.

'It is all right, lady,' he told her. 'I am able to take care of myself. Pray that I will do what grandfather wishes, and with great success.'

'Yes, pray,' his grandfather muttered. 'I will talk to you about this again. In the meantime you are not to mention what we have said to anyone.' His grandfather stood up. He looked as though he wanted to go lie down and resume his rest. The terrace was growing very hot. It was time to shut the blinds and turn on the air conditioners.

Abdullah made his way back through the bedroom, following his grandfather. There was more he had to say, but he didn't know how to begin.

'Grandfather,' he said. It probably wasn't the time to bring it up, but he was feeling suddenly crowded, as though there would never be any more time as there had been before, exactly. His life had so many things in it now, as a result of these past few minutes, that it felt as though it had virtually exploded. 'Grandfather, consider Layla.' He wanted to put in a good word for his sister before things got so complicated he couldn't attend to it.

It was, as he had sensed, a bad time to bring it up.

'It is settled,' his grandfather said.

'Grandfather, she doesn't *want* to get married; she doesn't like this man. Nobody as far as I can see has a damned thing good to say for this Saudi. Can't you let her wait a while longer, anyway? This guy is a real nit; he doesn't have the brains of an ostrich and he seems to combine all the worst lunacies of the Sauds. How is he going to treat my sister when he's been through half the whores in Cairo and Beirut? To say nothing of France and Italy!'

'Bibi –' his grandmother rushed in, caught him by the arm. 'Darling, not now! Not now!'

'It is settled,' his grandfather said shortly.

'Grandfather, she *hates* him, she'd rather not get married at all! Can't you just let her *not* get married, instead of marrying her off to this slob because of politics with the Sauds? Layla's the sort of girl who could give up sex if she had to. That is, not ever having had any, she wouldn't miss it,' he added. It seemed like a reasonable argument. 'She could become a – a – religious, a dedicated Moslem –'

'*Silence!*' his grandfather shouted.

It was obvious some of the newfound responsibility and trust wasn't working. Abdullah drew himself up tall, almost as tall as his grandfather, and met him straight on.

'Now look, Grandfather – honoured lord – I know Layla's only a female but she's my sister, too. I'm concerned with her welfare. She's serious; she doesn't *want* to get married!'

'*What?*' his grandfather roared, face contorted. 'Your sister does not *want*? What is this you are saying to me?'

'She's my sister,' Abdullah said stubbornly. His hands were sweating. 'Look, Grandfather, she's only a little girl –'

'ALLAH WILL –' his grandfather yelled.

His grandmother rushed between them, screaming. 'No, Ibrahim, don't!'

Abdullah backed away. God, his grandfather was getting ready to curse him! He had no idea the subject of Layla would lead to this. They were all under a terrible strain, that was the trouble. And dimly, he thought, He doesn't want her to do it, either, it's against his best judgment, but he thinks it's a good way to keep avenues open with the Saudis. He doesn't want Layla to go to that hellhole Riyadh and be locked up for life in a Saudi *hareem* like something out of the middle ages. But he's going to do it, anyway.

'ALLAH WON'T!' Abdullah yelled back at him. 'God won't help you in this, old man! You'd better reconsider!' His grandfather had better do something – he didn't need the marriage all that much for one thing. There were other ways to cosy up to the Saudis.

'AAAhhhrrrr!' his grandfather roared, lunging for him.

His grandmother hurled herself at Abdullah.

'Are you trying to kill him?' she shrieked.

Abdullah was startled. Kill him? The Emir stood there with his arms raised over his head, his face a ripe purple with rage and frustration. Not the least of which was this confrontation with his grandson after he had given him the responsibility of an all-important matter. His nose was the colour of eggplant, the veins standing out in it like knots.

'Make him go lie down!' Abdullah yelled at his grandmother. 'Before he has a goddamned stroke!'

He flung himself at the door, felt the servant and the two bodyguards rush past him into the bedroom. At the bottom of the steps that led to the corridor and then the central hall he stopped and leaned up against the wall, panting. He closed his eyes.

Two screaming rows in one day, and God knows the consequences! It seemed he wasn't going forward so much as zooming backward at a great rate. His grandfather would have apoplexy, now, thinking about his decision to send him to meet with GAROC. And to make matters worse, it really looked as though his grandfather didn't have anyone else to turn to.

I've got to go to see my mother, he thought.

THREE

It was noon and a hundred and seven degrees Fahrenheit in the shade, time for lunch and certainly too hot to travel anywhere. But Abdullah roared out of the garage on the Harley, recklessly cutting through the Emir's precious park and the grove of banana trees instead of taking the road, hitting the mud and water of the irrigation ditches and chopping off leaves and fruit as he went. A few gardeners, caught unawares in the greenery, ran for their lives. Abdullah came out of the garden and on to the highway, shearing in front of a truck and just missing a taxicab in the other lane. The taxi driver leaned out of the cab window and shook his fist and screamed and then, seeing who it was, quickly ducked back in again.

Well it doesn't matter, Abdullah told himself. I've done what I've done and it either works out or it doesn't. I've been in some kind of trouble all my life, nobody's ever treated me like anything but a child or a potential lunatic. But in spite of what's happened I know I can go to the U.S., I know I'm capable of meeting with the executive board of GAROC, and who knows? I've got some sort of chance of swinging it. Anyway, Hakim is out. He's pushed himself out in front with OPEC and the Arab League trying to make the world think that he's the real brains in Rahsmani. Instead of my grandfather.

Passing between two cars, Abdullah allowed himself to dwell bitterly on family ties. *My grandfather.* We make such a big deal of the Arab family and the bonds of kinship but when you come right down to it, he's a hard man to get close to, a hard man even to like. At the core there's something ruthless, untouched by sentiment. He hadn't hesitated to kick his own father off the throne when the time came.

You had to realize that in a lot of ways his grandfather came close to what the Westerners saw as the stereotype of the bloodthirsty Arab, cunning and cruel like old ibn Saud and the rest of the old-timers. Before attacks of the gout had slowed him down the Emir and his cousin Sheik Fuad used to hunt the desert gazelle with hawks from the back of a jeep: the hawk swooped down on the racing gazelle and slashed out its eyes with its talons, then the sheiks picked off the blinded animal with high-powered rifles as it staggered around on the sands. It was a bloody mess but they called it sport and enjoyed it immensely. They were genuinely unable to see why foreigners were so horrified. And in the old days his grandfather used to preside over executions, death being the penalty for practically everything, watching a man's head being lopped off without turning a hair.

And it's still in him, Abdullah thought. He's cruel and ruthless, he doesn't hesitate to use anybody when he has to. Even now he's using me, using Layla, even Hakim. When my grandfather needed somebody to deal with the oil companies he let Hakim handle it, letting him go as far as he could as long as he was useful. Now that Hakim's power is getting too great, he's going to bypass him.

If he can get away with it, Abdullah thought. If he doesn't carry it off, we're all in for a big change. Things certainly won't stand still.

For a second Abdullah wondered what it would be like if his grandfather were deposed and Hakim al Asmari declared himself Emir, taking the government into his own hands. It wasn't the most unlikely thing in the world. The way politics went in the gulf sheikdoms it was the rule rather than the exception.

I'd be out in a hurry, he told himself. If they were smart and pulled a bloodless coup to keep looking good in the eyes of the world then Grandfather would be shunted off to some place in the desert where they could keep him safely locked up, and I'd be lucky if they'd give me some money and let me go into exile. I'm not much of a political force; that's probably what would happen. Then I suppose I'd live abroad. He tried to think of some possible places. London. Paris. Rome. None of them struck a spark. He couldn't see himself living out the rest of his life as some fossilized political refugee. He could live in the United States, maybe go back to college and take a Ph.D. in something. But he hadn't been all that fond of his college days, Yale University, in fact any place that came to mind.

The trouble with me, he told himself, is that I don't know where home is. It sounds silly, but it's the truth. I've been all over, lived in the East and the West – half of my head is either one or the other – and I've had enough money to visit every place and buy anything I wanted to and I don't know where to find home. The thought jarred him. Everybody had to have a home, not to have a home was absurd. But Rahsmani? Why was it that Rahsmani, where he had been born and where he had lived for three-quarters of his life, didn't seem like home, either?

The highway traffic was thinning out a bit in the noonday heat, most of the cars cutting off the side roads into the city. He was passing along that stretch of road where the shoulders had been planted with miles of brilliant oleanders. Beyond the hedges stood the palaces of all the Asmari family, who had been given easy government jobs. The residences looked like copies of the Rahsmani Hilton, set behind high walls of concrete studded with broken glass to keep out intruders. And with good reason. As the road swung north it passed through the shantytowns that had sprung up in the last few years, filled with the Egyptians, Iranians, Iraqis, Jordanians, and Saudis who had come swarming into the country in search of work and who now made up almost half of the population. Most of them had no trouble finding jobs, as the desire to do a hard day's work was fast going out of the Rahsmanis.

Abdullah never passed the shantytowns without a feeling of revulsion. In a country that had more money than it could handle it was incongruous to come on these miles of shacks standing out like scabs on the landscape. Not all the outsiders lived here. The better educated, such as the Palestinians, found office jobs, a lot of them high up in the government, and they worked hard, ignoring the Rahsmanis, who gave nonsensical orders and often didn't bother to show up at their desks. But the rest, the unskilled poor who swept the streets and washed the dishes in the hotels and the other dirty jobs the Rahsmanis wouldn't stoop to, these people backed up in the slums. They couldn't buy land or go into business without a deadhead Rahsmani partner or even get a doctor without paying for it. While for the Rahsmanis, virtually everything was free.

What Ameen Said kept telling them was true enough – you couldn't put it out of your mind just because of the jargon about struggling masses and imperialist domination. This was what it was all about, the people who lived in the shacks under the constant stink of burning oil, with no water or sewage, the houses lit only with primitive gas flares at night. Nothing about the way these people existed was going to make them love the Rahsmanis.

Not that the Rahsmanis were 100 per cent happy in paradise, either. As the Harley roared past the skyscrapers of the Emir Ibrahim Medical Centre he remembered the reports that the outpatients in the mental wings had risen from a couple of hundred in the sixties to nearly twenty thousand the year before.

You couldn't drag an impoverished desert people out of nothing and into a billion-dollar fairyland without having something give. There had been some talk about the deterioration of the national character and the takeover of so many high-level jobs by the immigrants. Some of the *ulemi* of the mosques had even suggested to his grandfather that some way should be found to slow it all down, give the Rahsmanis some time to catch up emotionally and culturally with their money. As, for instance, a cutback in the lavish government benefits, offering bonuses for those who took real jobs and worked hard at them. But his grandfather knew full well that wouldn't work; he'd have the whole country against him. Besides, no one had figured out how to do it. Even the Emir had a hard time keeping up with all the money.

I've picked a crazy time and place to be alive, Abdullah thought. There's no doubt about it, Rahsmani is like something my father would have dreamed up in his craziest moments.

As the highway left the outskirts of the city and entered the desert it was better, as it always was. Abdullah adjusted his goggles, opened up the Harley, and took a deep breath of relief. The desert stretched away on both sides in a glitter of heat waves and sand dunes and occasional clusters of limestone rocks eroded by wind and sand. The sky at midday was a colourless void, burning like a furnace. On the horizon in the west showed the barren hills of the Rub' al Khali, the Empty Quarter of the Saudi Arabian desert where nothing lived. Along the road, which had been the original oil company highway, he passed corrugated huts and sites of the dry wells, the tombstones of millions of dollars spent for so many years looking for the oil in the place where it wasn't.

As always, his spirits rose with the sense of space and speed. There was still some kind of desert blood in him, he told himself, the same sort of stuff that ran in the veins of his grandfather and old Fuad and all the desert people who had pitched their black woollen tents out here in past centuries and had lived by the rising and setting of the sun and wherever one could find water and pasturage for the sheep. He breathed freer, his blood began to rise, and if it wasn't for the need to keep his grip on the handlebars of the Harley at the speed he was going he would have liked to throw his arms wide and let out one of those long, undulating yells of the Bedouin. Something in him really responded to the desert and the vast aloneness – if one had no home, how about No Home, No Place – the emptiness of the soul and the peace of spirit that was out here? I think I could live a long time in the desert, he told himself exultantly. This isn't Rahsmani or the rest of the world; it's the absence of everything, it's a place where you either find yourself or you lose yourself. But one way or the other it doesn't matter. Here you can have a life without meaning, but really *empty* of meaning and not just all screwed up. Just to lie flat on the sands and look up into the stars and dissolve into nothingness – maybe that was the answer.

He slowed the Harley down to about fifty, took his hands off the handlebars anyway and just rode along, his arms flung wide, feeling the heat and the wind tear through his hair, lick at the flesh of his face, and press his clothes against his body. If a truck or a car came along right then, he would really look out of his mind, shades of poor Prince Tewfik, but he didn't care. Shit, this was the place to get it all together, in the great No Place, flying along like a bird, his hands cutting the wind like wings!

'Ullah – ullah – Allah – Allah – Allah Akbar!' he yelled, the rolling consonants coming out in a burst of intoxication. God is great, there is no God but the One God! The Arab's call to God, who dwells in the desert whirlwind and the burning sun.

He rode on, his arms held out, his knees gripping the Harley under him until he could begin to feel the strain. But he didn't mind; the moment was so good he couldn't bear to cut it short. He yelled again.

Something went by him, a bird or a desert locust that he couldn't see, and he grabbed the handlebars quickly. Something like that could throw you off. He didn't want to crack up out there so far from anything. Something went by him again, invisible, but with a small rush of wind, faint sound. Then he thought, Hey, what was that? What was that? Then there were more than two of them and something seized the front wheel of the bike, cracking it like a sledge-hammer and trying to rip it out of his hands.

He was lucky he had slowed down. The front wheel went berserk, turned sideways, and he felt himself going up and forward over the handlebars as if a giant hand were dragging him inexorably, to fly in the air, since to fly was what he had wanted so much.

'Hey!' he said in horror and surprise. The earth came up to deal him a terrible smack and he felt his body shaking and flopping against the rocks, finally coming to rest in a small pocket of wind-scooped sand.

Another bird or locust came by with the same rush of sound, and then there was nothing more.

He lay there for about fifteen minutes, his eyes closed against the sun, a spray of sand on his dry lips, thinking, Some son of a bitch, some unclean offspring of a camel was shooting at me with a rifle. I know what a 30-30 sounds like. Some son of a bitch was shooting at me out here from behind some rocks or something and he was trying to kill me. Some son of a whore of the streets was trying to take my life. He tried to stop it, to get control of himself, but his breath was coming in big ragged gasps that sounded like sobs. I'm just shaken up, I'm not dead, I don't think I'm even hurt. So stop it.

Still, it was a long time before he could roll over and get to his knees, wondering if whoever it was, was going to fire again. After a time he crawled along the shoulder of the road and took a good look at the Harley, lying half upright against some rocks. He inspected the front wheel. Some of the wire spokes were broken but the wheel itself looked as though it could hold up. The tyre wasn't flat, nor the frame bent out of shape. The bullet had just caught the spokes.

He pulled the machine upright, looked it over carefully a second time and then slung his leg over the seat. I've got to get out of here, he told himself. I'll pass out with sunstroke if I stay much longer. And the only way I'm going to get out is on the Harley.

Allah is great, there is No God but the One God, he prayed and kicked down the starter. The machine came alive with a great rattling, some damned thing torn loose, and he hoped it wasn't anything important. If someone still had a rifle on him out there he had no time to worry about it.

The wheels spun on the sand and he tried to kick the Harley along with one foot. He got the machine up to the shoulder of the road and it slid back down again once but then, the rear wheel finding a grip on some pebbles, it suddenly roared forward and up on to the road. If somebody was still out there behind the rocks they still had another chance for a shot at him. It all depended on how fast he could get out of there. The Harley skidded from one side of the road to the other, the damaged front wheel bumping erratically. He couldn't do over thirty-five, he found, wrestling with it, but it had to get him away from there, that's all there was to it.

Gradually he got some speed into the machine, the wheel still bumping and shying as he turned north down the highway. Behind him there was only silence.

Two miles that side of Ras Deir and the neat, modern city the Gulf Arabian Oil Company had erected was a little dispensary, dating from the early days of oil exploration. The building wasn't much, just a pleasant concrete villa that had gone to seed under the sandstorms and winds of the desert. The dispensary wasn't going to be repaired, there was already a plan to move it into a new building in the oil city itself. But for the time being it was just as Abdullah remembered it. It was also the first place one came to on the highway.

The last half mile he had to push the Harley; it had broken down completely. Now he shoved it into the dispensary yard and left it leaning against the porch, and came heavily up the steps and inside. One of the little Indian girls on the practical nursing staff took one look at him and squealed, and then ran off to get help.

Abdullah kept going. He knew his way around the place. The dispensary had been opened when Ras Deir was just a makeshift settlement of Nissen huts. It had come into being to deal with what the early oilmen called the Second Baby

Syndrome among the Rahsmani women, the oil company volunteering the building and the staff because of so many calls, in those days, for company doctors to help women dying in childbirth. Atresia, which was its medical name, was the result of stuffing the Rahsmani women's vaginas with rock salt after childbirth, to insure the husband's sexual pleasure after the first child was born by inducing a thick, constricted layer of scar tissue on the vaginal walls, tightening it back up. Since most of the girls had submitted to circumcision, anyway, with most of the clitoris and labia sliced off, they took the rock salting stoically. They saw it as divorce insurance. It was only when the second child was about to be born that the trouble started. The walls of the vagina were so thick with scar tissue the birth canal would refuse to give, usually with the mother and child dying in agony and exhaustion. The Second Baby Syndrome was so horrible to the early oilmen that they pressured the company for funds not only to build a dispensary to perform surgery on mothers in labour, but also to set up a clinic to educate them out of the practice. Now the little villa concerned itself mostly with the dispensing of birth control pills and condoms and was gradually shutting down operations.

Abdullah walked into the back examining rooms and Sally Boggs was there, winding a bandage around a cut in a Bedouin woman's arm. When she looked up and saw him standing there she said nothing for a few seconds and then, 'Go into the other room before you scare somebody to death.'

He had to grin. That was pretty cool, when she hadn't seen him in so long a time, not for about four years. You couldn't shake up Sally.

The summer he was eighteen he had been sent up to work a few weeks in the oil company fields – work that actually turned out to be more of a VIP tour than anything else – and he had got to know the dispensary nurse pretty well. She had bandaged him up once or twice when he had got cut in the fields and her impact on him had been considerable. She was tall and blonde, somewhere in her thirties, with a wide mouth and a steely, casual air that implied she could handle anything. But she was gorgeous; she was almost as tall as he was with long yellow hair that was silk in the hand, a whole skein of it, and round, heavy breasts and magnificent buttocks. And she wore glasses. At that time he had never been close to an American woman. He had only the usual contacts of his two years at prep school with faculty wives and girls at mixers, which were hardly contacts at all. When she bent over him to put a piece of surgical tape across his arm he had held his breath, sickeningly dizzy at her closeness.

Now she came and turned on the water at the sink to wet some gauze and only said, 'Abdullah, long time no see. Have you taken a look at yourself in the mirror?'

'Not yet,' he told her.

'Then don't. You're a mess.' She started to work on him, pulling back his sleeves and his pants legs to find cuts and scrapes he didn't realize he had. 'You want to tell me what happened to you?'

'I cracked up my bike, the Harley-Davidson,' he told her. 'About five miles south on the highway.'

'You would.'

She still moved like the essence of American sexual queendom, the blonde amazon who ministered to men on World War Two cinema battlefields while shells shook the field hospital, who wisecracked and sang like Barbra Streisand while chorus boys lay at her feet and who tortured James Bond with a gold-tipped cigarette as he lusted for her. It was incredible that she should turn up in a starched nurse's uniform in an oil company dispensary in the desert, but there she was. Well now, he noticed, she looked a bit older, maybe forty, and the backs of her hands were tough and worn.

'What have you been doing, Abdullah,' she said, 'in all these years since last I saw you?' She took a lighted instrument and looked into his eyes. 'Hit your head? You don't feel concussed?'

'No,' he told her, wincing from the light and the crack on both knees she had dealt him to test his reflexes. 'I, uh, have a son, now.' He couldn't think of anything else to say. His voice sounded alarmingly shy.

'Oh? First baby?'

'No, second.'

She looked at him quizzically. 'How old are you, about twenty-two?'

'Twenty-three.'

You see, she always had this effect on him; she interrogated him like some inspector of secret police. She also made him feel that she was standing in judgment somehow, and that he was always trying to measure up to some ideal she held that no one could really measure up to.

'And how old is your boy? Any cracked ribs?' She squeezed him painfully through his chest.

'No. Four,' he said. He was sure he was all right.

She gave a sigh. 'You people! I suppose you already have a couple of hundred wives.'

No one else among the oil company people would dare to talk to him like that, he knew. Not that they thought so much of him personally, but he was the grandson and heir of the Emir. Even the lower levels of the Asmari family were treated like grand dukes. Stupid grand dukes, but grand dukes nevertheless. But Sally Boggs talked this way to everybody. He was tempted to tell her what had really happened to him. He had to tell somebody, he was still in a state of shock.

'I was married at fourteen,' he told her. 'Only one wife. My wife – she had the first child ten months later and it died. But it was only a girl.'

'Oh *come* now,' she said.

Well, that had just slipped out. It was the Arab side of him talking.

'Listen,' he said. He opened his mouth to tell her that someone had shot at him on the road and that it had shaken him up so that he could hardly think straight. It wasn't every day that somebody tried to kill you.

'What?' she said.

It was too complicated. He had better leave her out of it.

'I'm thinking of sending my son to nursery school,' he said.

She looked at him over the top of her glasses.

'I don't want him to be raised in the *hareem*,' he told her. 'You should know what it's like. He doesn't get to play with other children, only those dumb brats of my cousin's, and he's four years old and I think he should be talking fairly well, but he isn't.'

'And the mother?'

'She's a cow. Listen, have you ever seen Sesame Street?'

'Sure, we have it here on videotape.'

'That's what I want for my son. Pictures, stories, seeing other types of kids. He's got to be prepared for the world he's going to live in, not a bunch of women living in the Middle Ages.'

'Why don't you just buy it?'

'Buy what?'

'Sesame Street.'

He turned a dark red and she saw what was happening because she gave a click between her teeth. 'Okay, Abdullah, cool it, it was only a smart crack. None of your temper tantrums, okay?' Before he could say anything she went on, 'If your kid's four he ought to be talking very well unless he's got, one, some sort of physiological problem; two, he's a little retarded mentally; or three, he's retarded socially. How do you feel about him? Has he got all his marbles?'

'Yes,' he said slowly, 'I think he's very bright.'

'Nothing wrong with his health?'

'No, no, he's got all the doctors in Rahsmani.'

'Then you're probably right. If his mother's not doing much of anything for him and he doesn't get to play with other kids maybe he needs nursery school.'

He hadn't thought about that. It would be difficult, though. None of the Rahsmani families that he knew sent their children to nursery school. The traditional attitude was that the mother should have the son with her in the

66

early years. It was one of the ways that she could be assured of his being tied to her later on. No conservative family would think of breaking the custom. He knew his grandmother wouldn't. Not to send her baby grandson down in the city to mix with the foreigners and force some idiotic premature schooling on him. Look at the problems the Americans had with bad, disrespectful children and juvenile delinquency, she would say.

'It's going to be tough. Traditional families don't do that sort of thing. They think any child under five is a baby, really a baby. And that the mother should have a chance to spoil them rotten before they get away.'

'Then organize one of your own. That's what the wife of President Kennedy did. She had a nursery school for her little girl right in the White House.'

Abdullah shut his eyes. He, a male, organizing a nursery school? He tried to think of someone who could do it for him. All of the women of the Emir's household were too confined. They wouldn't know how to organize something like a nursery school. His grandmother could, but she'd be opposed to it and wouldn't. He would have to get Sam Crossland to suggest some American woman living in the city. He would have to get approval from his grandfather to have a foreign woman do this. He didn't even like to think of asking approval for such a project with the Emir.

He sighed.

'Is there a telephone?' he asked her. 'I will have to call back and get someone to come for me with a car. Can I leave the Harley where it is?'

'Of course,' she said, and led him into the dispensary office.

Abdullah called his office, told them merely that the Harley had broken down on the road to Ras Deir and to send the bodyguard, Wadiyeh al Qasim, with a car right away, as he was tired and wanted to get on with it. He wanted to see his mother and then start back.

When he came out of the office Sally Boggs was nowhere in sight. He wandered along the hall until he came to a room where a group of the Indian nurses were gathered around a woman on a table, who was groaning loudly, and Sally Boggs was down at her spraddled legs trying to lift one foot into a metal stirrup. She looked up only long enough to give him a wave of her hand and he rushed away. He didn't like to see things like that, a crowd of women and examinations or other things going on. They shouldn't have left the door open.

That summer when he was eighteen he had come back to see Sally Boggs at the dispensary, at an hour when he knew she was locking up. He had thought it all out, it was his last night at the oil fields and he knew he was returning to the city to leave all this behind, and it didn't matter what he did. He had come at her in the little examining room like a lion, taking her by surprise. There was no room to get past him. At eighteen he had grown to his full height and he was as tough and lean as a Bedouin. She had gone down sprawling on the floor of the dispensary, no fighting or screaming but still trying to match her strength against him, and he had clawed at her clothes until he had some room and then he had simply driven himself into her and had continued to do so, again and again, until he could hear the slap of her buttocks on the tile floor from the force of it. Then she began to go, Oh God, Oh God, because he was pounding her to the fullest limit, this Great Goddess he was holding down under him, her glasses knocked off, her big breasts sticking out from her open uniform. But he had had her. And he had done it to prove, he supposed, that she was just like any other woman and being who he was, he could have her. But afterward it was like nothing had happened at all. She got up while he was still lying there trembling and buttoned up her uniform and, putting on her glasses, said, 'Beat it.' That was all.

She was incredible. Nothing would ever really conquer her. She would look Death itself in the face and make some sarcastic remark, or stare it down.

His mother's house was ten miles past Ras Deir. When

Wadiyeh al Qasim the bodyguard came with one of the Cadillacs from the fort they drove straight through the oil city and its serene ranch-style houses, the swimming pools and the tennis courts, the movie theatre and the community centre and all that made it look like some modern American city transplanted here in the desert. It grew bigger as GAROC opened the new wells. At least there was no separation here between Rahsmanis and the others: Americans, English, Pakistanis, Indians, Rahsmanis, and other Arabs lived together, side by side, sharing in everything the city had to offer. It was one of the few places Rahsmanis flocked to and worked hard, and the ones who lived here were far different from those in the rest of the country. The population of the city was thirty thousand, and still growing.

About fifty miles to the north the Japanese combine was drilling offshore in the Persian Gulf, the first of the new concessions on the underwater shelf. The Japanese had paid enormous rates for the drilling rights but they, too, were trying to break the hold of the international oil companies who sold to them. Now they were exploring in the gulf states; they were smart and well organized and, it was to be hoped, would put some pressure on the oil monopolies. At least so his grandfather figured.

His mother's house was back from the road in a settlement of her branch of the tribe of Asmaris. It was the usual gaudy new house in a vague Mediterranean style, surrounded by the smaller, ordinary bungalows the government provided. It was strange how the various tribes still clung to their territories. There was nothing much to recommend this part of the north except that it was where this tribe had always lived even when they camped in black woollen tents.

The front garden was empty and Abdullah had trouble getting into the house because the front door was locked. He went around the terrace, past the empty, neglected swimming pool, trying the windows and the door handles until he found one that was open. Down the hall he found a woman crouched against a door and he sent her to look for

69

his mother. There was a radio going and the smell of cooking and he looked at his watch and wondered if he had come at a mealtime. It was three o'clock.

At last his mother appeared, drifting toward him with a great shyness, a small fattish woman in a satin Western-style housecoat that he realized she had put on just to meet him. She had on lipstick, but it was hurriedly smeared.

'Mother?' he said. It was always this way, this rising note in his voice, as though he was afraid he wasn't going to know her. She smiled, ducked her body, and then reached out to snatch his hands and bring them to her mouth, covering them with kisses. Some women, probably her sisters, lurked in the hallway, hiding their faces with their head-cloths.

'Come and eat,' she said softly, tugging at him. Her fingers touched his dirty clothes, the tears in his shirt and a smear of blood, and she gave a small cry of dismay.

'Do not concern yourself, lady,' he said quickly. 'I fell from my motorbike.' He was not sure she knew what a motorcycle was. Had she ever seen one? He translated it into Arabic as the two-wheeled machine with the gasoline motor that runs on the highway and she nodded and smiled, yes, yes, until he was not sure if she understood what he was saying at all.

He refused something to eat and she was disappointed. They sat down on two ornate chairs by an empty fireplace, their knees touching, and her sister brought in a platter of dishes and bottles of Coca-Cola, which he refused. Abdullah took his mother's hand in his and looked into her face. He had come this long way to speak to her but the sight of the brown, plump face with the inquiring expression completely distracted him. All he could think was, they married her to my father, my grandfather did, and she slept with my father the lunatic in all his violent madness and submitted to sex with the man who would bend over her in the heart of the night laughing like some demon from hell while holding a knife at her throat. Or fire. My father's great talent was for fire. He loved to get up while everybody else was asleep and fix little surprises, set fire to the bedclothes and the curtains and heap the clothes from the closet in the middle of the room to get a bonfire started. Once, they tell me, he filled a bathtub with water and tried to drown me in it. She was married to all this in the name of getting an heir and if she expected something more from life, she's never mentioned it.

She was looking at him happily, her eyes full of admiration.

I wonder what she thinks of me, Abdullah thought. Other than the great lord, the Emir's grandson, this man before her now who, for all she knows, rides horses like the wind in the desert as her brothers did, deflowers hundreds of virgins and performs other mighty deeds in the world of men. Does she remember anything of *me*, even as I was a child?

'Mother,' he said, 'come down to my grandfather's house and be with Layla, my sister.'

She drew back, her mouth a round O in her face. Ehe covered her mouth with her hand, looking away.

'Lady, listen to me speak, it is of most urgency. I wish you to be with my sister, to comfort and soothe her as she does not want this marriage, it is something which makes her heart weep.'

Speak to my grandfather, dammit, issue an ultimatum. Raise hell in the *hareem* if he says no and get all the women to screaming and wailing and breaking up the furniture the way it's been done a thousand times. His mother knew full well that his grandmother didn't want her there. His grandmother had eased her out once she had done her duty because his grandmother didn't like the northern Asmaris; she considered them to be an uncouth, backward bunch of people. But his mother could swing her weight if she wanted to. Fuad was her uncle.

'Bring your sisters,' he told her. 'Gather the women unto my sister, let them be true kinswomen to her in her time of unhappiness.'

But his mother had assumed a blank expression.

71

'It is forbidden,' she murmured.

'Nothing's forbidden,' he told her. 'I wish you to come down for a while and stay with my sister. Your daughter needs you, O Mother. Open up your heart and listen to my words. I am your son; I say that you should. Come to your daughter and help her, for she does not want this marriage.'

But his mother regarded him curiously, as if for the life of her she could not understand why he should ask such a thing.

'Allah is good,' she said. 'God provides. It is therefore not to grieve.' She touched his hand hesitantly with her finger-tips. 'Do not worry yourself with this, my flower, my beautiful leopard. Layla is a woman, she must do what women do.'

He sat staring at her for a moment and then he threw himself back and clutched his head in complete despair.

'Oh, HELL!' he shouted. This from his mother, now, the one who had been shipped down from the north and married to his crazy father when no other woman in the country would get near him! Of all the people in the world, she was the one who should have the most understanding.

God, he didn't even have any influence with his own mother; his grandmother pulled more weight than he did! He got up, gave the chair a kick and it fell over on its back. His mother had drawn away in alarm, her hands thrust out protestingly, little fat fingers spread. The sisters beyond the door gave a concerted wail.

'Crap!' he yelled. 'Don't start that – I'm not going to start throwing things around!' No one spoke English here, it only made it worse. They looked as though a *djinn* had possessed him. 'All right, all right,' he said, striding up and down the room, 'just give me a minute. I've got a lot on my mind. I've got a goddamn headache.' He didn't know how to deal with them. Maybe he should send for a truck, round them all up, and force them to go back with him. But he knew that wouldn't work. They would just lie down on the

72

floor and scream and refuse to budge, like so many obdurate bundles.

One of the women brought in a tray with a large brass pot of Turkish coffee. Everything on it was rattling as she set it down. She was shaking all over. Abdullah glared at it. The temptation was great to pick the thing up and hurl it against the wall.

'Mother,' he said. 'I do not wish to take coffee. Nor dates. Nor candy, nor anything else. It is not my stomach which is empty but my heart. I wish you to come and help my sister. That is what I desire.'

But his mother just sat, looking frightened and blank. He could tell it was no use.

Abdullah dispensed with the formal good-byes. It would have been a nice gesture of respect; it would have smoothed things over, but he was shaking in frustration and disappointment himself, and he did not trust himself to stay any longer than he had to. He gave her an obligatory kiss and strode out of the house. A faint smell followed him, sesame seed oil, frying meat, the incense with which they freshened the rooms. It made him sick.

Abdullah slept in the car and woke only when they were coming into the city. It was late but the hard bright sunshine of evening still held. The air was exhausted with heat; no breeze from the sea moved anywhere. When Wadiyeh started to turn off at the road to the fort he stopped him.

'No, I do not desire to go there,' he said. 'Drive around.'

He still had his headache and his muscles were beginning to stiffen up from the fall from the Harley. He needed some time. It was better, the shape he was in, to come in after dark and go to his rooms unnoticed. He was too damned tired and confused to handle anything else.

'Lord –' the Bedouin began.

' "Drive around," I said. "Anyplace." '

They circled through the city, past the beachfront hotels, the plaza, and the park with its veil of water sprays pumping to keep it green. Past the banks and office buildings of the financial district, all hot, hard, smooth surfaces. The people in the streets looked sun-beaten, hurrying to the nearest air conditioning. Some of the shops were already putting down their metal shutters.

'Mansur, that's it,' Abdullah said suddenly. 'Take me to my cousin Mansur's house.'

'Oh no, lord Abdullah!' the Bedouin protested. He knew better than that.

'Take me, or I will break all your fingers,' Abdullah told him.

The Bedouin smiled then, faintly, but he turned off to the right. It wasn't far. They went down the Boulevard Hakim al Asmari and out the flat stretches of the coast where the great rich had their villas. The lights of the Rahsmani International Airport winked in the distance. Mansur's palace was the last on the right after the turn. Abdullah got out in the parking lot and walked up to the house himself. A servant in a scarlet *ghandourah* let him in, looking surprised but discreet.

'Where is he?' Abdullah wanted to know.

'Lord, let me take you.'

They went through the front part of the palace, which had been designed by a Swiss architect. Through a courtyard echoing with a splashing fountain lit by underwater lights, planted with palms and oleanders, and filled with the recorded strains of the music from *Dr Zhivago*, and finally into another wing of the house.

It was quiet in the back, heavy carpeting, the hall lined with a nice collection of nineteenth-century art. When the servant opened the door at the end of the hall the noise hit them like shock waves. His cousin Mansur and about a dozen men were playing cards at a large table. There was music here, too. Throbbing French songs from Paris played full blast through quadrophonic speakers. Several European women drifted in and out, one a girl who had taken off the top of her evening suit, her naked little breasts jiggling. The room was thick with the smell of *hasheesh*.

His cousin got up from the card table quickly.

'Abdullah, in the name of God!' Mansur looked him up and down. 'You look like you've been in a train wreck.'

'Right the first time,' he said in English. 'Listen, get me something to drink, will you? I want to go someplace quiet and sit down and have a drink and think.'

His cousin raised his eyebrows. Drinking was forbidden, of course, under strict Moslem law. If Abdullah had come to tie one on, it was plain Mansur wished he had picked some other place.

'I'm not going to get you in any trouble,' Abdullah said. He looked around the room. 'That is, any more than you're in.'

'Yes, but that's *me*,' his cousin said. 'Not you. I don't want to get both my hands cut off for corrupting the youth of the nation.' He gave a grin.

'Come on,' Abdullah said impatiently, 'take me someplace quiet, will you?'

'Feeling a little claustrophobic?' Mansur said, taking him by the arm. He knew how it was. All of them who had been abroad, who had finished their education in the American or English universities, knew how it felt. The feeling that you are smothering.

His cousin led him out of the card room and back down the hall. Not too much light now, the thick carpets dragged at Abdullah's feet. Mansur opened a door and they went in. It was a suite like something out of a Hollywood musical, swaths of white satin drapes with gold ropes and tassels, white fur underfoot, crystal lamps. And a gigantic bed with a white satin bedspread embroidered with crystal beads.

'What is this,' Abdullah said, looking around, 'the bridal suite?'

His cousin looked cryptic, gave a shrug. He went out and returned with a bottle of Johnny Walker Black Label and some glasses.

'There's water in the bathroom. You want some ice? I'll send somebody.'

'No, God, keep the servants away from me. This country is just one big wagging tongue as it is.'

'Did you bring anybody?'

'Only Wadiyeh.' Abdullah sat down in a satin-covered armchair and broke the seal on the bottle of Scotch and poured himself half a glass of whisky. He was thirsty from the long drive and took too much in the first mouthful. It seared his dry throat going down.

'*Ya*, Abdullah, take it easy, huh?' His cousin looked nervous.

'I'm okay, I told you. I've just got a lot of problems and I want to be by myself.'

'Yeah, sure.' He backed toward the door. 'If you want anything, let me know.'

'I'll be out of your way in an hour,' Abdullah promised. 'Don't worry.'

When he had gone Abdullah leaned forward and put his head in his hands, the glass of whisky pressed against his forehead.

How did everything manage to come at me at one time? he asked himself. Yesterday I was living in a vacuum, not really doing much of anything, and now the whole world's on top of me. I'm not doing anything for myself; I've been just standing there letting things happen to me. I can't help Layla, I'm not going to be of much help to my son, and I don't know if I can live up to what my grandfather expects. I'm not much help to myself, when it comes right down to it. I don't have any great drive for anything. I don't have any great raving taste for women and that's an unspeakable lack in this part of the world. Nor, he added, even any lust for boys that I know of.

There's not anything I really want. I haven't really wanted anything in my whole life, it's always been there even before I needed it and too much of it at that.

Now they're shooting at me. I never did any harm to anybody.

The only time I ever feel like I'm really living is when I'm on the Harley in the desert and nothing can touch me, I'm all alone. I'm all alone and free as a damned wheeling buzzard up in the sky. Nobody wants anything from me because they can't touch me.

The problem is that I'm getting too close to my grandfather now. I'm coming up fast. I'm not Bibi the family darling anymore, and they already know it. It only took them a couple of hours but they know it. It couldn't be my dear uncle Hakim; he's too gentle a soul. Nor his militant mouthpiece and his Egyptian and Palestinian friends. My grandfather must be in more trouble than I thought for them to want to cut me out so fast. I could have broken my neck out there in the bike wreck and nobody would have known the difference.

Or it could be some of our friendly neighbouring sheiks to the south and north. Annexation's always a threat.

Or maybe since my grandfather is going to push for participation in GAROC the rest of the gulf states will see that it can be done and follow suit. A lot of radical political manoeuvring would go down the drain.

Or anything.

He sat back in the armchair and poured himself another drink.

I need somebody, he thought, and in all this crowd of relatives there's no one to turn to. Fawzia's a sow, she doesn't understand when you talk to her, and my mother's the same, poor fat little lady. My son's only a baby. My grandmother's loyalty is to my grandfather. My sister's the only friend I've got in the world. She'd let me talk to her and tell her what happened out in the desert today and the real reason for my grandfather sending me to the States, but I've let her down and I can't face her. That's about it.

He took the bottle to the bathroom, which looked as though it had been designed by Cecil B. DeMille, and put it on the washbasin. He didn't want it to turn over and make a stain on the fur rug and all the white crystal. He was feeling pretty light-headed but not all that drunk. He looked at himself in the mirror.

Well, what are you going to do? he asked himself.

The face, his own face, looked back at him. When he had a couple of drinks his eyelids drooped down just like his grandfather's. There's the old man in me, he thought, leering at the image. Crafty, not dumb. He peered more closely. His nose was not like his grandfather's; it was long but it was straight. But there was something awfully familiar about the mouth. It was a deceptive mouth; it looked as guileless as the old man's. And everybody knew about that.

What they're trying to do is kill me when I haven't even decided what I want to do with my life, he thought. I ought to have that chance at least, it's only fair. *I'll* decide if I want to be the next ruler of Rahsmani or not.

There, it's coming out, he saw, amazed. Something had turned the trick. God, something darkened, blazed back at him from the face. Something cruel, as if he had struck a long-buried note somewhere. Is that what's in me, then? he wondered.

You couldn't take anything away from the Asmaris; they'd hard-scrabbled in the desert too long. It didn't matter much what it was — women, money, horses, a stray piece of camel dung. What was theirs was theirs. Forever, and it's in me, too, he thought. When my grandfather gets too old and doddering, will I toss him, too, off the wall and into the sea? And chop off Uncle Hakim's hands and hang them up over the post office?

He was deadly serious; he stood there holding on to the washbasin with both hands, swaying a little, staring back at his face. So that was you all the time, he told himself. Another brigand, just like the rest.

He went back to the crystal-and-satin Hollywood bedroom and sat down on the edge of the bed and lifted up the white telephone. He dialled the number and it rang a long time. There should be somebody home. He looked at his watch. It was only ten o'clock.

When a voice answered he said, 'May I speak to Sam Crossland, please?'

When the American came on the line Abdullah said, 'Listen, this is Abdullah,' in English. There was a pause and then the American voice said cautiously, 'Yes, Abdullah, what is it?'

What the hell – the hesitation puzzled him and the tone of the voice. Did everybody know what was going on? That is, everybody but himself? Abdullah looked at the telephone frowning, then put it back to his ear.

'Look, Sam,' he said, 'I want all the books you've got and all the reports on oil participation and nationalization. I want to look over how the Iraqis have been making out since they nationalized their northern fields, and whether they're making any money. And the same thing in Libya, if the BP fields are able to come up to prenationalization production. Get me some downstream figures, they'll show. And I want every speech that Ahmed Zaki Yahmani's made to OPEC and the oil companies on participation and exactly what Yahmani thinks it should consist of. And anything else.'

'Why sure,' Crossland said pleasantly. 'I'll get them together for you whenever you want.'

'Now. Right now,' Abdullah told him.

'What, tonight? Most of that stuff's down at my office. Have a heart, Abdullah, I wouldn't know where to begin to look for it at this hour.'

It wasn't the first time Crossland had been asked to do something at night, had been told to produce something on a moment's notice, Abdullah knew. His grandfather made a practice of dragging his old friend up to the fort at all hours. It was just that Crossland knew he didn't have to do it for *him*, that was all.

Bibi darling's got a surprise for you, you old son of a bitch, he told himself grimly. If I'm going to go to New York with you, you're going to have to learn to toe the line. Just like with Granpa.

'Now, Crossland *sayid*,' he said smoothly, changing to Arabic, 'permit me this small favour, that you will bring me these books tonight, that you will be as good and loyal friend to me as you have been to my kinsman, the Emir, so that I will grow to love you as he does. It is wise to look into the future, is it not, and see the face of good fortune continuing? I desire the books TONIGHT and I desire that you bring them YOURSELF. Even if you have to walk up here in your GODDAMN PYJAMAS!'

There was another pause, but a short one.

'Sure, Abdullah, you don't have to yell,' Crossland said quickly. 'I didn't know it was that important. See you in about an hour.'

'Thank you very much,' Abdullah said politely, and hung up.

FOUR

Half an hour before the Boeing 707 jetliner began to approach the Madrid airport Adam Russell, the assistant to James Brooke-Cullingham, went back to knock at the door of the private bath.

'It's open,' Abdullah yelled.

The young Englishman opened the door and stuck his head in and then paused, his mouth slightly open. The quarters for the staff were forward in the plane and Russell had not yet had a chance to come to the rear to view the interior of the private suite of the customized jet. It was something to see. A large sunken tub of imitation black marble took up most of the space in the bath, the floors were covered with four-inch-deep-red carpeting, and the gold-veined black mirrors that lined the four walls made it the equal of anything to be found in a luxury hotel. The airplane nosed down slightly and the bath water, carefully perfumed by the bodyguard, Wadiyeh al Qasim, sloshed over the side a bit.

Abdullah had been lying with his feet stuck up near the taps, for the tub, like most bathtubs, was a little too small for him. He held a *Penthouse* magazine in one hand, but he hadn't been reading.

'We have our landing permission, sir,' Russell said, almost apologetically. 'Madrid coming up, in about twenty minutes.'

'All right.' Abdullah turned the handle marked DRAIN with his big toe. 'I'm coming out right away. Any messages?'

He was still trying to get in touch with his sister Layla, but without much luck. He had been sitting in the bathtub for the past hour thinking about all the radiotelephone messages he had ordered sent from the plane's communications centre since they had been airborne and all the messages before that, in Rahsmani, shortly before they left. You would think there would be some response; after all, Riyadh, in Saudi Arabia, was not the end of the world in spite of all the jokes about the Saudi's backward capital. But there had been nothing. It worried him. The understanding was that he could communicate with his sister at any time. Otherwise he wouldn't have agreed to anything. Not one damned thing.

'Two messages from Mr Ali Hassan in Madrid,' Russell was saying. 'Several from New York, the ones confirming arrangements for the most part. Especially the Waldorf luncheon for the UN delegates being organized by Mr Hamid Asmari. He's sent the full menu, asking if you'd like to approve it.'

Abdullah knew his cousin Hamid's communications; they never ran less than two typewritten pages on any subject.

'You do it,' Abdullah said. 'Strict Moslem food and no booze.' The Waldorf could handle such things, they had plenty of experience. But not serving any liquor would come as a blow to some of the delegates, even though they were mostly from the Arab oil-producing countries surrounding Rahsmani. But, Abdullah thought, it wouldn't hurt them any. Although some of the Arab delegates on the UN cocktail-party circuit were as hard drinking as any you could find, the luncheon was an official affair of the emirate of Rahsmani and as such was going to adhere to strict Moslem observance. It wasn't exactly going to be austere, but there wasn't going to be any champagne sipping, either. His grandfather wouldn't have it any other way.

'And the other message,' Russell said. 'Mr Hassan assures you he will be there when we put down in Madrid. He confirms last night's telexes, and he is bringing two young ladies.'

'I'll bet he is,' Abdullah observed.

Ali Hassan never had less than two young ladies in tow,

even on a transatlantic flight. It was part of his internationally famous romantic cinema image – an image that didn't cause him too much agony to live up to. Actually, as Abdullah knew, the Egyptian actor had a very nice Egyptian wife and a fourteen-year-old son living in Cairo, to whom he was devoted. But he also took care of his internationally famous reputation as a lover, too. That was what brought in the important screen roles. It is a fortunate man, Abdullah thought, who can learn to love his work. 'Nothing from my sister?' he asked.

The assistant shook his head.

'No, sorry, but we're still trying. We can raise Riyadh with no difficulty, it's just that we don't get any response from the party you're calling, Prince Azziz Saud.'

That figured.

'All right,' Abdullah said, 'I'll be out in a minute.'

When Russell closed the door he stayed where he was, watching the bath water slowly emptying from the tub. He opened his hand and let the *Penthouse* magazine drop to the rug. He hadn't even read the thing, although there had been an especially beautiful girl in the centre sections. Or so one of the Iranian secretaries had said when he gave it to him.

Abdullah was not in the mood to do anything but just sit. He was still trying to recover, he told himself, from the events of the past few weeks, which had seemed to reach a peak of frenzy when they had left Rahsmani. It was as though he had been on a damned merry-go-round. He was sure he had missed several nights of sleep somewhere, and although he supposed everything had been accomplished, nothing had seemed to turn out very satisfactorily. There had been the seemingly endless consultations with Brooke-Cullingham to get the trip to New York and California organized, the settling on an agenda that included not only VIP luncheons and receptions in New York but also the briefings with the commercial agents there about the possible bank purchases, and all the details of that business. And then there was the schedule for Los Angeles when they finally got there – a tour of Hollywood film studios arranged by Ali Hassan, a reception on the set of a movie being filmed that starred Robert Ellsworth and Raquel Wales, dinner at Chasen's with the congressional representative from California who had been connected with J. Paul Getty and who was said to be receptive to the problems of the oil industry, and much more. Abdullah couldn't remember all of it. There was an appointments book just for the California visit alone that Russell had prepared. It listed their projected activities day by day, hour by hour, and looked as thick as the telephone directory. And on top of all this there was the hard work Abdullah had done alone and in secrecy studying reports and reference books on the Middle East oil industry to prepare for the executive board meeting with GAROC when they returned East. At the last minute they could all see there had been too much scheduled to take care of efficiently, and they had to drop the proposed trip to Disneyland, to the great disappointment of practically everybody on board, especially the Bedouin guards. But Abdullah had ruled it out. To hell with Disneyland, enough was enough. It was the only unpopular thing he had done so far.

He felt, Abdullah told himself, as though he was a million years old. It was amazing how all the pressure and responsibility could wear a person down. A load of work such as he had taken on since his grandfather had delegated him for the trip, the continuing strain of making decisions right off the top of his head when he wasn't used to it was enough to make him grow old before his time. In some ways he had grown to appreciate his former status as the sort of student of the family – the unready, unlikely member of the Asmari tribe from whom nobody had expected much and who always had plenty of time on his hands. Now there wasn't enough time to go around. He felt as though he had been walking a tightrope for the past two weeks, surrounded by members of his grandfather's circle who were watching him closely to see how he was taking his new role.

Well, he was taking it slowly. As slowly as they would let him, throwing as much of the work as he could on to Brooke-Cullingham and the assistant, Adam Russell, and the crowd of secretaries who had been picked to accompany them. And he was finding that leadership consisted in large part of making other people do the jobs they were getting paid for, instead of hassling you about it.

The worst part of the past two weeks had been in trying to deal with his sister's wedding. Fortunately it hadn't been the all-out state and tribal affair it could have been. His grandfather seemed to have restrained himself somewhat, but it had been bad enough. They had had more than the usual number of banquets and receptions for the Sauds and the obligatory fetes where the northern tribesmen were brought in to stage camel races and death-defying feats of horsemanship to prove that the Rahsmanis were as good desert Arabs as anyone else, these followed by the parties at the hotels in the city hosted by the Sauds to show that they had as much money – maybe more – than the Asmari family of Rahsmani could ever hope for. At the end of the celebrations there was a parade through the streets of the city followed by the day for the men's party in honour of the groom, the day for the women's party in which the dowry and the bride's trousseau was displayed at the fort, and the final day for the biggest party of all when the Saudi groom finally and officially came to claim his bride. There hadn't been anything like it, everyone said, since the spectacular affair staged for Abdullah's own wedding. That kind of unfortunate observation hadn't made him any happier.

As far as Abdullah had been concerned his sister's wedding had been a nightmare. He hadn't had much time to see his sister; he had been neatly tied up with the details of the plans for the trip to the States and it was as though he never completely caught up with what was going on. He had a suspicion that it had been deliberately planned that way. At times Wadiyeh al Qasim had practically thrown his clothes on him while he was still busy with Brooke-

Cullingham and the secretaries, to get him ready for some Saudi wedding dinner.

Or perhaps, he had told himself since then, he had let what was happening steam-roller him because there really wasn't anything he could do to help his sister. He had managed to find time to tell her that, if she wanted him to, he would openly defy his grandfather and take her to the Rahsmani airport and put her on a plane for London. He supposed he could have got away with that much. But they both knew his grandfather would probably find her without too much trouble and just bring her back again. They really didn't have any friends abroad who would risk taking her in, at least for any length of time.

When you came right down to it, he tried to tell himself, nothing would have made any difference. Layla had said so herself. But she had given in, agreeing to everything without argument, as pale and curiously uncaring as though she had suddenly become a stranger. That had worried him. He hadn't expected her to surrender so completely. He supposed he had come to think of his kid sister almost as an extension of himself; they had lived together through a family life that anyone would have described as a nightmare of uncertainty and in doing so, they had developed a kind of partnership against loneliness and defeat that was more than the relationship between most brothers and sisters. It was impossible to think of her not being around when he needed someone to talk to. But then, Abdullah told himself, he hadn't really expected the damned marriage to take place – it had seemed like one of those things in the future that conveniently stayed in the future, an unpleasant event that with luck would never materialize. It shocked him to find that, as frantically busy as he was with other things, it was all on top of them at once.

When he went to his grandmother to talk to her about it she was as elusive as she usually was when anything opposed his grandfather's wishes. He had his duty to do was all she would say, his grandfather was depending on him. And he should stay out of matters that concerned Layla. He couldn't make her see the injustice of that, either; she only hustled him off to look over the ceremonial clothes she had ordered for the wedding. It was just like it always was – in the madhouse of Arab wedding arrangements naturally no one was going to listen to anything he had to say.

On the final day of the celebrations the Saudis had come in a fleet of Cadillacs to claim the bride. The groom, Prince Azziz Khaled ibn Jamil, had never been anything much in Abdullah's opinion, and meeting him again did nothing to change his mind. Azziz was a younger son of a younger son living uselessly on a fat pension of the civil list, a nothing even as Saudi princes went, and even his relatives treated him as such. It didn't help, either, that he was on the fat side and, from all he said and did, not too damned bright either. This was what bothered Abdullah most, that they had picked someone for his smart, pretty little sister who certainly deserved better, a half-educated twit who looked as though he didn't have brains enough to add up his monthly allowance. On top of that the Saud acted as though he was doing them all a favour to take Layla off their hands. Something that even his grandfather noticed. Abdullah carefully kept his distance. He knew if he got too close to him he would be tempted to shove his fist into the Saudi's fat, arrogant mouth. Layla stayed away from him, too, as much as possible, and that was a bad sign. When the Saudi took her by the hand you could see she shrank back a little. But it had all been pretty strange. It had upset Abdullah a lot, and there were times when it was hard even for him to recognize his own sister. She hadn't looked like herself at all, weighted in the traditional Rahsmani bridal clothes, gold coins clinking at her cheeks, encased in layers of pearl-encrusted fabric that seemed as stiff as wood. Layla was a little girl, not tall at all; she had seemed to move like a lifeless, gilt-spattered doll. The last he had seen of her, bound for the airport, was a small bundle of gold-embroidered clothes with a purple silk veil thrown over it in the back seat of one of the Cadillacs. Abdullah had wept openly there on the terrace in front of the fort and before all the crowds and his grandfather had been so angry he would not even look at him.

The tub was empty. He found himself sitting in a small puddle of cold water, staring at his feet. The nose of the jetliner was down, they were coming into Madrid. He supposed he had better get out of the tub before someone sent Wadiyeh to drag him out of it.

When he came out into the main cabin he found that most of the staff in the forward compartment had already buckled themselves into their seats. The communications centre was shutting down; Adam Russell and the telex operator were still on their feet, putting away some papers. The jetliner, from the private Rahsmani fleet of planes, was the flagship, the one usually reserved for the Emir, who rarely travelled anywhere. It had been handsomely customized by a United States firm and was as comfortable as an unlimited budget could make it. In the back of the 707 was the private suite with bath and bedroom, complete with king-sized bed and its own telephone system and then, coming forward, the dining and lounge area and then the staff compartment and communications centre. The plane had been outfitted in a style that was vaguely French–Italian–Egyptian, although it was hard exactly to place it. But it was as big as a hotel lobby, all gold and red and black, the Rahsmani colours, with built-in teakwood cabinets, reclining armchairs in red leather and black velvet, carpeted with the Emir's favourite Hamadan rugs from Iran, and with a wrought-iron partition separating the private suite from the rest of the plane. There was not another customized 707 jet like it, Abdullah often told himself, except perhaps in Abu Dhabi or Kuwait or Saudi Arabia or Bahrein. He had heard one of the Bahreini sheiks had a sort of airborne yacht with lots of chrome and white bearskin, real zebra-hide upholstery, a Swedish crystal dinner service, and two Klees and a Picasso. But he had never seen it.

Brooke-Cullingham was seated in a red damask Reclinolounger, already strapped in. Wadiyeh al Qasim was in a jumpseat by the staff lavatory, huddled in a knot. The black-and-red-checkered kaffiyeh had fallen over Wadiyeh's face and Abdullah could see that he was praying. The Bedouin hated jet travel; they never got used to it.

As Abdullah strapped himself into a lounger beside Brooke-Cullingham the Englishman said, 'We've got a spot of trouble with your luncheon in New York.'

'What kind of trouble?'

Brooke-Cullingham looked out of the window, carefully, to watch the plane's angle of approach as they descended. The narrow, slightly greying head and sharply defined chin and nose inclined away, handsome and imperturbable as ever, but there were deep lines about the mouth. Abdullah was not the only one who was tired.

'Cancellations. Rather odd, considering all things, but there you are. So far Kuwait, the Trucial States, Aden, and Oman send their regrets. They say the Delegates themselves won't be able to attend but they'll send the undersecretaries. However, the Saudis are firm – the full Delegate accepts with pleasure. Don't know about the remainder yet, but I suppose we'll see more of the same – regrets, and undersecretaries.'

Abdullah didn't find it odd. Unexpected, yes, but not so damned odd. If the Arab oil countries' UN delegations were backing out of the luncheon and sending only the undersecretaries, then it meant zero confidence on any given scale. And not only for himself but for his grandfather, too. By Arab measurement in such things it was bad. Not so bad as to declare war or commit suicide, but one got the point. His uncle Hakim's second or third oldest son, Nasir, was the current UN Delegate from Rahsmani.

There was a saying that when elephants fight, the grass gets trampled. Their friendly neighbours were just playing it safe. But the cut was substantial. It would be bad form to try to ignore it.

'Shall we cancel out?' Brooke-Cullingham murmured. 'The schedule's quite crowded as it is.'

Abdullah took a moment to think it over. He could

always call his grandfather while they were down in Madrid and ask him what, since they were mostly their own Arab oil-producing friends, they ought to do about it. However, complaining to his grandfather before he even got halfway started was not the smartest thing in the world, even he could see that. There had to be some other way. Either I keep, he told himself, a tight grip on everything from the beginning, or I might as well go home.

Cancelling the lunch wasn't the answer, either. Abdullah knew Brooke-Cullingham was waiting to see what he would do. He was fairly sure the decision to send the undersecretaries hadn't been made in New York; he'd bet the overseas telecommunications lines from the UN had been busy checking with the home governments to see what course of action to take – stick with the Emir's heir apparent, or hang in there with Hakim al Asmari and Ameen Said.

'Is my cousin Nasir coming?' he wanted to know.

'Oh, I imagine the honourable Delegate from Rahsmani will show. Be a bit too obvious if he didn't, don't you think?'

'Then you take it,' Abdullah told Brooke-Cullingham. 'You take over for me. I think I'm going to have a sudden attack of urgent business appointment.'

The Englishman turned away from the window to look directly at him.

'That's right, I'm going to be called away on another matter,' Abdullah said. 'Urgent business is all you need to tell them. That's very bad form, you know. These people regard anything less than a skull fracture as a poor excuse for a host's absence. It violates all rules of hospitality. But it's better to go ahead and give the lunch as planned so they can all get *my* message. Which is, "Up yours, too." Since you're going to pinch-hit for me,' Abdullah said deliberately, 'that will make it even better. You're not one of *us*, and that's even more uncouth. But since your Arabic is as good as anybody's, they won't even be able to make naughty comments under their breath.'

Brooke-Cullingham thought this over, then gave a slight smile.

'I'll say,' he drawled, 'that you've been called away to Trenton, New Jersey. That has a nice sound – terribly *déclassé* – no one will believe a word of it.'

'And another thing,' Abdullah said. 'Let's cancel out some of these other lunches and dinners while we're at it. As for instance the lunch with Roehart and Simpson to talk about bank buying. I'm not American enough to eat and deal at the same time. It gives me acid indigestion. Make a lot of appointments to do business in the office, preferably in the afternoon. There's not all that much to do, anyway.'

'Remember, Roehart has asked to go with us to California,' Brooke-Cullingham reminded him.

'I'll think about it,' Abdullah said, and closed his eyes. They already had quite a group: three Iranian and two Jordanian secretaries who also doubled as bodyguards, the telex operator, the jetliner staff of English pilots and two Italian stewards, plus Brooke-Cullingham and Adam Russell, as well as the two Bedouin, Wadiyeh al Qasim functioning also as Abdullah's personal servant. He was beginning to feel a little crowded. If they picked up any more people in New York they would qualify as an invasion.

The plane made its final swoop toward the runway. Abdullah thought, That takes care of things for the time being. But the little hassle over the luncheon for the UN Delegates was fair warning: it wasn't going to be the last time they would find something like that cropping up, he was sure.

The 707 hit the airstrip with a slight bump and turned its nose in the direction of the Madrid general air terminal. While they were still rolling past the lines of charter jets Abdullah saw a landing stage break away from the terminal bays and start toward them. You couldn't miss Ali Hassan – he was standing at the top of the portable stairs with a trenchcoat thrown over his shoulders, waving a pair of mounted bullhorns with some ridiculous red ribbons attached. Two grinning ground servicemen were pushing the landing stage as fast as it would go.

Abdullah's frown melted away. Even at a distance the actor radiated a devil-may-care, fun-at-all-costs attitude that was catching. Hassan was the last person in the world to give a damn what anybody thought. There was nothing, he thought fondly, more irresistible than this crazy Egyptian.

It took a few minutes to get the forward door to the jet-liner open. They could hear Hassan shouting greetings and rude remarks to them in Arabic from the outside. Three of the secretaries moved to the front part of the plane, fol-lowed by the Bedouin, who placed themselves in front of the stewards. The security measures had been worked out by Adam Russell; too many things had happened at airports for them not to be careful. The Iranian, Ramzi, who was also a member of Rahsmani Secret Security, slipped his hand under his jacket to touch his shoulder holster.

It took Ali Hassan a moment to push through the crowd. Someone picked the trenchcoat from Hassan's shoulders as he came through.

'Friend of my heart!' Hassan cried in Arabic. 'Mother of my liver and careful guardian of my soul – may the *houris* bless you with a thousand orgasms when you have gone to heaven!'

'For God's sake,' Abdullah said, laughing. But he was genuinely glad to see him, as always. 'Be careful, will you? You always sound like you're saying something blas-phemous. The *bedu* are strict Wahabi, they'll cut out your tonsils if you don't watch it.'

'*Ya*, Wadiyeh al Qasim,' Hassan shouted, thrusting the bullhorns and ribbons at the Bedouin, 'a present for you from the sacred cattle of Spain, O pearl of thy mother's womb, peerless warrior and possessor of an unblemished heart! How many widows have you seduced this week?'

Amazingly, the giant Bedouin guard shook with helpless giggles. Ali Hassan always had this effect, Abdullah marvelled. No one could resist him. Not even the simple-minded men of the desert who could barely understand the Cairo street dialect the actor was throwing at them. But the two Bedouin knew perfectly well who he was; they had seen the movie posters in Cairo and Beirut and they allowed him anything.

Abdullah embraced him. They put their arms around each other in the traditional fashion, touching each other's cheeks lightly with their lips. Then Hassan held Abdullah away at arm's length to get a really good look.

'Baby, you've grown a foot,' he said admiringly. 'What are they feeding you back home, sheep's testicles and Vitamin E? How big do you people get, anyway, out there in the ass end of the Empty Quarter?'

To his annoyance, Abdullah blushed. The girls had come trailing in, two breathtakingly lovely women barely out of their teens in tight-fitting pants and large hats and trailing scarves.

'There are women here,' Abdullah said awkwardly.

Ali switched to English. 'Permit me to introduce,' he said, 'Delores Monteverde, the French cinema's answer to Marilyn Monroe, as you can see. And the promising young starlet, Marta Hochman, who was with me on this last accursed film. Ladies, permit me to present the Sheik Abdullah al Asmari, the richest and handsomest young man in the world.'

'Delighted,' Abdullah said, and kept smiling. But he felt like an idiot. Damn Ali anyway! He could feel the heat in his face and knew that he had turned a dark red.

The girls glowed back at him. He was fascinated by the way they looked, their slender bodies in their tight, continental-style clothes, the dashing big hats. Their faces had some sort of pale burnish, their eyes rimmed knowingly with black paint and long artificial lashes. Even their lips had a smooth, pearly gloss. They looked as though they had been gone over carefully with a jeweller's cloth and polished to a high lustre.

But Ali was the same, he noted, the same fluorescent white smile that had lit up so many movie screens, the confident, suntanned magnetism one found only in millionaires and movie actors.

'We've just come in here from Greece,' Hassan was say-

93

ing, 'where we've been shooting some damned epic. I play Czar Nicholas the Second of Russia. Spent two weeks looking all over the Macedonian mountains for enough snow for the serfs to drag me through. I tell you it was hell. I'll be playing my own grandmother next.'

Abdullah could believe it. To his knowledge Ali Hassan never turned down a role. His passion was horse racing and gambling and he went from one movie contract to another, signing up for any kind of film that would pay the sort of salary he commanded. The Egyptian was really broke, according to the rumours. That is, the way one can be broke while living like a movie star. But it didn't matter. He was still, Abdullah thought, the handsomest man you could find anywhere. Part of that was the Hollywood veneer, the expensive styling of the coarse curling black hair, the Gucci shoes, the London–Paris clothes, the regular steambaths massages, and workouts, but there were also the liquid, mesmerizing eyes that had made his fortune, the rugged, athletic body – there was always one scene in every film where Ali stripped down to the waist, either in the bedroom or out on the desert while fighting the blowing sands – and that damnable, clownish, ingratiating white-toothed grin that made women swoon and men grudgingly admire him.

All the same, Ali Hassan was not really an Arab but an Egyptian Coptic Christian, which was something entirely different in their part of the world. The blood of the Pharaohs, the Copts called themselves. His real name was Constantine Moushmoun, and Hassan had converted to Islam and changed his name when he began to star in his first Arabic films. Abdullah was damned glad to have him with him crossing the Atlantic; and then of course they would see each other later in Hollywood.

'I told them to bring aboard a case of Dom Perignon,' Ali was saying. 'Man, this is some airplane, I haven't seen the inside of one of these Arabian Gulf specials before! Is that a movie screen? Tell me you're going to show *Sword of the Pathan* and I'll point out to you the scene where I nearly made myself a eunuch falling off a horse!'

94

'We've got plenty to drink aboard,' Abdullah told him. 'Or we will have, we're putting it on here in Madrid. Sorry we don't have your film. Russell tells me we're showing *Sound of Music*. Is that right?' He turned to try and find the English assistant.

'And three Roadrunner cartoons,' Russell's voice came from the crowd behind them.

'I can't bear it!' Hassan threw himself into a Reclino-lounger and put his feet up. 'Hasn't culture reached your part of the world yet? How about X-rated flicks?'

'We're lucky to have anything,' Abdullah told him. As Hassan knew, his grandfather didn't approve of movies, either.

'You never told me you lived like this, Abdullah *effendi*,' the actor said, leaning back and putting his arms behind his head.

'I don't. It's all done with credit cards.' Abdullah sat down beside him while the girls went back to supervise the putting away of their luggage in the staff compartment. 'Listen,' he said in an undertone, 'don't call me the richest man in the world. That's a hell of a way to introduce anybody. And besides, I'm not.'

His friend gave him a sharp look. 'That's not the way I heard it.' Hassan switched from English to Arabic. 'From Damascus to Cairo the very air breathes in whispers. They tell me you are about to become a great man. And that your esteemed country sits on the biggest lake of oil to be found in any kingdom of the Prophet's True Believers. Is it true that you have a big Japanese oil combine of Mitsuki and Mitsubishi right on top of a gusher about to come in?'

'That's a lot of horseshit,' Abdullah said quickly. 'Any oil company that's out there drilling expects to make a strike, naturally. That's what the Japanese are spending their money for. But this drilling is offshore, in the gulf, and gulf drilling is anybody's long shot as the oil companies will tell you. In case you've forgotten, my country's had a long history of bringing in dry wells. My grandfather used to have his wives sew up the holes in his ceremonial robes so he could go down to the city to pick up his drilling rights cheque. That wasn't so long ago.'

'Everybody,' Hassan said, rolling his eyes, 'has tales of what it was like when the family was poor. Next you'll be telling me you used to be on welfare. Me, I'm a rich kid myself, my father was a cotton broker in the delta, I went to private schools. I've led a sheltered life.'

But Abdullah didn't smile.

'What else did you hear?' he wanted to know.

'That you were making this trip to buy a bank in southern California. Is this for real?'

'My grandfather needs something to put his money in. The old strongbox is getting a little crowded.'

'I believe it.'

The steward came by, asking them to check their seat belts. The long twilight that had followed them from Rahsmani with the shifting time zones was fading now. The stop to refuel in Madrid had allowed sudden night to catch them, and the airport lights were suddenly strung like diamonds beyond the jet's windows. They would be serving dinner as soon as they rose out of the mountains of western Spain.

'What else did you hear?' Abdullah insisted. The women were settling in behind them in the lounge seats, exclaiming in French and Spanish over the electrically operated foot-rests and switch-button lighting connected to each chair. The NO SMOKING lights came on in English and Arabic.

'All men know the ninety-nine names of the Prophet,' Ali Hassan quoted, 'but only the camel knows the one-hundredth. Which accounts for the look on his face. But you'll notice, baby, he never tells.'

'Don't fool around,' Abdullah said, displeased.

Ali Hassan went everywhere and, like most Egyptians, he was a great gossip. Cairo was the centre of all rumours. As Ali had said, in the Arab world the very air breathed in whispers. If you put any faith in such things, it was wise to listen. He already knew about the bank buying.

'What do you want me to tell you?' Hassan raised his

hands in a truly Arab gesture. 'Lord Abdullah, I don't know anything – you know me, I'm full of jokes and stories, good for a couple of laughs, that's all. I'm just a good-natured devious Egyptian. It is written.'

'Don't make a big deal of it,' Abdullah told him. He was growing annoyed. He couldn't see Hassan's face very clearly in the diminished light for takeoff or he would have realized his friend was genuinely reluctant.

Hassan hesitated.

'Okay,' the actor said finally. 'It's this. Be safe; don't trust anybody around you.'

'What, *now?*' Abdullah quickly looked around the plane at the staff, Brooke-Cullingham and Russell, the stewards, the Bedouin settled into their jumpseats.

'Now, and all the way,' Hassan said in a low voice. 'It is said you are living very dangerously.'

'That's nothing new,' Abdullah told him. 'In my part of the world that's normal.'

But the Egyptian said nothing.

Later, at dinner, Ali Hassan was in good form. It had been a good idea to pick up the actor for the first leg of their trip, across the Atlantic, for, as Abdullah knew, it would have been a dull time without him. As it was, the plane took on a party atmosphere.

The teakwood table in the dining area was pulled out to seat all of them, the two movie actresses, Brooke-Cullingham, Adam Russell, Hassan and Abdullah, waited on by the stewards and the two Bedouin. The chicken and rice, which had been prepared for them by a Madrid restaurant, was excellent, the wine was good, the pilot had been told they were at dinner and held a steady course. The electrically lit candelabra stood beside a large arrangement of fresh roses and Spanish lilies and the service, while not quite up to the Bahreinis' custom-made Swedish crystal, was Spode, nevertheless, and the silver setting had once belonged to the Austrian royal house of Hapsburg. Abdullah did not take any wine or anything else to drink, observing his grandfather's strict Moslem custom, but the others worked their way into the case of Dom Pérignon that Ali had brought aboard. By the third bottle of champagne Hassan was flushed and roaring with laughter, and Brooke-Cullingham had told some of his best stories, including the one about the time old King ibn Saud's *hareem*, in a cavalcade of Cadillacs, had got stuck in the sand between Riyadh and Mecca. Which Brooke-Cullingham only did when he was pretty well oiled. They were all good talkers, the evening was immensely pleasant, and Abdullah sat back and enjoyed himself. As he looked down the table he thought, It's all my ball game now, I'm the host, the captain, the commander. If I wanted to order the plane to fly around in circles for an hour or two to stretch out the good time here at the dinner table, it's within my power.

It was a far cry from the recent times when he had been shunted back and forth across the Atlantic just to go to school.

By the time the Arab coffee had been served they were all howling with laughter at Hassan and his wicked stories. There was, the Egyptian told them, the great singing cowboy who was afraid of horses and who screamed with terror whenever one of them moved. The movie studio had ended up shooting his closeups on the back of a specially built mechanical horse while a double filled in for the outdoor action scenes. And the dignified British actor who had had his face lifted once too often and found himself minus half his repertory of dramatic expressions as a result. And the producer who could have seduced a hundred willing starlets but couldn't because he was impotent, and the great romantic film idol of all times who really preferred boys and not girls. Not to mention the all-powerful gossip columnist who, in spite of being married to a urologist, still wet her pants at unfortunate moments, once when she sneezed on stage at the Academy Awards.

Finally, when Hassan had grown slightly hoarse and they were all more or less exhausted themselves, they moved forward in the plane to settle in their chairs for the movie.

Abdullah did not join them. Instead, he slipped away to the private suite in the back and stretched out on the big bed to enjoy the rest of the trip by himself.

It was pleasant to be alone for a change. They were flying over the Atlantic Ocean in the night and through the bedroom window he could see the sea below them shining like a metal sheet, reflecting the moon like some vast spotlight. He wasn't sleepy, he told himself. They would be putting down at JFK in about three or four hours and besides, the bed was full of books on the oil business and some notes he had been working on earlier that, he told himself, he should finish.

Abdullah lay on his side, careful of the papers about him, and stared out the window at the brilliant moon and the almost starless sky.

For better or for worse, he thought, we're under way. Here we are, thirty or forty thousand feet up in the air, flying to New York. And from there I go on to Los Angeles where Ali Hassan tells me he will show me Hollywood as nobody has ever seen it before. But before that I'll be checking into the Waldorf in New York and Brooke-Cullingham will see to it that Adam Russell sees to it that the secretaries stay up all night putting the bank purchase analysis in working order for the New York lawyers and Roehart and Simpson. But I've still got an unfinished bunch of notes on the presentation to the GAROC board because I'm still reading OPEC recommendations on participation and I don't understand a hell of a lot of it. I'm not a very good student, I proved that at college.

A sudden picture of the refinery at abu Deis where he had played tennis with Dallman all those months came back to him, the towering spheres and cylinders where the Rahsmani oil workers had come out to watch them from the heights of the flying catwalk. It seemed like a long time ago. I wonder, Abdullah thought idly, what life would have been like for me if I had been born an ordinary Rahsmani, working in a refinery, instead of what I am? He tried to picture himself in a white canvas suit and checkered *kaffiyeh*, looking down from a refinery catwalk at the Emir's grandson playing tennis. How would I feel about the one with the tennis racket, walking around underneath?

I'd feel, he told himself, that I was a hell of a lot better than he was.

He yawned. He still wasn't sleepy. He knew he could go out and invite one of the girls Hassan had brought back to the bedroom with him. They were there for that purpose, naturally. But he really wasn't interested.

He must have dozed, because some time later he woke and heard a sound at the door. He called out in Arabic but no one answered. When he got out of bed and opened the door the narrow passageway was empty. There was only Wadiyeh al Qasim a little farther down, half asleep but faithfully guarding. The main cabin was dark; the noise and flickering light of the movie the only thing.

Abdullah ran his hand through his hair. He didn't know what had waked him but he had a feeling someone had tried the door handle. It was a curious thought. He yawned again.

Just because you're paranoid doesn't mean they aren't following you, he told himself. And paranoia is part of the job. He went back and stretched himself out again on the bed.

FIVE

The luncheon at the Waldorf turned out just as Abdullah anticipated. Although the Delegates cancelled out almost to a man, they sent the second-stringers, the undersecretaries, the press attachés, who showed up prepared to enjoy the situation, whatever it might turn out to be. What they got, though, was not the Emir of Rahsmani's disappointed grandson but that undersecretary of all undersecretaries, the unflappable James Brooke-Cullingham, former representative of the ill-remembered British Protectorate in the Arabian Gulf, a fluent Arabist and pastmaster of Middle Eastern political chess games. While the delegations' second teams were still thinking this over, the Saudi Arabian full UN Delegate – who was, inevitably, a cousin of Layla's husband – arrived with a retinue of ten, plus several Bedouin bodyguards, every last one of them in gorgeous formal turnout of gold-encrusted gowns, ceremonial daggers, and snowy *kaffiyehs*. The presence of the Saudis, done up to the teeth as though for a state visit to the White House, set the place on its ear.

'The Saudis stayed to the bitter end, of course,' Brooke-Cullingham said. 'Naturally none of the second-raters dared to leave until *they* left. They're all scared witless of the Sauds. You should have seen the consternation. There was quite a bit of running back and forth to the telephone in the men's loo to check with the office and tell them what was happening.'

'And did the Saudis have a good time?' Abdullah wanted to know.

'Oh, stood around like a pack of bored lions – you know how they do put on – noses in the air, drinking gallons of orange juice. They might have been amused, although it's hard to tell. In my opinion the Saudis are a particularly humourless lot; that damned Wahabi fundamentalism holds them down. They wouldn't know a joke if they tripped over it.'

'Don't fool yourself,' Abdullah said. 'They'd appreciate this one.'

He had scored one, he knew, and it hadn't done him any harm with the Saudis, either. His stock had gone up since the point-counterpoint in New York.

As soon as they had got to New York and had set up the telecommunications system in the hotel Abdullah had tried again to get in touch with his sister. But the whole stay in New York, like the flight over, had been interrupted almost hourly to tell him the same message: Riyadh city was responding but the party they were calling at the address given did not return these calls. Riyadh telecommunications had even, at their request, sent a messenger with a cablegram form out to the Saudi's residence and someone there had signed for it, but there had still been no answer.

If he ever got his hands on the fat Saud, Abdullah vowed, he was going to kill him. That is, if he was the reason he couldn't get in touch with Layla.

Finally he decided there were more ways than one to get around the problem and it occurred to him that his grandmother was the best one to handle it. The trouble was, his grandmother was about as hard to reach as his sister, but for a different reason. There was no difficulty getting an overseas call into the fort, which had a worldwide system, and there were plenty of secretaries around to process it. The trouble came in getting his grandmother to take the telephone receiver into her own hand and talk into it. Telephones were just not his grandmother's thing. It was not exactly that the Lady Azziza was that old-fashioned, but as a long-standing veteran of *hareem* and political intrigues she was too suspicious to talk into any electronic device. As far as his grandmother was concerned the world was full of spies. As for radiotelephone calls going through the air and relayed by satellite – his grandmother regarded this sort of bare naked communication as being exposed to anybody in the world who had a portable transistor radio. That is, everybody in the Arabic-speaking world. Abdullah knew that even if he somehow got her to the telephone she would never talk to him about Layla.

The only logical thing to do was to sit down and write his grandmother a letter suggesting that as she was the person to handle domestic snags such as were being encountered with Layla and her fat parasite of a Saudi husband, she might just want to make a trip to Riyadh herself to see what the hell was going on. A regular traditional family visit that is, accompanied by his uncle Fuad and as many other male relations as would make the whole thing socially proper and acceptable. With lots of gifts and maybe a female cousin or two to tag along. Layla's husband couldn't turn down that sort of thing unless he wanted to start a family war.

But as he was writing the letter to his grandmother Abdullah was overcome with a sudden and unaccountable attack of despair. His culture prided itself on the strong bonds of family, but it seemed to him that one kept hitting these strange pockets of indifference when relatives abruptly appeared to turn their backs on each other, to leave one to fend for oneself. It had happened many times when they were left with their lunatic father. Now he didn't know why in the hell he had to keep reminding his family of their duty to Layla when he was thousands of miles away and they were so fairly close to her. Didn't anybody worry about his sister the way he did? Or had they already assumed the customary attitude that since Layla was married, she was her husband's responsibility and it would be wrong to interfere? If that was it, then he was damned if he was going to accept it. Unless he heard from Layla herself he was going to keep on thinking that something was very wrong. It wasn't like his sister not to answer his calls.

The letter was given to his cousin Hamid al Asmari, the

consular attaché for Rahsmani in New York, and locked into a diplomatic pouch that was then chained to Hamid's wrist. Adam Russell had driven the pouch and his cousin Hamid to Kennedy Airport where Russell had personally put Hamid aboard a Kuwait National Airlines jet. With luck, Hamid would be in Rahsmani in twenty-four hours. And as soon as his grandmother could write a letter saying she was getting ready to go to Riyadh and visit Layla, Hamid would be airborne again with her answer, final stop Los Angeles. Abdullah had told his cousin that he wanted to see him in LA within a week or he would have him knocked out of his consular job and his fancy East Side apartment and his expense account, and sent back home in permanent retirement. And for once Hamid didn't take it as a joke. They all knew how Abdullah felt about his sister.

Every day while they were in New York there was some reminder that this was usually Hakim al Asmari's territory. Everyone knew Hakim. Even the people with whom they made business appointments frequently got the names mixed up, if not the actual identities.

'I'm getting tired of walking in and finding out that the lawyers and bellhops and waiters and damned near every-body else expects to see my uncle,' Abdullah told Brooke-Cullingham after a check over the accounts at Citibank Foreign Exchange Services.

'It is a little alarming, isn't it?' the Englishman said. But he was making notes, busily hedging in the areas where Hakim al Asmari had, after several years, left the impression that he was the sole representative of the Rahsmani government.

We should have started two years ago, Abdullah thought. But in the semiweekly telephone conversations with his grandfather he confined himself to reports that all was going well, nothing was much of a problem. Brooke-Cullingham and he had agreed that this was the best course to take until they got back. New York was only a stopover anyway; the real business would be done in California and on their return.

104

At night the Iranian secretary, Ramzi Alam, who was also the Rahsmani Secret Police contact in the group, got on the telephone in one of the Waldorf suites and settled down for an hour for what was usually called 'family greetings'. The Iranian had a list of Rahsmani students studying at colleges in the United States and one by one they were contacted by telephone, engaged in pleasant conversation about how they were getting along both personally and academically, and reminded that their families in Rahsmani were waiting for them when they graduated. Rahsmani needed its educated youth – at least Abdullah's grandfather didn't want a large part of the group who went abroad to study to stay abroad, either to hang around idly spending their wealth or to attach themselves to some radical Arab organizations as some of them did, especially from other gulf oil countries. This was the Emir's way of keeping track of the sons of some of the larger Rahsmani families, making sure they returned home where he could continue to keep an eye on them. Although Abdullah knew his grandfather wasn't as successful at this as were the Saud family of Saudi Arabia. God knows what the Saudis threatened their students with, Abdullah thought, short of mass murder of their kinfolk. Every last one of them went back home when their college tours were up. Of course, like his cousin Mansur and the rest of the Rahsmani college graduates, he supposed the Saudis spent the rest of their life going nuts, too, when they got back.

The last few days in New York were hectic. They had scheduled the remaining dinners with officials who were relatives, and the Rahsmani Ambassador, who was related to Fawzia's family as well as Fuad's, flew in from Washington. There was an evening at the theatre during which Abdullah fell asleep. It was hard to remember what was going on and what was being accomplished; he relied on Brooke-Cullingham to keep track of it all. The season was early spring on the East Coast and New York had the tired and gritty air of a hard winter. It rained most of the time. They went from appointment to appointment in taxicabs and rented limousines and only once, when they cut across Central Park, had Abdullah seen anything besides concrete and rushing traffic and the grey faces of New Yorkers. Outside the Waldorf at 2 A.M., as Abdullah and Russell were getting out of the cars they were accosted by a pair of prostitutes, young and garishly pretty but wearing strange outfits of patent-leather boots and cowboy hats and transparent blouses that showed their breasts as plainly as if they had been naked.

The temperature was in the twenties, and it was cold. Wadiyeh al Qasim had come rushing up from the car behind them, robes and headdress flapping, to get in between and when the women saw him they fell on him like a circus, screaming and clawing. It was mayhem for a minute. Russell and Brooke-Cullingham had grabbed Abdullah by the arms to get him out of there, fast. The women quickly got Wadiyeh down on the pavement in front of the revolving doors of the Waldorf, trying to kick him in the face and head. The Waldorf doorman and the rest of the group from the cars had finally driven them off. Brooke-Cullingham had dragged Abdullah through the lobby at full speed.

'No trouble,' the Englishman said. 'We'd better get the Bedouin into business suits.'

But Abdullah had sagged against the lift door in a fit of laughing. Militant whores! They hadn't even given Russell or himself a chance to say yes or no before they started fighting. It didn't make any sense at all. But it was just as he remembered New York; it hadn't changed at all.

It was even raining when they left.

The morning they arrived in Los Angeles, Abdullah woke with a hangover. Which was strange since, following the usual protocol, he hadn't had anything to drink the whole trip. But it was a hangover, nevertheless. His joints ached, his mouth was dry, and his head hurt. The only good thing about it all was finally to wake up in California after all this long time, after thousands of miles of airplane travel, and look through the glass sliding doors of the bedroom and out into the garden where there were real palm trees and a high, heavy hedge of hibiscus and oranges and lemons surrounding a green lawn, and beyond that, a private swimming pool. The clock said 10 A.M. and the California sun was already high and hot in a blue, desertlike sky, and the air was sweet and only slightly perfumed with the gassy smell of automobile exhaust drifting from the freeways.

It was a joy and a delight, Abdullah thought, finally to discover southern California. Coming in from the airport, it had hit him as nothing had in a long time – the arid hills and the flat openness of the land, the scramble of the expressways and the cars, cars, cars everywhere, the feeling of freedom and space, the stretches of palm-lined boulevards and Spanish-style houses that made it at first seem vaguely European and that turned into mile after mile of Howard Johnson used car lot Western Motel orange juice McDonald's Golden Arches clicking across the eye like a pinball machine, leaving one with a sense of stunned excitement. Welcome to LA. Hollywood City Limits, Home of the Stars. Route 12 to Burbank. But most of all the sense that the desert was near. It was as if someone had up-ended a bag of urban sprawl, flowers, houses, and freeways and dumped it down in an empty section of Rahsmani.

As Abdullah's limousine was stopped for a red light a man and a woman in a Maserati drove up next to them, both in evening clothes, the woman with diamonds around her neck, and both eating large, dripping slices of pizza. The man and the woman in the Maserati kept staring at them until they drove away. On the corner of another street they saw a middle-aged woman in shorts and high heels with two Borzoi hounds on a leash, pushing a pram full of grocery bags.

It was just what he had supposed southern California would be like.

In spite of the hangover symptoms, Abdullah unfolded himself in the bed lazily, feeling his joints creak, and took a long, slow yawn. It felt good. Everything felt good here, better than it had in a long time. And part of the good feeling was that it was past ten o'clock and no one had done anything about it, whereas in New York they had always been routed out by seven to make some damned business meeting. Obviously, life here in LA assumed its own shape, just as he had heard. It even tasted good, in spite of the condition of his mouth.

The feeling of a hangover that plagued him was a mystery unless he thought, you could chalk it up to being dog-tired for at least a couple of weeks and add to that being out nearly all night the first night in Hollywood. Thanks to Ali Hassan, who had met them at the airport, they had got off to a flying start with dinner at Chasen's, where Kirk Douglas and his wife were at one table, David Niven at another, and so many film stars generally that Abdullah had a hard time paying attention to the food. From Chasen's, with Brooke-Cullingham and Roehart, the New York agent, they had made a tour of the Sunset Strip, followed by a stopover at a Laguna Beach house party where the crowd of movie people was younger, the air filled with pot smoke, and a mass skinny-dip was announced for later, which they did not stay for.

After Laguna Beach, Brooke-Cullingham and Roehart decided to break off for a quiet nightcap and a return to the hotel. But Abdullah and Hassan went on to a nightclub–discotheque called The Candy Store, which, Ali assured him, was where the action was to be found. The place was pleasant enough and made a big noise about being exclusive; what made it interesting was the crowd of enormously good-looking women and the people one would recognize from having seen their faces on the screen. Although from the ages of some of them, Abdullah realized, this must have been some time ago. Hollywood seemed to be full of famous movie sirens of yesteryear with handsome anonymous young men, and ageing male screen stars with adolescent dates. For the first time Abdullah saw the subjects of Ali's scandalous anecdotes firsthand. Everyone knew Ali; they greeted him with screams of affection. The girls practically threw themselves at the actor's feet. That is, until Ali introduced Abdullah as a sheik from the oil-producing country of Rahsmani, and then he attracted more than enough attention in his own right. A famous film star tried to get Abdullah into a conversation about gurus and Indian religion, evidently confused about where Rahsmani was, exactly, and the difference between Hinduism and Islam. While Ali was dancing with a star Abdullah only dimly remembered from a recent musical film, a man who introduced himself as a film producer laid his hand familiarly in Abdullah's crotch and invited him to go home with him. An Academy Award-winning actor on methadone was taken out forcibly by his male nurse when he got violent. By two in the morning Ali was pretty drunk and Abdullah had to talk him out of taking one of the girls out to the car in the parking lot, which Abdullah didn't think was a very good idea, especially since Wadiyeh and one of the Jordanian secretaries were waiting patiently in the front seat. Although the girl didn't mind. She kept inviting all of them.

The number of beautful women in Hollywood was amazing. Abdullah couldn't get over it.

'Is it always like this?' Abdullah wanted to know.

Ali cocked a drunken eye at him as they were getting into the limousine.

'Miles of women,' he said thickly. 'The streets are paved with women in Hollywood. And all of them available. It's a true Arab's dream.'

It had been a great evening. Driving back in the night there had been the scent of fresh flowers blooming and the sky overhead was like the desert sky, vast and filled with stars.

Abdullah slid out from under the sheets and Wadiyeh, who had been sleeping on the rug in front of the glass doors, heard him, and got to his feet.

'*Al salamu alaykum*,' the Bedouin greeted him.

'Get out of here,' Abdullah told him. 'Go and fetch some coffee.'

The bodyguard gave him a confused look. He had been sleeping in his robes but his headcloth was off and his long hair, divided into a dozen tight braids, gave him a curiously girlish look. He had no English, couldn't use the telephone to call room service.

'*Ya*, aged sheep of thy father's worst flock,' Abdullah said, 'there is a small kitchen in the hall where coffee is to be made. Gather your wits about you and go and see what is to be done.'

When Wadiyeh had padded off down the hall in his bare feet Abdullah opened the glass doors and stepped out on to the small terrace that overlooked the hotel garden.

They had taken three bungalows in the back of the Palm Aire Hotel in Hollywood. Abdullah and Brooke-Cullingham and the two Bedouin bodyguards were in one, Roehart, Russell, the telex operator, and the secretaries in the other two. Each bungalow was surrounded by its own garden, and Abdullah's, called a deluxe villa, had a private swimming pool. To rent even one bungalow was enormously expensive but worth it, as the hotel assured maximum privacy with complete service. They had only to lift the telephone to order two Martinis, a Hawaiian luau for fifteen to be set up around the swimming pool, or the services of a masseur available twenty-four hours a day. A complete business service, including stenographers and a communications centre, could be set up within a few hours. They had brought their own secretaries with them, but the communications lines, including the telex, had already been installed in Russell's bungalow. Additional security guards had been provided by the hotel to supplement their own. There was even a butler available if they wanted.

Like everything else in California, the quarters pleased Abdullah immensely. The bungalow had been designed by a well-known southern California architect. Most of the exterior walls were sliding-glass panels that let in the floodlit green of the surrounding gardens by night and the California sun by day. There was a huge fieldstone fireplace in the living room, and great brightly coloured slabs of abstract paintings were hung all through the house. Abdullah wanted to make note of it; if he ever decided to build a house, he told himself, he would want it to be like this one.

The secretaries were supposed to use the main hotel swimming pool, where they could order drinks from a cabana reserved for them and watch the world go by. Abdullah supposed that was where they all were. He could hear Wadiyeh looking for the kitchen, but apparently there was nobody else in the house.

He pulled up a reclining patio chair and let himself sink into it. He had put on a pair of tennis shorts but the top button was undone, comfortably, and his feet were as bare as Wadiyeh's. The fake hangover was fading and he was feeling positively happy. He lay there feeling the sun soak into his bones, that clear burning light so like the sun of the desert that penetrated deep into his flesh. For the first time in a long time – at least since New York – he felt really warm. That was a hell of a relief. A small bird came down from the hedge of palms and lemon trees and skimmed across the swimming pool, hitting the bright aquamarine water with a spray of light and then flashing back up again into the green.

A sense of being on top of everything swept over Abdullah and he leaned back and put his hands behind his head, luxuriously. They hadn't done too badly in New York when all was said and done. And it looked as though things were going to be even better in Hollywood. At least he felt that way. Being in command of things could be a great burden most of the time, but it could also bring great satisfaction, as he was discovering. It was true, to appreciate anything you had to work at it, and he had been working pretty damned hard the past few weeks.

I should have come here sooner, Abdullah told himself. He had been to California once before, during his second year at college, but at the time he had been the guest of the Rahsmani Ambassador and several cousins from Fawzia's family, and they had travelled across country in the usual tribal group, out to San Francisco and back. After three weeks Abdullah had had enough. They had covered the face of America by plane and rented limousine and had seen the Grand Canyon and the Golden Gate and the Mormon temple in Salt Lake City, and he was glad to get back to fall semester at Yale. He had missed Southern California completely. Now, Ali Hassan's Hollywood, the eye-jangling lights of the Strip, the mansions of the movie stars set back in the hills, the great sprawl of Los Angeles, even the sight of palm trees again, filled him with a strange exhilaration. This was better than anything he had seen in the south of France, better than Majorca, Greece, or the Canary Islands. Southern California had a great open presence that invited you to spread out, enjoy all your senses, live it up, never stop going. He considered whether or not they should try to get Disneyland back on the schedule. It would be a shame to miss any part of this place.

In a couple of days they would be going out to the San Fernando Valley to look at one of the banks recommended by Roehart and Simpson. Abdullah was looking forward to the trip. Seeing the bank itself was not all that important. In the end he could throw it all over to Brooke-Cullingham to make the final selection and concentrate on arrangements for his meeting with GAROC back in the East. But the opportunity to see more of California outside the city of Los Angeles interested him. This rich, arid country reminded him of Rahsmani. He wanted to see what had been done with it.

Wadiyeh came padding back with a cup and saucer and the long-handled brass coffeepot, which steamed even in the warm air, and a copy of the Los Angeles *Times*, which he laid across Abdullah's stomach.

'Lord, regard the news journal,' the Bedouin told him. 'Inside, with thy picture thus.'

Wadiyeh couldn't read but he always went through the newspaper to look at the photographs and the comic strips.

Abdullah sat up quickly, taking the coffee with one hand. The Bedouin was absolutely right; on the fourth page there was a photograph of Ali Hassan and himself sitting at a table. There was no story, only a paragraph under the picture that identified him as Sheik Abdullah al Asmari of Rahsmani, oil potentate from the Persian Gulf, and international film star Ali Hassan. Snapped at a party at The Candy Store.

He sat looking at the picture for a long time, curiously. Once or twice in London he had had his picture in the newspapers, but this was different. Perhaps because he was with Ali. Behind them stood two predictably beautiful girls stooping over to get within the frame and showing a lot of cleavage, looking straight into the camera with large, gleaming smiles. Ali looking straight into the camera, too, the same large smile, looking as handsome and magnetic as he did in any wide-screen technicolor film epic. Everyone, Abdullah noted, managed to look photogenic but himself. The camera had caught him with his head turned slightly away, showing the length of his nose and the hair along his neck, which needed trimming. He looked tall even sitting down, slightly darker than the Egyptian, and with a remote, somewhat discontented air. It was an interesting study. I look, he thought, like one of my grandfather's fledgling desert hawks, talons tied and slightly cracked. Is that the way people see me? There was obviously some professional trick to having your picture taken at one-thirty in the morning and when you weren't expecting it. He didn't even remember a photographer being anywhere around. But he tried a few of those straight-on, dazzling smiles to himself and felt his jaw muscles strain. You had to practice, too, that was obvious.

Over the top of the paper Abdullah saw a girl come out of the thick fence of trees at the left of the garden and walk toward the swimming pool in front of him. She stopped by the diving board and unzipped her orange beach robe and dropped it on the grass and stood for a moment before she bent forward and did a flat racing dive into the pool. She didn't have any clothes on at all, not even a swimsuit.

Abdullah sat up straight in the chair and let the newspaper drop. He blinked once and then twice and she was still there. The girl was real, improbably enough, and actually doing what she was doing. It was no hallucination or trick of the bright sunshine in his eyes.

The girl swam several lengths of the pool, which was fairly large, and then stopped at the far end to put her hand up to rest a moment. Wadiyeh had seen her, too. He came to the door of the bedroom.

'Remain,' Abdullah told him under his breath.

He got up out of the chair and walked down the grass toward the pool. The girl saw him coming because she pushed off, treading water, and held her hand up to shade her eyes from the sun so that she could watch him.

When he got to the edge of the pool she said, 'Sorry, I didn't know anybody had moved in. Do you want me to get out?'

Abdullah stood there, looking down at her curiously. The water was clear as sapphire and he could see the pale gold of her legs treading water, her arms flung out and her hands moving gently. Her faintly gold breasts floated pleasantly before him, perfectly visible. She didn't seem bothered by the fact that she was nude and the water was as clear as a mirror; she simply kept treading water, her eyes on him. Her wet reddish-gold hair was flattened against her head and streamed down her neck in rattails. She had a bold, wide mouth without any lipstick and greenish eyes that were enormous in her face, eyes outlined with long spidery black lashes. Abdullah was slightly amazed to see that, even as these good-looking California women went, she was quite beautiful. He wouldn't have believed it possible.

He found that he couldn't do anything but stare at her. Obviously she had come through the gardens with the intention of taking a swim in the bungalow pool, that was clear enough. But now that she was here, what was to be done? She didn't seem to be greatly worried at being discovered. If he ordered her to get out, would she come out naked as she was or ask him to throw her the robe? If

Hassan's Hollywood stories were to be believed, he could expect anything.

'Is this your bungalow?' she asked him. 'I don't see anybody around.'

Abdullah knew Wadiyeh was watching them from behind the glass doors of the bedroom. The other Bedouin guard, Bisharah, was somewhere around. And there was supposed to be one of the Jordanians stationed a bit farther down the path between the bungalows. He wondered how she had got in. For a moment Abdullah couldn't think of a word in English, it was as though that language had fled from his head. He was busy watching her and her large breasts, which floated before him like fruit.

'Take your time,' he said finally.

She gave him an odd look.

'You're not American, are you?'

Abdullah shook his head.

'You have sort of a British accent.'

He supposed he had.

She turned then and swam over to the ladder and, as he watched, fascinated, she climbed out. She came out in a leisurely way, making no effort to cover herself. Her skin was covered with suntan oil, as the water beaded on her smooth flesh. She was beige all over except for the faint marks, he could see now, of a very small swimsuit that had barely covered the triangle of hair between her thighs and the matching triangles over her breasts.

He had never encountered a woman like this before, naked in the bright sunshine, a woman so beautiful it was impossible not to look at her in every detail. He could hardly believe what was happening. Out of the corner of his eye he could see that Adam Russell had come up behind Wadiyeh at the glass doors and he got a fleeting impression of the look on the Englishman's face. From where they were standing they could look out and see him talking to a perfectly naked girl by the swimming pool who was wringing out her long hair casually while she looked up at him. Well, he didn't know what to think either.

'Listen,' Abdullah heard himself saying. He felt rather silly, but on the other hand a sort of exuberance was in him, too. This was a part of the world where anything could happen, Hassan had told him so repeatedly. Everything was make-believe, not real at all. In spite of the audience at the glass doors and the incongruity of standing like that in the sunshine with a naked beautiful girl in front of him, the inevitable was happening, he would have been made of stone for it not to happen. He wished he had brought the newspaper with him to hold in front of him nonchalantly. What the hell was he supposed to do?

He felt the blood beating in his temples. She was looking at him speculatively, her lower lip caught between her teeth. Then she smiled, a rather knowing smile. It was the smile that did it. It came over him suddenly, a realization that after all he was who he was, with money and power in his hands and he could, if he wished, do exactly as he pleased. For no reason at all except that he felt like it. And at the moment he felt like it. After all, it was his damned schedule.

'Listen,' Abdullah said again, 'come and use the pool anytime.'

'Okay,' she said, still smiling.

It was a fairly stupid conversation, even he realized that. He started to ask her what she was doing later and then it occurred to him that there might not be a later. He would be even more stupid to let an opportunity rush past him. He reached out and laid his hand on her shoulder. She came willingly, the tips of her breasts still cool from the water against his bare chest. He felt himself begin to tremble. He knew it was crazy. It was as though he was suddenly drunk and without a care for anything else in the world. Let somebody else worry. He could hardly find her mouth; he took her face between his hands and a shudder ran through his body and into her and she leaned into him greedily. I haven't had a woman in a long time, maybe a month, he thought. I don't remember when it was, and it's getting to me now. And this girl from the swimming pool is doing her best to help it along.

Why not?

'How about coming inside?' he said to her, taking her by the arm. The faces at the door melted away as they came across the grass. When they went through the doors they found the room empty, the door to the living room shut.

SIX

'You lunatic!' Ali yelled at him later, as they were driving out to play tennis. 'How could you do a dumb thing like that? It might have been a two-bit whore – the Palm Aire's full of hustlers! It might have been a blackmail setup. She comes in, scratches herself all over, falls over a chair to get bruised up, and then claims you tried to rape her! That would have cost you a bundle of money, you know that? She might have been an assassin with a bomb up her pussy! It might have been a kidnap attempt – did you ever stop to think that while you were balling her two or three terrorists could sneak in and wrap you up like a loaf of bread and hustle you off to a plane like they did the oil ministers in Vienna? Don't you know better than to do something as goddamned stupid as that?'

'No, I suppose I don't,' Abdullah said evenly. 'Besides, she said she knew you.'

'Anybody can say that! Man, my face is on a million movie screens; anybody can say they know me! Besides, what the hell do you mean, you suppose you don't? You've had women before – don't tell me you haven't got away from your grandfather long enough to have had at least *some* – didn't it ever occur to you that you shouldn't get friendly with strange women that have just wandered in through the bushes somehow? And in LA of all places? This is a weird town. You haven't seen enough of it to know how crazy it is. Nobody in his right mind would take chances like that!'

They were speaking English because both the bodyguards, Wadiyeh and Bisharah, were in the back seat of Ali's Mercedes with the tennis rackets and the carryall with their change of clothes. But Abdullah switched over to Arabic. The Bedouin knew perfectly well what was going on. What had happened with the woman from the swimming pool had undoubtedly been a prime topic of conversation in the bungalows since then. Everything he did was a matter of record. As far as Abdullah was concerned he was still living in an extension of the lap of the great Arab family. He had never left it. Even Hassan, with his outraged yelling, was a wonderfully familiar part of it.

'Don't shout,' Abdullah told him. 'It is done, and to my mind it was done very well. I do not regret a moment of it. On the contrary, this girl gives a high degree of pleasure.'

'She's a *kook*!' Ali continued to yell. 'Of all the kinky people in Hollywood, Barbra Burchard is the Queen of Kink! Take my word for it. She's into some kind of ethnic marathon – last year it was Mexicans, the year before that, Greeks. Naturally when she saw your picture in the paper she practically climbed in through the window. How did I know this was the year for True Believers? But don't get excited; the word is that she's really frigid, she keeps looking for somebody with the magic flute to turn her on. If I mentioned you casually, which I don't remember doing, her brain lit up like a pinball machine. For which I am sorry. Please accept my humblest apology. I wouldn't have done a thing like that to my worst enemy.'

Abdullah smiled to himself. 'It is the wise man who can discern truth even in the mouths of others.'

'Oh go to hell.' Ali down-shifted the Mercedes as they turned a corner into the centre of Beverly Hills. 'I'm really surprised at you though. That wasn't a very smart thing for you to do, taking her right off the top without even knowing who she was. I don't care if she was walking around in her skin in front of everybody. If that's what turns you on, let me introduce you to some nice girls, nudists, skinny dippers, strippers; there are millions of them. But not Barbra Burchard. I know her. I know what I'm talking about.'

'She says that she is a movie star. That she has appeared

in many films. But I do not recognize the names of them.'

'Movie star?' Ali snorted. 'She's been in films, everybody out here has been in films, so what? What's a movie star, anyway? She plays the girlfriend of motorcycle freaks that gets gang-raped. She plays the type who comes in and takes her clothes off; that's her specialty. She plays hippies and hustlers in the flicks that never get off the bottom half of the double bill at the drive-ins. Movie star! That's a good one. No wonder you never heard of her.'

'Nevertheless,' Abdullah said, remembering the girl as she came out dripping from the swimming pool, 'she is very beautiful. With such beauty it is not surprising that she was able to become an actress in the films.'

'*Allah*, you amaze me, friend. I keep hitting these layers of pure innocence in you that I can't believe. Besides, she's not all that beautiful. She's had her nose fixed and a tuck taken in that big fanny and her snatch surgically tightened until I hear it's harder to get into than a Swiss bank. And she's been on uppers and downers; she takes a little coke now and then for the fun of it – in other words, she's just your average All-American Hollywood girl. You don't know how people live out here, baby, you just think you do. You've got to be careful. You can't afford to get mixed up with anything loud.'

Abdullah cocked an eyebrow at him. 'These are fine words, O friend of my heart,' he said lightly, 'considering their source. It is you who wished to enjoy the delights of the flesh in the back of the automobile last night, only you were too bombed to accomplish it. At least I indulged myself on the inside of the house, with the curtains closed.'

'That's not –' Ali began.

But Abdullah had half risen in his seat.

'Hey!' he shouted. He pointed straight ahead through the windscreen. 'See that? Stop there! I have been struck with a sudden inspiration.'

And he had. He saw a familiar sign among the shops in Beverly Hills and it had come over him all at once what he wanted to do. The sun was shining brightly, the day was warm, and he felt in an expansive mood. Also, he was tired of being yelled at.

He pounded Hassan on the back with his free hand.

'Stop the car, old mother of camels! Stop the car, I wish to go into Van Cleef's.'

'For what? Sit down, Abdullah, don't do anything funny or you'll attract a crowd.' Hassan threw up his arm to protect himself from the pounding. 'Are you nuts? Listen, I've got the courts reserved for us at the club – they won't hold them if we're late.'

It did no good. Abdullah continued to hit him, ordering him to stop. Somewhat savagely, Ali Hassan jerked the Mercedes to a stop at the kerb in spite of the large NO PARKING sign.

'Look, there's a parking lot in the back,' he began, but Abdullah was already out of the car. 'At least let's change our clothes,' he protested, but Abdullah had opened the car on the driver's side and was hauling him out by the arm.

'Don't preach. It doesn't go with your face.'

They went into Van Cleef and Arpels that way, Hassan protesting, Abdullah with a firm grip on his elbow. The actor was recognized right away. Two of the sales staff came up; some people at the counter in the forward part of the shop turned to stare.

'It's my friend,' Ali explained. He gave them the famous smile. 'He wants to buy something.' As they went toward the back he said, 'It's my friend, the Sheik Abdullah al Asmari, he wishes to buy something. It is quite all right.' They were joined by two jewellers, who ushered them into a private showroom.

The trouble was Abdullah was not sure what he wanted.

'Tell me, what does this woman remind you of?' he asked Hassan in Arabic. 'She reminds me of something gold-coloured. A shower of gems like topazes. But topazes are cheap, are they not? Something yellow, anyway.'

Hassan looked around him a trifle uneasily.

'Okay, Abdullah, I hear you, don't wave your hands around. Try to take it easy.'

'Don't be nervous,' Abdullah said, clapping him on the back again. He was beginning to enjoy himself enormously. A sense of power, such as he had felt in the morning beside the swimming pool, was returning to him. Hassan would see.

He drew up a chair at a small table and they sat down in the midst of the crystal chandeliers and mirrored cases.

'Something nice,' Abdullah said, running his hands together and grinning. He extended his arms at full length and waggled his fingers as though he expected a shower of gold to sift through them. 'Lots of diamonds and stuff,' he said to the jewellers.

They returned very quickly with several trays of necklaces and bracelets. 'Don't groan,' Abdullah said to Hassan in an undertone. 'You sound like you're giving birth.'

His friend rolled his eyes in mock disbelief. 'What do you think you're playing, *The Godfather*?'

Abdullah laughed.

The Van Cleef staff watched from a discreet distance as, in their tennis shorts and bare knees, they bent over the gems.

'Well,' Hassan admitted, touching a wreath of diamonds on a black velvet cloth, 'this is quite a display of goodies. I see they didn't bring out the cheap stuff.' But he was beginning to get into the spirit of it. He grinned his famous grin, full of delight. Then, in Arabic, 'It is hard not to be touched by such beauty. Allah is indeed good. Are we to be concerned with the price?'

'Only the colour.' Abdullah reached down and scratched his ankle thoughtfully. He had done this before. He was quite aware of the excitement and tension they had brought with them into the shop and the way the Van Cleef people, sensing it, had responded. He could do things like this when he wished, Abdullah told himself. It was a complete ego trip but it was worth it. It was great to stir things up, shake everything out of its ordinary everyday mould and watch people trying to cope. With all the strings leading into his own hands. Jump when I tell you to jump was the message.

Even Hassan, who should have been used to it, had been caught off balance.

'I wish more stuff in yellow,' Abdullah said. 'How about yellow diamonds?'

He was laying it on pretty heavy. He knew yellow diamonds would be hard to get in any matched size and on such short notice. He wanted something right away – he had enjoyed himself that morning and wished to send this gold-coloured girl something to express his appreciation.

For a moment, he allowed himself to drift back again to the recollection of what it had been like with her. Total strangers, they had come together on the bed in his room in a great hurry. He tried not to be in such a rush, but that was the way it was, and she had done nothing to hold him back. In fact, her fingers and mouth on his flesh had driven him to near frenzy. It was exciting to make love like that in a mysterious, quite impersonal manner. She was astonishingly tight and he was, perhaps, more than she had counted on. 'Oh God, oh God!' she had cried, a little too loudly. And then, finally, she closed her eyes and her body arched up at him, digging her feet into the bed, and he had let himself go with her. It was over almost before they had begun. They rolled across the bed and dropped off into the deep rug, still moving, finally subsiding. Slowly.

'Look at these,' Hassan said, holding up earrings that were a fountain of light between his fingers. 'Something to wear to the supermarket, right?'

He had wanted more of her then, and that night, and for as many days as he could count. At that particular moment, holding her firm, cool, lovely body in his hands, he was suddenly worried about not being able to see her as much as he would like. The California trip was going to be a short one. He was a man inexplicably burdened with time, now, which was something of a disaster.

They were beginning again when there had come a soft knock at the door.

'The luncheon approaches,' Wadiyeh's voice had said in

Arabic, 'with the American statesman. I am told to tell you this.'

Abdullah had stopped what he was doing.

'You'll have to excuse me,' he told her. 'I can't get out of it. I've got to keep an appointment.'

You see, that was the way his life was shaping up. He had power, yes, for all the good it was doing him. He told himself that he just had to learn to use it for his own purposes. There was no use having money if you couldn't get some pleasure out of it. The diamonds would explain it somewhat.

The manager of the Beverly Hills Van Cleef's came up to ask if they would like to see some loose stones.

'No, this is all right,' Abdullah said. He lifted his arm and looked at his watch rather deliberately. 'I've got to get in some tennis before it gets too late.' Then he poked at one of the heavier bracelets with his finger. 'Give me this, and I want you to take out the things in the middle. What are they, rubies?'

They were rubies. The bracelet was made of double interlocking whorls of diamonds set in platinum with a string of large rubies down the centre.

'And put in some topazes where the rubies are.' It took him a moment to describe what he wanted. It wasn't necessary for him to look over the topazes; he would take their word for it that they were good stones. Van Cleef and Arpels was a reliable shop. His grandmother had had quite a few pieces made for her, mostly bracelets and rings, by their Kuwait outlet. Abdullah knew if you paid a bit more they would put someone right to work on the bracelet and have it ready to deliver within hours. Night or day. He wanted it sent to Miss Barbra Burchard. He had to ask Ali Hassan to give them the address.

There was the problem of how to pay for it. Abdullah didn't have any identification in his tennis clothes, not even a driver's licence.

He looked at his Egyptian friend mock-seriously, giving the invisible strings of power a playful tug.

'How's your credit?' he said in a hoarse whisper.

But Hassan wasn't going to play along. He merely shrugged.

'Not me.' The actor touched a blaze of diamonds with his finger. 'A nice autographed picture is the most I do. Or maybe if it's serious, a little Swiss watch. Or *two* autographed pictures.'

'*Ya*, wondrous one, I am not so beautiful as you. My autographed pictures are worth nothing. There are those of us, alas, who have to pay our way.'

'I'll bet,' Hassan said soberly. 'This is a hell of a thank-you note.'

'She was worth it. I'll tell you something Hassan *effendi*, they gave you a bum steer, whoever told you she was frigid. You have my word on it.'

Hassan didn't look up. 'No kidding,' was all he said.

Abdullah settled it by having the Van Cleef manager call the Bank of America to verify the account and then the Palm Aire Hotel to have Brooke-Cullingham come down and sign for it. That was, as he knew, all that was really needed.

'It was nothing,' Abdullah called to the staff as they went out. He waved his arms expansively, so that the people in the shop all turned around and stared. 'Wait till I come back with some cash!'

'Oh come on, you damned clown,' Hassan told him. He practically shoved him out the door.

But as they were getting into the Mercedes they both broke into loud laughter.

'You damned desert lizard!' Hassan shouted as he threw himself behind the wheel. 'What an act! I'm going to have to take lessons from you. That is, if I ever want to play *A Thousand and One Nights*. What a throwaway – the whole business! I can't believe it.' But he was nearly bent double with laughing. He could hardly find the key to turn on the ignition. 'Eighty thousand – was it eighty thousand? – like buying onions. You wowed them. It's hard to do that in Hollywood these days, but you did it!'

'It takes years of practice,' Abdullah said modestly. 'I started training in prep school, a few thousand here and there, just to see what it was like. And my grandfather threatened to beat hell out of me when he saw the bills. He said it didn't show proper respect for either money or good character.'

'And what does he say now?' Hassan asked as they pulled away from the kerb.

'Well, he's given up on my good character. But we sure do have the money.'

The fooling around in Van Cleef's had taken too long and there was no time left for even one set of tennis. His schedule was really cramped. He had worked in the appointment for a late-afternoon game of tennis with Hassan at Hassan's club with difficulty. Now there wasn't even time to drive out and look at the place. And he was due back at the hotel shortly for an evening of work with Brooke-Cullingham to catch up on the telex messages that had accumulated, a review of the lawyers' report on the banks, and a set of long-distance telephone calls. The important one, to a number in New York to see if Crossland had arrived, was scheduled for five-thirty.

But he didn't want to go back yet, Abdullah told himself, just to take a shower and lie around on the bed for a while until it was time to begin work. He was enjoying himself too much.

'Drive around,' he told Hassan. He liked to drive around sightseeing when someone else was doing the driving. 'I don't have a damned minute to myself these days. My life has turned into some kind of businessman's appointment book full of people I don't really want to meet, that's the hell of it. It's worse than being in college. You should have been with me at lunch, talking about oil embargoes with this congressman from California. He kept asking me if I understood him, talking very slowly, when my English is a hell of a lot better than his is. After all, I speak *English* English, I had British tutors, I'm not exactly an unlettered savage. And I don't think the son of a bitch even graduated from high school.'

'Who – Brietenbach, J. P. Getty's buddy? He graduated from high school all right; he's got a degree in law from UCLA. That folksy bit is just to impress the constituents, that's all. Dealing with somebody like you, I'm sure he felt the need to get even folksier. That's to show you, you foreign Arab slickster, that he's a good solid One Hundred Per cent American through and through. He's been on the oil payroll for years, hasn't he?'

'Yeah,' Abdullah said. 'He lectured me for an hour on how America wasn't going to be at the mercy of the Middle East oil situation no matter what OPEC dictated. He kept telling me how much oil there still was in Texas and the Gulf of Mexico, not to mention Venezuela. Even though Venezuela is a member of OPEC he didn't feel they were going to step out of the U.S. lineup. And how the United States was still Big Brother to world oil marketing. According to him, the backward Arabs just can't do without American technology. And then to top it off he told me the U.S. government was going to set up an oil buying plan to store heavy crude in the summertime when there was the least demand for heating oil, and light crude in the winter when people used less gasoline. He even quoted storage space per barrel. Then, after he had told me how the United States didn't need Middle East oil and could function very well without it, he ended up by delivering a sermon on the energy brotherhood and how we all had to work together in faith and love and hope to support oil reserves, which also means supporting U.S. foreign policy.'

'What the hell does that mean?' Hassan said.

'It means countries like Rahsmani had better keep kissing the ass of the United States and let the international oil companies keep pumping the oil without bothering them too much. In return, the U.S. might sell us some up-to-date jets for armies we don't need and a war we don't want. That is, outside of the crazy Egyptians and the crazy Palestinians. It doesn't make much sense, does it? I mean, how much time have we got left, anyway?'

'We've got,' Ali said, peering at the clock on the Mercedes's dashboard, 'about half an hour. From what you told me.'

'No, dammit, I mean how much time have we got, before the oil runs out, or the Egyptians and the Syrians decide to jump the Israelis, or the revolutionaries decide to take over my grandfather?'

'Oh,' Hassan said.

They had come through Los Angeles and the flat and shabby blocks of the central city, the business district, the county and city government buildings, the courthouse, the hospital, almost without realizing it. Abdullah tried to shake off the effect of his own words. This wasn't the day to let anything bug him. As he looked out the car window he thought. The size and structure of American cities is something you have to see to believe, Europe shrinks to midget size by comparison. Here the cities go on from coast to coast – New York, Cleveland, Atlanta, Saint Louis, Dallas – enough for a whole confederation of European nations. Americans didn't seem to realize the enormity of their land, they accepted it. The richest country in the world, in proportions to stagger the imagination, though.

'The city is not much down here, is it?' Hassan was saying. 'That's what you don't think about, a rich country with a lot of poor spots. I couldn't get used to it at first. Of course the city, which is tied into the whole of Los Angeles County is still making money like all of Southern California makes money, but what was once the big money maker, the film industry, is just a shadow. Everything moves fast here, boom, bust, decay. It's something people like us, from other parts of the world, find hard to grasp. All the big film studios, Columbia, Warner, Disney, Fox, have moved out to the suburbs, and mostly they shoot television films. The old-time movie stars are gone, too, or if they're still around they're locked up in mansions in specially patrolled areas of Hollywood, behind the gates and the attack dogs. Even if they came out they wouldn't recognize the place. Some of the old studios have burned down; they keep catching fire on the back lots where they used to shoot the epics, the sea battles, and so on. It takes half the Los Angeles Fire Department to keep it all from going up like one big torch. Nobody cares.'

'But they are still making films,' Abdullah said.

'Not like they used to. They shoot them abroad, or on location in the cities in the East. This is why, if you're an actor like me, you end up going all over the world to work.' Ali turned the Mercedes into the centre of Hollywood. 'Regard. This used to be called the Glitter Capital of the World. The very words I used to read in the movie gossip columns of Miss Louella Parsons and Miss Hedda Hopper in the Cairo papers when I was growing up. I thought when I started working in films that it would all be waiting here for me when I arrived. But in this country nothing lasts from one decade to another. It is a very strange feeling for one who comes from a country where the pyramids are still a short trolleyride from the centre of Cairo to find that here the streets are not the same from one day to the next.'

The Mercedes was passing down between blocks of gaudy sex shops with names like 'Mother's Fun Place', 'Stairway to Love', and 'The Academy of Sexual Education'. The doorways and pavements were filled with women. Even here the women were exceptionally good-looking.

'They're all hustlers,' Ali observed. 'Here in Hollywood there are more prostitutes per square block than in Times Square. What a sewer, hah? It beats Copenhagen or Hamburg.'

The Bedouin in the back seat had rolled down the windows to stick their heads out and get a better look. Dozens of little storefront theatres offered hard-core pornographic movies. The signs in second-storey windows advertised massage parlours, showed bodies of women in pasties and G-strings, all in lurid colour. Live action sex shows, pornographic book and magazine stores. There seemed to be miles of them.

'I'd never been to Hamburg or Copenhagen, so I wouldn't know,' Abdullah said. 'But I've seen a few sex movies in Paris. More when I was at Yale.'

'You haven't seen anything,' Hassan told him. 'All the French movies are soft core, there's nothing to them compared to this. And what you might have seen at college is old stuff. The budgets are bigger now, the women better-looking – no more breast and butts in action shot with a hand camera. Porno films have gone into class productions, costumes, erotic material with special appeal, S and M you name it. Strong men blow their minds. The deputy mayor of Los Angeles was in Pepino's Adult Theatre and got so carried away he started fondling one of the customers, who turned out to be an undercover policeman. It was very embarrassing. The deputy mayor got charged with lewd conduct and drew a conviction.'

'No kidding,' Abdullah murmured. He wondered if there was something he had missed. He was inclined to doubt it, but he was curious. 'How about taking a look?' he said suddenly. It was an afternoon to do anything. After all, he probably wouldn't have another opportunity. Not this trip, anyway. 'Hey, Hassan,' he shouted, 'show me something new, how about it? They won't miss us for a few minutes!'

'Are you crazy? Now? With the two *fellahin* in the back seat?' The Egyptian took a quick look in the rearview mirror. 'It would be easier to buy tickets to a porno movie for two elephants in drag.'

'Not them, mudhead – they're orthodox Wahabi, strict observers, you know that. They can wait in the car. But I mean *me* – I never have the chance to do anything these days, and I'm not going to have the time to do it later! Come on, if you think about it, it'll run away. Go give the manager of one of these skin flicks fifty dollars, or whatever you've got on you, I'll pay you back later. Get him to give you some tickets and let us in the back way. You ought to know how to do it.'

Now it was Hassan's turn to burst into raucous laughter.

'*Ya*, Abdullah, an Arab's curiosity is as great as the sea. It is written. Listen, you want to get me in trouble with your whole country? You've been raised a strict observer yourself. The Emir of Rahsmani would send somebody out here to California to chop off my *hasab* if he thought I was corrupting the flower of the family.'

'Bullshit!' Abdullah shouted. 'We've done a lot of things together. I don't see why you're giving me all this crap now. If you're afraid of something, go ahead and say it.'

Hassan said something under his breath.

'Allah preserve us from the uncouth brigands of the desert,' he said in Arabic, 'for there is no pleasure in them. Friend, if you wish to go see a dirty movie, who am I to deny your wish? I am happy to show you the delights of this fair land, wearing tennis clothes, naturally, and bribing a theatre manager, and with a face that thousands recognize. It is my honour. Only do not bare your teeth at me, please.'

'Sorry,' Abdullah said.

Ali drove the car into a parking lot behind one of the theatres and went to see what he could do. In a few minutes he returned and motioned Abdullah to get out. They cut across the parking lot on foot and into a driveway between two buildings where a man waited, holding open a galvanized iron door marked EXIT. As soon as they stepped inside he let the door close, led them down a hall that smelled of cigarette butts and urine, and then into a darker hole that was the theatre.

'Pick a space with empty seats on either side,' Ali whispered. 'We don't want any close company. I'm too pretty, and so are you.'

Not quite an hour later they came out of the theatre by the way they had gone in. The afternoon was growing late and it was raining slightly, the asphalt of the parking lot turned to a black mirror in a sudden shower. The Bedouin were as they had left them in the back seat of the Mercedes, Wadiyeh combing the pages of the Los Angeles *Times* that Ali had left there, looking for the photos and the comics.

'It wasn't all that good,' Ali Hassan said as they drove away. 'We should have waited for something better.'

Abdullah said nothing.

The movies, the last half of one and the first half of another, had been adequate, he supposed, if not the super-productions Ali had led him to believe. But then he wondered what you were supposed to expect, after all. However, the features had been followed by a trailer, offering coming attractions of the next film and this was what had left Abdullah sitting there in the dark with his mouth open, not able to believe what he saw. The credits announced that this was a real, authentic movie, shot in South America, of the mutilation of several young women – chopping off the toes of one was what he actually saw – and the exclusive, final murder of another. It all went by so quickly he wasn't sure what had happened, but he thought they disembowelled one of the girls. At least he saw a lot of blood and heard hair-raising screams. While he was still sitting there stunned the second film began, which featured, he would swear, little girls of about twelve or less running about in the buff pursued by a pot-bellied man in a costume and various villainous types.

Little girls! In the dark he turned to look at Ali, who was sitting somewhat sideways, his arm draped over the back of his seat, obviously bored with what was taking place.

Little girls? Abdullah looked back at the screen again and could see that they probably weren't as young as they were supposed to be, although they were young enough. The sight of the slender legs and muffin buttocks, the little pointed immature breasts was weirdly disturbing. Abdullah licked his lips, feeling both betrayed and embarrassed. It was dirty, all right. He was surprised at himself.

The movies were better, he supposed, as Ali had said. The people were certainly better-looking, and there was an air of slick finish to the productions that hadn't been there before. But Hassan had been right, his grandfather would have been outraged.

I was certainly raised differently, he thought. I was

brought up in the old sensuous Arab tradition that accounted women as one of the great pleasures in life, along with money and horses, to serve in any way that would bring the ultimate pleasure. And that didn't leave out much, it covered just about everything one would expect to find in a dozen pornographic movies. It was also a tradition that accepted that someone like his uncle Hakim could satisfy a taste for young boys as well as marry and produce a decent number of sons.

But it was another thing entirely to sit in the dark in a crowd of furtive strangers and have the technicolor details come rolling out at you, three times as big as life, and try not to break out in a bath of sweat. It was the most curious thing in the world not to be able to do anything about it. If these movies got any better, ordinary, warm-blooded Arabs like himself were in danger of having a heart attack.

He had been thinking, most of the time, about Barbra Burchard and, absurdly, what she would look like with her clothes on. It had given him a headache.

SEVEN

It was almost seven-thirty by the time Abdullah got back to the bungalow in the garden of the Palm Aire Hotel.

James Brooke-Cullingham, who had been waiting, drink in hand, for the best part of an hour and a half, heard the footsteps approaching on the flagstone walk outside and quickly poured another large splash of whisky into his glass. His instincts told him he was going to need it. His eyes made a last-minute check around the room, the dinner table set for three that had been put up before the fireplace, the fire burning against the chill of a rainy California spring evening, and the hi-fi murmuring in the background. Ali was serene. Probably the calm before the storm, he told himself

He was right. A moment later Abdullah, dripping with wet and a sweater thrown over his shoulders, came into the room. A gust of turbulence, like an invisible shadow, seemed to come in with him.

'Ah, there you are,' Brooke-Cullingham drawled.

But, he thought, observing the other, we've got a headache or a stomach ache or I miss my guess. Been gadding about, it's damnably late, and he's put out by something or other, probably doesn't know what himself. The Englishman stifled a sigh. Watch out for flying objects.

These people, as far as Brooke-Cullingham was concerned, were so damned difficult at any time, and the young ones were the worst. The very first time something went awry their precious sense of balance slipped and they were prone to carry on like one of their skittish Arabian horses. It took a firm hand on the reins and limitless patience to get things back in order. Suppressing of course, a forgivable desire to deliver a smashing kick to the ribs.

He had longed to do that with this one, many times.

'Game go well?' Brooke-Cullingham asked.

'Mmmmmm.' The other ran his hand through wet hair and looked around the room morosely. 'What the hell's going on? Who's for dinner?'

Ah, I see you've forgot that, too, Brooke-Cullingham thought, and that's rather too bad. I'm sure you're going to be thoroughly provoked with yourself and everyone else now – you weren't here at five o'clock to take your overseas telephone calls, you've got some telexes that need your attention, there are several items that have come up that are not exactly going to make you overjoyed, and your dinner's getting cold. On top of it all I see I've got a job ahead of me getting you settled down to do an evening's work, which I doubt you're in any mood to do. Eighty thousand dollars is a lot of money to spend on a tennis match. I was hoping it would make you happy, but I see that it hasn't.

'Oh, the usual and then some,' the Englishman said coolly. 'All things in due time.'

The Bedouin returned from the bedroom with clean clothes and began to strip Abdullah of his wet ones, laying the sodden garments on the deep oyster-white rug. Brooke-Cullingham took another sip of his drink, watching the operation without enthusiasm.

'Never mind in due time,' Abdullah said. 'Get to it now, and get it over with.'

Brooke-Cullingham shrugged. 'Your choice, of course. Well, your cousin Hamid called from New York to tell us that he'll arrive here in Los Angeles on the one-twenty A.M. TWA flight. I've arranged for Russell to pick him up. The Waldorf would like some firm dates on your return to New York as they say they don't think they can guarantee the same accommodations without advance notice. The Ambassador would like to know if you have made up your mind about the Washington stopover. The Los Angeles *Times* called to ask if we will hold a press conference. I told them no.'

The Bedouin eased a soft white *disdasha* over Abdullah's head.

'I can't give advance notice about anything and to hell with it,' Abdullah said. 'Tell them we'll stay somewhere else.' Then, suddenly, 'Hamid called? Oh shit. Was there a message?'

Brooke-Cullingham maintained his bland, affable expression. Yes, there certainly had been a message. Hamid al Asmari had taken time between flight connections in New York to go to a telephone and call Los Angeles about his mission, in the hope that Brooke-Cullingham would find a way to smooth things over. Brooke-Cullingham didn't relish the idea and he was not, if he could help it, going to bring it up until the air had cleared a bit. The news was only one of several matters that, like hurdles, had to be got over before the evening was through. It didn't look very promising.

'Nothing substantial,' he murmured. 'Are you going to take a shower and clean up a bit, or do you want to get on with supper? Roehart's due to join us.'

'Dammit, you know I don't like business with dinner! I don't see why in the hell you can't remember that.' Abdullah looked around the room, irritably. 'I'm going to have a drink,' he announced. 'Go fix me a large Scotch and soda.'

Brooke-Cullingham raised his eyebrows a bit but kept his pleasant half smile.

'Shall I go on?' When the other did not answer he said, 'There's been a problem with security again, I'm afraid. I suppose this is as good a time as any to remind you that, ah, when you find yourself someplace other than where you told us you would be, you'd best telephone us and advise us of the change. That's only common consideration, you know. It's hard on Russell, since he's in charge of security, to lose track of you the way he did this afternoon. Makes him dreadfully snappish. He brought up the business of adequate protection again, which of course he should do, that's his responsibility, but then it does make it hard on me, too, to have to handle any of this. Damned if I know what to tell him. You did promise your cooperation. And Russell is quite right, having the *bedu* with you is not enough.'

Bob Roehart came into the bungalow at that moment, carrying an umbrella. Since the Bedouin were not in sight the agent stood holding the thing, not knowing where to put it. A small puddle of water drained off the umbrella and soaked into the rug.

'Hello, am I late?' Roehart said.

'Fix me a drink,' Abdullah repeated.

Brooke-Cullingham acted as though he hadn't heard him.

'We've got to have an agreement on security,' he went on. 'Right now, since you want to get on with it. It's a matter of complete seriousness, I'm sure you'll agree. I'm sorry we have to keep going on like this about it, but it's actually no exaggeration to say that Russell and I are quite tied up with your personal safety. I'm sure I can't imagine what we would do if anything happened to you.'

'I was with Hassan. His car won't hold more than four people.'

'Of course. But then on the other hand you know perfectly well you must take one of the limousines if you are going out, and bring along at least two of the secretaries. They're carrying sidearms and you're supposed to make use of them. Otherwise all their training's gone to waste. And no slipping out, as you did today with Mr Hassan.' Brooke-Cullingham paused to look down at the drink in his hand. 'Now either we reach some sort of agreement on this or it gets a bit sticky. You have a telex from the Embassy in Washington in which it says that the U.S. government wants to inquire about your plans while you're in the States and offers to have the FBI cover the rest of the trip. But whatever, they want us to file a copy of our itinerary. I told them no; this is an unofficial visit and we'd keep our itinerary to ourselves, as well as our security makeup. But this means taking a bit more care, doesn't it, and not letting things get out of hand? We don't want a pack of FBI or Secret Service people hanging around.'

'Dammit, get off my back,' Abdullah said. 'I was with Hassan. We can take care of ourselves.'

Abdullah went over to the bar and poured himself a glass of Johnny Walker and threw in some ice. A few of the ice cubes missed, bounced along the top of the bar. He did not bother to pick them up.

'I'm quite sure Mr Hassan can take care of himself,' Brooke-Cullingham said. 'Not to mention Mr Hassan's lady friend, Miss Burchard. They make quite an interesting couple. I took the liberty of running a check on the lady this afternoon. You might want to take a look at it. Russell had it typed up.'

'You *what*?' Abdullah yelled.

'Maybe I'd better come back a little later,' Roehart said.

'On the surface it would seem they're more than just good friends,' Brooke-Cullingham went on. 'It's a bit difficult to evaluate. But at least the change from Mr Hassan's Hollywood address to her present one in Long Beach seems to be fairly recent. The mail's still being forwarded.'

'Goddamn you, I told you to lay off!' Abdullah shouted. 'Stay out of things like this! That's not security! I'm not interested in what might have happened a few – in the past out here.' But the information had rattled him. He threw more ice in the drink, then more whisky. The liquor wasn't doing any good. His head was pounding. He was dog-tired and everything was coming at him at once.

He couldn't understand why Ali Hassan hadn't said anything about this. On the other hand, Ali hadn't denied that he knew her, either. It left a sour taste in his mouth. Had they been lovers? If so, that was a hell of a thing, even considering Hollywood. Was he supposed to take this, as everyone took these things out here, with a great deal of cool? He didn't think he could manage it. He was infuriated to be confronted with it like this, without having time to think it over. Brooke-Cullingham was wrong, that was all.

'The money's nothing, naturally,' Brooke-Cullingham said. 'You can dispense gifts as you please. It's these sudden involvements that bear looking into. Sorry I had to do it, but people in your position are particularly vulnerable and for the usual reasons. Watch out for Hassan. He seems like a nice enough fellow but there are areas of his personal life that no amount of digging can account for. Besides, his credit rating's problematical, always has been. When you put two and two—'

'SHUT UP!' Abdullah roared. Something in him gave way, surrendered to nerves and the accumulation of several days' tiredness.

The glass of whisky flew past Brooke-Cullingham's shoulder, spraying amber drops, and exploded on the stone of the fireplace wall. The splinters of glass flicked soundlessly in the air for a moment.

Brooke-Cullingham didn't move. Almost absently he reached up and brushed away some drops of whisky from the front of his dinner jacket.

'Well, it's not the nicest thought, to be sure,' he murmured. But his grey eyes had gone steely, his lips barely moving. 'One hates to be suspicious about one's own friends.'

'Don't goad me, Englishman!' Abdullah shouted. 'Don't sneak around – farting your bits of gossip about things that are none of your damned business! Lay off my friends!'

'I'll come back later,' Roehart said. He grabbed his umbrella and fled.

'But it is my business,' Brooke-Cullingham said. 'Your grandfather called at five-thirty, or rather one of his secretaries put through the call. Nothing urgent, just a check to see how things were going. They'll call back to-morrow. We are also in receipt of a telex sent by the Mitsumi combine through the Oil Directorate – that is, Sheik Hakim's office – informing us that the Japanese hope to make an announcement shortly. There's only one sort of an announcement they could make. They're certainly not going to pull out; their contract gives them five more years to bring in a well.'

'When are we going to *eat*!' Abdullah raged. 'I don't want to listen to this – I want something to *eat*!' He turned to the dinner table, the candles not yet lit, the silverware gleaming, a bowl of fresh flowers at the centre. 'What do I have to do to get something to eat around here!'

He picked up one of the chairs at the table, held it at arm's length and let it fall. It turned over on its side.

Brooke-Cullingham had not moved from his position in front of the fireplace. Now he placed his drink carefully on the mantelpiece and turned to the figure in the white tent-like *disdasha* who stood glaring, arms at his sides, hands slightly trembling.

Well here it comes, Brooke-Cullingham thought. You can't hold it in much longer, can you? And at the pace you've been going lately, I suppose it was bound to come. A proper family-style row, hard on the crockery. Not that there isn't some justification – you're something of a misfit at home and you don't fit into this world too comfortably, either, and I suppose the pressure's bound to build up. God knows you go at it with breakneck speed, like all the rest of your kind. And I'm paid to stand here and look after things until it all blows over.

Although, he told himself, I'm getting rather sick of it. I've got enough money now, I ought not to be muddling about with these people year after year, it puts a damn strain on me, too. After all, I'm rather in the same boat myself – I've grown accustomed to travelling in two worlds, and while it's exciting it's a bit difficult to bear up under at my age.

Brooke-Cullingham had a house in Switzerland, a refuge against the ferocious British tax structure, and he spent two months of each year there. His long term of employment with the Emir of Rahsmani had made him a wealthy man in his own right and he had been ready for retirement for some time. But lately he had found that his luxurious Swiss home tended to pall after a few weeks' residence just as Rahsmani palled after each ten-month period. In recent years he had been impatient to get out of one place and into another, all with an equal lack of enjoyment.

We're both cut loose, he realized, from that stability and

sense of place that anchors ordinary people. But mine's by choice, rather. And your problem, if you can call it that, is that yours isn't.

'Brace yourself for some bad news,' Brooke-Cullingham said flatly. Might as well go ahead and get it over with. 'Your cousin Hamid tells me your grandfather the Emir isn't ready to send anyone to Riyadh on family business. Not at this time.'

Brooke-Cullingham stopped. The other was staring at him wildly. It was going to take a moment to sink in.

'Don't tell me that, you son of a bitch! What the hell is this, anyway?'

'Just what I've told you. The answer to your letter is no.'

'What the hell is this?' Abdullah repeated, disbelieving. He cast about the room as though looking for some sort of proof. 'Is this some kind of crazy thing to ruin my day?'

'On the contrary. I'm to break the news first and ah –' Brooke-Cullingham drew out the words, 'give you time to compose yourself.'

'You – you –' Abdullah stumbled against the dinner table. A sweep of the arm sent the dishes, silverware, tablecloth flying. Blindly, he picked up another one of the chairs and held it uncertainly for a moment, then he sent it toward the glass partition that divided the living room from the entrance hall and the terrace beyond. But the chair fell short, silently, on the deep rug. Infuriated, Abdullah picked up another chair and heaved it in Brooke-Cullingham's direction. The Englishman dodged it neatly. The chair hit the fieldstone panel with a satisfactory crash. One leg broke off, dropped to the hearth. Brooke-Cullingham moved unhurriedly to get to a large upholstered easy chair and manoeuvre it in between. The two Bedouin rushed in from the hallway, then stopped short and did not come any farther.

'I knew it –' Abdullah howled. He raked his fingers through his hair, despairingly. 'The old bastard! *Allah – Allah!*'

He picked up the remaining chair and advanced on the

Bedouin, who retreated open-mouthed.

'You two – pirates! Scavengers – accursed Arab *family* –'

Brooke-Cullingham kept a sharp eye out. He stepped carefully over the broken chair at the hearth. The Bedouin were terrified, he could see the whites of their eyes as they backed down the hallway. Well, it was really too bad, the boy had earned his tantrums. But they would never understand that, not with his family history. The Bedouin were almost supernaturally afraid of madness. They were completely demoralized. In spite of the mayhem it was almost funny.

With a howl, Abdullah rushed at them and hurled the chair down the hallway. The bodyguards turned and ran. That chair too, fell without a sound, muffled by the thick carpeting.

'Dammit, doesn't anything BREAK?' he screamed.

He pounced upon a heavy bronze lamp on a table ñearby, heaved it at the thick thermal pane of the glass partition. The lampshade flew off, the lightbulb exploded and the glass panel suddenly spread in a giant star-shaped crack at the point of impact, silently. Abdullah picked up the small walnut table on which the lamp had stood and battered it against the glass. He stood back, panting. A fairly large spear-sharp section of glass fell out of the sunburst crack, very slowly, and settled into the deep pile rug. Abdullah stared at it.

'What the hell's the MATTER with this place?'

There was a moment of absolute quiet.

'All right, that's about enough, isn't it?' Brooke-Cullingham said. But he kept the easy chair in between.

Abdullah still had the lamp table in his hand, staring at the glass pane.

'Come and sit down now, and I'll fix you a drink if you want it. I don't think,' the Englishman said judiciously, you're making much progress there.'

'You go to hell,' Abdullah said. His hair had fallen forward over his eyes. He looked at the lamp table as though he did not know what to do with it.

'Probably. But come and sit down, anyway.'

Abdullah still stared at the table in his hand.

'I don't want anything to drink,' he said. 'To hell with that, too.'

Abdullah went slowly to the front door, opened it, and tossed the lamp table out into the rain. Then he closed it.

Brooke-Cullingham lifted his voice so that he could be heard to the end of the hallway. '*Essma!* Come at once, you sons of Eblis, wherever you are lurking!' When the figure of one of the Bedouin appeared at the end of the hall Brooke-Cullingham shouted, 'Fix some coffee. We desire it immediately. And whatever there is to satisfy our appetites. We die of hunger.' Then, to Abdullah, 'Come and sit down, as I have told you. Give your spirit a rest. As well as your feet. This is all due to weariness, truly.'

'Damn you. Damn you,' Abdullah said.

He stood for a moment and then he came across the rug in his bare feet and stood in front of the chair Brooke-Cullingham had pulled up. Rather abruptly, he turned and sat down in it. He sat bolt upright, his hands resting on the chair arms, staring straight ahead of him.

'Nothing breaks in this place,' he said.

Brooke-Cullingham sighed.

'Don't be a fool. We'll get you something to smash up properly, next time.'

'You can afford to be funny. It doesn't happen to you.'

The same old fear, Brooke-Cullingham thought.

'Of course it does – did, rather. Bursts of temper, youthful high-jinks. Temper's fairly natural when one is young and prone to fly off the handle.' That was a pleasant way of stating the case, he thought. 'I used to spar a bit at college, at one time I fancied myself quite a brawler.'

Brooke-Cullingham pulled up another chair and sat down facing him. The Bedouin came to the far end of the living room, one with the brass long-handled coffee pot, the other with a large tray. The forgotten dinner.

'Put it down,' Brooke-Cullingham snapped. They stood there, wavering. 'On the *table*. Pick up the accursed table, put the food on it. Then go away! But give us the coffee, first.'

When they had the small cups of black sweetened coffee in their hands Brooke-Cullingham leaned forward to Abdullah.

'Now listen, my friend, bad news must be taken with some measure of equanimity. Otherwise one can be destroyed by disappointments, is it not so? Now that you bear much responsibility, you cannot afford to let this happen. I know you fear for your sister, perhaps unnecessarily, but all things change in good time. If she is unhappy, as you suppose she is, it would seem quite logical, then, that you are the one to restore her happiness. In this I quite agree.' Brooke-Cullingham had known Abdullah and his sister since they were children, shunted about in Rahsmani court intrigues. He knew the tie was extraordinarily strong. 'However, since you are not able to do anything at this distance, it appears that you must cultivate patience. Such is the first step to wisdom and self-control. You will not be separated from her forever.'

'Why not?'

'Dammit, man, there are airplanes!' Brooke-Cullingham said in English. 'When you're through here you can hop a plane to Riyadh and handle the situation yourself. As her brother, you have the power to bring her home if she's all that unhappy. But first you have to have proof that she is. Otherwise there'll be a dreadful stink.'

Abdullah stared at him, not allowing much hope.

'She wasn't ready for marriage,' he said, finally. The words were mumbled. 'It wasn't right to send her off with some fat oaf who was going to –' Here he stopped, swallowed. 'Who was going to do to her what only should be done if two people have some feeling for each other. That is, at least the woman should *want* to go to bed with her husband. And I know my sister – she didn't even want him to touch her *hand*, for God's sake! Can you imagine what it was like for her, the first time? What a hell of a lover *he'd* make! You could just look at him –' He choked.

'I don't think it's as bad as all that,' Brooke-Cullingham said.

'And my grandfather did it – *I* did it, too; I'm as guilty as anybody! I didn't do anything to prevent it and I could have. My sister would give her life for me. You know I'm not exaggerating, that's the truth! She's the only one who cares for me, really, it's always been that way. As I am the only one who cares for *her*,' he said, almost to himself. 'We don't really have any friends in this damned world.'

Brooke-Cullingham was silent.

There's not much that can be done here, he thought, if this is what's been gnawing at him for the past few weeks. I'm damned if I can think of any ready solutions. Family feeling runs deep in these people – obviously what we have here is a great sense of guilt fed by the usual abundant Arab reservoirs of emotion. All of which can be bloody tiresome.

Brooke-Cullingham could not imagine himself being so overwrought about his own sister, who lived quietly in Sussex with her accountant husband and four children. Nor, for that matter, being particularly concerned about her sexual adjustment – something which apparently bothered the other a great deal. But dammit, he thought, you have to give him credit. He loves his sister wholeheartedly, probably the only feeling he has that is not totally centred on himself. The whole thing had the undeniable ring of truth.

'Well now, as far as your grandfather is concerned, I don't think he had much choice, really. The pressure's on him to get along with the Saudis, you know. He's rather in a spot.' Even at that moment, to talk about the need to get along with one's powerful, enormously wealthy neighbours the Saudis, Brooke-Cullingham realized, was horrendously banal. But something was needed. 'This marriage of your sister's is not just a political arrangement for nebulous gains in the future, it's very much a matter of here and now. And regardless of what you might think, Prince Azziz wanted this marriage very much, and that goes for the rest of the Sauds, too. Your grandmother has a remarkable reputation among their women, they think of her as very much a political power. Under the circumstances I don't think the Sauds are going to let your sister be too unhappy.'

Although Abdullah did not appear to be listening too attentively, Brooke-Cullingham went on, 'You should try to think about these things more often, my friend, and realize your grandfather is playing his political games as best he can, considering the complications of it all. The Saudis still regard all the small gulf states like your own as part of their traditional territorial claims. And as the Emir so rightly sees, in the event of Soviet interference or a revolutionary takeover in any of the gulf states, the Saudis would be ready to move in to protect the oil supply. Backed by the U.S. military, of course. Now perhaps you see your sister as a helpless pawn in all this,' Brooke-Cullingham said gently, 'but in fact she's playing a very important part. As important as yours. You've got to get over this feeling you're being unfairly manipulated.'

He sat back to observe the effect of his words. Abdullah frowned.

'But nobody explained this to her,' he said huskily. 'It would have made a difference.'

Brooke-Cullingham couldn't help but smile.

'Perhaps she realizes now. In her own way,' he said, as sincerely as he could.

The telephone rang. Brooke-Cullingham got up and crossed the room to answer it.

'It's Russell,' he said. 'You have a telephone call from New York. Do you want to take it here?'

'In the bedroom.' Abdullah went down the hall and into his room and saw to it that the door was tightly closed. He sat down on the bed.

It was Crossland.

'I'm here; I have a couple of numbers you can take, in case you want to get in touch with me,' the voice with the familiar Texas twang said in the receiver. 'The letters were sent ahead a few days ago, and I've already been in touch today. We're asking for an executive board meeting and they're bitching about the short notice, telling me they can't get anybody together in a hurry. But they will.'

'Yeah,' Abdullah said.

'What's the matter, are you busy? Do you want to call me back?'

'No, no,' he said. 'It's all right.'

'How's the speech going? You get everything you need? Can I send you any material from New York?'

The speech? Abdullah looked through the glass wall of the bedroom to the floodlit expanse of green beyond the lights around the swimming pool. The figure of Wadiyeh al Qasim passed in between suddenly, going on some errand.

'I'm okay. I'll have everything together when I get there.' He hadn't touched the speech since he had been in California.

'Check in with me tomorrow,' Crossland said. 'Or do you want me to call you?'

'No, I can call. It's okay. I have a phone in my bedroom.' He had forgot the exact arrangements for secrecy with Crossland, anyway. 'Try me about five, that's when I get the calls — or if I'm not here, I'll call you back.' It sounded pretty messy. 'We'll work something out.'

When Crossland hung up Abdullah went to the bureau and took the papers on the speech for the GAROC board out of their leather binder. At some point he should get back to them, he knew. But he was really getting pressed for time, for thought, for everything. The gift from Van Cleef's should have arrived at Barbra Burchard's address by now. He wondered if she could call him through the hotel switchboard. Or if she would.

He thumbed through the papers of the speech twice, because he didn't remember them being in that order. And as he stood there he knew they weren't in that order when he left them last. The notes were on the bottom and an OPEC report by Ahmed Zaki Yamani had been on top. Now they were reversed.

He started to the door, intending to take the folder out to Brooke-Cullingham, and then he stopped. He didn't know what he should do, but telling Brooke-Cullingham that someone had been going through his files was not it. He didn't know why, but it wasn't. He would have to think about it.

As he was standing there Wadiyeh passed before the glass again on the terrace, with Bisharah and Ramzi and two of the secretaries. Abdullah went to the sliding doors to look out. They were going down to the concrete apron around the swimming pool. As Abdullah saw one of the secretaries dip his hands into the water of the pool and rub them on his face for the ritual ablutions he knew what they were doing. It was a little late, but they were gathering for the 'isha, or evening prayer. Under the fluorescent lights of the swimming pool he saw them get down on their knees, facing in what he was sure Wadiyeh had found was the east and the direction of Mecca.

Abdullah opened the sliding doors and stepped out. The terrace was wet to his feet from the recent rain but the stars were out and a cold breeze hissed in the palm trees. The air smelled good. The hem of the *disdasha* picked up the water from the grass like a sponge as he crossed the lawn, and flapped about his ankles. But when he got down to the lighted area he dropped to his knees carefully and pulled the wet edge of the gown up over the backs of his legs and out of the way. They had begun the *ghahada* or confession of faith.

There is no god but God and Mohammed is the messenger of God.

He missed his Harley. He missed the Harley and the clean, empty sweep of the desert where God existed, and probably nowhere else. For the first time he thought about returning to Rahsmani and it wasn't too bad, after all.

EIGHT

The next morning they started for the San Fernando Valley where at eleven o'clock they were to look over the Citrus-ville Community Bank, one of the three banks proposed in Roehart and Simpson's portfolio. It was another beautiful California day, the sun high and hot in a faintly hazy sky and with only a few layers of bluish smog in the streets of Beverly Hills, which the radio said would burn off by noon. Thanks to the step-by-step itinerary that Russell had drawn up for the day they were only a little late getting started, snaking out on to the Los Angeles Freeway in a convoy of Lincoln-Continental limousines that Brooke-Cullingham had ordered for the occasion and that came equipped with bullet-proof glass, fully stocked bars, and television sets for the back-seat passengers. In line with security a chart had been drawn up showing how they were to proceed. The first car held Ramzi, who was to be security chief for the day, to let Russell stay behind with the telex operator; Bob Roehart; one of the lawyers from the Bank of America Legal Services Department and a Jordanian secretary-body-guard. The middle car, which was Abdullah's was more crowded, since they had to squeeze in not only Brooke-Cullingham but also Wadiyeh, an Iranian secretary-body-guard, and his cousin Hamid. The last car got the leftovers – Bisharah, the rest of the secretaries, and a pile of brief-cases and attaché cases. They were, as Abdullah had ob-served, getting more and more like an invasion or a migrat-ing tribe. It had even worried Brooke-Cullingham, who had wanted security but a fairly low profile, too, if they could manage it. But when it came time to make up the list it seemed everybody wanted to go – everyone wanted to get out of the hotel and see more of southern California, and finally Russell had relented and ordered an extra limousine.

At the last moment, though, Brooke-Cullingham had decided to put the Bedouin into dark business suits and shirts and ties. Since nothing much could be done about their long braided hair he had had to let them keep their head cloth kaffiyehs. As Abdullah was getting dressed he decided he would wear a kaffiyeh, too. Not that *his* hair needed covering up – although he had been so long without a proper haircut that it was almost as long as Ali Hassan's – it was just that he felt like wearing a kaffiyeh for a change. It was something he rarely did at home. He put aside the fancy assortment of silk cloths with gold ropes that Wadiyeh had packed for him and chose instead a black-and-red-checkered Rahsmani kaffiyeh such as the ordinary tribesmen wore. Like the Bedouin, he wore a lightweight blue business suit. From the back it was hard to tell them apart, although the Bedouin were slightly taller.

Now, as they sped along the freeway, Abdullah kept fiddling with the checkered cloth where the edges fell against his face and got in his line of vision. He could see Brooke-Cullingham, slumped in his corner of the limousine, smiling to himself. Which made Abdullah slightly annoyed. He knew what Brooke-Cullingham was thinking, but it wasn't so funny. He hadn't really got out of the habit of wearing a kaffiyeh, it was just that it felt somewhat strange with a business suit. It didn't look bad, though. From time to time he had to turn and look at himself in the reflection of the car window and what looked back was reassuringly familiar.

His cousin Hamid was in the jumpseat immediately in front of Abdullah, his eyes on the television set in the partition, which was playing a game show from Los Angeles. A woman had just won a compact car and the limousine was filled with her faint, tinny squeals. Before they had left the hotel Brooke-Cullingham had brought up the subject of friends again, and interestingly enough he had mentioned Hamid as a likely candidate. At least while they were in the States. They could travel together, do any sightseeing Abdullah might want to do and eliminate a lot of complications. It would also make security a lot simpler.

'He's quite a reasonable sort,' Brooke-Cullingham had said. 'I think he admires you quite a bit. Anyway, there's no harm in thinking it over.'

On the surface, Abdullah supposed, it wasn't a bad idea. At least it was quite in line with that sort of Arab custom which the Englishman, being an outsider, sometimes grasped better than they did themselves. In this case, playing it safe with the old bonds of tribe and family, take on Hamid as close friend and companion and throw out unknown quantities like Ali Hassan. The trouble was, as Brooke-Cullingham should know after all his years in the gulf countries, tribe and family were usually the ones you could trust the least. Sure, the old tradition advised one to put one's faith in relatives and shun strangers. But the saying also went, *Beware thy brother.*

Well, he didn't have any brothers, but he certainly did have enough other relations.

'Ya, Hamid, turn that thing off,' Abdullah said to the figure in the jumpseat in front of him. 'This noise wearies me.'

But his cousin, laughing, couldn't hear a thing.

You could see that idea wasn't going to get anyplace, he told himself. Abdullah looked thoughtfully at his cousin, a cigarette in one hand, cackling over some housewife making a fool of herself on the television screen. God knows why Hamid should admire him, he didn't know where Brooke-Cullingham had got that impression. As far as he knew Hamid didn't think about anything much if he could help it, much less admire anybody; actually they didn't know each other well at all, in spite of being members of the same family. His cousin was tall and bony like most of the Asmaris, being Fuad's grandson, and while not exactly ugly he was hardly the family beauty, either. Hamid had the Asmari beak of a nose but his chin was small and out of proportion to the rest of his face. Instead of the hawklike look of most of the family males he managed to look something like a quizzical rooster. Which didn't inspire much confidence. His cousin was near Abdullah's own age, about twenty-five or twenty-six, and like most upper-class Rahsmanis he didn't have any special ambition that one could tell except to keep on doing what he was doing, which was to stay in New York City, enjoy himself, and hold down a job as cultural attaché to the consulate that demanded only that he come to work once or twice a week, if that much, and then not do anything in particular once he was there. Hamid had two or three years of college in the United States, but Abdullah couldn't remember what midwestern university he had attended; he thought it was Indiana or Ohio. At any rate he hadn't finished. Somewhere along in there he had played polo and had even taken a couple of medals in it. Hamid was a fine horseman, even his grandfather Fuad boasted of it. But apparently Hamid hadn't had the ambition to keep on riding, either.

What was really hard to understand, Abdullah thought, was why anybody like his cousin would want to ride along on a beautiful day with his face stuck in a television set. That was one big difference between them, anyway. Abdullah turned back to the window. The little towns they were passing along the highway were fascinating places, like scenes right out of the movies about the American way of life that Hollywood produced. He supposed some of them must have been shot there, on location, to make them look so familiar. As the freeway sliced through the countryside on elevated sections you could look down and see wide streets, comfortable houses set back in green lawns where people were out with their hoses watering bright flowerbeds. Once again he was impressed with how good life could be here, everything with a relaxed and satisfied air, much more so than the cramped towns of the northeast that he remembered from his days at school. No wonder a bank in southern California had been recommended. It looked like a good place to live and do business. They weren't the only ones – the Saudi Arabians had already bought up two banks, the Bank of Contra Costa and the Security National Bank in Walnut Creek, California. Abdullah had no idea where Walnut Creek was, but he thought it might be interesting to find out, to go up and take a look and see what the Saudis had put their money into.

As Brooke-Cullingham had pointed out, his grandfather was a little late getting into the investment business, but then the Emir, being an old-line gulf state leader, had always been conservative on that score. Also, the Saudis and the Kuwaitis had had a twenty-year start, as Rahsmani oil hadn't begun to flow in any quantity until recently. But now, thanks to Brooke-Cullingham's prodding, Roehart and Simpson had steered them into putting a substantial amount into Deltona Corporation's retirement communities in Florida, the purchase of five new condominiums in Torremolinos, Spain, and a couple of new office buildings in the central area of London. And, what with the politicking of the Sudanese wife in the *hareem*, there was also a controlling interest in something called the Modern Match Producing and Distributing Company, which wasn't as bad as it sounded, and ownership of the Africa Palace Hotel in Khartoum. His grandfather liked to put his money into property in the old style, liked to stay out of the stock market or long- or short-term bonds or currency manipulation or anything that wasn't solid and real. As a result they had had the luck to avoid the Investors Overseas Services and the mutual funds disaster of Mr Bernie Cornfeld into which so many Bahreinis and Kuwaitis had sunk their money in the 1960s. It was true the Rahsmani Overseas Investment Corporation hadn't made much money during its comparatively short existence, but his grandfather could say that it hadn't lost anything, either. It also hadn't had much to do. Whole months passed sometimes with the ROIC staff sharpening pencils or looking out the window or reading the international stock market reports and little else. Everything had always pretty much led into the Emir's own hands. And the Emir, like most of the other gulf rulers, still preferred to send the bulk of Rahsmani oil revenues through Swiss clearing houses where, after some juggling, they ended up in London banks on deposit in special accounts. There, in line with the Emir's strict Moslem beliefs interpreting interest money as usury, it earned something the British labelled 'commissions'. The British economy might be bad, but they were still smart about some things. The Americans had a reputation for haggling over interest money being called interest money and to hell with it; the British took oil revenues and stuck it in their banks and called it anything you wanted them to. That, and the way the British Protectorate had run their affairs in the gulf in the old days still entitled the English to a good bit of respect, even though some of it was grudging. As a consequence the Emir still used the British Bank of the Middle East and Barclay's Bank in London, even though Abdullah for a long time had thought they ought to put at least part of their money into First National City of New York and the Bank of America. For convenience, if nothing else. But as long as the money still led into his grandfather's hands they were committed to some odd operations. As for instance his grandfather had a big chunk of money in the Algemene Bank Nederland, an old-timer originally founded by the Dutch near Mecca for their East Indies tourists on pilgrimage. His grandfather remembered cashing some drafts there once in the twenties when he had visited the shrine, and still liked it.

Gradually, though, as oil revenues backed up, things were changing. Buying their own bank was a first step. And according to the descriptions worked up by Roehart and Simpson the Citrusville Community Bank was a nice modest beginning. It was formerly owned by a large rancher in the Valley named Eric Bjornberg, a conservative Swedish immigrant whose tight fiscal policies the Emir of Rahsmani would certainly have approved of. The bank was small but solid and Bjornberg had kept his finger on everything, a real family business. Fifty-one per cent of the stock was now held by the widow, the rest of the stock in small portions going to the Valley Citrus Growers

Cooperative, a local plastics industries plant, an aircraft electronics assembly company with several large government defence contracts, a group of local private investors, and the Citrusville Department Store. When he had looked over Roehart and Simpson's presentation Abdullah hadn't been able to find much wrong with it. The bank's assets were good and straightforward, the management hadn't gone into mortgages too heavily in the past few years and so had stayed out of the usual trouble. The widow, Mrs Bjornberg, had run the business pretty much herself and had followed her husband's tight-fisted policies. Now she wanted to sell out her interest and move north to live near her son and daughter-in-law in Berkeley.

'This looks like it,' Brooke-Cullingham said.

They had come off the highway and into a state road and passed a community college with brick buildings set in a pretty green lawn as big as a golf course. Just beyond the community college they were supposed to find one of the three shopping centres in Citrusville, this one with a brand-new giant Woolco store, a supermarket, and the Citrusville Community Bank. They saw the shopping centre almost immediately, laid out like a small city in its own right, surrounded by a plain of asphalt parking lot. The parking area was filled with automobiles and a minor traffic jam had backed up on to the road. They could see something was going on. There were a lot of strings of brightly coloured plastic pennants flying from the supermarket roof, and several ice-cream trucks were drawn up in front. They could hear a country-music band playing from the back of a flatbed lorry constructed to look like a giant frankfurter resting in a hot-dog roll. Along the side of the lorry that was the hot-dog-roll portion were painted the words OSCAR MAYER WIENERS. A girl in a red-sequined cowgirl outfit was singing 'Your Cheatin' Heart' into a microphone, brilliantly amplified over the parking lot by a battery of loudspeakers.

'What the devil,' Brooke-Cullingham said. He moved forward in his seat to talk to the chauffeur. 'Get the others on the telephone,' he told him, 'and tell them to go around the back. We seem to have hit some damned fair or supermarket promotion of some sort. There's the bank – keep on going. These places ought to have a back entrance.'

The lead limousine had already made a U-turn back on to the highway with the same thing in mind. The chauffeur was trying to get them on the radiotelephone. There was so much activity in the parking area of the shopping centre it was hard to locate the Citrusville Community Bank, but it came into view as they turned down the traffic aisle. It was on the corner next to Woolco's in a building considerably larger than the prospectus had indicated. The bank looked like a fancy, rather futuristic city hall with a glassed-in arcade filled with indoor plants and trees. Some part of a high school band in red and white uniforms had spilled over from the supermarket area with their drums and brass instruments and a few were sitting on the pavement in front of it.

After a few hot, dragging minutes back in the line of cars on the highway they were able to cut into another entrance of the parking area and head around to the back. The lead limousine had pulled out far ahead of them and Brooke-Cullingham, trying to relay instructions to the driver using the telephone, cursed. There was, as they discovered once they had got into it, no back way to the shopping centre; the far side had been constructed to face yet another secondary road. The bank looked as official and accessible from this side as it did from the other, as did the Woolco's next to it. The parking lot was just as full of cars as the other and a large crowd flowed along the promenade and down through the arcade in the bank.

'Where the hell's the other car?' Brooke-Cullingham said, turning to look behind. 'Didn't they turn in? Stop in front of the bank,' he told the chauffeur. 'Don't try to find a parking space, man, the devil with it.'

It was not at all the way they had worked it out beforehand. The plans called for them to drive straight up to the Citrusville Community Bank, which Brooke-Cullingham expected to be fairly clear of people at that hour and ready to receive them. Now the driver could hardly find a spot on the yellow kerb in front of the stores big enough to park the limousine. The limousine in front had given up, was making a turn down through the lot to try and come up behind them. The third car was not anywhere in sight.

Almost before they had managed to pull in to the kerb, some half-grown boys in blue jeans and motorcycle caps gathered to feel the polished sides of the limousine and examine the radiator grille and insignia. Behind the youth were some remnants of the high school band from the other side, mostly adolescent girls with paper pompoms and red and white outfits with extremely short skirts. A tall, deeply tanned woman of about fifty with big teeth and blonde hair and two men in the uniform of the Citrusville City Police who were almost as big as she pushed their way through the teenagers and tried to clear a space.

'You kids get off the car,' the woman said. 'My goodness, we were expecting you around the *front*,' she announced. 'Half the band's back there.'

Wadiyeh al Qasim jumped out the door opposite the driver.

'My God,' Brooke-Cullingham groaned. He threw open the back door of the limousine. 'Keep your seats.'

The Bedouin was immediately surrounded by the cheerleader squad. One of the girls grabbed at Wadiyeh's shoulder. 'Are you the prince?' she shouted. Wadiyeh struggled to get his hand inside the business-suit jacket. He was remembering New York. Brooke-Cullingham saw the gesture and scrambled out after him in alarm, missed the kerb, almost fell to his knees.

'Be calm,' Brooke-Cullingham cried in Arabic. 'Restrain yourself!'

The large blonde woman stuck her head in the front window.

'Hi, welcome to Citrusville,' she said. The front seat was empty, the chauffeur had got out to protect his car. 'Oh *hey*, there you are!' she cried cheerfully through the partition. Behind her, Brooke-Cullingham was endeavouring to keep the teenage girls away from Wadiyeh. The Bedouin's *kaffiyeh* had slipped to one side.

'Hey man,' one of the motorcycle youths said. 'Dig that hair.'

'I should help,' Hamid al Asmari volunteered. But he looked out the window where the girls were mobbing Wadiyeh. 'What is it these girls are doing?' he said, anxiously.

Abdullah had started to laugh. He supposed it wasn't all that funny, but he couldn't help it. This country was certainly mad. It was impossible to offer explanations when no explanations would do. The girls had turned their attentions to Brooke-Cullingham, who was backed up against the fender, holding on to Wadiyeh. More people seemed to be gathering on the pavement, craning to see what was going on. The country-and-Western band on the lorry constructed like a hot dog had turned the corner at Woolco's and took up a spot at the end of the traffic aisle. The band began to play 'The Tennessee Waltz', briskly. There were a lot of women shoppers gathered on the pavement in front of the bank, some with children in prams. Through the thickening crowd, like apples bobbing on water, were the heads of Ramzi Alam and the Bank of America lawyer from the first limousine and Bisharah's checkered *kaffiyeh*. From the clump of girls with the red and white pompoms around him Bisharah was having trouble, too. A man in a T-shirt with a television camera on his shoulder came out of the bank.

'You'll have to excuse the kids,' the blonde woman said through the front-seat window. She was shouting, although they could hear her pretty clearly in the back seat. 'There's a Honda shop on the other side, they're always hanging around.'

Hamid started to get out, then sank back in the jumpseat. A young man with a harried expression inserted himself in the limousine door. 'Mr Sheik?' The man with the television camera on the shoulder set was behind him. 'Could you say a few words for us?'

Abdullah left Hamid with it. He got out on the far side of the car, which was fairly clear, with some sort of idea in his head of helping Brooke-Cullingham. But the girls had spotted him. They came around the back of the limousine followed by the Citrusville City Police. There seemed to be, Abdullah noticed hurriedly, a great many pretty high school girls with long bare legs in this place. All amazingly well developed for their age. As they came up to him he could see that, under the scarlet jersey tops, they were obviously not wearing brassieres.

'He's the one!' the girl in the lead shrilled. 'Oh far out!'

'He's cute!' another cried and made a lunge.

Abdullah held his hands up in front of him to ward them off. For a moment he wondered how Brooke-Cullingham was doing with Wadiyeh on the pavement in front of the bank. It was the only thing, now, that really worried him. But there wasn't anything he could do. Whatever all this was, it had certainly got out of hand.

On the other side of the car Ramzi Alam spotted Abdullah. He practically slid over the hood of the Lincoln, coming down beside him in the group of shrieking girls.

'Be easy,' Abdullah told him. He didn't want anybody to get hurt. He fended off a girl who was trying to grab his *kaffiyeh*. 'It's a variety of welcome or reception,' he told Ramzi in Arabic. The Iranian should know how Americans, especially young American girls, could act sometimes. They were ganging up on him for some reason as they would a rock singer or pop-music star. Anyway, he didn't have time to talk. He pried away the hand of a girl who was trying to pull out his shirt. The Citrusville police was trying to keep the girls from climbing up on the hood of the car to get a better look.

A pretty young woman squirmed through the press of bodies and reached out a microphone and jammed it into Abdullah's face. He had leaned forward at that moment and the microphone hit Abdullah's front teeth with a distinct noise. No one seemed to notice. The noise of a television camera's whirling began.

'Hey,' Abdullah said. He reached up to feel his mouth. He supposed he was all right. Nothing was bleeding that he could tell.

'Are you with this party? Do you speak English?' the young woman said hurriedly. Her head was covered with short bouncy brown curls and when she spoke dimples flashed entrancingly at the corners of her mouth. But her expression was grim, businesslike. From what Abdullah could see she wasn't wearing a brassiere, either; her breasts swayed lissomly as she was jostled from behind. 'Is it true you're here to buy the Citrusville Community Bank? Why do you want to buy a bank in southern California particularly?' She was having a hard time keeping the microphone pointed at him, shoved about as she was by the beauties of the pompom squad. 'Oh, damn!' she cried, the dimples deepening in distress. 'Is there anybody here that speaks this language and can interpret for me?'

'I do, what do you want me to interpret?' Abdullah said. He couldn't help grinning at her in spite of his sore front teeth. She was a very pretty girl to be working so hard. A woman with a little girl shoved a piece of paper at him, wanting his autograph.

The pretty young woman with the microphone rewarded him with a sudden, melting smile.

'You're a doll,' she breathed. 'You must be the prince.'

'Call me sheik,' Abdullah said. It was hard to resist her. It was hard, even, to resist the squealing girls around him and the women shoppers with their sunglasses and the motorcycle kids pushing closer to get a better look. 'He's a tall bastard, isn't he,' one of them said. One of the cheerleaders had her crotch comfortably against his thigh. Abdullah could feel the warmth through his trouser leg. 'Actually,' Abdullah said, 'sheik is not a real title.' He paused, not sure of what he wanted to say, but feeling that he had to get on top of the situation somehow. At least before he got his clothes picked off his flesh by his admirers. 'It's not a title like "prince" in my country. The word for prince is *emir*, and that's what you call my grandfather.

The Emir of Rahsmani. If you want to call me something you can say sheik. That just means leader, boss, something like that. But my real name is Abdullah ibn Tewfik ibn Ibrahim al Asmari.'

He thought they would like that. The cheerleader squad, overcome by the sound of his voice, gave faint, muffled screams. In front of Abdullah the television cameraman was muttering, 'Great, great,' under his breath. He shoved the camera closer.

'It sounds complicated but it isn't,' Abdullah said, smiling endearingly. The girls screamed again. He tried to move his leg away from the cheerleader's warm body but there wasn't much room to manoeuvre. There was another girl on the other side. 'What it means is, Abdullah, that's me — son of Tewfik — that's my father — son of Ibrahim — that's my grandfather — of the Asmaris, which is the name of our family. How do you like that?' he said to the girl next to him. 'And Abdullah means Servant of God. We're a very religious people; we like to give nice names.'

Abdullah stopped, smiling, and the faces in the crowd smiled back. By God, Abdullah thought, Hassan should see me now. He couldn't do any better himself.

Another television camera had appeared. 'Mr Sheik,' the harried newsman said, 'would you say you're the prime minister of your country or secretary of state or are you more like the president?'

'They said you were going to hold a press conference when you get inside the bank,' someone else said.

The women with the prams on the edge of the crowd were making way for the Citrusville City Police and Brooke-Cullingham, who could not get to Abdullah fast enough.

'No interviews, no interviews,' Brooke-Cullingham was saying. When he got close he stuck one hand in front of the nearest television camera and took Abdullah by the arm with another. The crowd groaned in disappointment. 'Dammit, let's get out of here,' Brooke-Cullingham said. 'Half these people think you're some damned movie star.'

'Don't do that,' Abdullah said, pulling away from him. It

was all going down on film and Brooke-Cullingham, rushing up like that, made it look bad. 'They want a press interview. We'd better give them a press interview. I don't mind.'

'The hell you say.' Brooke-Cullingham was fussed. His jacket was unbuttoned and his tie hanging out. 'It's that damned woman's fault. Let's get in the cars and get out of here. We didn't bargain for this.'

Abdullah didn't see what harm there would be in answering a few questions. He was having a great time; these people obviously liked him. To drive off in a huff would only leave a hell of a bad impression.

'We came to see the bank,' he said. 'Let's see the bank. Don't get uptight, this is just the way people do things out here. I know. Come on,' he said to the television people, 'we'll see what we can do inside.'

'Abdullah,' Brooke-Cullingham began.

'Be quiet,' Abdullah said in Arabic. 'And send someone to get the telephone number of this newsgirl. That is one very interesting woman.'

Fifteen minutes later Abdullah was sitting on the edge of a table in the reception area of the Citrusville Community Bank while the television people set up their lights around him. Ramzi and the Jordanian were busy persuading the crowd to move back a little and make some room, and Wadiyeh and Bisharah, settled down somewhat from their earlier flap, had taken up watchful positions against the far wall. People were very curious about the Bedouin; the two had to be instructed to stand still while the crowd looked them over and asked questions about their age and their efficiency as bodyguards and expressed amazement that they could not read or write. Abdullah had signed dozens of autographs in English and Arabic. The blonde woman with the big teeth, who was Mrs Estelle Bjornberg, the banker's widow, had gone to get Abdullah a paper cup of Coca-Cola and a piece of homemade cake, and while Abdullah was waiting for the television people he ate the cake, drank the Coca-Cola, and helped himself to a plate of home-made candy one of the bank tellers had made for the occasion. The idea of food being served, especially home-made food, made him feel right at home. Mrs Bjornberg had planned a reception, and there was a big table in one of the back offices covered with things to eat. The bank teller who had made the candy was about eighteen and redheaded. Abdullah had looked her over appreciatively. If anything, the girls in the San Fernando Valley were even better-looking than the girls one found in Hollywood, if one could imagine such a thing. The women all had a superbly healthy, radiantly sexual look to them that was astonishing, and none of them seemed to wear brassieres. Perhaps it was the heat. It was turning out to be a very hot day. The red-headed bank teller explained to Abdullah that the candy, which was made from dates and chopped walnuts, was terribly healthy and all organically grown right here in California.

'No kidding,' Abdullah murmured. He smiled at her warmly. He was impressed that, on top of everything else, California had date groves. 'Dates, too.'

'Just like your country, I guess.' The excitement had made the bank teller a little flushed. Her hair was dark red and she had fine gold freckles. 'We grow lots of dates down in Anaheim, just lots.' She looked as though she wanted to say more but couldn't think of anything else. Mrs Bjorn-berg, smiling, was watching from a distance. But the bank teller's eyes, Abdullah noticed, were resting very apprecia-tively on him, also.

The high school band, which hadn't been able to fit into the crowded room, was playing a rendition of 'California, Here I Come' through the open bank doors. The cheerleader squad, exiled to the pavement, waved their paper pompoms at the large glass windows and mouthed silent cheers.

Abdullah put down the cake plate and the empty paper cup on the table beside him. This certainly was a remark-able part of America. Maybe it was just his impression of things but the women seemed to come right at you, their lips parted, giving off a soft body aura under revealing clothes that was distracting as the devil. He still had the feel of the cheerleader squad's fingerprints all over him. He was pretty flushed himself.

'What about the oil embargo? Do you think the Arab world plans to cut off oil supplies any time in the future?' someone said.

Abdullah blinked.

'No,' he said, 'not unless they're forced to.'

The television lights were in his eyes and he couldn't see the speaker too well but it appeared to be the television newsman. The question had come out of the noise around them like a pistol shot. For an uneasy second Abdullah could appreciate why Brooke-Cullingham turned down all requests for press interviews. These might be only a couple of local television crews in the San Fernando Valley, but he was going to have to watch his step.

However, he supposed he could take care of himself.

'The oil embargo,' Abdullah said carefully, 'was used as a political weapon in 1973. So that's pretty much ancient history.'

He was hoping that would get him past that, but it didn't. Both television newspeople spoke at once.

'You've got to remember the Arab oil-producing countries haven't had a political weapon before,' Abdullah said. 'Every country in the world has tried its political strength in international politics at some time or other; 1973 was the Arabs' crack at it. However,' he said, before the newspeople could break in, 'you've got to realize it was done at a price. My country didn't suffer a lot; we weren't one of the top-volume producers at the time. But that one week of holding oil off the world market cost the Saudis over thirty million dollars in revenues and the Kuwaitis about seven million. That's a lot of money.'

What he didn't feel it was necessary to say was that both of them could afford it.

'Mr Asmari,' the girl said, 'I understand some of the gulf oil countries like Kuwait have only a quarter of a million people, but their annual income from oil is about four billion dollars. How much would you say that was, per capita?'

That was a lot per capita and she knew it, or she wouldn't have asked. 'I'm sorry, I don't have the figures,' Abdullah said, and smiled at her. He wanted to give a brief explanation of the way Kuwait had put its money to work in education, health programmes, and building, which was similar to his grandfather's programme in Rahsmani, but he didn't know how to begin. It wasn't diplomatic to say that the average Kuwaiti or Rahsmani citizen had better health care than most Americans. While he was mulling it over the other voice broke in.

'What about the future? Mr Sheik, people in this country want to know if the Arab oil countries will shut off our oil in the future.'

Abdullah's smile altered. He was on guard now, and 'our oil' struck a sour note. It was an expression he had heard too often from the oil people.

'Look,' he said, 'I can't predict the future. But there's one school of thought that regards the world's oil reserves as belonging to everybody. Not just *your* oil, or *our* oil, or even Arab oil, but the *world*'s oil. Any talk about oil production is bound by its very nature to be reciprocal.' Abdullah found that the words came easily enough; he had grown up with phrases like this. But he was not sure exactly what he was saying. He tried to listen to himself and talk at the same time, which wasn't easy. 'I think I can speak for the governments of the Arab oil-producing nations when I say that the oil embargo of 1973 proved one thing and that is, when we cut our oil exports to the point where it disrupts the world money supply and imposes a severe hardship on the West, then the West suffers an economic recession and doesn't buy much oil in return. At that point everybody loses. We certainly need the world to buy our oil. Maybe not at the rate it's currently being pumped nor at the cheap prices of the past, but at least at some level of mutual accommodation. After all, it's no secret that there's just so much oil under the earth's skin and when that's gone, it's gone. So eventually there has to be a plan to conserve oil reserves everywhere, to maintain a balance between production at the well head and oil marketing and oil consumption. As a case in point, my own country pumps oil right now in greater volume than it needs to or wants to. But we're not about to shut it off.'

He wanted to go on from there and say something about the contracts with Gulf Arabian Oil Company that held them to high-volume pumping, and over which none of them had any control, but decided against it. Not before the GAROC board meeting, anyway.

'Why do you want to buy the Citrusville bank?' the girl wanted to know.

'I don't know that we're going to buy any bank right now,' Abdullah said. 'But it's a good idea.' He remembered to keep smiling. 'And *I'm* not buying a bank, I'm here because I'm chairman of the Rahsmani Overseas Investment Corporation and my country is always interested to invest Rahsmani capital.' Now he wouldn't let them interrupt. 'That should show that my country has every confidence in the economy of the United States and that we're certainly not going to do anything to undermine it. Also, I'd like to remind you that the United States invests its money, billions of dollars, overseas, too. We hope that Rahsmani, which is a small country, will be as successful in overseas investment as the United States has been.'

'How rich would you say your country is?'

'I don't have any hard figures for you.' Abdullah had them, but he was getting tired of hedging. In fact, he could hear himself falling back on some pretty time-worn expressions. He was beginning to sound like one of his uncle Hakim's speeches. 'But I can quote you some figures on the top oil-producing country in the gulf, which is Saudi Arabia. I suppose you know the American government has always backed Saudi Arabia, even as far in the past as the 1940s, and thanks to American loans and the technology of American oil companies, the Saudis have become very rich.

166

In the next five years the Saudi oil revenues will top two hundred fifty billion dollars. That's roughly about one-fourth of the American economy. Or about as much as the total supply of money in the United States.'

The crowd in the bank, which had been rather noisy during the interview, suddenly fell silent. Abdullah tried to look beyond the hot television lights to see what was going on. Maybe he had put things a little too bluntly but he had just wanted to drop a note about wealth and power, since they seemed to insist on it. And he hadn't said all he could have said about the Saudis, either. In ten years the Saudis would have damned near half the money in the world if they kept on going at their present rate. So will we, now he told himself.

'My country,' Abdullah said in the silence, 'is still in an under-developed part of the world, I think we ought to remember that. Sure, oil has brought us a lot of money and in most ways we weren't prepared for it. But we're still trying to catch up with hundreds of years of Western development. In Rahsmani we've only had about fifteen to twenty years to get started. Consider that most of our population still lacks basic education. And we need technicians, engineers, financiers, all the trained people America has in abundance. So we want to work and cooperate with you. If you want to know what our situation is, I'll tell you. The West buys our oil. We use some of that money for internal development but since we can't use all of it we return it to the West to be put in banks and to be used for investment. It's called the U-turn effect. But what's important is that although we're new to the game we consider ourselves members in good standing in the world financial community. Which is what we want to be.'

These were all oversimplifications and he was making a lot of mistakes, Abdullah realized, but if you had to talk on these terms he thought he wasn't doing too bad. Still, he had to get out of it somehow. There had to be some way of changing the subject.

'You haven't asked me,' he said quickly, 'how I like

southern California. You know, I went to prep school in New England and I graduated from Yale University – but only because Stanford turned me down. Now I see what I missed. I should have at least applied to UCLA.'

There was some scattered laughter at this and Abdullah relaxed a little.

'How long will you be here?' someone asked.

From the front of the room near the doors Brooke-Cullingham was watching all this with misgiving. He couldn't hear most of what was being said but he got enough of it, now and then, to keep him from being very happy.

'Say, he's doing all right for himself,' the Bank of America lawyer said. 'You've got to hand it to him, he talks well, he knows where it's at. He's quite a personality. Maybe you ought to put him on "Johnny Carson", or "Face the Nation".'

'Yes, he can be very inventive.' But Brooke-Cullingham was somewhat grim. Just a moment before, watching Abdullah, he had been remembering the chair-throwing scenes of the previous evening. It was all very well and good, but one had to consider it in the light of the other.

What was going on over there under the television cameras was, as far as he was concerned, merely more of the same. Certainly it was shocking bad policy to get up in public and talk about how rich the Saudis were. The words 250 billion had hit like a dash of cold water. One-quarter of the American economy, indeed. They were going to hear about that.

What our untried young hawkling needs, Brooke-Cullingham reflected, is one of those leather hoods put over his head for the next twenty-four hours, to shut him up and give the rest of us a well-deserved rest. Over the heads of the crowd he could see the figure in the well-tailored blue business suit perched on the edge of the bank's conference table, suit jacket open and one thumb cocked nonchalantly in the waistcoat, the other hand gesturing, palm upward. The television lights picked out the vivid colours of the red-

and-black-checkered *kaffiyeh*. It was all very exciting and just what any television news producer would want. Our family sport, Brooke-Cullingham thought, is having the time of his life. He's having one damned marvellous time talking his head off and people are listening for a change. And if some fool from one of the local stations thinks to offer five minutes of this nonsense to the networks the fat's in the fire, absolutely.

Ramzi Alam had come in through the doors behind them and now he tugged at Brooke-Cullingham's sleeve.

'The call's coming through from the hotel.'

Brooke-Cullingham followed the secretary out to the pavement and to the limousine parked at the kerb. He slid into the front seat and took the telephone from the driver.

'The news is breaking,' Russell's voice came over the receiver. 'At least we're getting the preliminary announcements from the Oil Directorate through the Washington Embassy telex. The official release will be out in about forty-eight hours. Are you listening?'

'Yes, dammit, I'm listening. How does it look?'

'It looks absolutely tremendous,' Russell's voice said. 'Mitsumi's brought in four spouters in the gulf and more to come. The Japs are as busy as an old biddy with all her eggs hatching at once, the lucky bastards. All the releases are couched in pretty technical language – after all, they've been a couple of weeks out there on the shelf trying to assess just what the hell they've got. But it looks bigger than anything else that's come along. My guess is that it will hit the Tokyo stock exchange tomorrow like an earthquake.'

'Bigger than anything since when?' Brooke-Cullingham said. There were people gathered around the limousine and he reached over and rolled up the window.

'Since the bloody Pleistocene Age, I should imagine.' Russell's voice rose with excitement. 'It looks bigger than anything the Saudis have by far. And that's about as big as there is, isn't it?'

Brooke-Cullingham didn't answer. They had been expecting something of the sort for days, weeks, since the rumours of the Mitsumi strike had started, and it was good to finally get confirmation. Now the reality was a bit hard to absorb. Bigger than anything the Saudis had meant, bigger than anything in the gulf. Bigger than anything in the Middle East. Rahsmani upped to Number One. That would shake everything up, Russell wasn't far wrong.

'What's the word from back home?'

'Rather mixed. Our Mr Ameen Said is in New York, I'm told. Then he goes on to Pittsburgh to break the news in person.'

'The hell you say.' That was a damned unforeseen turn of events. 'How did that happen? Where's the Oil Directorate Chairman?'

'That's hard to tell. Rumour says Uncle's in durance vile. Some say house arrest.'

'Christ!'

What the hell did that mean? Brooke-Cullingham sat, the receiver to his ear, trying to think. Rumour wasn't to be trusted, they would have to get on the overseas lines at once and stay there until they found out what was up.

He told Russell to do it. 'We're leaving for this damned movie party directly,' Brooke-Cullingham said. 'The itinerary copy is somewhere about; look it up. It has the lot number, Universal Studios. Keep in touch.'

And he hung up.

They came into the barn of the Universal Studios sound stage fully two hours late, but everyone was assembled there as promised, including the stars of the picture, various notables, stars of other pictures who had been invited to attend, two vice presidents from Universal Pictures Corporation and the film's publicity and promotion man. In a few minutes a reception line was got together for Abdullah and Brooke-Cullingham to pass down, shaking hands and smiling. It was much the same sort of thing that had been arranged on another sound stage the week before, the publicity man told them, for the King and Queen of Denmark. Only bigger. Abdullah had been briefed on the news of the oil strike in the limousine as had the others; the good news, on top of the hectic morning they had spent in Citrusville gave them all an air of concealed excitement that seemed to generate invisible sparks. They might as well have been European royalty at that. Ali Hassan rushed forward to grab and embrace Abdullah, Arab-style, and then stepped back to take a good look.

'Oh Eye of Beauty, what has transpired?' the actor wanted to know. 'Have you merely visited this bank or did you also rob it? What's up?'

'What do you mean, what's up? I've just had a good day, that's all. I'm getting on top of things. As for instance I just had my first press conference. Only right now my feet hurt.' Which was true. He didn't understand how fatigue, what there was of it, could seem to settle in his shoes as it did.

'Is this what makes you so late? I had almost given up hope for you. Half these people are bombed, they've stood around so long drinking up the booze. Their makeup's running.'

'We're always late,' Abdullah said wearily. 'We move like a goddamned army these days. It's getting hellishly complicated.'

Someone had put a glass of champagne in his hand and Abdullah drank it, thirstily, before he remembered.

'God, take it,' he said, thrusting the empty glass at Hassan. 'I'm going to blow everything doing something like that. Why don't you watch out for me?'

The cast of the movie assembled on the sound stage was still in full costume. They had, someone told them, been shooting since eight o'clock that morning and, as Hassan had remarked, the actors looked somewhat worn. The cavernous sound stage was not all that well air conditioned and the air was damp; the patient, tired people had had nothing to do for hours but wait for them. The picture was a drama of World War One and there were women in hobbled skirts and big hats, and men in khaki uniforms with wrapped leggings. Under the circumstances, everyone seemed to be extraordinarily uncomplaining and cheerful, something Abdullah noticed at once. A gigantic buffet catered by a Hollywood Swedish restaurant offered what appeared to be the world's largest smorgasbord. The table was fully fifty feet long. Ramzi and the others, who hadn't had anything to eat since breakfast, lost no time in going to fill their plates. The two Bedouin hung back, looking doubtful.

'For God's sake, somebody go help the *bedu*,' Abdullah told Brooke-Cullingham. 'Get them some plates with food they know they can eat and not be polluted.'

'Come and have something to eat yourself,' Hassan told him.

'I'm not hungry.'

'Then come and meet some beautiful girls.'

This was Hassan in his usual form, offering the delights of all Hollywood filmdom. He seemed right in place among the crowds of improbable people sweating in their World War One costumes.

Abdullah shook his head. The homemade cake and candy he had consumed in Citrusville and the gallon or so of Coca-Cola rested heavily on his stomach. And as for the beautiful girls, there had been plenty of those in the Valley. He was restless and filled with a mild impatience at all that was going on. He had been looking forward to the party on the sound stage but now that he was there it seemed artificial and flat. Up close, he had noticed, you could see how hard these people worked. It was not very glamorous, at least not as glamorous as it seemed on the screen.

While Abdullah was standing with Ali, the producer, Mr Herman Shoemaker, the director, whose name was King, came up and introduced themselves. The star, Miss Raquel Wales, was with them. At least Miss Wales was every bit as lovely as she was on film, if somewhat heavily coated with makeup. She wore a dress with a large pink rose that ended the V of her neckline just above the sash. Mr Robert Ellsworth, her co-star, came up and shook hands very briefly, said nothing, then sauntered off to get a glass of champagne.

'Mudhead,' Ali Hassan said to Abdullah in Arabic. 'He thinks he bestows roses when he pisses.'

Ellsworth was at least as handsome as the Egyptian actor, if not more so, and certainly much taller. He carried his head with an arrogant crook to one side. He was probably just as Hassan had described him but even so Abdullah found him interesting. Ellsworth, at least, had the air of a man who wanted no part of anything.

In one breath Mr Herman Shoemaker had slid from a very nice conversation about the plot of the picture into a list of figures. He was counting up distribution outlets and projected box-office receipts.

Abdullah excused himself and went over to the table where the white-jacketed barmen were opening the bottles of champagne.

'We met just a minute ago,' Abdullah said to him.

The chilly blue eyes touched him only briefly. 'That's right,' Ellsworth said.

'How much do they want?' Abdullah asked him.

Now the actor turned to him, a vastly different look in his eyes. He was silent for a full two or three minutes while he looked him over very thoroughly.

'How the hell should I know?' he said. 'From here we're supposed to go to Rhinebeck, New York, to rent the vintage planes, stage the dogfights, and all that. From what I hear, we don't even have the air fare.'

'What's Hassan, co-producer?'

'Something like that. He's your friend, didn't he tell you?'

'Make a thumbnail estimate,' Abdullah said.

The actor leaned against the table and studied the glass of champagne in his hand.

'You get to lay the leading lady; that's part of it,' he said between beautiful capped white teeth. 'Or we have a couple of starlets. Now that they've seen you they're even more together than they were before. They might even want it.'

'Just to the closest round number,' Abdullah said. 'Before I hear their estimates.'

Suddenly, looking at each other, they both burst out

laughing. Ellsworth's face changed completely when he laughed. He appeared to be a nice person.

'You're smarter than you look,' Ellsworth said.

'Don't kid yourself. Anybody could smell it when they came in.'

'Don't get stuck. They can go back to the banks if they have to. The trouble is the banks want great big options this time.'

'How do you feel about it?'

Ellsworth shrugged. 'It's a good picture. Nostalgia is big on the market right now, and King's not a bad director. Also, we have a good editor. Sometime, if you're interested in how pictures are made, I'll take you around and show you the people who really put a film together. The cutters and film editors.'

'Half a million?'

'More than that. Whatever figure they quote you, double it. Triple it, even. Cost overruns.'

When Abdullah started back to the others Hassan came up to him quickly and took him by the arm.

'*Ya*, Ali,' Abdullah said in a low tone, 'I have already heard the story; it is not necessary. Whatever it is, send it on to the Englishman and we will look it over. He makes up the money proposals.'

'It is not as you heard it,' Hassan assured him. 'I have everything in a book, with the figures, which I was going to show you. Believe me, it is a very sound investment. I am sorry it has started thus, with this son of a bitch Ellsworth. There is a man who truly does not know the name of his father.'

Abdullah threw back his head and laughed. When you knew what was wanted, it was easy to play this game. Only Hassan seemed really pissed off.

'Listen,' Abdullah said. He pulled his friend to a stop. 'How about you? You don't need any money, I mean personally, do you? You aren't broke?'

The Egyptian drew back, the famous obsidian eyes flashing.

'Camel! Do you think I would pimp to cheat you?'

'Don't lose your cool; I'm just asking. You're still my friend, I'd lend you money if you needed it. Just ask me.'

'I'll see you in hell first.'

'Okay, if that's the way you want it. But when I meet you there, the score is even.' They both understood perfectly. 'I just thought I'd let you know.'

Beyond Hassan he saw her come in through the tangle of cables and props at the far end of the sound stage. Her gold hair was pulled back very severely and the outsized sunglasses nearly covered most of her face, but he knew who it was. Abdullah kept his grip on his friend's shoulder in a perfectly affectionate sort of way but he had one more thing to say.

'Women are not part of the trading,' he said softly. 'My people deal in oil and money now and a few well-bred horses and Cadillacs. I can make my own arrangements.'

NINE

The figure came up from the steps to the wooden sundeck
from the beach, the moonlight behind her and moving softly
on bare feet, the sea wind blowing out the long trail of her
hair. Abdullah was lying on the bed of the empty beachhouse with the open doors to the sundeck in front of him,
watching the glimmer of his white shirt, which she had
thrown over her shoulders before she went outside. The
moonlight was brilliant enough to show the shine of her
naked legs and the tips of her breasts, the flat plane of her
stomach where the shirt blew open. But there was no one
around to see – Wadiyeh al Qasim and Bisharah were somewhere beyond them in the darkened house and Russell and
one of the Jordanians waited outside on the road in the
limousine, probably asleep. It was late, perhaps two or
three o'clock. Abdullah did not bother to lift his arm to look
at the illuminated dial of his watch. There was no use
worrying about the hours; he could catch up on his sleep
later if he had to.

'What are you doing?' he said.

The voice came indistinctly, blurred by the wind and
the sound of the waves on the beach.

'Seashells. It's as bright as daylight out here. You can see
everything.'

She came into the room and leaned over the bed, laying
out some small, cold sharp objects on the flesh of his
stomach. Her long, slightly damp hair fell forward like a
scarf, brushing his skin.

'You should see them, they're really beautiful. I should
come down here,' she said thoughtfully, 'more often. I

never get a chance to, and I should. I'm a Pisces – the things of the sea are mine.'

'Ummm,' he said, picking the cold wet shells off his stomach one by one and dropping them over the edge of the bed. He could hear them hitting the newspaper on the floor where he had thrown it earlier. They had bought the Los Angeles *Times* on the way out to Santa Monica that afternoon, Russell handing it to him without comment. The headline said: 'ARAB OIL POTENTATE SAYS OIL BELONGS TO EVERYBODY.'

The item was two days old, picked up from the television interview he had given in the Valley, a part of which had been rerun on ABC and NBC news nationwide. The story had been placed on the inside pages but that, Abdullah knew, didn't mean it wasn't going to be read and noted by a hell of a lot of people. It had cropped up everywhere.

Abdullah reached up and slid the white shirt from her shoulders. By the light streaming through the doors to the sundeck she was outlined clearly, all the slight curves of her body, the sharp elbows, the little breasts lifting outward in points. He could even make out the freckles like gold paint on her skin, which gave her the look of some spangled creature, all awkward elusiveness, swinging, as she bent forward, the dark fall of red hair. Her fingers moved on his thighs and his groin.

'Do you like that?' she whispered.

It was a moment before he could get his breath.

'Wait a minute,' he said huskily. One of the seashells was on the sheet under him. He pried it out and threw it away into the darkness of the room. When he started to speak again she suddenly put her mouth on him and all that came out was, 'Oh God,' and a groan. He put his hand on her hair.

Just as suddenly she stopped what she was doing and threw herself into his arms, the length of her body stretching out against his. Her skin felt very cool from the sea wind. Now her mouth was along the flesh of his throat, under his chin, and moving up under his ear, the wetness of her tongue trailing. Finally the feel of her teeth, faintly sharp, on the lobe of his ear. Her hand explored him, her body pressing down full weight on top of his.

'You're beautiful,' she whispered. 'Men can be beautiful, too. I think your body is very beautiful.'

Abdullah put his arms around her and held her where she was. This redheaded girl was very lovely and appealing but certainly hard to understand. One felt rather than thought with her; everything was emotion, and this was somehow irritatingly familiar. She had come into the empty beach-house that Russell had been told to rent for the evening carrying a large paper bag with more of the homemade candy of walnut and dates that he had said he liked, a jar of honey one of her friends had extracted from a wild bee-comb using a centrifuge, some sesame-seed wafers exactly like those that could be bought in Rahsmani city, and something called kelp, which Abdullah had sampled unwillingly. All these were gifts for him. That was unusual enough. She was very concerned about health and diet, as she had told him. Although she had decided that he had a very good-looking body – very strong and symmetrical, as she had put it – she wanted him to know that an organic diet, strictly adhered to, would make him immune to the common cold (which, when he tried to think, he hardly ever had), lung cancer, and heart disease. She was very glad he didn't smoke or drink.

There was such a grave, knowing air about her, just as there had been when he first met her in the Citrusville bank, that he found it utterly disarming. He knew on the spot that he had made a mistake, that the evening was going to pass in talk and lectures about health foods and with nothing at all concerning making love.

To his great surprise, though, they had gone off to the bedroom almost without any preliminaries. She had a fragile, awkward prettiness; she moved gently, her voice soft, she took down the amazing length of her dark red hair with one sweep of her hand, pulling out the comb that held it close to her head with all the cool, calm power of one who decides the matter with a sudden gesture. And somehow with all this he couldn't regard the health food in the large paper bag as funny after all. It was seldom that anyone thought to bring him, with all that he had, any gifts. One look from her eyes, her lips parted expectantly, sent a terrible heat sweeping over him. He had moved toward her to take her and kiss her and put his hands on her warm skin as slowly and as considerately as he could manage.

It had only been a passing thought to ask for the bank teller's telephone number as well. Now he was glad he had had the sense to think of it. For the television newsgirl, as it turned out, lived with her boyfriend and wasn't interested. But when he had called the redheaded teller she had replied very enthusiastically that she would love to come. She had been picked up by Russell in the limousine at the bank in Citrusville and brought to the beachhouse with no questions asked about the dinner that had been provided, which she did not eat, or the stock of liquor, all different sizes and flavours, which she did not drink. They had talked for a while on the couch in the living room and then she had got up and gone to the bedroom of her own accord, where she had taken off her dress, pausing once or twice to regard him softly, even timidly.

Now she slid her cool arms against his face and put her hands in his hair, cradling his face between. Her mouth descended on his, her tongue touching his lips.

'You're tense,' she murmured against his mouth.

'I have a right to be,' he said indistinctly. 'I hope you appreciate it.'

She laughed. 'I do.' Her hand had found him. 'Oh, I do.'

'That's not going to relax me, either.'

'Are you going to make love to me again?'

'In a minute. I'm in no hurry.'

He held her tightly, feeling the desire that had not left him all evening sweep up strongly again. Her response to him was astonishingly open – she seemed shy but actually she was not at all. When the heat came upon her she had little pretence, giving out very noisy moans of pleasure. His shoulders were covered with faint bite marks. She was, he told himself, a nice, loving sort of girl and inside him there was a hollowness at the thought of having to leave her. There was nothing for them beyond the time they spent during this California trip, he knew that. Nor did he want any more than that.

'Don't rush me,' he said halfheartedly. He wanted to linger with the moment a little. But she had slipped his flesh between her thighs and her mouth and body pressed down on his. Stretched out on top of him like that she was a cool, demanding weight.

'Okay,' he told her and rolled over on her heavily. She started to laugh.

Laugh, he thought. It was a lovely sound. She was like bathing in the warm sea of the gulf, she was comfort and fire together. He was a charging storm and she gave way under him, crying out.

Almost before it was over, she reached up and held back his sweaty hair with both her hands and murmured, 'What sign are you?'

'August tenth,' he said, breathlessly.

'A Leo.' Her eyes went wide in the moonlight. 'Leos are magnificent. But cruel, sometimes. The sun sign.' Her hands held his hair between her fingers, holding it out from his head, spreading like rays. She viewed him critically. 'Yes, I can see it,' she said. 'A Leo. Which comes out of the sun like a lion.'

'Don't,' he said, and tried to take her hands away so that he could drop back down against the sheets. Such talk made him uneasy. He lifted his arm to read his watch again. It was even later.

'But I can believe it,' she said. 'You have the look. Leos are kings, suns travelling across the sky. Glory and war and the clash of arms. That's what the books say. Also, Leos are very domineering.' She moved up against his body, threw one arm across his chest. 'The vibes are right,' she said against his shoulder. 'I would have guessed a Leo, actually.'

He lay for a long time holding her while she slept, not

knowing what to do. It was getting late, every once or twice he thought he heard Wadiyeh or Bisharah padding about the house in the dark. Probably checking things out, he thought, or going outside to see if the limousine was still there. The security went on, no matter what.

The redheaded girl's words hung in the dark corners of the room, away from the chill brightness of the moonlight. No wonder there was something peculiarly familiar about her. Echoes of my mother, he thought, restlessly. All those signs and superstitions and omens and the charted movements of the stars in the sky and their influence over men, as the desert people, too, believed. And it was all nonsense, he told himself. American girls read these things out of books, just as she had said. He remembered from his days at college all those diffuse, misty-voiced girls in long skirts and their mysterious other-worldliness, talking of the occult and Karl Marx all in one breath.

But in spite of this a cool, sombre thing like the great tides of the sea began to creep in his belly and flow upward toward his heart. Omens, signs, they were the shadows that lived in the dark, whispers that came to the brain when one was asleep. His aunts were all fortunetellers, necromancers in tents, divining by bones and sticks thrown on the sand. He had visited them as a child, women in purple wool dresses, clanking with silver ornaments cast in the cook fires.

Allah! The things that came into one's head in the night! The wind from the sea coming in through the open doors was cold and they had nothing to cover them, the sheets had fallen to the floor. He had been happy for most of these hours as he had not been happy for some time. And now this – lying awake while she slept, and it got later and later. Health food, and strange powers from the moon and the sky, and her cool certainty!

He moved slightly away from her and turned to look down at her in a curious sort of unease. Like a child she had curled up against him, innocently sleeping with her hand folded against her cheek. This was only some ordinary girl from this small town in southern California, he tried to assure himself. A very nice girl, if a little strange. Actually he preferred tall women with large breasts, invincible women with big mouths and driving buttocks and all that went with it. This confident tenderness opened like a flower, irresistibly. He wasn't ready for it.

In that moment a sense of danger such as hardly ever bothered him those days swept over him, and he felt his flesh prickle. To be alone in a house in a strange land in the middle of the night with nothing but emptiness and darkness was bad enough; now he felt his own momentum drain out of him, leaving him stranded on the edge of loneliness and sudden uncertainty. What the hell am I doing here? he asked himself. And Hassan's words returned to him, spoken on the plane when they had first met in Spain: *Don't trust anyone around you. You are living very perilously.* It was true, his life had been threatened, his friends had connived against him, he couldn't put any faith in relatives.

He bent over her, thinking to touch her and waken her, but his shadow fell over her like a dark blot. He was startled to see how black it was.

She was as slender as his sister Layla and for that moment as delicate and shut away as though ten thousand miles were in between. My God, he thought, looking down at the girl, and his shadow grew alarmingly before his eyes and it seemed to spread along her body down to her knees and the feet drawn up in sleep, uncovered in the cool wind from the sea. It's only my shadow, he told himself. But his teeth came together with a click and the whole flesh of his face trembled. He had no business being here. This was not the same woman but another woman, and the body changed under the shadow and the hair was some other girl's hair, not a girl who had come to bed casually in a beachhouse by the sea, in an alien country not his own. It was not his sister but some other girl just as fragile, and while he held himself up on one hand looking down and shaking at the great shadow spreading across her and on to the bed he felt a great stillness like the odour of flowers in a garden, a softness in the darkness that seemed to reach up to him. It was far away and in the future.

Abdullah shook all over and he felt his eyes drawing back into his skull painfully. A real omen – he was seeing it – and the whole of his soul rose up in terror and cried out to be let go. A darkness flowed from her form and into his like a cloud. Blood, darkness, and strange things, and a piercing sense of sweetness like perfume. They were all around him, things in the darkness; he was in peril and he could not go on living like this. He heard footsteps, distinctly, and the sound of voices. Fair warning. He must have cried out. There was a sound like a door closing somewhere in the empty house beyond.

The girl on the bed opened her eyes and then sat upright, bumping against him so that they had to grab for each other.

'What is it?' she said. And then, seeing his eyes, she drew back from him. 'What happened?'

He looked at her, this freckled girl with red hair, this nice girl who had no part in his life or the dangers it held. It was in his face because she put her hands up in something like fright.

'Don't be afraid,' he said, hearing his own voice like someone else's. He was shaking like a man with a fever. 'It's nothing.' Only night terrors. The shadow had melted. There was nothing on the sheets around them but moonlight.

'I have to go home,' she cried. 'I really have to go home.' She wanted no part of it. She jumped out of the bed and ran over and started gathering up her clothes from the floor.

'It was nothing,' Abdullah repeated. But he still sat where he was. He was not sure himself; he could never explain to her the dangers that surrounded him, and what they meant. He supposed he looked like a man who has just seen a marching horde of *afreets* pass through the room and yet cannot tell what he has seen. His whole body had turned cold.

It will go away, he told himself.

'No, it's all right,' she kept saying. She was throwing her

clothes on in a great hurry. 'What time is it?'

He didn't know what time it was; he had to look. 'It's four o'clock,' he told her.

He really wanted to see her again, but when he said this she turned and looked at him and wouldn't answer.

It was arranged that Russell and the Jordanian secretary would drive her home. The Bedouin would stay behind in the beachhouse with him and he could go back to bed and get some sleep. Abdullah looked back at the bed and it was white and empty by the light that streamed in from the beach. Whatever it was that had shaken him was gone; he could, he saw, sleep there very soundly after all.

'I'll call you,' he said. He picked up his trousers from the floor and put them on and took her out to the hallway and then to the living room, where Wadiyeh rose up in the dark and went silently on bare feet to open the front door for them.

'I have a few more days in LA,' he tried to explain. 'I'm waiting for some business to be set up in New York, but I want to see you again. I certainly want to see you again,' he repeated. His words disappeared in the dark.

'It's all right,' she said. But she looked behind him to where the figure of Wadiyeh stood, and beyond him the dark blur that was Bisharah in the hallway, and he could see that it was not all right. She opened her mouth to say something more, then thought better of it. She went down the steps into the street and to the limousine, a very slight figure in a pale dress in the night. Russell got out and opened the limousine door for her.

Finally, while Abdullah waited by the open door with the sea wind blowing cold on him, the motor started up and they drove away.

The next day he told Brooke-Cullingham, 'I want you to pick up a car, maybe an Audi Fox or something like that, and send it to this girl from the bank in Citrusville. Nancy. I think her other name is Sullivan.'

The Englishman did not even bother to look up from the

papers he was working on. 'What colour?'

'Whatever they've got.' But Abdullah thought it over and said, 'Purple, if they have it.' He thought purple would suit her. It would go with the red hair. 'But don't wait on a custom paint job. I want her to have it right now. And all the accessories. Fix it up good.'

'CB radio and gun rack?'

'Don't be funny.'

He had given it quite a lot of thought because although she had been a strange girl, she had given him a great deal of pleasure. The gifts, and her warm sexuality, were not easy to find. He felt very grateful toward her, he was sorry she had been put off by anything he might have seen or felt. A matter of night jitters. His lifestyle was bound to catch up with him now and then, even he recognized that much. He wanted to make it up to her. Besides, bank tellers didn't make any money, and she said she lived with three friends in an apartment over a dry cleaning store in the older part of the town. He could imagine such a place. She drove a car, but he understood that it was old and in bad shape. At least she hadn't been able to drive it all the way to Santa Monica and had asked that Russell come for her. Abdullah didn't want to give her a sports car or anything flashy that would take a lot of money to maintain.

'Also, get her a good sound system, quadrophonic speakers, the works, and find some store nearby that will arrange a charge account for all the records she wants to buy. Give them three thousand dollars or something and make them issue us an accounting.'

'That's a lot of paper work,' Brooke-Cullingham said. 'I don't think we have the time to keep track of three thousand dollars' worth of pop music. Why don't you just give her the money?'

'The staff can keep track of three thousand dollars' worth of anything if they're told to do it,' Abdullah said. 'Just tell them to do it.'

He had made up his mind that it was going to be done just as he wanted. And he wanted her to have the money for the music and not to pay up bills or spend it on her friends, since he imagined she had plenty of both. And he didn't want her to be cheated. 'Put ten thousand in the bank for her, too.'

'Don't you want to buy her a wardrobe?' Brooke-Cullingham picked up the pile of telexes and looked through them, the glasses riding low on the bridge of his nose.

'I don't know what kind of clothes she wears.' He couldn't tell if his leg was being pulled or not. 'And as you say, we can't handle every damned detail.'

The stuff was enough, he told himself, as he did not intend to see her again. The gifts were not worth as much as he had given to Barbra Burchard, but then that matter wasn't closed, either.

When he had woken that morning the feel of the omen was still strong in him. He had not been mistaken, it was a true omen. Ordinarily he didn't believe in such things, they were best left to his mother and the women of her tribe who took such stuff with great seriousness. Certainly women like his grandmother didn't lend themselves to magic and all that. However, this was an omen, no matter how much he tried to talk himself out of it, a glimpse of his fate. It was terrifying and he didn't understand it all; that was what made it so convincing. There had been another woman in that room, a smell of something sweet like perfume, and a warning of danger. Some hollowness, such as one has after any brush with the unknown, still lingered with him. Naturally he would rather be struck blind than admit to anyone that such a thing had taken place, or that he believed in it.

Now, looking across the desk in the living room to where Brooke-Cullingham sat going through the morning's accumulation of messages he thought, The Englishman stays out of this, at least. If I choose to sleep with fifty or a hundred women it's none of his business and he knows it. It annoys him. He thinks we should stick to what we came for and no fooling around, as the British would have it, but he can't say anything.

186

'Jim, let me fix you up with one of Hassan's women,' Abdullah said. He leaned forward in his chair interestedly to see what, if anything, would show on the Englishman's face. 'You might as well enjoy yourself while you're here.' He wondered sometimes what went on during those visits to Brooke-Cullingham's house in Switzerland, and if he had a woman or perhaps a boy waiting for him there. It was hard to tell with the English exactly what their preferences were or if indeed they had any taste for sex at all. In Rahsmani, Brooke-Cullingham lived the life of a hard-working civil servant; his private life was above reproach and any romantic attachments invisible. But that was probably to avoid blackmail and any kind of political squeeze. Still, Abdullah told himself, everybody had to have a sex life, sometime. Somewhere.

'If your shopping list's finished,' Brooke-Cullingham said, 'I think you should turn your attention to this inquiry from the New York office of the Arab Petroleum Exporting etceteras. OAPEC wants to know if you wish to comment on the news story they have seen on ABC and NBC, about your giving Arab oil to the whole world. Also, it seems they are complaining that you have been quoted as speaking for all the governments of the Arab oil-producing states in the Gulf, and they say they haven't heard that you've been appointed as any sort of representative to do that sort of thing. That's the essence of it. I spent quite a bit of time with Mr Farouk Mahdi on the telephone from New York, getting all this. Do you want to write them a letter?'

Inwardly, Abdullah cursed. He supposed he had the feeling that they could just slip by without anybody taking any particular note of some of the things he had said. They had sounded okay at the time.

'Sure, write them a letter. Say that I was quoted out of context. Say I'm young and inexperienced. If we move up to Number One with all the Mitsumi oil coming in, they're going to start licking our shoes, anyway. What's important is what my grandfather says. I suppose,' Abdullah said, 'we're going to hear?'

187

Brooke-Cullingham looked at him and shrugged.

'So far, as quiet as a mouse. All I have in hand is the usual, passed on by your grandfather's staff, and the bulk of that's handouts on what the Japanese are doing and what they think they've found. There hasn't even been much direct contact at that. Russell's been on the telex to the Embassy in Washington this morning and then on the overseas wires, and everyone is responding, but only routinely. I suppose there isn't anything in it, and of course they are tied up with the Mitsumi business, but for the last twenty-four hours we get only the word that the Emir is in council or has been in council and will call at the usual times. Nothing more than that.'

They looked at each other. They were both wondering what sort of council could be operating since he and Brooke-Cullingham were in California and Sam Crossland was in New York. That left Fuad and Hakim. Ameen Said was in the States.

The last time Abdullah had spoken to his grandfather was three days ago.

'What's the matter?' he wanted to know.

'Your grandmother sends word that your son has been in the hospital with a sore throat.'

'*What?*'

'Well, I'm sure that's something you'd want to know. However, that's all we have this morning. Plus a ream of material on the Mitsumi find.' Brooke-Cullingham put down the pile of telexes. 'That's the sum and total of everything that's come in.'

Abdullah was overcome with a sudden surge of rage. It wasn't the most important news in the world, but it was important enough to him. Every time his son was sick, thanks to Fawzia's indifferent mothering, Karim ended up in the hospital. It was a fine commentary on how things went when he was away.

'Tell me about it,' Abdullah said through his teeth.

'It appears to be another strep throat. He's being treated

with antibiotics and is responding nicely. The Lady Azziza says not to worry.'

He glared at Brooke-Cullingham. Well, that was better. For a moment he couldn't think of anything but his anger and then it occurred to him that what the Englishman had said was rather odd. With all that was going on, the only news was that his kid was in the hospital again and that his grandmother, the Lady Azziza, said not to worry. He supposed that was good enough : his grandmother would probably tell him if something was really wrong. But he was filled with the frustration of those who have to rely on long-distance communications to keep up with what was happening. It was like carrying on a conversation through a messenger on crutches.

'Nothing else?' He was still turning the matter over in his head. His kid was sick, his grandfather wouldn't come to the phone, and his uncle Hakim had dropped out of sight. Was that the way it really was?

Brooke-Cullingham leaned his elbow on the desk and fingered his chin as he always did when considering his words carefully.

'Crossland called this morning.'

Abdullah looked up from the telexes. Crossland had spoken to Brooke-Cullingham directly?

The Englishman saw the look.

'I think he'd put the call in last night at some ungodly hour, but you were at the beach house and couldn't be disturbed. Crossland heard of the new oil strike through his office, wanted to know what was coming in here. I told him damned little; we seemed to be on our own as far as current developments. His news from Rahsmani city's been as sparse as ours. He told me why he was in New York,' Brooke-Cullingham said. 'It was probably the best thing to do.'

Abdullah said nothing. His grandfather's secretiveness even with his intimate advisers was a matter of record, even though it often served no good purpose. Now Brooke-Cullingham knew what Crossland was doing in New York, and why. That wasn't the way his grandfather had wanted it. And no one had said they were going to tell him. All of a sudden it seemed that a peculiar drift had set in. They kept telling themselves that the Emir was busy with the Mitsumi announcement, which was, after all, the biggest news since Gulf Arabian had brought in their oil in the early days. Naturally the offices would be busy. But he was fairly sure OAPEC had sent a copy of their complaints home, too. That should have got his grandfather on the telephone right away. He never missed a chance to come down hard on anybody.

Looking at Brooke-Cullingham's neatly barbered head bent over some papers, the business suit and white shirt and tie in spite of the California morning heat, Abdullah thought: He's known what was going on all the time, Crossland didn't have to tell him. He wouldn't be where he is if he didn't make it a matter of routine to keep his fingers on everything, whether he was supposed to know or not. He knew that was what he would do if he were in Brooke-Cullingham's place. And he remembered being certain that someone had gone through the papers of the GAROC speech in his room.

And he has some guesses about what's going on back home, too, although he's not ready to say so.

'Crossland says that the noise of the Mitsumi strike, big as it is, is putting pressure on GAROC. They want more time to think about a meeting.'

'They're stalling.'

'That's obvious. But Crossland is fairly sure they're trying to find out what concessions have been made to the Japanese, since they're reportedly very liberal, and if they're more than GAROC is willing to give under a new agreement. So they want time.'

'They don't need time. They're going to be pushed out of the picture if they don't get on the stick. The Japs have got the upper hand now if they've brought in a bigger strike. GAROC can pack up and go home. We don't have to beg from them.'

'That's going to be a matter of some years yet, isn't it? The Japs still have to set up their fields and pipelines.'

They sat for a moment in silence, thinking it out.

I'm still going to go East and finish up with GAROC, Abdullah thought. It's time somebody got those bastards to hew the line. My grandfather's let OPEC dictate everything so far, and do it through Hakim. Now Gulf Arabian's got every right to be worried about the concession the Japanese are operating under. The guidelines are written right into the contract – maximal host country control, maximal revenues. The Japanese were so hungry they were willing to pay through the nose for the right to drill. Now we've both hit it lucky.

Naturally, Abdullah told himself, he wanted to sink his teeth into the GAROC business. After all this time and trouble he wasn't going to give it up. They still had to live with Gulf Arabian for a good long while, and the handwriting on the wall had to be made a reality. A shift in the balance of power, at least out of Hakim's hands, was what his grandfather had had in mind, and through GAROC was the way to start. Especially if things were to continue the way they wanted.

'It's not like my grandfather not to let us know something,' Abdullah said. 'He ought to be on the telephone giving his opinions about how much oil Mitsumi's got or raising hell about my television goofs or at least having his secretaries do it for him. Especially since nearly all of us are out of the country. And that bastard Said is over here peddling whatever it is he has to sell. Who's he talking to? What's he telling them? What the hell's been going on?'

'We have everything that's been sent,' Brooke-Cullingham said.

'We need more than that,' Abdullah fretted. 'Get Mansur on the line.'

The moment the words were out of his mouth he knew that wouldn't work, either. If anything was going on, his cousin Mansur wouldn't risk talking about it on the overseas wires. None of the family could be relied on absolutely in any choosing up of sides, that was the hell of it. The tribes reverted to their own.

'You've got some sources,' he said. 'What about those?' He'd be surprised if Brooke-Cullingham was without contacts in the network of English and American management that ran through the Rahsmani government offices as well as the GAROC fields.

The Englishman regarded him under slightly lowered lids.

'Hmmm. Well yes, I've checked, but all's quiet. Everything's running smoothly, actually – they claim they don't know what's going on any more than we do.'

Abdullah stood up from the desk and went over to the glass wall of the bungalow and looked out on to the terrace and the bright sea of grass that lay beyond it. The thick hazy day had dawned under a heavy layer of Los Angeles smog. Even the weather was impenetrable.

'Put somebody on a commercial flight to go back and find out what's up. Think of some good excuse to do it. My grandfather's all alone, and I don't like it.'

There was a moment while he tried to think of a likely candidate. Ramzi Alam was their secret police contact, but the Iranian pulled little weight in something like this. He was too far down the political chain of command. If his superiors were fence-sitting he'd get no place. He wouldn't even get inside the fort.

Russell was all right. He was an Englishman and more effective because of it, but he, too, was fairly minor as far as power went. Abdullah didn't trust his cousin Hamid – he could see Hamid taking to the desert in the north to sit it out if things got tough.

Brooke-Cullingham was the only one.

'I can't go,' the Englishman said flatly. 'That would be a gross breach of my instructions. I'm scheduled to stay with you until New York. Your grandfather was quite clear on that. Besides, we're only assuming a difficulty. Why not wait for a few days and read the signs? At least until Crossland gets you fixed up.'

Abdullah could see that Brooke-Cullingham was hedging.

He couldn't believe that the other had no ideas at all.

'No,' Abdullah told him. 'Look, in all these years in the gulf you ought to be able to smell something cooking a thousand miles away. You tell me what you think is going on.'

Brooke-Cullingham didn't say anything for a moment.

'You give me more credit than I deserve. Frankly, I can't give you an opinion when I damned well don't know anything myself. There's quite a bit going on back home, and apparently we're being neglected. That's about it.'

'That's not what I asked you.'

'What does it mean? Could damned well mean anything. Look, I'll be frank with you – when we left the situation was fluid. It had been left hanging too damned long, as you should know. Your grandfather hasn't been moving fast enough these past few years and his decisions about his –' he paused, '– political heirs have been somewhat muddled. Let's not go into past family history. Put it down to personal quirks of an ageing ruler, lack of confidence in your abilities, whatever you want. But what we have before us now is the obvious outcome of all this shillyshallying – not much real power anywhere and what there is, up for challenge. By God, there certainly should have been some policy to deal with this oil strike by the Japanese, since they bloody well held the contract and were out there in the gulf working their heads off drilling for it! And, I might add, there's a contract quite nicely effected by Hakim Asmari, a veritable gem of concessions worked out by a man who's done all the work now for years in this mess and got damned little credit for it. Certainly some provision should have been made for your uncle and your half uncle Said, considering how they would feel when so abruptly cut out of things. Sending you off to talk to GAROC was hardly the answer. I assume,' Brooke-Cullingham said quietly, 'you still don't have any idea of what your authority is, other than to go and make your speech when it's arranged?' He didn't wait for Abdullah to answer. 'The whole damned thing,' he said somewhat wearily, 'is what comes of running these governments like a bloody family rug shop.'

Abdullah stared at him, his mouth slightly open. This was a new side of Rahsmani's financial adviser showing itself. The bland, imperturbable James Brooke-Cullingham in an entirely new light. All he could think of was, Brooke-Cullingham must be going to quit, to voice his opinions as bluntly as this. His grandfather would want to hang him up by the ears for what he was saying. The thought of Brooke-Cullingham quitting or retiring at any time rattled Abdullah for a second. Then he thought, But he has the same view I have about this obsession with Arab family and tribe. So I'm not the only one.

'My authority's what I say it is, I guess.'

He took Brooke-Cullingham's silence for assent. The Englishman, though, sat looking at him rather sceptically.

He needed Brooke-Cullingham's advice. He couldn't have him back out of it now just because he was thinking of quitting.

Abdullah decided to try a different approach. 'Give me your heart,' he said in Arabic. 'I need your help in this now as my grandfather has counted it thus for many years. If this is the last thing you will do for my family, then do it for me. For a short time only, for as long as it will take to make this trip. I will make you this promise.'

Brooke-Cullingham said nothing.

Dammit, what did he want?

'And for this last intrigue of all the intrigues. Which may be the best.'

Brooke-Cullingham had to smile.

'Abdullah, you're a spoiled child, and totally inadequate for what's before you,' he said. 'But you're smart enough to tempt me with that, aren't you?'

'I'm plenty smart,' Abdullah said in English. 'I just don't seem to be able to convince anybody.'

The Englishman groped across the desk and put his hand on the morning newspaper. One of the Hollywood gossip columns had been circled with the black lines of a Magic Marker. Abdullah picked it up.

'Twenty-three-year-old Arab oil millionaire and business-man Sheik Abdullah of Rahsmani has been boosting California economy these days by his generous scattering of petrodollars on the Hollywood scene. Latest to benefit from Middle East oil wealth is luscious Barbra Burchard of film-land, who has been seen sporting a collection of diamonds. Sheik Abdullah is famous for his recent comments on television that Arab oil should be regarded as belonging to everybody. It would be hard to find anyone who would argue with that, but we are left wondering just how much of the world's oil wealth is going to be redistributed under Sheik Abdullah's plan.'

There seemed to be more, but Abdullah didn't finish reading it. He threw the newspaper on the desk.

'All right, I'm not smart all of the time,' Abdullah admitted, 'but I'm trying. And I'm not setting myself up as a saint, either. If any of this bothers you, get us a public relations outfit and tell them to buy us a retraction. Get them to say it was really some Saudi and not me.'

The Englishman continued to smile.

'Abdullah, there are some few things in this world you can't buy your way out of.'

'Not many. You can be in Rahsmani,' Abdullah insisted, 'in twenty-four hours. If nothing's going on, I'll see you back in New York.'

'My dear friend, I'm here on your *grandfather*'s orders. I'm afraid I can't budge until he says so.'

Abdullah took a deep breath.

'All I'm asking you to do when you get to Rahsmani is to look things over, that's all. No – if you find my grandfather's really not operative for some reason, don't wait. I want you to throw that son of a bitch uncle of mine in jail and arrange for him to have a heart attack. If you don't have any cyanide with you, pick up some before you leave.'

'My, my,' Brooke-Cullingham murmured.

But Abdullah could see something glimmering. He pushed for the advantage.

'I'll give you a letter empowering you to do anything you have to do.'

'A *what?*' Brooke-Cullingham regarded him, still smiling slightly.

'Under my authority. Listen, Englishman,' Abdullah said, but he kept his voice under control. By now, he told himself, he really didn't give a damn. 'Either you go, or I'll send Russell. Or if he won't go, I'll send Ramzi Alam. But either way, as I go down the line I'll fire every last one of you on refusal and kick your asses out of here. And if you don't like it you can complain to Rahsmani. That is, if you can get anyone on the telephone.'

The Englishman looked at him now quite soberly.

'You can't do that. It'd leave you in a damnable pickle.'

'Listen, you seem to think I'm some sort of idiot kid you have to lead around by the hand, but I want to let you in on the news – I can take care of myself. I don't need this damned caravan you and my grandfather have put together, I can get into a sweater and jeans and get on the plane to New York myself. I've done it before – you didn't know that – so I know I can do it again. And I'm going to meet with those Gulf Arabian Oil bastards and let them know they're dealing with the government of the world's richest piece of real estate, which is my country, and they'd better get off their butts and start moving. We've dealt with their fucking scorn and contempt for us long enough. Now that we're about to get so damned rich we'll have an option on most of the world's money, it's time they learned how to treat us. Which is, by engraved invitation to us to join up and tell them how to run their lousy business for as long as we're kind enough to let them operate within our borders. That's for starters.'

'Easy, easy,' Brooke-Cullingham said.

'You shut up. There's only one thing in this world money can't buy, they tell me, and that's love. Well, I'm going to ask GAROC for love, I'm asking them to get down on their knees and beg us to let them keep pumping our oil. I've sacrificed my sister to this shitty politicking, I don't intend to give anything more. From now on, everybody gives to *me*. I'm buying it.'

'*Ya*, Abdullah my friend,' Brooke-Cullingham said, 'all this is very interesting. You impress me. But do not become so excited. The way to statesmanship is not so simple.'

'Bullshit,' Abdullah said.

TEN

Midnight.

Someone had left the lights on around the swimming pool but the smog combined with a mist from the Pacific Ocean that lay over most of Beverly Hills turned the pool area into a faint, illuminated glow like a fogbound house or a ship that had lost its way. It was so thick outside that it was impossible to see even the palms or the lemon trees that bordered the garden. The bungalow's central air-conditioning system filtered out the worst of the inversion layer that choked southern California, but even so the curious stink of the freeways and ten thousand incinerators managed somehow to penetrate the rooms and weigh on the lungs. Bisharah and Wadiyeh were particularly affected. The Bedouin had been coughing like jackals for most of the evening.

Adam Russell sat at the desk in the living room going through the paper work which he now, in Brooke-Cullingham's absence, had to approve: bills from the hotel, bills for the maintenance and servicing of the jetliner at the airport, rentals on the limousines, telex and telephone charges, and all the miscellaneous items that piled up day after day. Russell was doing a good job by himself. The thin blond young Englishman, who was only a few years older than Abdullah, had kept things running smoothly since Brooke-Cullingham had left.

Abdullah was on the couch, his legs sprawled out before him, lobbing tennis balls off the far wall of the living room with low sweeps of his racket. Like any other place where one was confined too long, Los Angeles was losing its interest. The weather was rotten and he was sick of hurrying through the smog in a closed limousine to play tennis on indoor courts. He wanted to get out of southern California. He had so much to do once they got underway it made him nervous to sit and wait.

They were waiting for a telephone call from Sam Crossland in New York. Time differences made it past three A.M. in the East but Crossland was coming to the end of his negotiations to get the GAROC board together and Abdullah wanted to know about it as soon as it happened. These things sometimes went on through the night, hooked up by long-distance telephone lines to points in New York, London, and Amsterdam, where, in the never-sleeping works of the international oil companies the meshing of time zones was of no great importance.

Abdullah threw his tennis racket on to the floor and looked at his watch. Late, late, he told himself, and still no word. He got up from the couch and went down the hall to the master bedroom and opened the door.

Barbra was stretched out on his bed in one of his fancier *disdashas* watching television. Her long gold hair was screwed up into a knot on top of her head and she was smoking a rather crushed-looking joint held tightly between thumb and forefinger. The room reeked of the new-mown-hay smell of pot. She only turned to look over her shoulder at him, smiling, but she said nothing. She was already pretty high. Her eyes were red.

He closed the bedroom door quickly. It was probably a mistake to keep her around the house all evening but he was looking forward to relaxing a little after he got Crossland's call. Standing in the hallway, he was beginning to feel the first warm waves of anticipation. This woman, Abdullah told himself, could be habit-forming. With her, everything was sex and no emotion to get in the way, no tiresome demands upon him at all. Which was very satisfactory as far as he was concerned. He would feel no regret at all when he left her except, perhaps, that she was one of the most beautiful women he had ever seen, and damned agreeable.

The telephone rang, and he could hear Russell answering

it. He went swiftly into the living room. Russell was holding the receiver and looking down into it as though he did not know what to make of the noises coming out of his end.

Abdullah supposed it was Crossland. And what they had been waiting for, at long last. Russell held the telephone out to him, a curious expression on his face.

'It's for you,' he said.

When Abdullah took the telephone he heard the same odd sounds. It was a woman crying.

'I've been trying to get in touch with you all evening,' the voice said between sobs. 'But they said you couldn't be disturbed. Finally I told the man who doesn't speak English very well that it was an emergency and then they put me through. I don't see why it has to be so impossible to get you on the telephone.'

It was the redheaded girl teller from the bank in Citrusville. Abdullah held the receiver away from his ear and stared into it as though it had just turned into a scorpion in his hand. Then he put it back to his ear. She was making quite a bit of noise.

'Slow down,' he said. 'It's me, you're talking to me. But I can't understand what the hell you're saying.'

'— and my supervisor is just FREAKING out — there's this ten-thousand-dollar deposit in an account here in my name with all sorts of crazy implications and everybody thinks I'm going to SCREW things up or that I have some sort of interest in why they're trying to sell the bank and they don't know what to DO with me! I mean, you have to be here to see what's going on! And what am I going to do with this purple CAR!'

The sobs were coming like a flood. It made so much noise he could hardly keep his ear to the telephone.

'Calm down,' he tried to say over the uproar. 'Listen, those were only gifts. I want you to enjoy them.' What the hell, he asked himself, was he supposed to do about all this? 'Don't pay any attention to what people say. You have nothing to do with whether we buy the bank or not. In fact,

I think we're going to close the deal, so you can relax. Anyway, it's not very important.'

'You don't understand,' the voice wailed. 'I don't care whether people know we made love or not; it's just that everybody thinks I got PAID for it! You really screwed me up, you know that? And I was really great to you and you know it. How could you do this to me?'

'Look,' Abdullah began, but his words were drowned.

'But I guess something like that doesn't mean anything real to you. You're probably used to treating women like THINGS and you can't relate any other way, right? I mean, all this STUFF – what am I going to do with it? My friends are renting a lorry and they want to know where to bring it back to you – are you listening? They want to bring it up to LA to the hotel and just dump it. I don't need a quad hi-fi; we've got a whole sound system one of the guys here built that's way out ahead of yours!'

'Oh,' he said.

'And the money, too. I really couldn't explain to you that I don't need it, could I? Well, there are some people who don't think it's all that important. I mean, did you ever stop to think that money is probably making you a cold, turned-off person that's not ever going to be able to relate to anybody on a REAL one-to-one basis? I mean, EVER? Oh, I feel sorry for you!'

'Look, Nancy.' He was so upset he had broken out in a sweat. He didn't need to have any of this happen to him right now. 'I'm sorry I hurt your feelings. You're really a sweet lovely girl and I haven't got much time here, I just wanted to express –' he groped for some suitable words, '– what the evening meant to me. And don't worry, I can relate –'

'No you CAN'T. You're locked into a whole materialistic bag that inhibits your feelings only you won't face it. Well, you're going to have to find out there are some things money can't buy!'

That, too.

'It was all sort of a thank-you note,' he said hopelessly.

'FORGET IT! I mean, in some ways you can't help it; Leos are like that. I mean, they are far out, totally into themselves, into their own heads and they are absolutely nonrelating to anybody else's THING. It's a real bummer when you find a bad Leo. I'm a Pisces; our signs are absolutely noplace together. I should have told you.'

'Yeah,' he said.

'I'm going to say a mantra for you,' the voice on the telephone said.

When he heard the click on the other end Abdullah put the receiver back in its cradle. Russell was looking at him sympathetically. He supposed he had heard just about all of it, the way she was yelling.

'I think,' Abdullah said, 'some people are going to come by with a lorry. Get somebody to make a note of it.'

The telephone rang almost immediately. Abdullah let Russell pick it up.

'The hotel wants you to know Mr Hassan is on his way.'

Abdullah leaned against the fire place wall and stared at Russell. What an evening this was turning out to be! There was no one to stop him. The hotel would let Hassan pass because he had given those orders himself. And whoever was on duty on the path would let him go by, too, unless they were smart about it.

He didn't think they would be that smart.

'Ah,' Russell said, scratching his head, 'let me know if there's anything you want me to do.'

Abdullah continued to stare, trying to get his thoughts in some sort of working order. He looked down the hall to the bedroom. Hustle her out through the garden? It was all coming too fast; he didn't know what the hell to do. But, he told himself suddenly, he wasn't going to get into any kind of farce like that. To hell with it. He knew Hassan wasn't going to come down to the bungalow to make any sort of trouble, as there wasn't any trouble to make. They had settled all that.

Hassan was his friend, he reminded himself. In spite of all the crap that had gone on between them lately it was, after all, just about the most rewarding friendship he had ever had with anyone. That crazy girl from the bank in Citrusville was dead wrong. He could relate to people. It was just that all his life it had been very hard to find a person who could survive the wear and tear of his kind of friendship.

'It's okay,' he told Russell, 'I can take care of it myself.'

They heard footsteps approaching on the flagstone walk outside and Abdullah went to the front door of the bungalow and opened it.

It was Hassan all right, coming out of the smog toward him dressed in evening clothes and holding himself as stiffly as a British sergeant major at evening parade. The outdoor lights were bright on him and Abdullah could see there was not a hair out of place. Hassan was as handsome and dashing as ever. But he was also very much boozed up. The smell of alcohol flowed ahead of him like a blast of trumpets.

'*Al salamu alaykum*,' Abdullah greeted him. 'The blessings of God upon you, *Ali effendi*.'

Hassan stopped abruptly and looked at him with sombre, liquid eyes.

'And on you. I hear that you are leaving,' he said.

'Yes, soon. Perhaps even tomorrow if God wills it. It is enough, we have spent more than our full time here.'

'Profitably, I hope?'

'Yes, very profitably.' Abdullah could see that things were going to be very cool between them. It was not a fortunate evening.

'Permit me to come inside? It is my desire to take a proper leave of you.'

Abdullah hesitated, then opened the door wide.

When they came into the living room together Russell stood up, gathered up his papers, and disappeared down the hall. Abdullah turned to Hassan and saw real tears overflowing, rivulets of wet coursing down his cheeks.

'My dear friend,' Abdullah said, taken aback. He didn't want to see Hassan broken up like this over whatever the hell was wrong. He didn't want to lose his friend – what would he do without him? Ali was one of the jewels of the world; you could count on him to liven things up when everything else was down and dragging. Abdullah put his arm tentatively around the other's shoulder and embraced him. 'Do not be thus. It is true, I was going to speak to you on the telephone before I left. I would not go without that.'

Hassan was almost sobbing.

'I did not send this woman to you for any reason,' his friend said. 'I swear it, she came to you of her own accord because she had heard me speak of you and was curious. This woman is an abomination of sexual curiosity. If this were my own country I would beat her. I may beat her yet.'

'Let us not speak of it,' Abdullah said uncomfortably. He wondered if Russell, on his own initiative, had thought of getting her out the back way after all. 'It's not important.'

'What I said of her is true,' Hassan insisted. 'She is uncontrollable. She is not good for anything but to have in bed, may Allah forgive me. But in no way did I send her to you for gain.'

'It is finished. Besides,' Abdullah said quickly, making up his mind on the spot, 'I will finance this film to any amount you may need. It is a valid investment.' He would have to have it authorized, but they would get a wire off to ROIC in the morning. 'For this I thank you.'

'Do not heap the coals of thy generosity upon my head thus,' Hassan wept. 'I suffer enough.'

'Lay down your sorrow,' Abdullah told him, 'you have done nothing. It is the sins of my importunate nature that have laid this between us. I have the curse of a too-ready tongue.' But he sighed. He was getting a little tired of people in tears. 'Come and have a drink,' he said, without thinking.

He saw at once it wasn't the best idea in the world. Hassan was pretty well tanked up. He had lost some of his remarkable rigidity and was beginning to sway from side to side.

'I am drunk,' Ali said, openly weeping. 'Women and money, they are a curse to mankind. But the worst is the demon that tempts men to wine.'

It wasn't wine Abdullah thought. It smelled more like gin.

'Nevertheless, to have money in one's purse is to have a heart without care,' Abdullah quoted. 'Be happy. Now this film will be completed and make its way to glorious success and great riches.' He heard a door closing in back. 'We are friends, O Truest of the True,' he said, raising his voice. 'We should not let small things mar our friendship.'

Oh shit, he told himself. The gaudy black-and-red-striped *disdasha* was making its way down the hall toward them. Abdullah tried to step in front of Hassan.

'Come outside and let us stroll in the gardens,' he said hurriedly. Outside it was choking in smog. 'Or up to the cocktail lounge in the hotel, where we may talk further.'

It was no use. Barbra came into the living room and stood there for a long moment, simply looking them over. She was too stoned on pot to know what was going on.

'Hello, Ali,' she said, hardly moving her lips.

There was a profound silence.

'I guess you two know each other,' Abdullah said.

Hassan had staggered back. He put his hands up in front of him in a gesture that was pure Theatre Cairo.

'O whore of a thousand fathers!' he cried. 'Now you appear before me thus! A woman and my best friend!'

Abdullah sat down on the couch and picked up his tennis racket and began thunking his finger against the strings. 'She's been here all evening,' he said in English. 'You knew that when you came down here looking for her.'

'What's he saying?' Barbra wanted to know.

Hassan was screaming and beating the air with his fists in an agony of Arab betrayal and grief.

'He says that I am trying to unman him,' Abdullah translated. 'That is, I want to cut off his balls. He sees that you have just got out of *my* bed, obviously, and that he just had you in *his* this afternoon and that bouncing you back and forth between us like that is particularly offensive. Especially in the same day.'

'Oh,' she said. She blinked her eyes slowly. She watched as Hassan threw his head back and clutched at his hair with one hand. 'That's pretty heavy,' she intoned. 'If it doesn't bother me, it shouldn't bother him.'

'That's not the point,' Abdullah said.

The Bedouin had come from the kitchen and now stood at the edge of the living room, listening to Ali Hassan lay it out in detail. It was mostly about the woman and what she did with various men that were mortal affronts to his honour and the *bedu* could follow it perfectly, since it was all in Arabic. They drew back their lips, teeth gleaming. Hassan was in great form, even drunk.

'You have no importance, whore!' Hassan roared, descending on her. 'It is what you have done to *me*!' He grabbed Barbra by the arm and swung her against him. Being as stoned as she was, she couldn't keep her balance; she flapped one arm like a great bird enveloped in the *disdasha* and fell to her knees. She put her arms around Hassan's legs.

Abdullah got up from the couch. Wadiyeh and Bisharah moved toward them, interestedly. Ali had got Barbra to let go of his legs and was dragging her to the front door. He got it open with one hand and sort of rolled her out into the smog. She sprawled on the stone path.

'Come on,' Abdullah said, 'what do you want to rough her up for?'

He followed them outside and Hassan turned on him, shouting.

'Desert lice! Eaters of lizards! What do you know of wealth?'

When Hassan swung at him, Abdullah countered with the tennis racket. The Egyptian fell back into the tall hedge of oleanders that bordered the wall, almost disappearing from sight. Abdullah waded in after him, his clothes catching on the branches. They came through on the path of the bungalow next door. Barbra and the Bedouin were right behind, ploughing through the sticky leaves.

Ali got to his knees and then his feet and came to Abdullah in a windmill rush of blows. The Egyptian was no sort of fighter and Abdullah had had only a few reluctant rounds of boxing at school. He preferred the tennis racket. He hit Hassan a resounding whack on the side of the head with it. The strings hummed like a returned volley. Hassan reached up and wrenched the racket out of his hands and punched him in the mouth with it, grip forward. Abdullah felt a painful wet spread down his chin.

The bastard, Abdullah realized, had tried to knock his front teeth out. He hurled himself at Hassan and they fell on the walkway. He tried to land a punch on Hassan's perfect nose, but the actor's hands were in between. Bisharah bent down over them, offering his help.

'GET OUT OF THE WAY!' Abdullah shouted.

Hassan got away from him, scrambled to his feet, and then charged him again for another flurry of roundhouse punches. There were people coming up the walk to the bungalow and Abdullah dimly heard men's voices and then a woman scream as he dragged Hassan on to the terrace in a bear hug. They fell over a patio table and some iron chairs. It made a lot of noise. Then Russell's voice. People were coming and going in the oleander hedge and falling down in it.

Abdullah shoved Hassan up against the glass doors of the other bungalow and held him. He was taller than the Egyptian and had the advantage of reach, but Hassan was more powerfully built. Even drunk, he was beating the hell out of him. Abdullah had to get his breath. They glared at each other, panting.

'What is in thy head, Egyptian, that you come now to fight with me?' Abdullah said to him. He tried to cough some of the blood out of his throat. 'Hear me, I said I will give the money for the cinema. A million, two million, what does it matter?'

'You filthy son of a bitch *bedu*,' Hassan said between his teeth.

That was no answer. Or perhaps it was. For all the tears and embraces of friendship, Abdullah thought, it was possible that Hassan really hated him. And had to load up with a bellyful of booze before he could get it out.

Abdullah tried to look carefully at him. They were so close, jammed together like that, that the blood dripped off his chin and on to the shoulder of Hassan's tuxedo. He had his forearm against Hassan's throat to hold him.

'You're not friend, are you?' Abdullah said. It was a terrible realization that Hassan, too, like so many others, might not be his friend after all. He coughed. The blood and California smog were strangling him.

There was no answer.

He let Hassan go and the Egyptian swung at him. Abdullah stepped back in time to dodge the blow and then he reached out and brought his fist up and let him have it under the jaw. Hassan slid down quietly into a squatting position against the glass doors and regarded his shoes. He did not look up.

Abdullah looked around him wearily. Wadiyeh was picking a woman out of a nasturtium bed. She had her mouth open, speechless with horror. Barbra Burchard was holding the side of her face and Russell was half in and half out of the oleander hedge, trying to help her back through.

'Someone's called the police,' Russell said. 'We'd better get out of here.'

Abdullah moved toward him uncertainly, trying to wipe some of the blood from his neck and chin. It was flowing freely. Hassan had split his lower lip; the crack in the flesh there felt as though it was going to need stitches. He turned back to look at Ali, still squatting on the strange bungalow terrace. He didn't move.

'Fetch him,' he told Wadiyeh.

'My God, my God, who are these people?' the woman who had been in the flower bed kept shrieking. 'Where did they come from?' A man in a sports coat and a straw hat was trying to comfort her. Another man was sitting on the flagstones beyond.

Bisharah moved past them holding Ali Hassan rather awkwardly over his shoulder, as one carries a sack. One of Hassan's shoes had fallen off. The man in the straw hat shrank back as Bisharah and his burden disappeared into the oleanders. He put his arm around the woman.

'One of those things –' he hesitated '– stepped on my wife! What are you going to do about it?'

'Send us the bill,' Abdullah said. He made a dejected, sweeping gesture with one arm. 'We'll pay for everything.'

Russell reached out of the oleander hedge and grabbed Abdullah by the extended arm and jerked him, none too gently, through to the other side. Abdullah brushed the leaves from his bloodstained clothes. Coming up the path on this side toward them was a tall surly youth in blue jeans with long blond curls that flowed over his shoulders and down his back. His arms were full of a turntable and an amplifier with AM-FM radio. A hotel security guard trailed him.

'Are you the whatsit?' the one with the golden hair said. He stared in an unfriendly way at Abdullah, taking in the bloodstains and the figure of Wadiyeh looming behind. 'Where do you want me to put this stuff?'

Abdullah had an impulse to hit him, too, just for the look on his face. But he thought better of it.

'I don't give a shit,' he said. 'Dump it in the swimming pool.'

Even at that moment it was a dumb thing to say.

ELEVEN

From *The Hollywood Reporter*:   May 12th

A little fist fight between Arab friends over some of those famous petrodollars seem to have precipitated the hullabaloo at the Palm Aire Hotel in Beverly Hills the other night. International film star Ali Hassan, one of the reputed punch throwers says 'No' to everything, explains it was just a noisy way of friends getting together after a large party, Arabian Gulf-style. Playboy Arab oil millionaire handsome young Sheik Abdullah of Rahsmani could not be reached for comment but residents of the surrounding exclusive back bungalows of the Palm Aire say there was more to it than just Middle Eastern type celebrating. Mrs Margery Kearns, wife of Paramount Studios producer Joe Kearns, just happened to be passing by and was hurried off the spot by the large group of ferocious native desert tribesmen who surround the Sheik. In the scuffle, Mrs Kearns tripped and fell, sustaining a sprained ankle. Also on the scene, rumour has it, was Barbra Burchard, former great friend and companion of Egyptian movie star Ali Hassan, who has been seeing a lot of the young Sheik lately. What all Beverly Hills is buzzing about is that although those petrodollars seemed to be the subject of the brouhaha that woke the neighbours, Miss Burchard has been seen around town sporting a bruised eye her press agent says is the result of connecting with a stray tennis ball. Alfie Brown, pro at the Beverly Courts Club, says, 'She was all right when I last played with her.'

CONTINUED

and the future of the Sabah family of Kuwait, a future that is very much dependent on the stability of the moderate rule begun in 1965 by the present Sheik Sabah al Sabah.

One of the few to violate the secrecy that surrounds the activities of the oil aristocrats of the Gulf sheikdoms is freewheeling young Sheik Abdullah of Rahsmani, grandson of the present ruler, eighty-year-old Emir Ibrahim al Asmari. Heir to a vast Arabian Gulf oil fortune completely controlled by the Asmari family, Abdullah has recently been upped to a position of responsibility in international affairs, a role never allocated to his late father Sheik Tewfik, who died an incurable schizophrenic. Now Chairman of the Rahsmani Overseas Investment Corporation, the young Sheik Abdullah promoted the recent purchase of the Citrusville Community Bank in southern California and is currently backing the film *The F Squadron* produced by Herman Shoemaker–Ali Hassan, to be released by Universal Pictures next spring.

A graduate of Phillips Andover Academy and Yale University, Sheik Abdullah is reported to be a personally engaging and astute member of a family that has long represented traditional absolutism in government among the Arabian Gulf nations. But Abdullah's course so far has been somewhat shaky. His openness to the press, with the resulting quote that, 'Arab oil belongs to the world' has given him anything but the much-desired low profile of most Arab oil Government representatives. Unlimited wealth (the Japanese Mitsumi oil combine has just announced a strike of 'undetermined size' in Rahsmani offshore drilling that, added to the current Gulf Arabian Oil Company concession, may bring the country up to the Gulf's number one oil producer) has had its obvious drawbacks for the untried twenty-three-year-old heir to the Rahsmani throne. A recent stay in Hollywood did nothing to dispel Abdullah's reputation for fast living and wild parties with several thousand dollars' worth of diamonds going to one Hollywood film actress and a bill for thousands more tendered by the Palm Aire Hotel in Beverly Hills – which threatened a damage suit on discovery of considerable breakage in one of their bungalows and a late-model sedan submerged in the private swimming pool.

To date, Sheik Abdullah's antics have not threatened his standing in his own country; he has, in spite of a spotty performance, managed to establish himself as a fairly certain successor in the government so rigidly controlled by his grandfather the Emir, and has brought about a measure of success in his first Stateside trip to scout possibilities for Rahsmani investment money. However, the formidable figure of his uncle, Sheik Hakim al Asmari, looms large on the horizon of Abdullah's political future. Sheik Hakim was one of the founders of the Organization of Petroleum Exporting Countries (OPEC), which initiated the oil embargo of 1973, and the Organization of Arab Petroleum Exporting Countries (OAPEC), its offshoot. Hakim, in tandem with another uncle, Sheik Ameen Said, have long controlled Rahsmani oil policy in the outside world. Their fight to

CONTINUED

Memo: To the Sunday desk

Kill the above section.

J.P.

Memo: to Managing Editor James Pressman

Has this got anything to do with the guy from the State Department? I think we ought to let these screwballs have it. It was a purple Audi they dumped in the swimming pool. Also, some women got beat up.

Memo: to the Sunday desk

　　　　Kill it.

J.P.

'The thing you've got to remember about these boys,' Sam Crossland said as they got into the lift of the Oriental Oil Company Building, 'is that they're not bankers or financiers, they're oilmen. When you talk about production at the well head they know what you're talking about as well as you do, maybe better. Most of them have served their time in some-out-of-the-way part of the world before they got where they are now. You just try to keep that in mind.'

Abdullah nodded. He was looking around him at the lift, which was a curious piece of machinery, decorated around the walls and across the ceiling with a bas relief of gold metal dolphins, mermaids, oil derricks, and tankers riding a sea of golden waves, all of this set against the lift's jade-green and gold-enamelled walls. The Oriental Oil Company Building had been constructed during the Gulf of Mexico oil-boom days, which accounted for the mermaids and oil derricks mixed together in the frieze and the overall movie-theatre architecture throughout. This was the executive lift, one boarded at the nineteenth floor of Oriental Oil's headquarters in Pittsburgh to ascend to the boardrooms at the top of the tower. Considering the lift's age, Abdullah thought, you would think it would jiggle and shake itself to pieces making the final journey, but it didn't. The fancy old cage ran as smoothly as any modern installation, only it ran very slowly. There was even an ornamental brass lamp above their heads, and it didn't sway an inch.

There was a nice sort of message in all this if anyone cared to read it – a real clue to the type of thinking so entrenched in the older petroleum giants like Oriental Oil. The smooth-running antique, which some other corporations might have junked years ago in modernizing an old building, had been carefully preserved, like the Oriental Oil Company Building itself, with a fine disregard for cost or changing tastes. Set down in Pittsburgh where the oil age, with its ghosts of the first Rockefellers and Mellons had begun, the lift whirred slowly upward, powered by electricity and billions of dollars of insulation against time and the world outside.

Of course there was also a giant fifty-storey Oriental Oil Company Building in New York City that resembled a science-fiction grain silo paved with green glass, but that didn't count. Looking around the lift, anybody could see where the company's heart and soul really rested.

Abdullah caught Adam Russell's eye from the back of the lift where the assistant was squeezed in between one of the Jordanians and a State Department special security plainclothesman, and tried to give him a reassuring look. Russell, who carried the forty-seven pages of the speech to the GAROC board in his attaché case, had been up all night putting the finishing touches to it, and managed to look more nervous and strained than any of them. Although, Abdullah reminded himself, it was probably hard to tell just by looking at him how *he* was feeling: his cheekbones were still puffy from the fight with Hassan in Los Angeles, and while the stitches had been taken out of his split lower lip that morning the cut was not completely healed over. The doctor at the Waldorf had sprayed the break with some sort of medicinal plastic that held the edges together but the total effect, counting bruises, was not very encouraging. Abdullah saw Russell look away.

Well, they had all agreed there wasn't much they could do about the state of his face. There had been a lot of conversation about it that morning in the hotel while he was getting dressed, and speculation about how best to carry it off before the officers of the executive board of the Gulf Arabian Oil Company while looking like the victim of a mugging, and in the end they decided there wasn't any real solution. Sam Crossland had taken a good look at Abdullah before they had left New York and all he had said was, 'You look like a pretty tough character. That might not be too bad.' Which was to say that they were stuck with it. The meeting with GAROC, after all that time and pressure from their side, couldn't be postponed.

The lift was crowded and there was hardly room for Abdullah to lift his hand and touch his mouth to see if the plastic was still holding. He didn't want it to break loose in the middle of his speech. The lift held not only the two Bedouin bodyguards, Russell, Crossland, and himself, but also the State Department security men and the State liaison officer, who were now a more or less permanent part of their group.

The lift doors slid open and they stepped into the foyer of the executive tower. Several people were standing there and as they saw them they moved forward with hands extended.

The young man with the heavy British army-style moustache and light blue eyes was Knacker, assistant to the director of operations of Gulf Arabian, which oversaw all of Rahsmani pumping and refining. Charlie Averbach, head of Engineering, was also there and quickly introduced three of GAROC's legal staff. Abdullah gave the lawyers the briefest of nods; like his grandfather, he had little admiration for the corporate legal flunkies. But he knew Averbach, a longtime resident of the oil city at Ras Deir. It was good to see a familiar face. They shook hands warmly.

'Ya, Charlie sayid,' Abdullah greeted him in Arabic. 'How is evening? How long has it been since you have seen my esteemed kinsman the lord Emir?' Averbach was one of Gulf Arabian's pioneers and one of the oilmen his grandfather liked.

'In too long a time, God knows, and the blessings of peace be on him,' Averbach responded. 'All is well with him insofar as this knowledge is mine.' There was something in Averbach's heavily suntanned face that hesitated, not sure with only a few moments and all the people around them, whether to go on. 'I hear that Jim Brooke-Cullingham has returned to Rahsmani city. Anything new?'

'Only the usual affairs of business. For this, I suppose, God has given us airplanes.'

But Abdullah was curious. In their last conversation with Brooke-Cullingham the night before in New York the Englishman had said that there were demonstrations in the city again on the usual issues – demands for the establishment of a parliament and the continuing protests over the secret police – such as they had had the year before, but he had kept the details to a minimum. Hakim al Asmari was still under unannounced house arrest; no one knew much about that except that his grandfather had given the orders out of an apparent desire to keep Hakim in the country while the GAROC negotiations were going on. Now here was Averbach, who had obviously flown in to make a report to the Gulf Arabian board on current business, wanting to know if Abdullah knew what was going on. That was interesting.

'All is well?' Abdullah said. He couldn't find any better words. The lawyers were still hanging around and someone had him by the elbow, urging him to move on.

'All's quiet up where we are,' Averbach said.

Abdullah looked for Sam Crossland, who was somewhere behind. He would get Sam to look into it later. It would seem they needed a more thorough checking out on what was going on than they had been getting. There were GAROC people all around him, they were being gently moved forward to the doors to the boardroom. They were already more than an hour late. 'Don't rush,' Sam Crossland had cautioned him. 'Set your own pace and don't try to get ahead of yourself. Most of this game is in putting on a good face and knowing when not to back down.'

Abdullah couldn't help but smile. Putting on a good face was not the right word for it. Some of them hadn't caught up with his publicity; the GAROC lawyers had looked downright shaken.

He moved easily toward the double doors to the boardroom, the folds of the white *disdasha* billowing around him. It had been up to him that morning as to what clothes he would wear and he had chosen to go with the full traditional turnout of finely made cotton *disdasha*, severe and without any trimming, a heavy white silk *kaffiyeh* held by a gold and black rope, the ceremonial dagger, and even, though they were hard to manage and one usually wore Western-style black oxfords, the old-fashioned slippers with turned-up toes. Abdullah found that he was pretty comfortable dressed as he was. He was forced to move slowly, as Crossland had advised, and his head could only make the most dignified of turns without the *kaffiyeh* getting in his way, but that was all to the good. He was rather satisfied with the way the clothes set him apart from the others and linked him only with the Bedouin, whose black *disdashas* and red-and-black checkered headcloths were as sombre as his outfit was bright and kingly.

The double doors opened into a dark-green-and-gold-painted room that looked high out on to the city of Pittsburgh. The same theme was here, too, with a mural of oil derricks in the sea on one wall, the same frieze of gold mermaids and tankers around the ceiling. A large mahogany table surrounded by heavy upholstered chairs centred the big room.

Here finally were the men he was to recognize from Sam Crossland's descriptions: Henry Baker Lamborchard, president of Gulf Arabian International, a man who had once been as spare as Crossland but whom money and comfortable living had filled out to corporation size; Gilbert ten Doop, the handsome rangy chairman of the board of Jakarta Oil Limited and also an officer of Royal Dutch Shell; Robert Jamison Blair, the bald little Scot who was director and general manager for Anglo-Oriental Petroleum Industries. John Hubley Foxe of the legal firm of Foxe and Rhinebach, GAROC's lawyers, stood behind them. Except for the lawyer they all knew the Emir of Rahsmani or had met him at least once; they all knew Sam Crossland from Sam's early oil-prospecting days in the Middle East, and all of them together knew the giant interlocking network of acquaintances who ran the big international oil companies.

They had appeared before too many Senate inquiries not to be familiar with each other. There was a burst of talk and handshaking as they stood around the table, and mentions of when they had last seen each other and the people they all knew.

Very clubby, Abdullah observed. That was what impressed you most about oil people, the sense they had of all belonging together and that even finer attitude of having a monopoly on power and the knowledge of how everything should be run. It was hard to fight against, as the people in his part of the world had learned. They wanted you to feel that you were always an outsider.

Well he was an outsider, he told himself. That was why he had worn his traditional robes.

'I hear you had a very good time on the Coast,' Henry Lamborchard said to Abdullah. 'Hollywood's a damned entertaining place. I don't get there much more – we still have a little house in Santa Barbara, but the oil business keeps me so tied up I can't visit like I used to.' Lamborchard spoke in the usual east Texas twang of so many of the oil-men and he had developed a manner of standing slightly to one side so that he could incline his head as he talked, giving the impression of friendly intimacy. It was also a position from which he could keep track of what was going on. It was easy to see he wasn't concentrating on his words. His eyes followed Russell as Russell laid the attaché case on the conference table; they went to Sam Crossland talking to Gilbert ten Doop of the Dutch oil combine, and then the Bedouin as they looked for a place against the nearest wall. '– glad we could finally get together, sorry for the delays, I suppose your people have kept you advised –' Lamborchard's voice went on.

He's sizing us up, Abdullah thought, sort of smelling us out to see what we're up to. That is, anything other than what they've already mulled over and decided on. Crossland he knows. Russell doesn't get much attention, and after a few quick looks to see what in the hell's happened to my face he's filed me away for further evaluation. Probably while I'm making my speech.

'The Dutchman is the one to look out for,' Sam Crossland had said, 'although they're all sharp. Remember, they all got their heads together beforehand to see if they could guess what we want. They've reviewed everything you might want to come up here and raise hell about, including some things you'n me never thought of. And you can count on them being up to date on all that Hollywood publicity so don't waste your time worrying about it. Since they're oilmen they've most likely been in some fights themselves in the old days. They might think it's kinda cute.'

Abdullah felt slightly restless. He wanted to get his speech in hand and get it over with and then go on to the discussion that was sure to come after. No matter what Sam Crossland had said about his appearance, it didn't make him too comfortable. The Scot from Anglo-Oriental Oil had been studying him and could hardly hide his smile. Abdullah looked to Crossland to see if he had noticed, but the other wouldn't look at him.

Damn, he's feeling it too, he told himself. So you see, it doesn't do any good to tell me it doesn't matter when it does. Crossland knows they've already got us down for some kind of travelling circus, he got the message pretty clearly. And it was just what he was afraid of. Now he's trying to assess what this is doing to his own standing with these oilmen, to be caught like this with some playboy Arab kid in tow who wants to make a speech that nobody wants to really listen to. It all happened in those few minutes when they saw me for the first time and put two and two together with what they've already heard, and made up their minds. Just as big a farce as they'd expected. And if, as Crossland says, they've been briefed about me, then they certainly know the State Department has finally caught up with us and assigned enough people to keep me out of trouble. Or at least out of the newspapers. That little item has probably finished us off.

Abdullah felt a slow painful surge of blood to his face that gathered about the cut on his lip and made it ache.

It was all suddenly very clear. The moment of truth, Abdullah told himself bitterly. For a split second he regretted wearing the *disdasha*. Here I've been going along thinking I've been doing pretty well after all, give or take a few dumb accidents, and it turns out I haven't been fooling anybody but myself. No wonder my grandfather took so long making up his mind about me. The personality quirks of an ageing ruler, that was how Brooke-Cullingham had put it. But he had been referring to my grandfather putting any trust in me, that was what he really meant. Even Hassan had it all figured out.

What the hell do I do now? he asked himself. Here, in the midst of these people who, like Sam Crossland and Lamborchard, who have finally trained themselves not to call us Ay-rabs to our faces, but who deep down haven't budged an inch from their conviction that we are a backward and ignorant people who have lucked on to the world's largest puddle of oil and sure as hell don't know how to handle it? And now me, done up in *disdasha* and all the rest while they're having a hard time keeping their faces straight.

Abdullah looked down, not hearing Lamborchard's voice going on with its supply of condescending small talk, and put his hands on the smooth surface of the conference table. I'll be damned if I'll let them write me off that easily, he told himself. They're not dealing with one of the five or six hundred worthless princelings the Saudis have had to pension off to keep them out of everybody's hair, or a spoiled nitwit like some of the Sabahs in Kuwait, no matter what they may think. I don't give a damn what their experience has been in the past. I may not come on too strong right at the moment and I know I've made my mistakes, but I'm better than that. I've got to be.

Still, he told himself, it was no wonder his uncle Hakim and Ameen Said looked good by comparison.

Abdullah felt someone touch his arm and looked up to

find Adam Russell standing there, the papers of the speech in his hand. The young Englishman had a look on his face that said he, too, knew what it was all about.

'Carry on,' Russell said quietly.

The damned British.

'Right,' Abdullah said. But he noticed with some alarm that his own hands were shaking as he took the papers from him.

'First,' Sam Crossland had said, 'follow the old army method which is, tell them what you're going to do. Then you do it. Then you tell them what you've done. But start out slow and easy and give them time to settle down and get accustomed to the sound of your voice.'

The first part of the speech briefly outlined the development of oil exploration in Rahsmani in the bad old days when one dry well after another had been sunk in the desert and the Gulf Arabian consortium had to hold meetings every three months to decide whether to go on putting millions of dollars into what other oil companies had found to be a pretty futile venture. Gulf Arabian had been gambling against the worst sort of odds, following in the footsteps of all the drilling outfits who had found the place barren. Give credit where credit is due, Crossland had said. Abdullah gave it all he could muster. At the peak of the worst of it when the talk was that Gulf Arabian was about to pull out, the strikes had come in the most dramatic of ways, spouters one right after another with the crews fighting to get them capped, pouring light sweet crude of the finest grade with, remarkably, one of the lowest sulphur contents to be found anywhere in the world. And then, just not to be left out, a small pool farther south of heavy crude for fuel oil that had put them anyplace in the market they wished to be. For one hectic year it had seemed the northern desert of Rahsmani was spewing oil faster than anybody could attend to it. The GAROC find was big enough to put the country up to Number Three Producer in the Arabian Gulf right behind Kuwait. That was when the riches began to flow. His grandfather, who had been making what money he could on modest drilling rights fees from companies who had brought in nothing but dry wells, suddenly found himself with as much money as GAROC had oil.

Abdullah had been only four or five years old at the time; some of the men there in the GAROC boardroom remembered it all a lot better than he did. Still, he realized suddenly, it hadn't been so long ago, after all.

He went on to list the GAROC credits one by one. The programme of job training for those Rahsmanis who wanted to enter semiskilled work in the Gulf Arabian Company oil fields. The step-by-step advanced training for Rahsmanis that took them on to engineering degrees at company expense. He even had the number of Rahsmani engineers who had gone up through GAROC's training system – twenty-two – and the figures of Rahsmanis hired for skilled and semiskilled labour – over two thousand. Then, the schools and the first highways built with oil company funds, as well as the health services provided by GAROC not only in Ras Deir and other company towns but also the second-baby-syndrome clinics, the dispensaries, and the special team of five agronomists from Arizona State University whom Gulf Arabian had hired in the sixties to set up an agricultural experiment station to breed better strains of sheep and line with concrete the wells the Bedouin depended on. All this was on the credit side.

However, he went on to point out, this had all taken place in the days when GAROC oil profit figures were tightly held secrets. Although oil royalties were making his grandfather enormously rich, they were still very low by neighbouring oil-country standards. And GAROC knew it. Those were the days, although they were not to find it out till later, when Gulf Arabian Oil Company could produce Rahsmani's top-quality crude for not more than five cents a barrel and sell it on the market for one hundred times that much. Although it was true GAROC had spent millions to bring in the Rahsmani fields, their take had been in billions. Not much of a fair share had even been thought about in

GAROC boardrooms until Abdullah's kinsman Hakim al Asmari had joined together with the other oil-producing countries to found OPEC.

No one, least of all the international oil companies, had believed OPEC would really work. It was hard to consider that countries like Venezuela and Iran could band together with Saudi Arabia, Kuwait, and Rahsmani and stick together (this was the important part) in any sort of unanimity of purpose. That they could have any strength to press for a bigger share of oil profits or fight against manipulation of the world market by the big international oil firms. But the infamous cutting of prices by Exxon in the sixties had originally outraged them, and the scorn with which they had been received when they organized had strengthened them.

Abdullah looked up from his papers. It was not written into the speech but Henry Lamborchard of Gulf Arabian had voiced the attitude of the big oil companies when he had declared, 'We don't recognize this so-called OPEC and never will. Our dealings are with Rahsmani, and not with outsiders.'

Abdullah looked down the long mahogany table to see what effect the mention of OPEC's history was having and if Lamborchard was remembering how he had scoffed at it. But he saw, startled, that the president of Gulf Arabian International was talking in an undertone to Blair, the rolypoly Scotsman, and smiling and not listening at all.

There was a sudden silence. Abdullah found himself looking at ten Doop of Jakarta Oil, then at Sam Crossland, who seemed to have pulled himself away from what was going on, and then finally at Russell. The Englishman's face was slightly red.

'Sorry,' Lamborchard said in the quiet. He was smiling the most inoffensive of smiles, which said that no one with any experience in dealing in high places would take any notice of it. 'Please go right on.'

Abdullah couldn't go on. The slight might not be very big in east Texas or even in the boardroom of Oriental Oil in Pittsburgh, but he was sure Lamborchard knew the real measure of such crashing rudeness in Arab society. If they had all been sitting in the council chamber of his grandfather's fort in Rahsmani their remarks would be listened to with excruciating attention whether they chose to speak five minutes or five hours. Nothing else but such politeness was ever offered unless one was a savage or wished to render a deadly insult. Now Abdullah could only wonder what in the hell Lamborchard had thought he had done, anyway.

You've misjudged me, he told himself, if you think I'm going to put up with something like that. You people always seem to be making the same kind of mistakes, it just seems you don't ever learn.

'Yes, I will go on,' Abdullah said finally. He put the papers of his speech down on the table and pushed them to one side. The bulk of his ceremonial robes made him move slowly and deliberately. 'I was about to make the point that when you, Mr Lamborchard, heard about OPEC you said it wouldn't work because these damned people, as you put it, would be too busy fighting with each other to be any sort of threat. As it turned out, the petroleum-exporting countries have hung together very successfully after all, so you were absolutely wrong. The OPEC cartel has forced a lot of changes in the few years it's been organized that you never thought it would, including some stiff agreements on posted prices for their product. But your sort of talk is what most Arab oil countries, and Rahsmani in particular, have been accustomed to getting from you ever since we granted rights to drill our oil. And after this sort of continuing shit year after year,' Abdullah said, 'I'm beginning to wonder why my grandfather or my uncle Hakim have had the patience to go along with it. I think the Kuwaitis had the right idea in 56 – somebody should have torn up your pipelines a long time ago.'

'Well now,' Lamborchard said, his knowing smile growing broader, 'it hasn't been as bad as all that.'

Abdullah ignored the warning signals Crossland was making from his end of the table.

'I can't say how it's been, since I haven't been here before. But I was going to go on and say that after OPEC was organized my uncle the Sheik Hakim approached you directly with an offer to raise Rahsmani prices for crude and you told him to go stick his head in a bucket. OPEC's bucket, to be exact. And every time we have asked you to open yourselves to some sort of participation in regulating the market flow of oil, or conservation of oil reserves your reaction has been that you're not going to concede one drop of anything we can't forcibly screw out of you. I want you to realize you laid down the rules. We didn't.'

There was another long pause and no one said anything. But now the Dutchman and Blair were smiling, too.

I'm doing just what they thought I would do, Abdullah thought. They're expecting me to start some good Arab screaming right about now and lose all my cool. Then they can tell me to calm down, go home, and leave this to more experienced heads.

'Unfortunately,' Abdullah said, 'I haven't come to try to screw anything out of you this time. The day for slug-and-hug tactics – and that's your phrase, too – is over. In the speech I was going to read you I was going to give you all the arguments on the side of sweet reason and try to persuade you that my grandfather the Emir wishes to make some accommodation with you right now, as you are facing the prospects of a coming unstable situation. With some hard decisions about foreign oil ownership in our territory. My grandfather desired us to work together.'

'The whole Middle East,' the slightly accented voice of ten Doop said, 'is a highly unstable situation. The point is, whether it is still profitable for us.'

Make note of that, Abdullah told himself. When they talk about profits, that's always important.

'I know I'm only defining,' he went on, 'the current state of affairs in the light of my own perspective – there was an

225

audible snort from Lamborchard – 'and the political and economic views held by my grandfather the lord Emir. But there's no reason for us to assume that these aren't sound. The Emir knows perfectly well the dangers of a large non-citizen majority in countries like ours and the pressure of left-wing radical elements. He is also well aware, as I am, of the shifting balance of power in the gulf and the need for the political well-being of neighbouring nations. To this end, my country maintains good relations and ties with the Sabah family of Kuwait, the government of Abu Dhabi and, as you know, my sister is married to Prince Azziz of Saudi Arabia, a younger brother of the present ruler.' He heard himself saying it, as he had planned to say it, and only stopped for a second before he went on. 'I want to let you know that my grandfather is working toward that stability in the gulf which all our countries desire. It may not be apparent from your positions, but it's going on.' Abdullah took a breath. 'And I realize that to date most of the Gulf Arabian transactions have been handled by the chairman of the Rahsmani Oil Directorate, the Sheik Hakim al Asmari.' He wished to hell he knew whether Ameen Said had been in this boardroom in the recent past and what he had said, or promised. 'There's been a change, however. I'm here today to tell you that I am acting directly for the Emir Ibrahim. And this will continue until further notice.'

'We don't have any advisement of a change,' the lawyer, Foxe, said.

'There is a letter from my grandfather authorizing me to act in his place. Sam Crossland has had it forwarded to you.'

Ten Doop had his eyes on him. The Dutchman, at least, had been paying very close attention to what Abdullah was saying.

'There is no letter.'

For a moment Abdullah couldn't figure out what this was all about. Why wasn't the letter received? Sam Crossland had assured him that it was all taken care of.

I can stop here, he realized, while we haggle over whether or not there is any letter and whether I'm the authorized

226

representative or not. This is somebody's sandbagging attempt, and they're not going to help me out. He looked down the conference table. It's probable they've been in contact with Hakim through Ameen Said and my beloved kinsmen have offered the oil companies a whole new situation to deal with – a more representative, progressive government, some under-the-table concessions that will appease the Third World crowd while making the oilmen happy – there's no telling what. And with my family record and Hakim's assessments of my character, not to mention what they've read in the newspapers, they're probably not too enthusiastic about placing any bets on me. Or even on my grandfather at this stage.

But, he told himself cautiously, they'd be fools to go along with Hakim and any alliance he has got to get together with the radical Palestinians and Iranians inside my country to make it work. That's about as shaky as anything they could do. Unstable, shaky – what was it the Dutchman said about it not being profitable anymore?

'It's not important,' Abdullah said evenly, 'whether you feel you've been officially notified of any change or not. I'm telling you there has been.' He found that his hands had stopped shaking. To hell with it, he told himself. 'I'm here, and I'm the new representative in Rahsmani oil matters. In everything.'

Blair leaned forward to say something to Lamborchard, who took the cue.

'I understand you've said you speak for the rest of the gulf oil countries on the subject of oil, too,' the president of Gulf Arabian International said. 'Or is that unofficial, also?'

'I was misquoted,' Abdullah said shortly. 'I don't speak for the other gulf nations, only Rahsmani.'

Ten Doop made an impatient gesture. 'All right, all right, that's good enough.'

Ten Doop, Abdullah observed, was one man who was not going to fool around. The others sat back, still with their satisfied smiles. But the Dutchman kept his cold, judicious gaze on Abdullah.

'I came here with a prepared speech,' Abdullah said, 'but I'm not going to use it. Let's forget the formal structure of my telling you what went on in the past, and my listing all the philanthropic things your corporation has done for my country — that is, other than pump out our oil at rip-off rates while telling us we should be grateful to you for dragging us out of the twelfth century. I'm sure you're as sick of hearing about it as I am. So let's get down to what I came here for. We want to propose that you grant the right to the government of Rahsmani to buy into the Gulf Arabian Oil Company on a sixty-forty ratio with GAROC holding the forty, beginning the first of July of this year. With options for a one hundred per cent sale to us within the next five years.'

There it was, right off the top of his head. And far more than his grandfather had ever had in mind when he had sent him to these people to make a bid for participation in the GAROC structure as it existed. What he had been thinking about these past few weeks was participation as the Saudi Arabians had worked it out with Aramco — to buy in, with eventual plans for a complete takeover. One hundred per cent ownership and no chicken-shitting around. But he hadn't made up his mind until a few minutes ago. He could see Crossland's eyes widen with surprise, the shock on Adam Russell's face.

'You are speaking now,' Blair said carefully, 'of current Gulf Arabian operations within Rahsmani.'

'The works,' Abdullah said. 'Everything within the political and geographical boundaries of my country.'

The oilmen sat in profound silence, Lamborchard with his head thrown back contemplating the mermaids and tankers circling the ceiling; ten Doop with his hands clasped against his chest, regarding Abdullah from under heavy eyebrows; Blair busily writing notes on the pad before him. It was as though they were waiting for some invisible concord to flow between them.

They weren't looking for that, Abdullah told himself. Now they're working like hell to realign the figures on the balance sheet and come up with a whole new auditing. You can practically hear the numbers clicking in their heads.

At last Lamborchard sighed. It seemed to be some sort of signal. Ten Doop reached across the table and pulled a new stack of papers in front of him. He opened the top binder.

'One hundred per cent within eighteen months,' ten Doop said. 'The works.'

Now it was Abdullah's turn to fall silent. Capitulation, right off the wall! He didn't try to read Sam Crossland's face. Even the Bedouin, who only understood half a dozen words of English, knew something big was happening. They leaned forward to listen and watch the faces.

They aren't kidding, Abdullah told himself. And they didn't make up their minds right here on the spot, so I was wrong. Something has been going on all the time. I just blundered right into it. His thoughts raced ahead. He felt that he was chasing things that he only dimly understood, trying to catch up with them.

Like me, they can see the Aramco deal involves all of us. If the Saudis can make Aramco sell out to them, then the game is up for foreign oil ownership in the gulf. It's the handwriting on the wall.

But they're not so damned dumb they're not going to figure some way to come out on top of it, that's for certain. And the way to do *that* is to give over entirely, and let the gulf oil countries sweat out the political and economic ups and downs without the benefits of the old oil-monopoly structure. Now we'll be just another part of the oil suppliers in the world market, with all the headaches, while they go on to put their dollars into North Slope Alaska and the offshore drilling in the Atlantic. The U.S. government won't mind that, either. Very neat. That's what the 'unstable' part is all about. It's a big gamble for them to pull out while the Middle East still holds more than half the world's oil supply. But they figure it's worth it.

Abdullah knew it was time to say something. They were waiting. But not anything directly; to slide around it while he was thinking, as they would do.

'Naturally,' he began, 'my country's committed to a long-term programme of oil conservation under any new agreement. We would have absolute control over rate of flow, even if GAROC does the marketing.' Rahsmani reserves were estimated at over thirty years. More, now, with the Japanese finds. They would have to have binding contracts on marketing and distribution. They couldn't afford to get into their own world marketing yet.

'We need an agreement on technical services, managers, and skilled workers in the fields.' They hit me hard with this, Abdullah told himself, but they were probably just waiting to see who they were going to have to deal with. In the old days they would have shored my grandfather up politically and in any other way they could, like Aramco has always done with the Saudis, worked out tax deals for us, arranged arms sales if we wanted to start our own army. But now they aren't even going to think about sticking their necks out that far. Even the Japanese strikes haven't got them back into the game. Brooke-Cullingham was wrong, too. They're going to let the Japs sell their oil to the Far East and Europe, which aren't their prime market, anyway, and not worry about it.

'But before we consider working out any agreement,' Abdullah said, trying to choose his words with care, 'we need some assurance that you will continue to deal with the present government of my country and not any other agents. And by the present government I mean that of the Emir Ibrahim al Asmari, with me as his sole representative.'

They only stared at him.

Well, he was going to shove it through. He couldn't let them run with the thing all the way. 'I want it now,' Abdullah said. 'Before I leave the building.'

Lamborchard rubbed his chin. 'We don't have the —'

'Yes you do.' Abdullah knew better than that. 'Under the present contracts it's spelled out only in terms of what existed ten years ago.' He had read them thoroughly, he knew what he was talking about. 'What I want is a statement of continuing intent, under new definitions.' He raised his voice. 'Isn't that right, Sam?'

The heads turned to look at Crossland, who sat with his chin on his hand, staring down at the papers before him. He didn't look up.

'He's your sole representative for the government of Rahsmani,' Crossland said. The words were so low they could hardly hear him.

That's just too bad, Abdullah thought, looking down the table at Sam Crossland. It's just too bad he's not able to deal with us, but he should have stopped caring a long time ago what his old oil buddies thought of him and put his heart and soul into our side. Now the thought of all that oil going over to us really shakes him up. But that's his problem.

And as for the rest of you, he thought, looking around the mahogany table at the well-kept faces of the board of Gulf Arabian Oil Company, and beyond them, the lawyers and GAROC secretaries, you've been smart, but you haven't been as smart as you should have been. Because it's not the oil that's important in the long run, it's the *money*. You're so used to thinking in terms of petroleum your brains are jellied in it. But by the time you finish paying us for the last of the oil, we'll see who ends up on the top of the world. The Saudis will have half the damned money supply in the next ten years and my country won't be far behind. Then, if we need to go into the international oil business, we'll just buy it right out from under you. They said you weren't bankers and financiers but oilmen. They were absolutely right.

'Conservation,' he said, 'is going to be one of my country's top priority items in the next few years.' He knew they weren't really interested in conservation, but he had decided they were going to have to listen to it, anyway. Their approach to conservation had always been, buy up the drilling rights, pump out the oil, move on somewhere else when it ran dry. Abdullah also threw in his views on projected rate hikes and raised refinery costs under any new agreement, slipping in a forecast as to what GAROC could look forward to. More expensive oil prices upstream. They don't care about that, either, he thought. They'll pass on any new costs to the consumer.

'I need to recess now,' Abdullah said abruptly. 'I need some time to meet with my staff. Have somebody arrange to bring in some sandwiches.'

'We have lunch here,' Lamborchard said, getting up from his chair. 'We're looking forward to –'

'I don't do business at lunch. Make it sandwiches. I'll see you back here in an hour.'

Moving slowly, holding his robes aside with one hand, Abdullah got up too and moved away from the conference table. Sam Crossland hurried to meet him.

'I didn't know they were going to hit us with the whole thing,' Crossland said. 'We're going to have to hurry like hell to get this all down on paper before we get out of here. Unless you want to stay over.'

'No,' Abdullah said.

'Jolly good,' Russell offered. The excitement he was holding back made him sound more clipped and British than ever. 'I say, damned good show. You were absolutely tremendous.'

'I don't think you understand,' Abdullah said. 'We lost.'

TWELVE

'What do you mean, "We lost"?' Adam Russell said curiously, as he settled himself into the seat beside Abdullah.

The seat-belt signs had gone off and the 707 was making a steep ascent over the hills of western Pennsylvania, but it was already too dark beyond the windows to see more than the spangled spread of lights that was Pittsburgh rapidly receding away to the right-hand side, and the little patches of brilliance that were the small towns surrounding it.

'Because we got screwed,' Abdullah told him. 'These people are always one jump ahead of you and they want you to know it. They never let you get a complete victory. You always come away from these things with a couple of poison arrows stuck in your hide. Sometimes you drop dead afterward, when you think you've won.' He wasn't making jokes, he was deadly serious. Russell didn't smile.

While the Rahsmani jetliner had been on the ground in Pittsburgh they had received several messages through the communications centre, most of them from the Emir's information office updating them on the Mitsumi strike in the Arabian Gulf. These were the usual handouts to their embassies, to Roehart and Simpson in New York, Gulf Arabian and other connected oil interests, and the wire services; the prepared releases had a disappointingly impersonal air about them, like advertisements that arrived in the mail. Only one message, from Brooke-Cullingham, was of any interest. Abdullah wanted to talk to the Englishman as much, he was sure, as Brooke-Cullingham wanted to talk to him. The details of what had been done in the meeting with GAROC were going to come as a hell of a surprise, he knew. The fact that he hadn't talked with his grandfather

233

or got the Emir's opinion before he changed their demands was now beginning to bother Abdullah slightly. But it had all turned out all right, he tried to assure himself. Complicated but about the only thing they could do under the circumstances. Now he was going to have to think about how to explain some other items, such as taking over the Oil Ministry as his own domain and acting as sole representative for the government and all that. Brooke-Cullingham could get it straightened out.

Russell handed Abdullah the Mitsumi release from the telex printer along with the notation of Brooke-Cullingham's call and a copy of *Newsweek* magazine opened to a story on Saudi Arabian Oil Minister Sheik Ahmed Yamani. The *Newsweek* story covered OPEC's new call for a cutback in oil production to boost gulf oil prices and, in what the magazine called a 'remarkable gesture of solidarity' for the Arab oil nations, the Saudis' announcement that they planned to shut down two entire fields of heavy crude to cut any competition with Iran, which was having marketing troubles.

'The damned Iranians,' Abdullah muttered. He looked over the *Newsweek* article and then tossed it aside. 'The Shah is crazy. Their damned grandiose schemes are driving them into bankruptcy and driving the rest of the OPEC countries nuts at the same time. Only the Saudis have enough money to be able to bail them out. Next they'll be putting the bite on Rahsmani. That's the price of going it alone, dammit.'

Abdullah groaned, wearily. 'My faith in working with the Saudis and the Iranians and the rest of them is only a cut above Henry Lamborchard's when you come right down to it. But then my trouble is that I don't know too much about the oil business. That's the truth. It's always been my uncle Hakim's department.'

It had been a long day and he was tired. The telex in the communications centre forward was busily ticking out messages at top speed and the regular hum of activity up forward seemed even noisier to him than usual. Even the

Bedouin were standing around enjoying the excitement from all parts of the world as the response to the news of the Japanese oil strike came in on the printer. Abdullah was damned sorry he had missed Brooke-Cullingham's call. They had been tied up at the Oriental Oil Company Building until well past the supper hour. When he did finally get back to him, Abdullah promised himself, he was going to brief Brooke-Cullingham and then send the Englishman to break the news to his grandfather. It would be easier that way.

Coming back to the Pittsburgh airport in the limousine he had had a few quiet moments for the first time to think over what had been done and to tell himself that, as Russell assured him, he had done very well. God knows he had come on strong enough. It was just that nobody seemed to appreciate how badly prepared he was to deal with all this. He had spoken the truth when he had told Russell that it was all his uncle Hakim's department. Hakim had run that part of Rahsmani's business for so long that there wasn't anyone, not even Crossland, who knew how to pick up the reins and take over. Certainly not his grandfather. The Emir was the sort of person who dumped the whole damned problem on you, whatever it was, and told you to get it done without wanting to know how the hell you were supposed to do it. At least, he thought, my family should have had the foresight to steer me into some sort of preparation for this, a damned engineering course if nothing else.

Well it was finished, or just begun, whichever way you wanted to look at it, and now they could return to Rahsmani. Some things had been taken care of; he had tried to see that they wouldn't be left without any management and skilled labour when GAROC pulled out. The agreement hacked out in the boardroom that afternoon had defined arrangements for the present staff and skilled work force to hold their positions for four years, with individual contracts to be negotiated by the new Rahsmani Oil Company after that. But even he realized four years was a short time to get ready, to find replacements for people like Averbach and Knacker and all the rest of them, in the event they didn't want to stay. They would even miss the guiding hands of ten Doop, Blair, and Lamborchard. He couldn't see himself filling ten Doop's shoes quite yet. That was something he hadn't even thought about.

Abdullah closed his eyes for a moment, telling himself he was going to get up and go for his bath any minute and into a change of clothes. By the time he did this, with perhaps a stretch out on the bed to take some of the tiredness out of his body, they would be in New York. He would have to hurry. The stewards were setting the table for dinner, but the meal would have to be for the others. He didn't have time. And, he thought, looking ahead, he would probably be up half the night at the Waldorf talking to Brooke-Cullingham and waiting for his grandfather to call. There was a sharp burst of Arabic up forward where the secretaries and the Bedouin and a stray State Department man were gathered around the communications machines. He couldn't tell what was going on, the voices were too far away. He kept his eyes shut.

'Adam,' he said, 'go up and tell them to keep it down. That's a hell of a lot of noise.' He heard the other get up out of his seat and go away.

Then there was the matter of Sam Crossland. Maybe, he told himself, it was time to try to convince his grandfather that Crossland had outlived his usefulness. But, he fretted, Brooke-Cullingham was going to have to stay. I can't do it alone. I don't even know what potential business talent we have in the Oil Ministry, for one thing. We're going to have to lean pretty hard on GAROC in the beginning, and they're going to get their due share of laughs out of that. Especially after we've made a few thousand mistakes.

A low, peculiar noise from somewhere in the plane pulled Abdullah out of his thoughts. It was a strange sound, a shrill keening that might have been metal grinding, or a machine breaking down. But it was human. Abdullah opened his eyes. He saw a group of secretaries by the entrance to the staff restroom and further along, Ramzi and Wadiyeh and the State Department guard at the bank of telephones. As he stared Wadiyeh gave another long, burbling wail that was enough to make the flesh crawl, and broke loose and came running through the dining area. The stewards jumped back to let him through. Just past the dining table and at the entrance to the lounge Wadiyeh, still howling, threw himself full length on the thick carpeting, his hands stretched out over his head. He began to writhe slowly inching along the floor of the plane, bubbling howls issuing from deep inside his throat. He moved forward, on his stomach, toward Abdullah.

Abdullah did not get up. With the sound of those undulating moans that bubbled up into shrieks and then fell back again, the hair had begun to prickle across his scalp. He saw Russell make a futile grab for Wadiyeh and then stumble. The staff was silent. Only Bisharah, in the front part of the plane, bent over and threw himself down on the floor there and joined Wadiyeh's howls with his own. The copilot came out of the cockpit and then stopped, the door held ajar. The pitch of Wadiyeh's voice had managed to paralyse them all.

Abdullah pressed back against his chair. Deep inside him something had responded, he knew a moment of dread. Russell reached out again and tried to stop the Bedouin, moving toward them almost painfully, the brown feet in sandals digging into the carpet.

'Leave him!' Abdullah cried. Whatever it was, there was nothing Russell could do about it. His own mouth had gone suddenly dry.

'*Le, le, le,*' Wadiyeh shrieked. Flat on his belly, the hand reached out for Abdullah. The *kaffiyeh* had come off, the upturned face showed the eyes drawn back in the head like one in a trance. 'O accursed house of rulers! Sorrow of a possessed father, vengeance of the *djinns* and the evil ones visited first upon one generation and then the other! Sorrow of an ill-fated daughter, blight of the father – accursed! Accursed!'

For Abdullah it was as though there was no longer any

blood flowing in his veins. He had turned deathly cold. The dark shadow fell, encompassing the length of the Bedouin's body.

'Tell me then.' He could hardly move his lips to speak. It was as though he was already a dead man. 'Tell me, or I will have your throat slit.'

Wadiyeh rolled over, the braided hair falling away from his throat and face. He seemed to lie in a black mist. His hands reached for Abdullah's feet and locked themselves about the ankles.

'Thy sister!' he howled. 'Accursed family of sorrow!'

Abdullah allowed the hands to remain around his feet although they were like bands of iron. A great cold and darkness dimmed his eyes.

'What is this?' he said, barely above a whisper. He was aware of the stillness that had settled on them, with only the roar of the jet engines in between. Faces stared at him from the forward compartment as he regarded the Bedouin stretched at his feet.

'Thy sister, O unfortunate one – O most unblessed, thy sister!'

It was as though they had all stopped in midair, time stopped, no forward thrust of the aircraft, nothing. The telex made no noise. A black fog drifted over them. When Abdullah spoke no one heard him except the Bedouin grovelling before him, who answered. There was an answering shriek from Bisharah, his face buried in the rug by the communications machines.

Abdullah sat for a few minutes, staring down at Wadiyeh, before he gave him a heavy kick to the side of his head. 'Remove yourself,' he said.

He continued to sit where he was as the Bedouin got to his knees and crawled away, to come to rest doubled up at the iron partition that separated the lounge from the staff area. Finally Abdullah got up slowly as if he had forgot how to do so, and walked like an old man to the liquor cabinets in the dining area. He got a bottle of Scotch out of one of the cabinets and stood with a bottle in one hand, looking

238

back at the faces in the staff compartment. Russell started toward him.

'It was something coming in on AIRINC,' Russell began. He stopped.

Abdullah pushed past him, making his way toward the back and the bedroom there, Russell hurrying after him.

'I say.' Russell was worried about the bottle of whisky. Let me go back and check –'

He stopped short as Abdullah turned at the door to the bedroom.

'It's my sister,' Abdullah said. His voice was low and un-inflected. He kept his head turned away. 'I thought you understood Arabic. She's dead.'

'My God,' Russell exclaimed. 'Oh my God.'

'By her own hand. By her own hand,' Abdullah repeated. 'I can't talk to anybody.'

He went into the bedroom and closed the door.

When they landed in New York, Crossland got into the first limousine with Abdullah, followed by Ramzi, the two Bedouin guards, and one of the Jordanians. Russell and Sam Crossland had half carried Abdullah down the landing steps from the plane and toward the waiting cars. Abdullah couldn't walk. He had managed to down most of a fifth of Scotch and was a veering weight that several times threatened to break away from them and fall down flat on the asphalt of the landing area. Russell, worried sick, had checked him out several times for drugs and even gone through the private bedroom and bath thoroughly on the plane. It appeared to be only a massive drunk. There had been no sleeping pills, tranquillizers, not even aspirin aboard. Thank God for that, Russell told himself. He's young and he's healthy; he hasn't any need yet for that sort of thing. Mixed with alcohol, they would be in trouble.

What happened was still fairly baffling. The call had come into the plane from AIRINC communications centre in New York, originating in the Emir's office, although it plainly hadn't been put through by anyone in the family.

The caller identified himself only as one of the staff. Nor had the call that Brooke-Cullingham put through on the 707's plane radio as they were preparing to land at JFK been of much help, either. Russell took it up forward in the radio operator's spot, using the scramble box to assure privacy.

'Wadiyeh told him,' Russell said. 'The Bedouin overheard something when it came in. Nobody's that damned coherent about it now, in spite of being questioned several times over. It just happened. Afterward, we went a bit mad trying to get it confirmed.'

'It's confirmed,' Brooke-Cullingham told him. 'Your source may not be, but the news is.' The radio frequency they were using was studded with clicking and sudden fadeaways, adding to Russell's frustration. 'I don't know who took it on themselves to let you know, but I expect we had better find out. You can't imagine what's going on here. The family's in an uproar. No one's paying attention to local matters, in spite of fighting having broken out. Worse than last year.'

'What?' Russell shouted. He couldn't hear. He flicked the radio switch over to Brooke-Cullingham.

'I said, we're busy with our own little problems. The girl's death doesn't help any. Put your friend on; I'll speak to him.'

'He's out, dead drunk. Went to the rear compartment with a bottle of whisky. I had to take his pulse.' Russell kept shouting. 'I'm thinking of having his stomach pumped out when we put down in New York. These damned State Department people are into everything. They want to read all our communications log for the evening.'

'Keep them out of it.' There was a roar of interference on the company frequency that almost drowned Brooke-Cullingham's voice. 'Adam, don't let our prima donna do anything foolish. He'll take this very hard. Don't forget, it's his beloved sister and all that. Rely on Crossland and the Bedouin. How,' Brooke-Cullingham's voice said faintly, 'did the GAROC business turn out?'

'Smashing,' Russell told him. They couldn't go into all that right then. 'But a bit complicated. We'll have to get back in touch with you in New York.'

Now, getting into the limousines, there was quite a bit of confusion.

'Let's get the hell out of here,' Sam Crossland said. He, more than any of them, didn't want the State Department moving in too close. 'I'll go with him. You keep the State Department happy in the other car. Pull up as we leave and stay right behind us.'

Russell was somewhat rattled. Abdullah had fallen to his knees in the back of the limousine and the Bedouin were trying to haul him up on to the seat. Crossland was not exactly in charge, but he was right; they didn't want the U.S. government taking over any of their private problems.

Coming through Grand Central Parkway toward the city Abdullah's limousine suddenly cut down an exit ramp and into the dark streets of Queens. Russell got on the car telephone to call to them and they responded fairly promptly. It was Ramzi Alam.

'We're making a toilet stop. He's been sick. We have to stop and clean up a little. We're in a Mobil station.'

They could not get back immediately for directions. The Iranian had hung up. The driver of Russell's limousine took them around for a few blocks looking for the Mobil station and finally they found them. The leading limousine was drawn up in a pool of bright lights beyond the gas pumps. All the doors were wide open; everyone had got out of the car.

Russell opened the door of his limousine and was out of it before it had stopped moving.

'What's happened?' Russell cried. He knew something was wrong by the way they were just standing there, the car doors flung open on both sides.

Sam Crossland turned to look at him. The night was warm. Crossland's face was shiny with sweat under the arc lights of the Mobil station.

'He's gone,' Crossland said. 'He went to the bathroom and he didn't come back. He can't get far. He must be around here somewhere.'

Russell stared at Crossland, unable to speak.

'Don't panic,' Crossland said. He reached out and touched Russell on the arm. 'He probably wanted to break away to be by himself for a while. He's had a bad jolt. He'd do something like that.'

'I don't think he had any shoes on,' Russell said. He couldn't remember if they had put shoes on him before he got into the limousine at JFK. Abdullah had changed his clothes, that much he was certain of, but he couldn't remember about the shoes. Or if he was carrying any money. 'How drunk is he now?'

Crossland looked uncertain. 'Well, might be he lost the best part of it in the car. But still pretty plastered.'

'Damn!' It had been a big mistake, not to have gone with them. Right behind in the other limousine was not good enough.

'It's not as bad as it could be,' Crossland said. 'The Bedouin's with him. Wadiyeh.'

THIRTEEN

'It would be best,' Adam Russell said into the telephone, 'if you could persuade Number One not to call for a while. I'm running out of excuses. Also, we had the Lady Grandmother on the overseas line a while back and it was pretty difficult to handle. My Arabic's not up to it. I'm afraid all I could say was that he knew, and that he would call her back shortly.'

Russell was not feeling too well. It was not just that he was over-tired, which he was, or that the last cup of coffee had given him heartburn, which it had; it was just that the strain had not let up for one damned moment and from what he could see it was getting worse. It was hard to keep the overseas telephone callers at bay, and in due time he supposed the word of Abdullah's disappearance would leak out to the UN offices and the consulate in New York and eventually to the Embassy in Washington and then those interested parties would be sure to descend upon them, too.

From where he sat in Abdullah's room using the bedside telephone Russell could look out into the main part of the suite and see the crowd that had already collected there, with Sam Crossland going from one group to another doing his best to keep some kind of order and suppress any outbreaks of undue emotion. Beside their own staff there was now the Waldorf public relations man and his assistant, two hotel detectives to keep out strangers, the State Department liaison man and his plainclothesmen busy on their call to Washington, and a sprinkling of the blue uniforms of the New York City Police Department. A hotel telephone installer was on his knees at the baseboard of the sitting room running extra telephone lines into the other bedrooms. It had been thought best to have a few extra telephones put in, in case Abdullah should try to call them and find their regular phones busy.

'I don't think she'll get back on,' Brooke-Cullingham said. The telephone hookup from the Waldorf was much better than the radio they had used a few hours earlier. Brooke-Cullingham's voice, a few thousand miles away now, was perfectly understandable, although lagging with fatigue. 'I'm surprised she got on the telephone in the first place. She has a horror of electronic devices.'

Adam Russell hadn't had any sleep himself, he could sympathize with Brooke-Cullingham. He looked at his wristwatch. It was now ten AM in New York City, late afternoon where Brooke-Cullingham was, in his office in the Rahsmani Overseas Investment Corporation. Two days without sleep, the other had said.

'The Saudis have come in,' Brooke-Cullingham went on, 'so that should keep everybody off the telephone and busy for a while. A delegation flew in from Riyadh including the bereaved husband and I suppose, considering the furore when they got here, there'll be a sweatbath of explanations. Not that there's much to explain. The girl was damned unhappy; that's about the sum of it, and Azziz tried to keep it quiet until he could think of some way to cheer her up. I understand the Saud family rallied round, promised her a trip to Paris, honeymoon, shopping excursion, whatever she wanted, if she would only calm down. By the time they all got around to taking her seriously, it was too late. It's rather a mess,' Brooke-Cullingham said drearily. 'The Sauds are having a nervous breakdown en masse. They've even brought Azziz's mother and sisters with them; the fort is filled with screaming women. But they're not off the hook that easily. One must realize that it's as big a scandal for the Sauds as it would be for us. Then there's the political side of it, too.'

'Of course.' Russell couldn't think of anything else to say. He had been thinking of Abdullah as Brooke-Cullingham spoke and wondering if, wherever Abdullah was in New

York City, he had sobered up enough to want to come back to the hotel. Or even telephone. And presuming, of course, that he hadn't fallen afoul of any sort of trouble. The whole business was so damned upsetting for everyone. Naturally the news of the sister's death was bound to leave them all shaken; even the way Brooke-Cullingham was rambling on showed he was under pressure. Abdullah's wandering off without a word to anyone made it damned near intolerable.

Brooke-Cullingham already knew their State Department people were on the line to Washington, making their report. Once their news was released into the toils of the United States government, God knows what would happen. Brooke-Cullingham could only curse. Neither one of them knew whether the CIA or the FBI would be called into it, but one just couldn't lose a sheik of one of the leading Arabian Gulf oil countries in New York City for any length of time without setting up a stink. 'Try to wait another two or three hours before you notify the police,' Brooke-Cullingham had advised, 'he might show up yet. He's boasted he can take care of himself.' Russell had yet to tell Brooke-Cullingham the police were already there.

Russell put his thumb to his mouth and gnawed at the edge of it tentatively. He realized he hadn't bitten his nails since he was a child. He wiped his thumb on the edge of the bedspread. His brif description of what had gone on at the GAROC board meeting had only brought groans from Brooke-Cullingham. 'Of all the beastly damned fool stunts. Of course it's all right. It's a peck of trouble, though. It wasn't what was wanted.' They had decided to leave that part of it over for tomorrow. We're both worn out, Russell told himself. He found that it was getting difficult for him to keep track of things, he wanted desperately to lie down on the bed and just listen, holding the telephone to his ear. Brooke-Cullingham seemed to be absorbed in his own problems. Russell supposed it was difficult from that distance, halfway around the world, for Brooke-Cullingham to grasp all at once what sort of an infernal jam they were into. And there was even more.

If I can just get a word in, Russell thought.

'Number One's not holding up too well,' Brooke-Culling-ham was saying. 'He's catching it from all sides right now, poor old devil, and at his age that's hard. As a consequence all sorts of things have come unravelled. The damned secret police have been allowed to run wild, they've been routing out all the People's Democratic Socialist factions and beating them up on the spot. Last night they came down on a local group of left-wing Palestinians, mostly government supervisory types. That wasn't too bloody clever.'

Russell looked up at Sulman, the Jordanian secretary, who had just come in. Sulman bent down to whisper in Russell's ear. 'Jim?' Russell said into the telephone.

Brooke-Cullingham didn't hear him. 'And I've got the GAROC people in my hair wanting to know what the hell's going on. They've heard a rumour there's been gunfire up at the beach hotels. They also know there's a flock of Sauds up at the fort, but they don't know what for.'

'Jim,' Russell said urgently. 'We've got a little trouble here. Ramzi Alam's gone.'

There was a pause on the other end.

'Are you sure?'

'We've been looking for him since we set up breakfast at about seven-thirty. Naturally you know we're in one hell of an uproar. We assume everybody's somewhere about or on one of the telephones. His bedroom's been checked out. The bed hasn't been slept in, but then none of us have had any sleep.'

'It's not possible he took it into his head to go out and look for our friend himself?'

'Not bloody likely. Besides, he's our secret police attachment. They don't do that sort of thing.'

'No. Hang on.' Brooke-Cullingham was talking to someone in his office. He came back on the line briskly, all tiredness gone. 'Tell me, how did Mr A. look when last you saw him?'

'When last I saw him?' Russell remembered half-carrying Abdullah down the steps of the landing stage from the plane, the trouble he and Crossland had getting him into the back seat of the limousine. 'Dead drunk. Almost off his feet. They tell me he brightened up after vomiting all over the car. At least enough to get out and walk to the toilet himself. Wadiyeh was right behind him. It was dark around the side of the building; no one saw much after that.'

'No drugs?'

Russell suppressed a sigh. It was getting on his nerves, to have to go over the same thing so many times. 'He killed the best part of a bottle of Scotch. That's not bad, considering he's not a drinker. I checked out the plane. Apparently there wasn't even a bottle of aspirin aboard.' Obviously he hadn't thought of one other thing. 'But I suppose that doesn't mean someone else couldn't have had something with them.'

There was a fairly long silence.

'You might be right,' Brooke-Cullingham said. His voice had gone low and careful. 'We might have a bit of trouble there.'

A few minutes later Adam Russell went out to the sitting room of the suite to shake hands with Deputy Inspector George Horgan of the New York City Police. This was the third member of the New York City Police Department Russell had spoken to in nearly as many hours. They were going up the ranks, he noted. They had begun with a detective out of the midtown Manhattan precinct, then there had been a captain from headquarters. Now Deputy Inspector Horgan. They came back into the bedroom and closed the door and Russell took his seat on the edge of the bed.

Inspector Horgan reminded Russell once again that one usually had to wait twenty-four hours before filing a report on missing persons.

Russell nodded. He understood all that. He also understood it was important enough for the New York City Police to send yet another detective. Inspector Horgan took out his wallet, extracted a small piece of scrap paper from it, and began to write with a ball-point pen. He put down the date.

'How about a description of the missing party?' Inspector Horgan said.

Russell gave him a wary look. He wondered what the hell had become of the descriptions, lengthy detailed accounts, he had given to the other two. But he wasn't going to argue.

'Well, Sheik Abdullah was barefoot. He was in the process of getting dressed and I don't think he had quite finished.' Russell ran his fingers through his hair. 'Twenty-three years of age, six feet one.' He found he was so tired he couldn't convert British stone weight into pounds. 'One hundred and seventy pounds, or one hundred and sixty-five, something like that, polo shirt – knit shirt, short-sleeved, I think it's white. Tan trousers. He has an olive complexion, brown eyes, longish black hair, slightly waving. Mediterranean type, rather good-looking. There might be someone else with him.' Russell hesitated. 'They're both Arab, of course. The second man is a bit taller, six foot four or so, rather heavier. This one is interesting, he's a Hammasseh tribesman, a Bedouin. Wearing Western-style clothes. But his hair –' Russell made a circling motion around his head with one hand. 'If he's not wearing a head-cloth, his hair's unmistakable. Black, oiled with something, about twenty tight braids ten or twelve inches long all around. It ought not to be terribly difficult.' Russell suggested. 'One's probably still drunk and barefoot and the other has quite remarkable hair. That should help in spotting them, shouldn't it?'

Deputy Inspector Horgan looked up from his small scrap of notepaper. 'In New York City?' was all he said.

'I see what you mean,' Russell murmured. He looked into the light blue eyes of Deputy Inspector Horgan, eyes that were as perpetually tired as his were at that moment, and came to a decision. Russell stood up.

'I'd like to bring Mr Harry Bascom from the State Department in here, if you don't mind.' Russell ran his fingers through his hair a second time and looked down at the man in the chair opposite the crumpled bed. 'I think I should talk to you both at once. You see, there's a possibility that Sheik Abdullah didn't just wander away. Or if he did, there were persons – people, around who might take advantage of the situation.'

Inspector Horgan looked up at him, his terrier-blue eyes wrinkling at the corners.

'You mean you think he's been kidnapped?'

'We probably should consider it,' Russell said.

The weather had turned beautiful that morning. Spring had finally come to New York City in a telescoped burst that had shoved the raw, windy cold of May into the sudden, melting heat of June. A faint summerlike breeze, full of grit and luminous with smoke, moved over the city; the air was full of the songs of strange Latin music, joined with the screams of children playing stickball somewhere out of sight, and the tinkle of broken glass. From the point where he could pull himself up from the bed to rest his chin on the windowsill Abdullah could look out into a corner of the curious elevated tracks of the IRT subway lines and the mellowed yellow brick of an old tenement-style building that showed opened windows and boarded-up frames of windows filled with galvanized iron in series, like normal and blinded eyes, across its front. When you looked closely, he could see, there were pots of plastic flowers in some of the windows that opened and glowed in atomic colours and then shut themselves back up again like sea creatures or the sudden night-blooming plants of the tropics. In this amazing building even the bricks moved. In fearsome rows like numbers the bricks massed and aligned themselves into columns, dividing by fours, twos, eights, and sixteens, stretching out sidewise to regroup in long lines that ran off the walls and into the air to connect with walls farther down. Watching the bricks was astonishing, each seen so clearly that the grains of sand and clay that had gone into them were perfectly distinguishable. Marching bricks, up and down and side by side and, if you waited long enough, beautiful diagonal formations in numberless patterns. He had never realized bricks, marching bricks, were so beautiful and interesting. He had watched them a long time although he had some trouble now and then focussing his eyes. Above the walls of intricately matched brickwork the sky stretched into a hot grey and blue tent breathing the small white clouds of summer.

Abdullah let himself fall away from the window and back down on the bed, sinking and then rising slightly with the weight of his bouncing body, but always as free as a balloon. Comfortable and quiet as he was, shut away high above the strange elevated tracks of the subway and with the warm, faintly odorous wind blowing in on him, he had nothing at all to worry about. There was even a cockroach beside him on the sheets. He had watched it walk back and forth over the folds of the cotton cloth for a long time, maybe months or years. The cockroach had no place to go, that was why it was so restless; it was an unhappy, inquisitive wanderer. It would have a mental breakdown if it continued to live its life that way. He knew about such things.

One summer when Abdullah's father had been in a sanitorium in southern France they had lived in an apartment high above the streets like this, his mother with two French servants and an elderly male cousin who was also a relative of his uncle Fuad's. His mother didn't like to use the lift – it frightened her – and she was uneasy in the streets without something to cover her face, so she rarely went out. The cousin did the shopping and the French servants looked after them, and there had been many days when he and his sister had spent their time like this, lying on the floor of their room playing with toys or reading picturebooks and listening to the hot wind in the heavy-leafed plane trees outside in the street. Sometimes they would climb the stairs to the apartment-house roof, where the maids hung out the wash to dry. The roofs of the city in southern France were filled with billowing laundry, like sails in the wind. They used to pretend that they lived in a harbour surrounded by sailing ships. His sister Layla was so young at the time he explained everything to her. She was full of a thousand questions. As always, they lived isolated from other children; they had only each other for companions.

When I grow up, Abdullah told her, *I will buy a big ship. Grandfather will give me the money, and we will go around the world to see what it is like.*

On the other hand, there were jungles where naked people in leaves danced to the frantic drums of mambos and merengues and it was not safe to go out at night. Terrible things happened there, and there was always the sound of automobiles clashing in the streets in the dark and screams, and once the shriek of a fire engine.

'Put it on the sugar with the dose of strychnine on the top to up the effect,' someone said in English. 'How much have you got there?'

'You are going to kill him.'

'He is mad. You can't kill a madman. Get the *bedu* to come in.'

It was good to see a friendly face. When he was older Farid had been retired, since someone more vigorous was needed for a growing boy, and Wadiyeh had come, only a youth in his twenties then, sent by Fuad from one of the subordinate Bedouin tribes that came over the borders from the Rub' al Khali. The backward Hammasseh nomads whose honour was unbreakable iron, stupid but faithful. Not stupid, the old shiek had said; all of the men of the desert are simple. Never offend them.

'Wadiyeh,' Abdullah said. '*Allah*, it is good to look upon you.' His voice was hoarse because the stuff they had given him was now stuck in his throat. The Bedouin's face loomed over him, a dark face, but glowing like a lamp from the light of the open window. He put up his hand to touch Wadiyeh's face but could not reach it, his hands were floating away.

'Wadiyeh!' he yelled, because they were pulling his clothes off him. He could see his naked legs on the bed.

'O defiler – will you not listen?' the voice of Wadiyeh al Qasim cried. 'Accursed blasphemer – whoremonger, thou hast taken the gods of the unbelievers, and turned thy face from the true God! Thou hast cursed the name of Allah in thy mouth! Madman. They father's son, truly!'

Hey, that's my own body down there, he tried to tell them. That was his own body down there, they were letting it fall to the floor, a flurry of blows upon it.

'Drunkard! Blasphemer! O most accursed of all evil – you are damned! Evil the day a kinsman would send you to lead us! It is finished!'

Why do you do this to me? he moaned. The cut on his mouth had come open again, there was blood all over the floor. Wadiyeh's eyes, strange and large as black moons, filled up his sight. *You can see who's mad*, he tried to tell them. It is not I, it's this Wahabi fanatic. His own servant, bound to him on blood oaths that dripped on the rich carpets of his uncle Fuad's tent, never to be broken. Except when one has renounced God, broken the laws of God beyond redemption, and one is no longer worthy of loyalty.

I didn't do that, he said, crawling about on the floor. I *didn't do any of those things. You've got it all mixed up. Besides, he's my own body-guard, Wadiyeh al Qasim – and the bedu are never supposed to betray you.*

It felt strange to be down on hands and knees, naked on the floor, crawling about like a cockroach, poor unhappy seeker, a cockroach nervously scuttling about with not a friend in the world. Other cockroaches do it. Abdullah rolled over and sat up and started laughing, kept laughing and holding his head against the kicks.

'His soul is rotten. He stinks of alcohol,' someone said. 'He is dog shit, corrupted with the shit of the oppressor. This is what you see. Behold, the leader of thy people!'

'Be careful with the face. We need the face to be recognized.'

It was only that the music was so loud. He put his hands over his ears. *Cut off the music*, he told them. *It hurts. Take me home.*

Later he said with perfect clarity, 'You son of a bitch betrayer. They will cut off thy fingers and nose for this, and then the ears and so, in little pieces thus, until they kill you! I will see to it, I promise you.'

And his own bound man Wadiyeh kicked him in the face, making more blood where it was already slippery on the floor around them and said, 'Dog! Thou hast murdered thy sister!'

Only then did he begin to scream.

Adam Russell went down to the coffee shop in the hotel because he needed to get away from the crowd in the rooms upstairs and in particular Mr Harry Bascom of the U.S. State Department who, with the men from the New York office of the FBI, were making the life of Deputy Inspector George Horgan miserable. Not that Horgan couldn't defend himself well enough, Russell thought; there was just no need for him to put more strain on his own nervous system by staying around to listen to it. When Russell had left the suite the FBI men were going over a list of terrorist organizations known to be operating in New York City, some of them with only tenuous connections to Middle Eastern political factions, and Inspector Horgan was denying that the New York City Police Department had ever heard of them, or if they had, that they were now outmoded and had been replaced with other, newer organizations. By way of proof Inspector Horgan had produced his own list, brought up from NYPD Headquarters in downtown Manhattan, that he said was more up to date than anything the FBI had on hand. Russell had left them trying to find out whether to eliminate such operations as the Puerto Rican Socialist Independence party and the Japanese Communist-oriented groups, the latter since someone had inadvertently mentioned that the Japanese were drilling offshore in Rahsmani territorial waters in the Arabian Gulf. The PLO, FLN, JAR, PFLP, and others had already been set aside in an 'active' pile.

Still, the FBI had been arguing, there was no real evidence

that there had actually been a kidnapping. No ransom note had been received, nor had there been any announcement to the newspapers or the New York television stations, taking credit for such an act. It had been more than twenty-four hours; notifications of terrorist kidnappings were usually quick in surfacing. And the Sheik Abdullah al Asmari had been, according to reliable witnesses, exceedingly drunk when he was last seen heading for the men's room in a Queens Mobil service station. The FBI was thoroughly acquainted with Abdullah's newspaper publicity and the news of the family death. So there was still a large margin for error, the FBI maintained. Until proven otherwise, they still had to take under consideration that a foreign national was off on an informal excursion somewhere in New York City.

Early that morning the Rahsmani Ambassador had flown in from Washington and, in spite of an announced desire to keep a low profile, had brought enough of the Embassy staff with him for them to have to reserve yet another suite on a floor below. With the demands of the current unsettled political situation in his country, the Ambassador planned to fly back and forth on the New York–Washington shuttle for the rest of the week. The Rahsmani consulate staff, based in New York, could go to their office and their homes with comparative ease; they had set up a gathering place in Russell's bedroom. Only the Rahsmani delegation to the UN was sparsely represented. Nasir al Asmari, the Delegate and one of Hakim's sons, had already flown back home.

That should tell how things were beginning to shape up, Russell thought grimly. In spite of the still orderly outward appearance of the Embassy people from Washington, the New York consulate staff, and the United Nations crowd, all was confusion within. None of them, perhaps with the exception of Nasir al Asmari, had any conception of what was really going on. For the time being it seemed to be the New York and Washington people tentatively lined up with each other, and Nasir's UN faction waiting to hear from their boss, who had flown back to Rahsmani. At least in the top levels, nearly all of them were related.

The CIA had come in to the Waldorf that morning, had gone out, had left word that they would be back again. The CIA had had a hard time deciding which of them to deal with as the accredited, most responsible agents of the government of Rahsmani: the Ambassador, Crossland, the Consul, or himself. Ordinarily the Ambassador would have been in charge, but Selim al Asmari was an old man and notoriously without power; the same thing could have been said of the Consul, who was only a second cousin of the Lady Azziza. All of them had taken their orders directly from the Emir. That left Crossland and himself, and the CIA had instructions to deal only with Rahsmanis. They had gone to check back with Washington to see if the situation could be better defined. But the Rahsmani International Airport had been announced closed as of midnight, and reports of fighting in the streets of Rahsmani city by several factions, including the National Police and the Rahsmani People's Liberation party, were in the city edition of *The New York Times*.

In the past day Russell had stopped drinking coffee, had briefly switched to tea, and was now experimenting with Pepsi-Cola and glasses of milk. That was one of the side hazards of tension, he knew; eventually you start to eat again, but it's the long stomach-burning time in between that takes its toll. He could remember how it had been during his days in the navy.

He saw the figure of Sulman come through the doors of the coffee shop, pause to look for him, and then find him at his booth.

'Brooke-Cullingham has called,' the Jordanian told him as he slid into the opposite seat. 'He is going now to the fort, and we are to reach him there from now on.'

'What's the matter?'

Sulman shrugged. 'Obviously he no longer has the desire to remain at his offices in the city. Perhaps it is not safe. Also, he has informed the family now of what has happened. It is very sad.'

Adam Russell frowned, looking down at the small puddle

of white that still remained in his glass of milk. He did not care much for milk, he thought. If Brooke-Cullingham was retreating to the fort the situation wasn't improving.

'Also, the Saudi Arabian Ambassador,' Sulman said, lowering his voice, 'called from Washington. *Sayid* Crossland took the call, but I lifted the extension in the other room, as we agreed, and listened to it. The Saudis have offered their help in any way we might think effective. They were most discreet. They did not say that they knew the lord Sheik Abdullah was missing.'

'What kind of help?'

'They did not say exactly. They talked a lot, but I think they would have preferred to speak with *sayid* Brooke-Cullingham.'

I have no doubt, Russell thought. So would I. 'Did Crossland keep his mouth shut?'

'Oh yes, he thanked them also, but told them that the New York visit was proceeding smoothly. *Sayid* Crossland has been long enough in the gulf to know to do that.' Sulman paused. He was a young Jordanian, sharp and aggressive; he was not the type to hold back when an opportunity presented itself. And, like the others, he was probably wondering where he stood in all this and if, in the coming days, he would still have a job. It was the hour of speculation for all of them. 'Do you think he is dead?'

Sulman appeared to hesitate. 'No, of course not,' he said quickly. 'I'm a loyal employee.' But still he hung on, eyes lowered. He could not resist. 'Why do you not go back and question the other Bedouin again?' he said softly.

Russell stared at him for a long moment, trying to read into the words everything that should be there.

'Jesus!' Russell got up from the coffee-shop booth in a hurry, flinging down his change. Damn them, why do they wait so long to come out with these things? he asked himself. Is it because they want to wait and let the situation ripen, like fruit, before they make up their minds?

He rushed out, leaving Sulman sitting there.

*

Eat your food,' they told him.

Ramzi Alam was not eating, either. He sat watching Abdullah, who was weeping again, the tears sliding down his chin and dripping off into his plate. He looked around uneasily. They were having trouble with the waiter, who stood regarding them at a distance.

The rest were nervous, too. 'This is awkward. We are not going to be able to manage it.'

'Yes, it is going as planned. We don't want them to see us arguing.'

Abdullah only wanted to go forward, to put his head in the dishes in front of him and bury the despair, which was overwhelming him now, and in his ears was a roaring like a storm at sea. There was no need to go on with it, they had told him. His sister was dead, that was his fault. He could hear them talking.

'It is better to kill him.'

'That will take care of itself. Dead, or a lunatic, it does not matter.'

Not too subtly, the one on the side pulled him back up again. Now, they decided, was the time.

'Get up, madman. Show them what we have come here for.'

It was a large room, overlooking the city, and there were many people in it. Once they let go of him Abdullah got up from his chair in a rush of release, but uncertainly, a glass in his hand. He threw it across the room. The place tilted as one would tilt a board and all the people ran together, the tables overturning, and much shouting and noise. But to be free of it was all he wanted.

But getting free was not that easy. He jumped from one place to another, on a chair and then a table and fell on the far side in a crash of silverware. It was a very big place, there were a lot of things in his way. He ran out by the lifts and then back again, passing Ramzi Alam and the others. They did not wait, they opened a fire door and went down the stairs. He was in a kitchen, he ran through a kitchen as big as a ballroom and out into a service area with garbage cans.

Naturally, they came to hold him down.

Stay away from me! Abdullah yelled. They didn't know how fragile he was, as breakable as all the glass around them. If they touched him, he would break into a thousand pieces, he felt it, and they would spend hours picking up those pieces without any idea of how to put them back together again. To be free of them, to get away from them, was all he desired. They were gone, now; there were only these other people trying to corner him at the doors where there were all of the tables and chairs overturned.

'He just went crazy,' somebody said. 'There were people with him.'

He stopped, panting. It was quiet now; the shouts, screams, faded away.

Beyond was the sky. To be at one with the sky, to swim into it as one would swim into the warm, caressing sea, was the only true freedom. A vast crowd, such as those who always surrounded him, the secretaries, the bodyguards, the stewards, Brooke-Cullingham, Russell, Crossland, pressed in with a thousand hands, reaching out to catch and hold him if they could.

'Take it easy, man,' they said.

'Watch out, don't let him get out there!'

But he couldn't let any of them touch him again.

'Easy, man, easy,' they said, these strange people in this place. They were backing him into a corner, trapped, this time, not to let him out.

He threw himself sidewise. The door broke. He went through glass and out into the air and for a brief second as he fell, only as long as it took to register on the surface of the eye, he saw the great blue arc of the sky and the city spread under it, all of the city from high up in the air as one would see it on postcards or in travel films. The glass showered around him, as glittering as ice, and a sound like millions of small bells, ringing and piercing.

FOURTEEN

Adam Russell and Sulman had taken Bisharah into the bedroom and locked the door behind them. Deputy Inspector Horgan had tried to follow them in, wanting to talk to Russell, but Russell had been in a hurry, almost shutting the door in Horgan's face. Now Russell was sure the Deputy Inspector stood outside, if not actually eavesdropping, then at least intensely interested in what was going on. Horgan knew something was up.

'There is only one way to do this,' Russell observed. 'And I suspect the *bedu* knows damned well *I* won't do it.'

Russell handed the Smith and Wesson back to Sulman, who opened the gun rather ostentatiously so that Bisharah could see what he intended to do, and shook the bullets out, throwing them in turn on the bed so that there was only one left in his hand. He inserted the remaining bullet into the chamber and then flipped the gun closed.

'There are other things we could try,' Sulman said. He looked around the bedroom. 'But not here.'

Russell could imagine. 'Get on with it,' he told him.

The Jordanian looked down at Bisharah, who had fallen to his knees on the carpet, his hands clasped before him in the traditional gesture of supplication. But there was no particular pleading in the Bedouin's face. If anything, he regarded the Jordanian as if speculating whether or not Sulman was the man for this and if so, how far he would go.

'Oh, hell,' Russell said almost to himself. 'The whole thing's so bloody melodramatic. Why don't you,' he said, addressing Bisharah in Arabic, 'speak to us of what you know; It is thy lord Abdullah's life that is in danger.'

'I know nothing, Russell *sayid*.' The Bedouin looked straight ahead. 'This is the truth.'

'Nothing breaks them,' Sulman said. 'Even those other things I spoke of, unless they desire to speak. Give him time to consider it. But first, we must show him that we are serious.'

The Jordanian put the barrel of the Smith and Wesson against the Bedouin's temple and pulled the trigger. It clicked, but on an empty chamber. Only Adam Russell had winced.

Bisharah looked thoughtful.

'Speak to me,' Sulman ordered.

There was a long wait.

'Wadiyeh al Qasim knows that the lord Abdullah is mad,' the Bedouin said softly. 'This he has told me, many times.'

Russell eased out his breath. That looked hopeful. But Sulman shook his head, no. He kept the barrel of the Smith and Wesson pressed against the temple, prodding him to say more, but the Bedouin was silent. Deliberately, Sulman pulled back the hammer with his thumb.

They stood waiting. Still there was nothing. The Jordanian let the hammer fall, and again there was an empty click. The Bedouin stared straight ahead. He had not even blinked his eyes.

'It is not allowed,' Bisharah said finally, 'under the oaths, for Wadiyeh al Qasim to let any evil thing befall the lord Abdullah. To imperil his life is to imperil one's own soul.'

'It is understood,' Russell said quickly. 'What is done, is done. But consider thy soul now, which must answer for it.'

The Bedouin's eyes altered slightly, considering. That might be reasonable.

'Do *you* think he is mad?' Russell insisted.

'Russell *sayid*, it is not for me to judge these things. I repeat only what Wadiyeh al Qasim has told me.'

'You will kill the lord Abdullah, thus, by not speaking. If he is not dead already.'

Now Bisharah looked down, dropped his hands and

spread them out against his knees. 'He cannot be dead. They have promised that they would not kill him. Only thus would Wadiyeh al Qasim agree to it.'

'Dammit,' Russell cried, exasperated, 'I knew it! All this damned time, and not one damned one of them would open their mouths! Speak to me, man,' Russell cried, 'or this time I swear – I will blow thy brains out myself!'

The Bedouin caught the ring of conviction. He threw himself flat on the rug and spoke to them, his words muffled, very sincerely. 'I know nothing, Russell *sayid*! It was not my burden to know any of these things, I swear it!'

'Agree to what?' Sulman said, bending over Bisharah.

'That they would not kill him – only put him in some place, as with his father!'

'Put the gun down,' Russell said. 'And to whom,' he said to Bisharah, 'do we go now, to ask? To whom do we speak of such things, to find out what has been done, thus and so?'

Bisharah shook his head, face pressed into the rug. 'Lord, I cannot! It is not mine to know! The others, that is all that has been told to me. Those others, who say that the lord Abdullah is *shirk*.'

Russell turned, baffled, to Sulman, who was putting away the Smith and Wesson in his shoulder holster. The Jordanian shrugged.

'A zealot, like all the Wahabi. Thus they have used Wadiyeh al Qasim, it is to be supposed.'

'Used him?'

'It is the only sin for which one is damned, for which one is excluded from Paradise. The worst of all sins, the acknowledgment of other gods than God. In this case, who knows?' The Jordanian shrugged again. 'They think that he is mad, he is *shirk*, that his soul has gone rotten with the evil gods of the Unbelievers. It is true that he drinks.'

'Good lord,' Russell said.

'One name,' Sulman said, looking down. 'Those who speak with honour have the love of God. Otherwise, they are also damned.'

'Verily, I know no names,' Bisharah said. He began to

weep, the tears flowing freely. 'It is evil, this thing! I have turned my face from it!'

'One name,' the Jordanian repeated. 'They will only kill him, not put him in some place for lunatics. This you should have known.'

There came a low, smothered wail.

'It is not for you,' the Jordanian said with distaste, 'to be known as the betrayer, also. It is enough for there to be only the betrayer among the *bedu*.'

'Hamid, the cousin,' the low, muffled voice said into the floor. 'Hamid knows. His heart is not with them; he does nothing wrong, but is afraid to speak.'

All around us, Russell thought. Ramzi Alam. Wadiyeh al Qasim. Bisharah, at least to some extent. And now cousin Hamid. Probably our friend Nasir, the UN Delegate. And certainly the uncles. The classic pattern.

'Get on the telephone and try to find Hamid,' Russell told the secretary. 'He's probably gone underground, too.'

Sulman looked at Russell, eyebrows raised. 'He's right outside. In the other bedroom, with the consulate crowd.'

A sudden thundershower had come up over mid-Manhattan, breaking the heat, heavy enough to drench the ambulance attendants to the skin in the short run from the back of the ambulance to the emergency entrance of Roosevelt Hospital. The wheels of the stretcher bounded as they hit the concrete, and if their cargo had not been well strapped in, he would have fallen out. As it was, he let out a low, vengeful roar.

'What have you got for me?' the emergency room nurse said, as they wheeled quickly past her.

The New York City uniformed police officer who had come out of the back of the ambulance with them said, 'They said he tried to jump out of the Top of the Nines, landed on a terrace about twenty feet below the kitchen. It was a good try – a couple of inches more and he would have had the whole thing. Nineteen storeys.'

'No kidding?' The emergency room nurse was half running along the stretcher as they went down the corridor. 'What's wrong with his knee?'

'All these acidheads think they can fly,' the attendant said. He was a short, swarthy man with raindrops in his curly black hair. 'That's some heavy OD. I took his pulse; it's doing *salsa* music. *Qué tal, hombrecito?*' he asked, bending over the stretcher and wiping his wet hands on his jacket. *'Piensas que tú eres una canaria?'*

'Le, le, ana Rahsmani,' Abdullah croaked. He couldn't tell where he was, only that he looked up into bright, throbbing lights filled with shadows that bellowed and roared, swelled into giants with huge heads and even bigger hands. His teeth rattled. The world was filled with terror.

'Man, another Dominican,' the swarthy man said. 'Thassa incredible accent, ain't it?'

'In here,' the nurse told them. They wheeled into a crowded room, a bed in one corner surrounded with young doctors, pounding a cardiac arrest, the other two beds blocked by people, some weeping and praying in a foreign language, a still figure hung with intravenous feeding bottles like a spider web. 'Do me a favour. Check out his identification,' the nurse said. 'I've got a multiple fracture outside. And watch him – the eyes twitching means he might convulse.'

'I need some coffee,' the swarthy attendant said to the other as they lifted Abdullah to the ward bed. 'Don't take the straps off,' he said to the policeman. 'Get Rosalie to put some leather restraints on. I think you're going to need them.'

But Abdullah lay quietly as the policeman went through his pockets. In the corner of the emergency ward a beautiful sunset was breaking over the door marked EXIT. He watched the colours spread across the walls and on to the ceiling, dripping like spilled Dayglo paint. He could feel the warmth of the sunset as it washed across all four walls, slowly, and over the floor and toward that end of the room, lovely reds and oranges and lemon yellows, rising up against the edge of the bed where he lay, and his bare feet sticking out.

'Nothing,' the police officer said when the nurse came back. 'No ID, no driver's licence. No money, nothing.'

'Poor baby,' the nurse said, standing close to the bed to get Abdullah's pulse. She looked for needle tracks along his arms. 'No bread, huh? No shoes? Why doesn't your girl-friend look after you better?'

The cop said, 'She probably kicked him out.'

One of the doctors went by, pushing a machine on wheels. 'Rosalie,' he said, 'I think you've got a thing for junkies.'

'No, this one is cute. Hey, *Abra tus ojos*, right? *Quieres hacer* pee-pee? I don't want to have to put a catheter in you, sweetie. Or maybe I do.' She bent over Abdullah, try-ing to pry one eye open with a finger. 'Well, well,' she said suddenly, 'we're going to have a problem. Hey – Marvin? Get me an oral airway, cardiac monitor! We're going to have a big one!'

Abdullah let out a roar. The colours of the sunset had treacherously attacked his feet with waves of fire. Flames were rising around the bed in a flickering, leaping ring. *Let me out of here!* he yelled. All he wanted to do was get out of there. He didn't want to be burned alive.

'SHIT!' the nurse yelled. 'Marvin! Dr Feingold!'

'I'm busy,' a voice said from the other side of the room.

The nurse and the New York City policeman threw them-selves on Abdullah and managed to hold him long enough for Marvin to come up and poke a metal thing into Ab-dullah's mouth.

'Where did you get *him*?' Marvin said, when they had finished. 'He kill somebody?'

The machine they had put by the bed in the emergency room began to pipe a small busy noise as lighted blips, like erratic ping-pong balls, bounced across the screen.

'Oh hell,' the young resident said, coming up, 'I hate to see them going like that.' He stepped back and regarded the cardiac monitor for a long moment. 'Let's do a toxic screen for starters. What's the vote?'

'Acid,' the nurse said. She hesitated. 'With maybe something added, for a booster.'

'STP,' Marvin said. 'Nobody's doing acid anymore. Really.'

Dr Feingold was putting an intravenous needle into Abdullah's arm.

'I hope,' he said, 'we don't bomb out over here. I'm down three already tonight. It's my time to win one.'

There had been nothing on the noon news on television except a passing reference to the 'continuing political unrest' in Rahsmani and a brief rundown on the Mitsumi oil strike in the gulf, the latter information easy enough to get, Adam Russell supposed, from the wire-service handouts the past few days. But there were no film clips on television of the fighting, and only the briefest of looks at a map of the Arabian Gulf on the rear screen behind the newscaster and not a closeup at that. *The New York Times*, interestingly enough, was not much better. No photographs, a description of the political factions thought to be involved in the street fighting giving prominence to the Left-wing Rahsmani People's Liberation party and its alleged connections to Palestinian radical groups, a lengthy biography of the Emir Ibrahim and the al Asmari family in general that was, Russell could see, accurate and thorough, and a less thorough, less accurate assessment of Hakim al Asmari's role in the political split. Ameen Said was not mentioned. No hard news, then, Russell told himself. On the telephone that morning Brooke-Cullingham had told him that the fighting was confined to the central part of the city along King Qabus Street, and there had been several large fires. At the abu Deis refinery the National Police had put up security blocks, and there was talk of issuing arms to the GAROC people.

Russell got up from his chair, pushing aside the wheeled table with the remains of his lunch on it, and stepped around Deputy Inspector Horgan, who was sitting on the floor talking into the telephone. Russell threw *The New York Times* on Abdullah's bed, which was already covered with the litter of their several days' occupancy: clothing, newspaper, checklists, looseleaf paper with notes, telex printouts, a sandwich in a wrapper, and someone's toothbrush. Russell hadn't let the Waldorf people come in; there hadn't been time to vacate the bedroom even for a cleaning-up.

Inspector Horgan put his hand over the telephone receiver. 'Do you want to go down to the morgue again?' he wanted to know.

Russell shook his head. He had already been down to the morgue once on a false alarm. He didn't want to have to go back any time soon if he could help it.

'Can you send somebody?'

Russell considered it, briefly. 'Later,' he told Horgan. 'What have they got?'

'Some corpse with a cut on his lower lip. They say about thirty, forty, but only maybe. Apparent suicide. Out of the river.'

'No.' Russell shook his head again. 'That doesn't sound like anything. But we'll send Crossland to see. Later.'

There was a knock at the bedroom door and Bisharah went to unlock it. Sulman came in. 'The State Department people want a conference.'

'About what?'

'They want to review what they have on hand, which I think is nothing, and to look over some stratagems with the FBI.'

'Later,' Russell repeated. He looked at his wristwatch. As always, when he checked the time like this, as he did several times during the hour, he tried to compute the hours since Abdullah's disappearance, and then examine once more the reasons why it should be so long without a single clue as to what had become of him. They could have put him on a plane, he told himself. It may be all over. He may be dead. After a couple of days, Inspector Horgan had said, the chances of finding him alive go down fast. It nearly always works out that way. You can start assuming he's dead. Now Russell caught himself using the past tense. The bedroom *was* the Sheik Abdullah's. Those *were* the Sheik Abdullah's clothes.

The telephone by the bed began to ring. There were now three telephones installed in the bedroom: Inspector Horgan was using one as he sat on the floor; another stood on the night table; there was still another phone on the bed itself. Russell picked up the wrong one, cursed, put it down, and picked up the right one.

'Listen, Adam Russell,' the voice began without identifying itself, 'listen, I said I would inform you, and I am informing you, I wish you to remember that! He is not dead – they have gone to the hospital to look for him!'

'What?' Russell recognized the voice as Hamid's. 'Say it again.'

'He is not dead; he is not dead!' Hamid shouted. 'This is what they are telling each other. They were in the office a moment ago. He is not dead. Now they go to the hospital to claim him.'

The nurse brought in Abdullah's lunch and put it on the swing table over his bed. Although he was still weak and dizzy, Abdullah managed to raise himself up on his elbow, grab the tray by its edge, and throw it toward the door. The lunch was Canadian bacon and an omelette; he could smell the pork the moment it came in the door and he knew it would make him sick.

The nurse turned in the middle of the narrow room and said, 'I'm going to put the restraints back on you if you act like that.'

Willie, who was in the other bed, said, 'Woman, he's a brother; he can't eat that shit! He's a brother. He don't look like it, but he's a brother! He told me so hisself. You go get him a kosher diet like the brothers get.' Willie sat up in bed with difficulty. He had come into Roosevelt Hospital the same way as Abdullah, through the emergency room, but OD'd on heroin. 'You hear me, woman? You get him something dietary to eat or I'm going to WHIP YOUR ASS. I AM GOING TO WHIP YOUR ASS.'

'You shut your big mouth,' the nurse said. The nurse, too, was black, and took no nonsense from Willie. But she came back to pick up the lunch tray and the plastic plates from the floor.

'I don't want anything to eat,' Abdullah said. Now that he was a little more awake he found that he was being attacked by waves of nausea. With some vague idea of looking for a bathroom he put his legs over the side of the bed and stepped down. But he discovered his legs were useless; there was a sudden sharp pain in his right knee and he slid rapidly down the side of the bed and on to the floor. He sat on the floor, the back of his cotton gown open so that he could feel the cold of the tile on his flesh, but he couldn't move. Abdullah leaned his head back and rested it on the edge of the bed, weakly. 'I have to get out of here,' he told them. 'They're going to find me, and this time they're going to kill me.'

'That's right,' Willie said from the other bed. 'This cat's got problems. He told me so. His family's trying to kill him.'

'Get back in the bed,' the nurse said to Abdullah. But she didn't try to help him up from the floor. She was the regular Drug Dependency Ward nurse; she knew better than to try it by herself. 'You haven't got any clothes on. You're sitting in all this mess.'

'I have to leave,' Abdullah said, trying to convince her. 'I'm serious. If they find me, they'll kill me this time. Don't you see how they beat me up?'

'They tell me you jumped out a window,' the nurse said. 'You better get your stories straight when you talk to the police officer.' She didn't try to wipe up the food; that was a job for the aides. 'They tell me you tried to fly out of a window in a restaurant. That's why you're all cut up. Watch your knee, you can't put much weight on it yet.'

'Listen,' Abdullah said faintly. The bacon was beside him on the floor. 'Can't you pick up some of this stuff? It's making me sick. I think I'm going to vomit.'

'Then you shouldn't throw it around like that. Make a mess and then want to sit in it.' But she picked up some of the bacon between her fingertips and took it into the bathroom and flushed it down the toilet. She started for the door, then turned and looked back at Abdullah. 'You better get back in bed,' she warned. 'Dr Parathi's coming. He doesn't want to see you like that.'

'Please,' Abdullah said. He put his head against the bedspread and flung one arm over it to keep out the glare of the overhead light. His eyes hurt. 'Please, somebody call the Waldorf and get in touch with Adam Russell or one of the secretaries. I don't know the number, but just ask for Adam Russell. I've got a whole string of suites on the twelfth floor, the Waldorf will know. That's the truth.' It was the third or fourth time that morning that he had made such a request from the hospital staff. He didn't have much hope.

'Man, I told you,' Willie bellowed from the other bed. 'This cat is one of the richest men in the world. He told me so hisself. He's so rich, his family's trying to kill him!'

'I'm going to do something to him, too,' the nurse said, 'if he doesn't get up off the floor.'

'Well,' Willie said when she had gone out, 'you get a bitch like that, man, and you don't get nothing. She's got a big ass on her, which I am going to beat, one of these days. They make me cold turkey this time, I am going to beat *somebody's* ass before I leave. They better keep me on methadone.'

Abdullah closed his eyes. Every now and then, even though he supposed he was getting better, the room faded from view and it was as though he sat suspended in a roaring void, like an airplane caught in a hurricane or a body catapulted into space. Not much of voices, outside noise, came through; he was spinning, turning, shot through outer space like an astronaut. And he was mortally, deeply sick to his stomach.

Some time later he opened his eyes to find that he had

been put back in the hospital bed and a dark young doctor, big-eyed and very skinny, was taking his pulse. The skinny dark young doctor's eyes were so black and expressive he was reminded, with a pang, of someone else.

'Ali Hassan is my friend,' Abdullah murmured. 'You look something like him.'

'I like Jane Fonda, myself,' the doctor said. He had a very slight accent. 'I have you down here on my sheet for an interpreter. Aren't you the one who needs a Greek interpreter?' Before Abdullah could answer the doctor said, 'There's nothing wrong with your English; it's as good as mine. I'll scratch it out. How are you feeling?' He began to press on Abdullah's abdomen. Then he lifted Abdullah's legs and flexed them. 'You had a lot of LSD in you. Your blood and urine were saturated, and we found traces of strychnine. You nearly died. Don't you know better than to do something like that? A good-looking young man like you, is it worth ruining your brains and your body, to dose yourself up with these terrible drugs?'

'They're trying to kill me,' Abdullah said. The light was fading slowly in the room and the roaring had increased; it was hard to keep his eyes on the doctor's face. 'My uncles are trying to kill me, and my bodyguard, too. You've got to get me out of here.' Abdullah reached up in the dark and managed to grab the doctor's arms with both hands, nearly pulling him into the bed with him. 'Listen, who are you?' he said, suddenly full of suspicion.

'I am Dr Parathi,' the doctor said. He didn't struggle. He calmly lifted Abdullah's hands away and straightened up. 'Take it easy. They're not going to get you. They never do.'

'You're not an American!' Abdullah shouted. His voice blared out weakly, circled the bare hospital room like a bird, returned to settle on his lips.

'I'm a Pakistani,' Dr Parathi told him. 'But don't let it bother you. Now, let's see your knee.' He pushed the call button at the head of the bed. 'You nearly fractured that kneecap. Did you give a urine specimen this morning?'

'Listen to me,' Abdullah said. But someone had come in

to hold his hands and arms down while Doctor Parathi moved his knee. It hurt, but Abdullah did not scream. '*Allah, Allah!*' he managed through clenched teeth. And then he remembered that Pakistanis were Moslems. 'Listen,' he said into the dark, 'please call the Waldorf. I'm a Rahsmani. My name is Abdullah ibn Tewfik ibn Ibrahim al Asmari. Please, I'm telling you the truth.'

'Be quiet a minute,' Dr Parathi said to the other person. 'I'm trying to hear what he's saying.'

But Abdullah was drifting back into the roaring chaos again. It was as though he was slipping away from life itself, into some place full of rest and peace.

'In the Name of God, the Merciful, the Compassionate, please call the Waldorf,' Abdullah told them. It was completely dark now. He couldn't see a thing, but he was still conscious. He could hear them talking. 'Praise belongs to God, the Lord of all Being, the All-Merciful, the All-Compassionate, the Master of the Day of Doom.' He knew his grandfather would be proud of him, to remember all that. And there was more of The Opening: he pulled the remaining phrases out of his memory, like unwinding threads. 'Guide us in the straight path, the path of those whom Thou hast blessed, not of those against whom Thou art wrathful, nor of those who art astray.'

'What language is that?' the nurse said. 'It certainly isn't Greek.'

Am I one of those, Abdullah was asking himself, against whom God is wrathful? And if so, what the hell for? Why not a little wrath for Hakim and Ameen Said? And why not a Day of Doom for Wadiyeh al Qasim?

Dr Parathi straightened up and put his stethoscope back in his pocket. 'He's reciting the Qur'an. The beginning of it, anyway. And that's about as much as I recognize in the original Arabic.'

Adam Russell, Deputy Inspector George Horgan, Sulman, and a detective sergeant from the midtown Manhattan precinct stood on the floor below the Asmari suites at the

Waldorf, waiting for the lift. They were on their way to Bellevue Hospital, and they had walked down one flight of stairs to catch the lift on the eleventh floor in order to avoid the attention of Mr Harry Bascom of the U.S. States Department, and the FBI assistant director of the New York office. Particularly the latter. The FBI man had been hanging around doorways for the past twenty-four hours and listening in on telephone conversations, and Adam Russell was thoroughly fed up with both the FBI and Mr Bascom. The FBI had accomplished nothing, as far as Russell could see, except spend most of its time in negotiation with State and the CIA to see whether the unproven but possible kidnapping of a foreign national, allegedly by other foreign nationals within the boundaries of the United States, fell under their jurisdiction at all. The State Department felt that if there had been a kidnapping, the repercussions in the Middle East would certainly disrupt a delicate economic and political balance and was trying, somewhat ineffectually, to put pressure on both the FBI and the CIA to come up with a clarification of what, if anything, they were all supposed to do. But in some ways, Russell thought, it was probably too late. They had received a call in the hotel that morning from the Washington bureau of the Los Angeles *Times* checking out a rumour that one of the sons of an important Arabian Gulf oil country had been kidnapped in New York City by members of one of his country's terrorist political groups. The *Times-Mirror* was trying to put two and two together: they had Abdullah's newspaper clippings on file and remembered his stay in Hollywood very well; there were also the continuing disorders in Rahsmani. The State Department people at the Waldorf had handled the call, issuing a denial but sending it back to Washington to be announced there. Russell had been enraged. The Los Angeles *Times* would be more interested than ever, with a denial issued not on the spot but out of the State Department press offices in Washington. Such bungling was beyond belief, Russell told himself, but not beyond what he had been told to expect.

The worrisome part of it was that the story, apparently was leaking. It was bound to, he realized, as more and more people were cognizant of it, especially within the damned octopus-like structure of the United States government. Inspector Horgan had agreed with him.

'But nowadays the newspapers will lay off,' Horgan said. 'Especially with a kidnapping. We get pretty good co-operation because newspapers have got too many people killed that way, rushing into print. The kidnappers get panicky and decide to get rid of the evidence. Of course this story's got international implications, that might make it different. But I don't think so. Still, I know how you feel about these bureaucrats. I've been on a case with the FBI more than once. They spend more time trying to beat your time than they do keeping up with their legwork.'

Just as the lift doors opened, one of the Iranian secretaries, who had come down the fire stairs, came running toward them. He was waving a paper.

'Regard this before you go,' he said very rapidly, in Arabic.

'We're going to Bellevue,' Russell told him. But he took the paper. 'We have had a call from the police. They are sure that the one we look for is there.'

'I do not think so.' The young Iranian was out of wind; he had run very hard, and he had only guessed that they would be waiting for the lift on the floor below. 'Of course, it is a very mixed message. I wrote it in a hurry. Someone called from the Roosevelt Hospital just this five minutes ago and said he was only doing this because there were two private doctors there with two other men, trying to remove a patient from the care of Roosevelt Hospital, a patient who said he had been living at the Waldorf. At first the Roosevelt Hospital doctor did not believe the patient, but when he saw the two doctors giving the patient injections of pheno-barbital, which he did not approve of since the patient was a drug overdose case, he became suspicious. And the two men with the patient say they are relatives. They wish to take this patient away in an ambulance, to a private hospital in New Jersey, where these other doctors are from. They have the papers.'

Inspector Horgan had been holding the lift doors open; now he motioned for all of them to get in. Russell took the long typewritten sheet and started to read it, eagerly.

'This doctor was a Pakistani,' the secretary hurried on. 'Mainly he called here because of the doctors giving pheno-barbital shots to the patient. He says this is not done with a drug overdose patient and he warned them, but the strange doctors would not listen. They told him they were the family doctors and it was all right. But the Pakistani thinks this is irresponsible medical practice. So he took it into his mind to call the Waldorf himself. He had your name correctly. See there – Adam Russell.'

'How old is the patient?' Inspector Horgan said.

The Iranian was very excited. 'He says it is a young man, about twenty-five years of age, who speaks Arabic.'

'Is the doctor going to hold them?' Russell asked.

'The doctor said he could do nothing. These doctors and the men who say they are the relatives have the necessary papers. They say it is a court order.'

'A *court order*?' Russell cried. 'They've got to be mad!'

They all came out of the lift running.

FIFTEEN

Dusk had fallen on Manhattan, that hour when the lights along Broadway had suddenly become visible as running streams of coloured neon, white flashing buttons of electric bulbs on theatre marquees, a fluorescent blue glare of juice stands open to the warm, gritty twilight, the solid shine reflected in glass-sided skyscrapers. Traffic in midtown Manhattan was heavy. Coming up toward Columbus Circle, Adam Russell leaned forward to tap Deputy Inspector George Horgan on the shoulder and motion for him to turn off the patrol car siren. They were all slightly deafened by the noise, and it seemed no one outside was paying any attention to it, anyway. Russell could see that the jam of taxis and lorries took the presence of the New York City Police Department coming at them with siren and flashing red light quite indifferently, as did the pedestrians, who jumped out in front of the patrol car and ran through traffic as though daring anything to challenge their right of way.

Russell was beginning to realize it was true that the New York City Police apparently did rely on the siren to get about the streets, which was a rather peculiar phenomenon to anyone familiar with London. Logically, a siren going full blast would only serve to warn off anyone attempting to take Abdullah al Asmari from Roosevelt Hospital, or at least advise him the police were in the neighbourhood. Inspector Horgan, sitting up front with the uniformed driver, had also been on the police radio, asking for backup support. Holding on to the door handle with both hands as they sped along, Russell had visions of a fleet of New York City Police Patrol cars converging on the hospital, sirens going, gunshots ringing in the night, perhaps a wild chase through the clogged streets of the city. This was exactly how he had seen it in the cinema many times, and now he was afraid it would all come true. But he had no right to be critical, he told himself, as long as the damned operation worked. That was what was important.

The police car slowed down as they turned west. The driver was from the lower Manhattan police precincts, Horgan explained, and was not familiar with Midtown West. There were a few anxious moments while they got lost in the side streets, but finally they came upon the great red-brick pile of Roosevelt Hospital ahead of them in the deepening twilight. The patrol car circled the block, looking for the emergency entrance and the ambulances.

'They bring them out the side door, right where the ambulances park,' Horgan was explaining to the driver. 'There.' He pointed. 'Okay, there are three of them lined up; we've got three to choose from.'

As soon as the police car had swerved to a stop Russell, Sulman, and the other police officer bounded out of the back seat, Inspector Horgan out of the front. The ambulance in front of them was unloading a visibly pregnant woman; a car, presumably her husband's, was drawn up carelessly, blocking the drive. Horgan began to shout for someone to move it.

'Excuse me,' Russell said hurriedly, trying not to fall over the woman on the stretcher directly in front of him. At that exact moment a large blue and white ambulance was pulling out to the right of the driveway to get around the illegally parked car and Russell, anxious that it did not escape, jumped in front of it, waving his arms for it to stop. His heart pounding, Russell told himself that this ambulance could only be the one. The blue and white ambulance swerved to avoid him and its front wheels mounted a small divider kerb. The motor gunned noisily, but the ambulance itself came to a stop. A New York City Police patrol car, evidently answering Inspector Horgan's call for support, red light revolving and flashing, its siren echoing down Sixty-first Street, drew up to block the Roosevelt Hospital emergency drive at the other end.

The driver of the blue and white ambulance stuck his head out the window. 'What the hell's the matter with you people?' he yelled. 'You trying to get killed?'

The ambulance was empty. Even from where he stood on the raised edge of the concrete divider kerb Russell could look up and see the stretcher inside with its neatly made up sheets and plumped pillow. And somehow in all this he had lost track of Inspector Horgan and Sulman. Now the patrolman from their car came up and said, 'False alarm. Let's check inside the hospital.'

They went across the driveway and into the emergency entrance together. There was no one there but the emergency room nurse checking in the woman about to have her baby. 'What do you want?' the nurse said to them.

'I'm looking for a young man, about twenty-three years old,' Russell began hurriedly. He realized he was talking too fast; his accent evidently confused the nurse, who was frowning. And the premature jump in front of the ambulance outside had rattled him – he was out of breath. 'The – the – the people with the doctor from New Jersey, I think, who want to take a patient –'

'They went outside,' the nurse said over her shoulder.

Russell and the policeman rushed back out the doors of the emergency entrance. They were no sooner on the pavement at the drive than three or four dark figures emerged from the upper left, running hard toward them. Thinking that it was Inspector Horgan and Sulman and perhaps the other cop, Russell stepped out to shout, 'Where are they? Which way did they go?' He was about to join them when he realized they were coming straight on, and it was not Sulman he recognized in the dim light but Ramzi Alam. For that moment as he saw the Iranian he couldn't move, couldn't shout again, couldn't do much of anything, but some part of his mind was still alert enough to search for the rest, for Wadiyeh al Qasim or even Ameen Said. But they were not there. The Iranian secretary, in a white shirt

277

which gleamed in the dusk, ran as though all the hounds of hell were chasing him. The others were close behind, their shoes pounding the pavement of Roosevelt Hospital driveway like pistol shots. Russell dived toward them, grabbing wildly.

'Halt!' the cop shouted. He had drawn his pistol but did not raise it to fire.

As the running group passed someone shot out his hand and caught Adam Russell in the face. Russell went down to his knees and then fell to his right side, trying to catch himself. It all happened so rapidly that when he was able to scramble up again the running figures were into Sixty-first Street, passing around both sides of the police car blocking the driveway there and scattering like chickens into the stream of traffic. They disappeared into the night and blinking lights.

'Jesus Christ!' Russell got to his feet, saw that the knees of his slacks were torn out, the skin scraped and bleeding underneath. He was shaking with rage and disappointment. They had made a mess of it, incredibly enough – the others had got away by the simple expedient of running like hell. 'Why didn't you shoot?' he yelled to the cop by his side.

The other stared at him. 'What the shit for? It was his family, wasn't it? With a court order?'

'Never mind!' Russell cast about him frantically. There was another ambulance parked farther up the driveway. They could just make out someone holding the back doors of the ambulance open with hands. Another uniformed figure was at the side.

'It's all right,' Inspector Horgan called as they came running up. 'We found him.' He threw away the cigarette he had just lit, the small red tip arcing off into the dusk. 'They panicked – that was pretty stupid, but they did. Just ran off and left him.'

There was a small auxiliary light on in the interior of the ambulance. Russell could see Sulman bending over the stretcher. Abdullah was inside. *We found him*, Inspector Horgan had said.

Adam Russell allowed himself to sag against the warm slick metal sides of the ambulance in sheer relief. He had broken out in an anxious sweat; perspiration was running unpleasantly down his back, soaking his shirt. He's here, Russell told himself. We found him after all. The sense of satisfaction almost choked him.

Inspector Horgan had climbed into the back of the ambulance with Sulman. Now he appeared at the doors, looking out. 'He doesn't look too good,' the Jordanian began. 'Perhaps we had better have a doctor look at him.'

'He had a shot of phenobarbital,' Russell offered. 'That's what one of the doctors here said.' He was trying to remember all the details – they might be important.

Horgan wasn't listening. 'You're right, he looks sorta blue. We better get him out, quick.'

Russell stood aside as the New York City policemen and Sulman lifted the stretcher out of the ambulance. In spite of the heat the body was covered with a heavy plaid wool blanket, strapped down with leather restrainers. Abdullah's eyes were closed with the deep stillness of drugged sleep or death. The stretcher was wheeled down the pavement at a fast clip, the policeman turning it quickly into the emergency entrance of the hospital. The little nurse with the clipboard was right inside the doors as though waiting for them. She almost jumped out of their way as they rushed past.

'Let's get on it!' Inspector Horgan barked. 'He's drugged up!'

'In here,' the nurse told them. She peered to look, too, then straightened up quickly. She started running alongside the ambulance stretcher as they wheeled it down the back corridor and toward the emergency ward. 'Put him on the bed here,' she ordered.

In the other corner of the ward a group of young doctors bent over a bed attending a patient with a seizure. At another bed a circle of youths in T-shirts watched a young man writhing as an attendant put a blood pressure pad against his arm. The emergency room was bright, the glare of overhead lights hard on the eyes. Russell and one of the cops lifted Abdullah out of the stretcher, the plaid blanket and leather straps falling away.

'Damn,' the nurse muttered. 'Where's his pulse?'

'I think he's had a shot of phenobarbital,' Russell offered. It seemed that he was saying this without getting anybody's attention. 'There's a Pakistani doctor in the hospital here who –'

But the nurse was busy with the policemen. 'Hold on to him,' she was saying. 'I want to put an IV into his arm. DR FEINGOLD!' the nurse yelled at the top of her lungs. 'We need you!'

The young resident came slowly, still making an entry on a chart, stopped and looked down at Abdullah spread-eagled against the hospital bed draw sheet, his head fallen to one side, his mouth open and a stream of spittle leaking out. The doctor looked again, then bent down to look a third time, squinting in disbelief. 'That's the same damned one,' the doctor said. His tone was quite peevish. 'That's the same one!' It was a warm night. The resident was sweating profusely, clad only in a skivvy shirt and faded-green operating room trousers. The more he stared, the more the whole thing appeared to offend him mortally.

'Listen, I don't give a shit who you people are,' Dr Feingold began. He was having trouble getting his voice under control. He looked around at Russell, at Inspector Horgan, at the two uniformed New York City policemen standing by the side of the bed. 'I don't give a damn who you are – I want this kid put on a drug rehabilitation programme!'

After so many hours, or perhaps it was almost two days, the dreams went away entirely, even the fantasies of drift-ing through time and space and stars, tumbling end over end like a space rocket that cannot find its way back to earth, or the giant swollen heads and hands that tended and prodded him painfully, or even the voice of Willie Struthers wander-ing through the withdrawal symptoms of smack. After so long a time the world turned gradually calmer, but a calm filled with a tiredness that soaked itself into undreaming sleep at last, waking to find out that people had come and gone and had turned off the television set left blaring at night, and there was food to be eaten without much interest, trips to the bathroom, or merely lying in a state that was not exactly a stupor but blissful uncaring, watching the glowing haze of New York City summer sunshine come in through the half-drawn window shades. *I'm going to take him off the Thorazine,* the voice said, the Pakistani doctor who had taken care of him in the hospital.

That last glimpse, however, remained, the dream of the face he had not recognized all at once: the infuriated delicacy of the long straight nose so much like his own, nostrils flaring, the curved lips and elongated eyes that were the mark of the mother, the Egyptian concubine. But also, as he was to note with some alarm, a curious reflection of his own, young and turbulent, enough like him to be his brother. For the first time he had regarded Ameen Said as though he, too, could be someone like himself and not just the enemy.

What the hell are you doing here? he had wanted to know when, it was to be supposed, he knew perfectly well what it meant to wake in a hospital room in New York City and see the face of his half uncle burning down on him in the late afternoon light.

You have had an unfortunate happening, but not unexpected. A psychotic breakdown such as affected your father when he was alive. And I have a court order. It is done.

And for that time and place Abdullah supposed that it was reasonable enough. It was what they all knew and had all predicted; he was ready to believe it himself. This was the reality, his half uncle and the doctors and the legal documents, after the memory of the room and Wadiyeh al Qasim raining blows upon him and the others' shouts that he was a madman. And the death of his sister. After all these long years of waiting it had finally happened.

Not quite.

'No, I'm NOT,' he said, and came wide awake in his own

bed in the hotel. Awake and sensible for the first time in days.

Fortunately the dream was just fading so that he could grasp the last of it, catch and hold on to it so as to examine the details and find out what it was all about. As Ameen Said and the others buckled him into the stretcher with leather straps he had said plaintively, *Why do you do this to me?* the same words he had used with Ali Hassan, and as with Hassan there was no answer, only that cold look of hatred which he was coming now to expect. And as he turned it over in his mind it was a great relief to know for once and for all that this hate which he saw so often now in the faces of others was not for him as he thought of himself and as he was coming to know himself, but for what he was, apparently, in the eyes of others. And also for what he had – meaning money – which the others had not. One took up this burden, he told himself, because one had to. It would be this way forever.

'I can learn to live with it,' Abdullah said out loud.

Adam Russell had heard him get out of bed and come out into the sitting room, Bisharah following, for now Russell came out of his own bedroom, red-eyed and only half awake.

'You shouldn't be up,' Russell said thickly. 'Not for another day or so, anyway. You don't want to overdo.'

Abdullah turned away from the window where he had been looking out into the night of the city and the fantastic lights beyond, thinking very hard and still pursuing what he was going to do.

'I've been up for a couple of hours. I feel fine.'

He did, that was the amazing part of it. Not only as good as before but perhaps even better. He felt charged with energy, the feeling which comes, he supposed, from having escaped death by a narrow margin. The world was suddenly a very real place to be alive in.

Russell was only half awake. He groped for his wrist-watch, held it close to his sleep-swollen eyes. 'Good lord, it's only three am,' he groaned. Then, aware of Abdullah standing in his pyjamas and bare feet, 'For God's sake, let Bisharah fetch you a robe. You'll get pneumonia.'

'No.' Abdullah didn't want to be covered up; he was all right as he was. He scratched across his bare chest, meditatively. 'I was watching "The Late Show" and then the television news. They say we've gone into the United Nations Security Council. How did that happen?'

Russell paused for a long moment, trying to get his thoughts together. 'Saudi Arabia and Kuwait. The Soviets are supplying the rebels after a fashion; the Saudis are afraid Russia will intervene if things get worse. They want a debate.'

'Christ!' Abdullah paced back and forth in the sitting room, favouring the bad knee. 'It doesn't pay to be out of commission around here for very long! What else has happened? Where's my grandfather?'

Adam Russell watched the pacing with a certain wariness. The doctor hadn't said anything about this, the electric vitality that bordered on the manic. He wondered if it was another drug reaction. The day before, Abdullah had been flat on his back in bed, dreamily agreeable under the effects of the tranquillizer. Now this. It was quite a change.

'Where he should be,' Russell said. 'At the fort. Don't jump to conclusions,' he added, 'everything's pretty stable. These situations don't go bad all at once, you know. They rather seesaw around for a time. Brooke-Cullingham reports the city's in rather good shape, the buses are still running, people are still trying to go about their jobs, the telephones are working in most places. The large spots of trouble seem to be in the dock area, where the fighting is still going on. And with the National Police, who seem to be emerging as a far right faction. At least they don't seem to be solidly on the side of the government.'

Russell felt a sudden surge of aggravation. He was damned tired, the past week had been hell on everyone, and he certainly wasn't prepared to come stumbling out of bed at three o'clock in the morning to wrap it all up in a few sentences. He tried to get a grip on his patience.

'I've got,' Russell said, 'all the reports of the past week and all the transcripts of Brooke-Cullingham's calls from the tapes. It's all there, but I can't do it justice at this hour, you know. Why don't you,' he said, 'go back to bed and plan to catch up with it all tomorrow? Or,' he added quickly, catching the other's look, 'go to bed anyway and I'll come and sit beside you and tell you all about it. But I do think you ought to get off your feet.'

'Knock it off,' was the rejoinder. The voice had a pronounced edge to it. 'I'm only going back to bed to sleep, and I don't feel sleepy right now.' Abdullah reached up and raked his fingers over his upper arm. 'There's a lot of important things I've got to take care of. For one thing, I need to get the hell out of here. It's not safe. If I hang around here they're going to come back, and this time they won't go to all the trouble of trying to put me in a funny farm someplace. They're going to want to see me dead.'

'Well, the middle of the night,' Russell began, 'is no time –'

Abdullah wasn't listening. 'I've got to get the hell out of this damned country. The women are crazy, the air is poisoned and you can't take a breath without choking, and there's some bastard waiting at every turn to screw you. Not counting relatives. They can have it!'

'Why don't you –' Russell tried again.

'Listen to me – I'm TALKING! I woke up thinking about it, and I've got it figured out. I'm going back right now.'

'Takes some arranging,' Russell murmured. He didn't feel up to all the pacing about, the strident voice with a ring to it.

'No, dammit, it doesn't. That's what I'm trying to tell you! I'm going alone.'

Now Russell could only stare.

'That's right. We can't fly the jet into Rahsmani – the airport's in the hands of the terrorists, according to what I hear. And I'm not about to try to land that monster in Riyadh or Kuwait. I don't intend to end up as a guest of our loving neighbours until they make up their minds about

284

my political future, if any. And as for those damned Sauds – they think they own the peninsula, anyway. They'd love to annex me and my country and get it over with. I'm going alone, it's the only way. They'll be expecting,' he said, looking down at the Bedouin sitting on the carpet, his feet drawn up under him, 'me to be travelling with all my nursemaids. They'd never think to look for me alone.'

Russell merely shook his head.

'What's the matter?' Abdullah wanted to know.

'This sort of brainstorming leaves me cold, I'm afraid. For one thing, you're just out of the hospital. Be sensible.'

Abdullah smiled. They couldn't accustom themselves, he thought, to the idea that he could do something by himself. He looked down at Adam Russell, the Englishman who was not more than five or six years his senior, after all, and kept smiling.

'Nobody can stop me,' he said softly. That was the truth, and the other knew it. Russell looked up at him.

'At least let me arrange to get the Gulf Arabian people to fly you into Ras Deir or some other oil town.'

'Not on your life. I'll be damned if I'm going to come flying into my own country on the wings of GAROC. That's a lousy way to get started; it looks like I haven't got any brains of my own. No, I'm going to take a commercial jet into Kuwait, say BOAC. I want you to get in touch with Brooke-Cullingham and have him get somebody to meet me in the north, at the border. Somewhere near the highway where the Bedouin cross back and forth. I can pick up some *bedu* clothes on the way.'

Adam Russell watched Abdullah as he began to pace again, scratching feverishly, and could think of nothing to say.

'Getting into Kuwait is the problem. They'll be looking for me to try to come into my country from one of the neighbouring gulf states. I need,' he said suddenly, 'a different passport. One with another name on it. You're in touch with British Intelligence, aren't you?'

The question took Russell by surprise. His face reddened.

'I don't know what you mean,' he said stiffly.

Abdullah smiled. It was only what his grandfather had said many times – either Brooke-Cullingham or Russell, perhaps both. The British government didn't overlook the advisers to Arab governments; they were much too smart for that. It was a time-honoured tradition.

'I know you can fix things up if you have to,' Abdullah said. 'Look, I was born under the British Protectorate. If British Intelligence scratches around a little I know they can come up with a passport – that's the least of it. After all, London is where we bank our damned money. And God knows England needs our oil.'

Russell rubbed his fingers over his eyes tiredly. 'You can't throw these damned things together in a few hours,' he said. 'To begin with, you haven't had a damned bit of experience. You can get into all sorts of trouble unless you know what you're doing. It isn't like the cinema, you know.'

'The hell it isn't! Anyway, I haven't got time for a course in political cloak-and-dagger work. I either get out of here or I'm stuck. It's just a matter of time.'

'You couldn't find a decent disguise, actually.'

'Yes, I can. I'm going to get on a commercial jet and pass myself off as an Indian with British citizenship visiting relatives in the Middle East, or a salesman, or a student – whatever you can come up with. And keep the stupid Americans out of it. After what you've seen of the State Department and the U.S. intelligence outfits, I shouldn't have to argue with you about that.' Abdullah suddenly looked down where his scratching had left long raised red marks across the bare skin. 'I itch all over,' he observed. 'It must be some allergic reaction. I thought they got all that crap out of my system.'

'Now, you see. What if you have some sort of relapse of some sort?'

'Ummm.' Abdullah looked up, remembering. 'Listen, I want you to take care of something else for me. It's important. I've made up a list. I want you to take care of it just as you've done before, in Hollywood and other places.

Okay, the nurse on night duty in the Roosevelt Hospital Emergency Room is named Rosalie Donato. She lives on Long Island. I understand she has three kids and her husband is a fireman or something like that. I want you to buy her a house. Get her a nice house, the kind you see in American magazines, somewhere on Long Island.' Abdullah had a picture of it in his mind; he had been thinking about it while he lay in bed watching the last of 'The Late Show'. 'Make it one of those white colonial-style houses with lots of big green trees around it. I want you to set up an Overseas Investment Company dossier on her, see that she never goes hungry.'

'What –' Russell began, but Abdullah cut him short.

'This is important, I told you! The other one, the one named Marvin, you'll see what I've written down for him. A trip to Europe. See that,' Abdullah said delicately, 'he gets to the right places, the opera, the Folies-Bergère, the transvestite bars, stuff like that.' He started to laugh. 'Put some money in the bank for him, too.'

'My God,' Russell said.

'And the doctors. Buy them their own hospitals – I mean it. Something nice for everybody, especially the Jewish one.' But he paused. 'I've thought about asking the Pakistani if he wants a job with the Medical Centre in Rahsmani. We have plenty of Pakistanis there now. They seem to like it. He could be chief of staff, hospital director, whatever the biggest job is. You find out about it. I have never,' Abdullah said slowly, 'been in a hospital before in my life. There's never been anything wrong with me. You don't know what a damned shock it was, to wake up and find out that I had nearly died. It's something to think about – that my life was in other people's hands, strangers, and they worked like hell to keep me from dying without even knowing who I was. They thought I was some junkie off the streets.'

'It's their damned job, after all,' Russell said. 'That's what they're supposed to do.'

'No, that's not the way to look at it. I've changed,' Abdullah said. 'Things are different now. A person can't come that close to dying without its making some profound changes in the way he thinks. I know what I'm talking about.'

Abdullah regarded Russell for a long, thoughtful moment.

'I want you to take care of it right away, too, so give it top priority. I have everybody on the list including the New York City detective who helped you when the other people didn't. I don't know some of the names – I've just written Officer A and Officer B and Officer C and so forth. Watches, television sets, new automobiles, pay up any debts they might owe. You can leave the actual purchasing up to Sulman and the others. You don't have to bother yourself with the details. And that leaves only you.'

Russell looked up, startled.

'Since you're an employee of the Rahsmani government, that puts you in a slightly different category. I don't know what the usual thing would be, a bunch of money, I suppose, but I'm thinking about it. It goes beyond money. If you hadn't stuck with the New York City detectives and come to the hospital when you did, I wouldn't be here now. I owe my life to you as much as to anyone else.'

'I wish you wouldn't,' Russell said. He was very red now. 'I'm not asking for any reward.'

'Oh, that's all right.' Abdullah's tone was matter-of-fact; he rubbed his chin, his eyes far away. 'I want to express my thanks. It's only a little thing; it's only my life. "And what is a man's life, that he is not grateful for the keeping of it?" You must remember, Russell, my friend, I'm a true Arab. I'm not ashamed of it.' He paused, beginning a smile that showed all of his teeth, ferociously. 'Wait till you see how I reward my enemies. It's going to be a work of art.'

SIXTEEN

As they moved across the desert floor before the orange and brown shale of the plateau that edged the north, a small whirlwind no bigger than a horse and rider accompanied them, moving on the right and parallel like some watchman of the empty country. There had been no warning; the whirlwind had materialized before their eyes like an *afreet* and was simply there, with the unexpectedness of all things in the wastelands. For a long time Abdullah kept his eyes on it as he had a healthy respect for whirlwinds as well as desert vipers, dust storms, and other aberrations of the vast No Place of the world. Sakir, the Bedouin in front of him, rode with his transistor radio to his *kaffiyeh*-wrapped head, enveloped in the tinny sound of popular Arab music from Radio Kuwait, and took little notice. This was all that happened for at least ten miles by Abdullah's reckoning: the sun shone down on them in the blinding glare of morning; the silence — except for the pocket radio — was profound enough to make the ears ring, and the steady shuffle of the racing camel's stride was like an agonizing carousel, back and forth and swimmingly upward, a sealike motion that racked the spine and made the stomach uneasy.

The bad knee, full of half-healed lacerations from the fall in New York, hurt so much that from time to time Abdullah reached down and massaged it cautiously with his free hand. At least the knee was on the side that allowed it to hang straight; his other leg was crooked over the wooden horn of the camel saddle, much as Victorian ladies once rode their horses, and had gone numb from lack of circulation. On the free side also, the M-16 with a supply of box magazines in a woollen bag with fringe bumped against the camel's ribs. Sitting like that and guiding his mount with a nose rope on the left and a long reed wand on the right, Abdullah had ridden most of the night and now out of the dawn and into the hot early day. The camels were beginning to tire. They had stopped to rest them three times since the first light. Behind Abdullah rode Sakir's brother Khaz'al. In all the miles in every direction and as far as the eye could see, there were no other moving things but the three of them and the camels.

Don't dream, the Bedouin had warned him when the sun came up. This is a long journey and arduous, even for desert people. So think of many things as you go and keep the soul busy, for it is easy to fall into that curious sleep of the mind from which it is difficult to return, and dangerous.

It was easy enough to keep his soul busy and think of a lot of things, Abdullah realized; as Adam Russell had foreseen he had made a lot of mistakes, it was a miracle that he hadn't blown the whole business a thousand times over. When he had come through customs in Kuwait city, a critical point for everything, he had been weeded out by the customs officers at once, made to go through the line twice, and the second time he could have sworn they were on to who he was. Nothing came of it, though. The customs police had taken his passport and examined it thoroughly, especially where he was described as a Pakistani with British citizenship travelling to join relatives. While they did this he had lost his head and had talked too much, had fallen all over himself being agreeable, and that alone should have made them suspicious. He was amazed when they finally passed him through.

After that, going to buy clothes in the *souks*, the shops in the old city, hadn't exactly been a roaring success, either. He had damned near forgot how to bargain in Arabic – after all, everything he needed was always purchased for him by others – and he had stumbled over the business of prices to where the shopkeeper had finally raised his eyebrows in disbelief at such clumsiness. He had paid more money for the clothes than they were worth. But the necessity for haggling according to custom when he was sure the police were somewhere nearby had nearly driven him crazy. It had all been accomplished eventually, but he had cursed Russell at every turn. The Englishman was right, of course; you could hang yourself hourly if you didn't know what you were doing. Only luck had seen him through. In the last hours in the city a fit of anxiety had overtaken him. It got to the point where he could not be sure whether he was being followed or not, but he suspected the Kuwaitis were keeping their eye on him.

But once he had stepped into the alley of the Kuwait city *souks* to put on the second hand Bedouin robes and cover his head with a ragged black *kaffiyeh*, everything changed. It was as though anonymity settled down on him like the wondrous Cloak of Invisibility from the tales of the *djinns*. When he came out again into the streets of the old quarter he was like a fish that has been put back into the sea again to swim with the other ordinary fish. People took no notice of him at all. Except for an occasional shove in the back when he didn't move fast enough he could have been anyone. This took some adjusting to. For once in his life he was now someone else; he had turned into a face among many hundreds of faces, a part of the great mass of poor looking for work, a wandering Bedouin lost in the city, no one. It was a wild, unsettling feeling. He had just left a life where there were too many people trying to organize and control everything he did, and now here he was, no one of any consequence, and alone. It had, temporarily at least, changed his whole character. When he went to buy a ticket for the bus southward he took the scorn of the ticket seller meekly. And he was so wrapped up in being no one at all that he forgot to buy something to eat to take on the bus trip and as a result had damned near starved in the midst of passengers eating bread and smelly sausage and fruit and other things that made his mouth water and his stomach rumble.

At dusk he left the bus at Mina Asmari, the last village before the border, and had walked along the highway for about three miles until he managed to hitch a ride on a lorry going southward to the oil city at Ras Deir. The lorry driver was a young Iranian from the port of Kuwait city, a little bit older than himself, had a large family, and was making a living trucking Indian foods and cotton cloth to the shops that catered to the Pakistani oil workers at the Ras Deir fields. Their talk was all of the disturbance centred about Rahsmani city and the troubles of the Emir's government.

'I hear it upon the radio, on the news which is given every hour,' the lorry driver said, 'that this is now a very unpredictable place to be, this country, and dangerous to everyone. The last time I was stopped at the Rahsmani border by the National Police, but the time before that the police were not to be found and those who stopped me were but brigands, anarchists with submachine guns and no other authority, and they wished to search my vehicle for contraband. Allah only knows what is contraband! It changes with the moment, especially with the lawless ones; so I fell by my lorry in the sand and prayed until they were through and they had satisfied themselves. It is fortunate I was carrying only curry and cloth for the Indian shops, which are not part of the oil company.'

'Truly, a grave situation,' Abdullah agreed. 'It is to be hoped I will find my family safe. Who are these brigands?'

The driver threw up both hands, letting the lorry barrel along the highway by itself. 'Who knows? It is the curse of Rahsmani that many fight at once – those who say they will liberate the people and fight in the name of the masses; the National Police, who think maybe to set up some sort of military state; and the rest of the Rahsmanis, who follow the old man whom many say is too feeble to lead his government. Two of his sons wish to take the throne. They have an alliance with some of the rebels. And there is a grandson, a young man and promising, but he is cowardly and has fled the country. And there are even others. This is

292

the trouble, that there are more fighters than one can count. All strangers are enemies once the border is crossed. That is why I carry this.'

The driver opened the glove box of the lorry long enough for Abdullah to get a brief glimpse of an old Luger pistol inside.

Abdullah thought about it for a while as they sped down the highway.

'Naturally,' Abdullah said, 'as you see, I am travelling alone. And I do not know what I will find when I get to my village. Would you consider perhaps selling me your weapon?'

The Iranian laughed.

'I could make a fortune if I had more, verily! This country thirsts for arms. The people will pay any price. But I will have to hide this when I approach the border, and to carry it at all is dangerous. Men will kill for it. It is all I have.'

As Abdullah asked, the driver dropped him off about four miles north of the Rahsmani border. When he jumped out of the lorry Abdullah pointed to the west, across the darkening waste of the desert to the rim of the plateau in the distance. 'Now I must go this way,' Abdullah told him, 'until I come to my village.'

'The peace of God go with you,' the Iranian told him formally, leaning out of the cab, his white teeth flashing in the twilight. 'You are lucky to be going home. When all is in confusion, the men of the desert dwell in good order.'

'And the peace of God on you, also,' Abdullah responded. 'It is good order I hope to find, when I once more see my family.'

But he knew the other was watching him. The Iranian probably wasn't fooled, especially by a hitchhiker who wanted to buy a gun and who wanted to drop off before the border station. Abdullah heard the lorry start up again, the progressive changing of gears as it picked up speed, as he stepped off the highway and started to move into the desert, limping. His knee was bothering him a bit and he went slowly. If he's looking in the rearview mirror, Abdullah thought, the sight is enough to reassure him. The clothes, the nondescript headcloth, the limp, should have placed him safely among the nothings of the world.

Now, in the twilight, he was not sure where he was going. That was another thing that had seemed simple enough in New York – to get off the highway and strike off to the west until about even with the border and then wait for someone to pick him up. But he had forgot how vast the desert was and how impossible to determine the direction even with plenty of light. He kept his eyes on the plateau until the last sunlit colours faded into grey and disappeared all together and then he was alone, going forward, but with his feet slipping on pebbles and sand and small patches of desert grass. Finally he sat down in the dark and looked at his watch. It was almost ten o'clock. The light lingered long in the empty country.

He didn't know what in the hell he was going to do. He supposed he could stretch out and sleep until dawn broke, but he was worried that whoever had been sent to meet him would be wandering around looking for him at about the same time he was looking for them, perhaps going in opposite directions. Then where would he go, what in hell would he do in the middle of the desert?

As he was thinking this, out of the darkness, and with not even a rustle or an indrawn breath to warn him a voice said, 'O lord Abdullah, thy servants greet you.' And as he squinted, trying to make out any figures in the dark, he saw that they were right under his nose, prostrated before him on the desert floor, the dark shapes of camels rising like hillocks behind.

The murmuring went on, the blessings of God invoked, all the formal greetings, and he found he couldn't make any answer. It was like something out of a dream: the Bedouin grovelling, the camels now and then adding a low, warbling rumble, all in darkness. He felt his skin prickle.

May your night be blessed.

May your day that is coming be fortunate.

We are your servants, O lord Abdullah, and you are now the light of your people.

The one God be with you.

It was as though he had been suddenly grabbed back into the ancient past, as this very thing had happened for hundreds of years with his kinsmen. It's too damned dark, he told himself. It's not a dream, but I've got to watch it. Next I'll be hearing the Voice of Destiny speaking out of the wilderness.

'Get up,' he told them.

They scrambled up, two of them, and as they were right at his knees he could make out their faces, Hammasseh tribesmen from the pattern of their *kaffiyehs*, probably just out of their teens but full-grown men as it was reckoned. Abdullah knew what was coming, he knew what they were going to say even before they said it. They grabbed his hands to kiss and he couldn't pull away.

'Who is it?' he wanted to know.

'Oh lord,' the young voices said, speaking at once and overlapping each other, 'we are the brothers of Wadiyeh al Qasim, thy slaves, now, to atone for that one's great wrong. We have begged to be allowed to come to you, as you see us thus. That you may forget, in your great mercy, the name of the accursed betrayer.'

Their voices were loud in the dark, and anxious.

'One will kill himself now, so that you may see that we have honour, and this will wipe out the shame of our family. It has been too much for our father to bear, this terrible thing. He has sent us to do this.'

'Oh damn,' Abdullah said. He saw the metal of the knife blade catch a stray spark of light from somewhere and he reached out in time to catch it across the knuckles. But he stopped it. He supposed that the other had intended to cut his throat or something of the sort. Or at least make the gesture.

'Don't do that,' he said crossly. 'It is not necessary to kill yourself and leave dead bodies for my enemies to find, and

295

you have cut my hand. Such is the penalty for foolish acts, that you have wounded me.'

'Say that yours is forgiveness,' one of the shadows said.

'I do not wish to speak of any of this,' Abdullah told them. All this emotion in the dark left him feeling badgered. He had not even thought for a moment of treachery when the knife appeared; they were too damned buggingly earnest. 'I wish to speak to you,' he said, 'of acts of treachery and who will pay what and thus-and-so, when we are out of here. This is what you have been sent for, to get me out of here. Not threaten to kill yourselves. Do you wish me,' he said, peering beyond them, 'to ride one of those?'

'They are of the finest beasts, O lord,' they assured him. 'They go where the lorries and automobiles cannot; they are the pure racing stock of the King of all Camels, brought out of the great Empty Quarter, the Mother of all Deserts, which breeds beasts of surpassing swiftness and with flesh of iron. All men know this.'

'Their souls desire only to bear thee, lord Abdullah,' one of them said, 'until their bodies are broken in thy service. They want only speed, and death.'

'The lord ibn Sullakh, sheik of the lowly Hammasseh and of the great tribe of the al Asmaris has bidden us choose only the finest, pearls from the loins of the greatest of –'

'I want to get the hell out of here,' Abdullah said violently. He had run out of patience. 'I have injured my leg and it is an abomination of pain, and I am hungry.' He remembered the long bus ride from Kuwait city and his stomach growling with emptiness. 'What have you brought to eat?'

Now, suddenly as they moved across the desert floor, Sakir threw up his arm, brandishing the transistor radio, and cried, 'Down! Down – or the beasts will run away!'

There was a flurry of yells and blows with the reed wands on the necks of the camels. Before Abdullah could get his leg free from the saddle horn Khaz'al was on the

296

ground and had forced Abdullah's camel to its knees, almost throwing him off. Abdullah slid down to take his place with the Bedouin, who huddled close to the sides of the animals, the sleek hairy ribs expanding and contracting with a symphony of camel garglings and groans and melancholy ruminations. Abdullah hadn't seen anything at all, and hadn't heard a thing. For a brief moment they waited expectantly. Then, from a great distance, there came a chattering that grew louder and two helicopters, American-make Hueys making routine sweeps over the tableland, circled, saw them, and swept down toward them. The racket grew deafening, then unbearable, and the helicopters drew down on them low enough to sweep their clothes with the wind from the rotors and make the camels throw up their heads and roll their big squatted bodies hysterically. The Bedouin wrestled with the camels to keep them from breaking away.

'WHO THE HELL ARE THEY?' Abdullah shouted, his mouth against Khaz'al's ear.

'THE SAUDS.' Now Khaz'al placed his mouth against Abdullah's ear in return. 'They do this several times in the day, to see what is going on, and to watch the fighting.'

Abdullah lifted his head to watch. They're violating our air space, he thought grimly. The arrogant bastards. Just keeping a watch on things, huh? But they've got no damned business this far over our borders.

The sight of the Hueys, at last turning their tails and chattering loudly off toward the mountains, had made him thoughtful. The American equipment was just what they needed. The source was close; all they had to do was figure out a way to get it.

'Get me to my uncle Fuad's camp now, as quickly as God will allow it,' he said to Khaz'al. 'How far is it now?' The sun was high and the heat had become fierce. His face was covered with dust, not all of it thrown up by the helicopters, and his lips were beginning to crack. 'Will these beasts last long enough to get us there?' With racing camels, they were still only covering the ground at about six miles an hour. He had no idea where they were, or if the Bedouin brothers could truly take them where they were supposed to be before the camels dropped dead.

Khaz'al only laughed, the easy laughter of the *bedu*, and Sakir came up and joined in.

'Over the broken land,' Khaz'al said, pointing. 'Before the midday meal, we will see the place! Our lovely ones are fresh, they have not yet begun to walk – now we will make them run!'

His uncle Fuad's base was located at Salwah, in a large valley set between low barren hills and around a small green oasis, as it had been for three hundred years or so since the al Asmaris had come out of the Armah plateau of what was now Saudi Arabia to settle there. Salwah was not quite a village nor yet entirely a Bedouin camp, for it had permanent houses of the standard Rahsmani government construction, but most of the population was transient, the tribes coming in to the oasis to set up their black tents and water their flocks, then leaving, not to return for months. What permanent town structures there were, were strikingly ugly: the combined post office and telephone exchange of dirty pink concrete erected under the British Protectorate; the old army barracks that had once been used as a school and was now a garage for the sheik's hunting jeeps and Cadillacs; the new school; the small two-storey hospital surrounded by dilapidated, unwatered palms; and a gigantic water tower, gift of the water-loving Emir and which most of the Bedouin took, seeing its somewhat unconventional shape, as a public monument to Sheik Fuad's legendary virility.

Abdullah had been in Salwah many times. It was one of the few places in his grandfather's money-glutted country which, like old Fuad himself, showed the minimal effects of wealth and progress. The camels, smelling home, water, and feed, began to gallop down what served as the main street, past the water tower and the post office. Abdullah tried to rein in his camel but Sakir's and Khaz'al's, wallowing with excitement, went around in circles until finally the Bedouin gave them their heads, letting them run wild into the oasis and spurring them on with yells.

Riding a camel, Abdullah told himself, was like trying to control some damned prehistoric monster. He tried to do something workable with the rope in one hand and the neck wand in another, but nothing much helped. He managed to come to a stop, finally, in front of the sheik's garage, the damned beast's head turned completely over its back with his tugging, and its body wobbling from side to side like a mountain about to collapse. It was, he saw, the hour for the midday meal and the main street of Salwah was fairly deserted. There were only a few women coming out of the tents to watch his struggles, and a girl in a refinery workman's jumpsuit approaching, a basket over her arm.

'Dammit!' Abdullah cried. The thing was really trying to fall down flat where it was. And then to the girl, since she had stopped to watch, too: 'The blessings of Allah upon thee and all that sort of thing, and tell me quickly, how does one get this animal to kneel?' He had been slapping the camel on its pretzeled neck with the reed wand and now the head was almost completely turned around. It stared him straight in the face, looking at him through gigantic long-lashed eyes, seductive and disdainful.

The girl regarded him silently. Obviously she had never seen anyone ride out of the wastes and dangers of the great desert who didn't even know the basic commands to control a camel. Well tough luck, Abdullah told himself, she was seeing one now.

'Give me your assistance, if you know how to do this,' he said politely, but he was trying not to grit his teeth. She was not a bad-looking girl, quite small and slender in spite of the refineryman's workclothes. Her long hair was braided into two plaits and covered with a red bandana. Her face was delicate, the eyes large and rather beautiful, and she reminded him of someone. But he didn't care at all for the supercilious expression.

Suddenly she stepped forward and without even bothering to put the basket down she seized the nose rope forcefully and cried, 'Yik! Yik! Lallah, lallah!' and the camel swivelled its head back to position Normal, gave a sentimental yodel, and sank to its knees in the dust.

'Crap!' Abdullah said under his breath. 'Just like that – yik, yik, lallah, lallah.' It was amazing.

The girl seemed to know who he was, and disapproved.

'It's a wonder you got here if you don't know how to ride a camel any better than that,' she said.

It took Abdullah a moment to realize the girl had spoken in English. He slid down from the camel saddle, the M-16 under one arm and the ammo boxes in his free hand, and stopped to look at her. It was true, she looked somewhat like his sister, although perhaps a little prettier in a bolder, more vivid sort of way. And from her manner he would judge that she knew very well that she was exceptionally good-looking. He had never seen anyone so damned assertive.

'Congratulations on your English,' he said. 'It's very good.'

She shot him a totally unappreciative look.

'I received my education in the English language,' she said loftily. 'I graduated from the Henry Baker Lamborchard High School in Ras Deir and I will go to college when this revolutionary fighting is over.' She hesitated, then added quickly, 'My father is Farid al Asmari, supervisory foreman at Twenty-four Well, Hamzah.'

'Congratulations to you both, then,' Abdullah said.

While they had been standing there some men had emerged from the tents across the way, throwing back on their heads the *kaffiyehs* they had removed for the midday meal. Now they ran toward them, joined by a small crowd of Bedouin women and children tagging along behind. The first men to cross the road came up to Abdullah and threw themselves flat in the dirt. Abdullah backed away hastily, but the camel was right behind him. They were joined now by men, women, and children coming from all directions, all hurrying to prostrate themselves. The nurses from the hospital came out and gathered on the front steps to watch what was going on. Now Abdullah could see some of Fuad's district government people jogging toward them from the headquarters building. When one of the clerks threw himself in the road at the edge of the crowd, Abdullah frowned. Something was going on, more than just a welcome. He looked at the girl, who was still on her feet, watching him closely.

'What's up?' he asked her.

Abdullah felt hands clutching at his ankles. He tried to move back, but the camel let out a small warning gargle. The Bedouin in front were trying to kiss his feet.

'They are calling you Emir,' she told him. But she held her head to one side thoughtfully, and her expression seemed to soften. 'You do not know, do you?'

'I do now,' he said. Suddenly Abdullah could not make his throat muscles work well enough to speak. It was not the first time in the past few years that he had felt like a very small child, suddenly beleaguered and alone with his woe. He wanted to put his hands to his face and bawl. Nothing lasts, he told himself. The world changes and finally leaves you alone in it. Now this is gone, too.

A moment later Hussein al Asmari, who was district commissioner for Salwah, came up and took him by the elbow and led him away from the crowd. Hussein was visibly upset.

'It is distressing; you were meant to know about this in a different way,' he said. 'But then, it could not be helped.'

'Be at peace,' Abdullah told him. 'Tell me only how my grandfather died.'

Another member of the district government staff joined them, then a handful of clerks, as they walked through the sun-bitter dust of the street, the village crowd trailing behind.

'That is distressing, too.' The district commissioner was a short man but slender like all the al Asmaris; his large black moustache covered a mouth working with emotion. 'They were terrorists from the streets, the ones who call themselves the Children of the Fire, and they attacked the fort with hand grenades at a vulnerable hour, an hour when one would not expect such a thing. It was the hour of darkness before dawn. The residence has sustained much damage, you would be greatly angered to see what was done. It was him, of course, that they came for. And they found him getting out of bed and they killed him, thus.' Hussein covered his mouth with his hand for a moment, overcome with grief. There were tears in his eyes. 'It was said he resisted them, and also the bodyguards thought to fight, and the men who were stationed in the fort, but it was of no use. It was a daring raid.'

'What did they do afterward?' Abdullah kept his head down. His voice was more controlled than Hussein's. He didn't wish to give himself over to any public display of emotion. People were watching them; no doubt they guessed what was being said. Abdullah felt as though his neck were being held in iron bands.

'The Bedouin died by his side, naturally. But the success of the attackers was this, that they picked a time when the Englishman was in the city and Sheik Fuad was leading his fighters. Otherwise they would have accomplished little. Your kinsman blames himself, only. He has vowed to exterminate them all.'

'I said, what did they do then?' Abdullah repeated.

'Do not ask me to tell such things,' Hussein implored. 'It is best to learn of sad events slowly, not to receive news in the street.'

But the clerk from the district office who was walking on the other side said, 'They threw the body off the wall of the fort and into the sea, as in the old times. Hakim al Asmari ordered this. Then it was pulled out of the water and taken away.'

Abdullah stopped short to look at the speaker. The clerk was a young man in his twenties, moustached, with a dark and angry face. 'Who are you?' Abdullah wanted to know.

'Al-Malih al Asmari.'

'Are you a cousin?'

The other didn't need to answer; they were all cousins in Salwah. They had come to a large black tent in the green outer edges of the oasis, set in the first rows of date palms. It was a very beautiful spot.

'Enter,' Hussein al Asmari said, looking relieved. 'All will be explained inside.'

It was cooler under the black wool canopy of the tent and dim after the glare of the noonday street. An old woman stood in the centre of the tent by the ridgepole, barefoot on the jewel-coloured Persian carpets that were his Uncle Fuad's pride and joy. The elderly woman had improbable orange hair, streaked with grey and untidily arranged, and she was wearing the black Bedouin woman's gown with coloured embroidery across the bosom. She had once been handsome, one could see that, and she had on several diamond bracelets and a pair of diamond earrings that flashed in the sudden gloom. The way she held herself was very familiar. They squinted at each other. Abdullah had forgot how he was dressed, in Bedouin clothes and carrying the M-16 rifle in one hand.

'Grandmother?' he said, finally. He couldn't believe it. In spite of the moment he wanted to laugh. She looked like a worn peacock, colours still brave, her great courage rising out of the ruin. Her lipstick had been laid on with a heavy hand, the eyes thickly dimmed with mascara. She looked awful, and very dear to him.

'Oh Grandmother,' Abdullah said again, and his voice broke. He would have to watch himself. This would bring him down, the sight of her like this, as nothing else could. He stepped forward and put his arms around her as he would anything fragile, and she allowed it. But she stayed drawn up rigidly like an old mare ready for battle, or a queen, and would not relent.

'I prayed that you would come. I prayed that you would live to come here again,' she said. The voice was high and under great pressure, but perfectly even.

'Lady, I honour you,' Abdullah said formally, and let her go and stepped back. If this was the way she wished it to be, a distance between them, then it was all right. His grandmother could be full of steel when she wanted to. 'The blessings of God upon you, peace be with you.'

The district commissioner and the clerks now turned to go, but his grandmother stopped them with a lift of her hand.

'Stay!' she commanded. Then, to Abdullah, 'Your son is here.'

'My God!' That had taken him by surprise. He was so full of the shock of his grandfather's death that he hadn't even thought about his son, and the others. Now it rushed on him, anxiety and joy all at once. 'Fawzia? Where is the Englishman, and my uncle Fuad? My mother?'

'Come he waits for you.' The hand with the sparkling diamonds took his wrist in a strong grip and moved him after her, toward the back of the tent. It was difficult to walk on heavy rugs in shoes. Abdullah stumbled a little. They went through a hanging tent flap, decorated with tassels, and into a little room that had been made in the rear area, the room usually reserved for the women. There was a small table with blankets on it, and his grandmother gestured toward it. A thing the size of a large animal, perhaps a dog, lay under the blankets. A wizened face looked up at Abdullah as he bent to see, the eyelids stuck together and the sockets sunken, little white teeth showing like exposed pebbles. It had been this way for some time and the desert air had worked on it, leaching out the moisture and the body fluids and turning it to rot and leather.

'Behold your son!' His grandmother's voice was trapped in the folds of the tent over them, the agony muffled.

Abdullah bent closer to get a good look, at first not believing it at all. It's true, he realized, with a wrenching inside of him that was like his heart being torn to pieces. It's my son. Oh God, it's Karim. Now there would be no more books for Papa to read, no nursery school, no more heavy jumping weight in his lap that invariably trod in his crotch, no more sticky hands to smear his lovingly. I never even started being a father to my son, and now it's over. It's gone.

'Mourn!' his grandmother cried.

Abdullah looked up, startled. His grandmother was standing there like any old woman at a tribal death. She had loosened the front of her clothes, her hair stood out around her face, and she held her hands up, palms outward. She wants me, he thought slowly, to fall back and howl and tear my clothes, too, and beat on my flesh until I'm hoarse. Then, when I'm properly worked up, vow my terrible vengeance.

But they were not all like that, the al Asmaris. His grandfather had been as cold and direct in his rages as suddenly bared steel. It was then that he always spoke softly. It was what he was feeling now. His grandmother could put down her hands, wait for some other time to rip her clothes, he decided.

'And the mother?' he wanted to know.

'Dead! They are all dead! In my arms your son died, while I was carrying him. Here –' she swept back the blanket. One leg was missing. And from the appearance of the rest of the body it seemed to have been caught in a machine-gun burst. 'This shows what was done!'

They stood in silence for a second.

'He needs to be buried,' Abdullah said. 'In this you have broken the Law, to keep him thus. And what,' he said, calmly, 'was done with the body of the lord Emir?'

Now his grandmother took down her hands and stared at him, the small net of lines deepening at the corners of her eyes. She seemed puzzled. 'They took him through the streets, dead and naked.'

'That's what I thought.' Dragged behind a lorry, he had no doubt, so that no one would forget. 'Is there anything else, lady?' he asked her.

His grandmother kept staring at him. Finally she moved very close to him and stood and stared into his face as if wondering at what she was finding there. Abdullah stood still and let her examine him. As she looked, she grew less certain.

'It was not necessary, grandmother,' Abdullah said finally. 'But I understand what you desired to do. Nevertheless, I will take care of it. I would have, anyway.'

'Allah,' she breathed. It was as though someone had thrown a violent light into her eyes. She blinked.

'*You* mourn,' he told her. 'I haven't got time. Get the women in, and get him ready to bury. It's against God's Law not to have buried him before. Besides, he's only a little boy. I don't want him lying around like a damned national monument.'

'Abdullah, my darling,' his grandmother said suddenly. She gave vent to a low, trembling moan. 'Aiieee, my beloved – do not look at me like that!'

'I can't help the way I look,' he told her. He went to the tent flap that divided the women's area from the rest and lifted it and came out into the main part beyond. He still had the M-16 in his hand and he stooped to put it down carefully on the cushions.

'I have seen my son,' Abdullah told the group standing there. 'And I have found out what happened to my grandfather's body, and that my wife is dead. Sit down,' he told them, and motioned to the cushions where he wished them to sit. When they had settled themselves he said, 'Where is the Sheik Fuad, my uncle, now?'

His uncle Fuad had been in the camp a week ago and had returned to the city with as many of the lorries as could be mustered, and more men recruited from the tribes of the Hammasseh and the al Asmari. Brooke-Cullingham was in the city; the government forces controlled the area around the Medical Centre. There were many cousins and other relatives involved in the fighting: Mansur al Asmari, Fawzia's family, the students – the recital was long and Abdullah cut it short. He wanted to know about telephones. The lines to the south from Salwah had been cut many weeks ago and had not been repaired, but at Ras Deir the oil company still had theirs in working order. The GAROC people were busily flying in and out of the company air-port : already the first list of women and children had been evacuated to Dharan in Saudi Arabia and waited there to see if they would be sent on to the United States. The oil fields were armed to prevent any disruption or attempted takeover.

'Try the telephones here, first,' Abdullah told Hussein. 'I wish to place a call to Riyadh, to the Prince Azziz ibn Saud who, as you know, was the husband of my sister. I have seen the helicopters passing over. Now,' he went on, 'as to the men of the tribes here who have volunteered to go and fight in the city, this is all well and good, but I see many strong *bedu* who perhaps are not as strong and passionate as they once were but who are good fighting men, neverthe-less. We need a new recruiting programme. And this is the new recruiting programme – that we go about with lorries and fill them up with every man who is not so old that he will fall down when required to hold an automatic weapon. If the Rahsmanis are to survive and not lose their country to these damned outsiders. we must have every man avail-able. I will lead them myself.'

'There are no lorries left,' Al-Malih said. 'They have gone south.'

'There are lorries at Ras Deir, with the oil company.'

'But they will not let anybody in – they have armed the oil fields like fortresses!'

Abdullah smiled slowly.

'We have just bought them out,' he said. 'Everything that once belonged to them now belongs to us. I must go and tell them the good news.'

SEVENTEEN

'I was going to kill you,' Abdullah said in English, 'but there's something you're going to do for me, so I'll get back to that later.'

'Who is this?' the voice of Prince Azziz demanded.

'You know damned well who this is, you recognize the sound of my voice, so don't play dumb. Now listen, you little wart, let's see if you can do something other than abuse young girls and make their lives miserable. You have a large debt to pay.'

There was a choking sound on the other end of the wire as Prince Azziz tried to cope with his rage. 'I owe you nothing,' the voice said violently. 'I do not abuse young girls. If you had been there when I came to your country you would have seen me and I would have told you the facts. Believe me, she was uncontrollable; nothing would pacify her. The conditions of my marriage were utter lunacy! My mother will tell you –'

'I don't want to talk to your mother. I want to talk to you,' Abdullah said. Just the sound of the other's voice made him angry. He was standing at Charlie Averbach's desk in the administration building at Ras Deir and in front of him the sweep of the glass wall of Averbach's office overlooked the oil city with its tree-lined streets and lawn sprinklers and swimming pools, and the eastern section of the oil fields beyond that, and the far purple rim of the mountains of the desert in the distance. It was a great view. It was hard to imagine, as one looked out on it, that there was anything else going on in the world other than this sparkling vista of industry and modern living placed side by side in the desert. Abdullah reached across the desk and pulled Averbach's scribble pad toward him, picked up a pen and started making notes. 'You're violating our air space, you and your helicopters, and the next damned Huey that comes over without proper clearance is going to get shot down.'

'I have nothing to do with helicopters!' the voice shouted. 'Why are you calling me? Are you mad, now, as with the rest of your accursed family?'

'If you don't have anything to do with helicopters, then find somebody who does. I understand one of your cousins is a general in your half-assed air force or army or whatever it is the Americans have given you.'

'I'm going to hang up,' the voice yelled. 'And do not call me again, I do not wish to receive harassing calls from lunatics!'

'You better not hang up,' Abdullah said softly. He tucked the telephone receiver under his chin so that he could hold the notepad with one hand and write on it with the other. 'I'm going to come up there and kill you yet if you don't pay attention. And you know how that is – all the al Asmaris are lunatics and desert creepers. You'll never have a safe moment, never draw an easy breath again even in your own bathtub if you don't listen to me now. I want your cousin to bring about ten of those UH-One-H Hueys I saw coming over the border yesterday with about five hundred M-Sixteens with standard ammo clips of twenty rounds and grenade launchers, as many as they can pack on board. Also, we need some military field communications, walkie-talkies, whatever will work for street fighting. And military personnel carriers. If you farts haven't already been sitting over there thinking about what we need then you better get off your asses and do it right away. I want them by dawn tomorrow morning.'

There was a pause and then the voice said, 'That's ridiculous! It's impossible for us to violate our neutrality. You don't know what you're talking about.'

Abdullah laughed. 'You were never neutral, you bandit. You people haven't been neutral for the last five hundred years. Listen, last month when I was in the United States I got a message that if I needed anything just to let your family know. They were extremely sorry, then, about anything that might have happened to my sister. In the old tradition, this was a point of honour. How's your honour today?'

'Do not talk of honour,' the voice said. 'We have honour. We have had honour when your tribe was stealing women and sheep in the Armah.'

'Ah, then you know your grandmother,' Abdullah said rudely. 'I'm glad she got back. Look, I can hop a plane and be in Riyadh in a few hours to cut your balls off, if necessary. But first I will get on the telephone and call our mutual neighbours and tell them I know from experience that you and your family are camel shit, and your honour is what the goats have left behind.'

'You do not know how to talk to civilized people,' Prince Azziz said. They had both been shouting; now the voice in Riyadh made an effort to lower itself somewhat. 'We can't do anything that might compromise us. You understand I am not a military man. I am not even an official in the government.'

'I want the drop at Salwah, at my uncle Fuad's camp. That's not much of a trip – the helicopters can hop over the border and be back again before your pilots have time to wet their pants. That's two dozen Hueys,' Abdullah shouted. He switched to Arabic; it was a better language for yelling. 'And a thousand automatic M-Sixteens with ammunition, grenade launchers – and you can drive the personnel carriers in to Salwah, if you can't figure out a better way to do it. But all this must be here by tomorrow morning. Attend me – all I desire from you is one word! And that one word is your stinking honour, which binds you!'

'You are mad!' Prince Azziz yelled back.

But there was a long pause, a standoff, and Abdullah waited, and then the voice said, 'Where can I call you back?'

That was better. Abdullah gave him Averbach's number

at Ras Deir and hung up. Charlie Averbach, who had been listening, sitting in one of the black leather conference chairs across the room, now got up.

'That's what,' Abdullah told Averbach, 'you call doing business on a high level, government to government.' He managed a smile. 'You can put that conversation in your memoirs.'

'Abdullah, hadn't you better take it easy?' Averbach surveyed the figure before him in a borrowed T-shirt and denim jeans, the corners of the checkered *kaffiyeh* tucked up into the headrope to keep it out of the way. The automatic rifle lay on the desk where Abdullah had put it down, among the telephones and the intercom system. 'How much sleep have you had?'

'Don't talk to me like that, or I'll shoot up your office,' Abdullah told him. 'I'm not a kid. Listen,' he said, 'some of these calls I'm putting down I'll have to make myself. These people won't believe a damned thing unless they hear my voice. Like the consulate in New York, and that damned geriatric case we've got for an Ambassador in Washington. But for the rest of the calls, there's a smart young guy who's one of my uncle's district office people and I'm going to get him to bring in some of the clerks from over there and help me.'

Abdullah picked up the notepad and looked it over quickly. At the top of the list he had put Adam Russell's name. Nothing could be done without getting back to Russell in New York and, he thought with a sense of relief, what he was coming now to regard as his own group of people – Sulman, the secretaries, Bisharah. It was strange now not to have them around. Russell could take care of a lot of work from New York, notifying Roehart and Simpson as to the new head of government, the Bank of America in California, Chase Manhattan, the banks in London, the Swiss International banking exchanges and so forth. It would be easier to do it from New York. Russell had the staff to work with there and they could coordinate time zones and office hours. Russell could decide what wording to use but the message was essentially the same for all of them. The death of the Emir would be announced and the succession of the new ruler. And a statement from the new Emir to the effect that the government of Rahsmani was in the process of establishing order and would issue a bulletin shortly on new appointments. There would have to be, Abdullah realized, some contact with the Japanese combine in the gulf, and press releases to *The Times* and the Washington *Post*, and the newspapers in Paris and Rome. The remaining problem was to figure out some way of getting in touch with Brooke-Cullingham.

'I've got to contact the member nations of OPEC, too,' Abdullah said out loud. 'Damn, some of these things ought to go by telex. That's the trouble with not having some sort of trained staff with me – I don't know how to do it all by myself. How's your overseas switchboard?' he wanted to know. 'Can they handle a bunch of calls, or do you need to put extra people on?'

'We're okay,' Averbach said. 'A lot of the equipment is automatic dial.'

'And listen, I want to use your Rahsmani telephone lines to the south, since they tell me they're still open. I want to call the ROIC offices and the Oil Ministry, just for the hell of it, and see who's answering the phones. That ought to be fun. How about here?' Abdullah said, looking around. 'Can we move in here, or do you have a better place for us?'

'Now look, Abdullah,' Averbach said, 'you're putting me in a hell of a spot. You came in here and said you only wanted to make a few telephone calls. It's not that I don't want to offer you a base of operations, exactly, but we're on an emergency alert of our own, and we're in a bind. I'm trying to keep a low profile and keep some of the crazier terrorists from blowing up our pipelines. You realize that's a danger, don't you? And when the pipelines go the gas and power for the city goes, too. We're sitting on a load of dynamite as it is, and now you want to put my ass right on top of it.'

But Abdullah wasn't listening. 'Charlie,' he said, 'I don't

want any more GAROC personnel flown out of here. It's bad for national morale and it shows a distinct lack of confidence in the new government. I've been thinking that maybe some of your people won't want to come back again, just when we're going to need them the most. So keep your planes on the ground. I'm taking all of your lorries. I'm going to commandeer everything around here except the bicycles.' Averbach opened his mouth to say something but Abdullah went on, 'Get on the phone and call the fields and tell your supervisors to go round up all the Rahsmani nationals and have them report in. All Rahsmanis have just volunteered to go to the city and fight.'

'Now you just wait a damned minute!' Averbach's flat Oklahoma accents rose appreciably. He leaned across the desk and pointed his finger at Abdullah. 'I need every damned worker I've got. And I'm not going to force any of my people to go south with you if they don't want to. Every damned job is accounted for; we're working on a stripped-down basis as it is. You take my Rahsmanis off, that leaves us with a majority of Palestinians and restless Iranians that I've taken out of essential areas, anyway, and they're not too damned happy. So don't come in here and tell me what I'm going to do!'

Abdullah looked down at the finger pointed at him and for a moment Averbach saw something in his eyes that flared up bright and hot as a match flame, then died.

'Don't point your finger at me,' Abdullah said evenly. 'Just try to adjust yourself to the idea that I'm the new Emir. And, like my grandfather, that means I'm next to God almighty in this country and even better – because my grandfather didn't own the Gulf Arabian Oil Company, and I do. You've read your telexes. Well, I've just moved up the takeover date. It begins right now.'

Averbach took his finger down and only stared, speechless. Finally he appeared to collect himself. He cleared his throat. 'Now, don't fly off the handle like that. For God's sake, man, make some sense!'

'I'll write you an executive memo,' Abdullah told him, 'if

313

that will make you feel any better. So get the field supervisors on the wire. I want every Rahsmani worker you've
got to report in. Immediately.'

'I can't do that – be reasonable!'

Their eyes met, and held.

'If I have to shoot you,' Abdullah said, 'I guess I can still
keep everybody here at their jobs, one way or another. But
I can only leave Al-Malih or my cousin Hussein al Asmari
here to try to run things from the top. And that will really
screw everything up. They don't know how in the hell to
run a bunch of oil fields. I hope you don't force me to make
a choice.'

The M-16 was between them on the desk. Abdullah could
see that Averbach struggled, not knowing whether to believe him.

'Okay,' Averbach said, 'have it your way for now. God
knows we want to get this damned thing over with as much
as you do.' He took out a pack of cigarettes and shook
them out and lifted one to his mouth. His hand holding the
lighter did not shake. 'Abdullah, there's been a hell of a
change in you,' he said, smiling slightly. 'I mean, physic-
ally, too. I didn't know you at all when you came through
that door this afternoon.'

'I'm only a hundred years older, that's all,' Abdullah said.
'You have to get used to it.'

They worked through the afternoon, Abdullah and Al-
Malih and the district commissioner and some of the clerks
from Salwah, bringing in Averbach's two American secretaries, finally, to type up the reports of what had been
done by telephone. At first Charlie Averbach left them, saying that he was going down to the cafeteria to get some
lunch. When Averbach returned Abdullah was into his
second hour of conversation with Adam Russell at the
Waldorf in New York, and Averbach stopped only long
enough to leave a message that he was taking the rest of
the afternoon off to play some golf, and they could have
his office as long as they wanted to use it. The Ras Deir golf

314

course, watered by artesian wells, was rated one of the best in the Middle East.

'Tell me how the hell you're going to get over here,' Abdullah said, as he took Averbach's message from one of the secretaries and read it. 'I sure as hell need you. I need Brooke-Cullingham, too, and I wish to hell I knew where to find *him*. But the damned telephone lines have been cut out of Salwah. Listen,' he said, 'I've been trying to think of something, like putting the seven-oh-seven down in Riyadh, but I don't want to push my luck with the Saudis too far. If the goddamned airport were open, that'd solve everything. But I can't do anything about that until I get into the city and blast the insurgents out of it. Adam,' Abdullah said, lowering his voice, 'how the hell do you fight a guerrilla war, anyway? I mean, you've had military training, at least in the British navy, tell me how to do a few smart things.'

Later that evening at Salwah, Abdullah walked over to the hospital to see what he could do about getting some sleeping pills. His whole body had been fearsomely alert and almost sleepless since he had left New York and, as Averbach had noticed, it was beginning to show. He felt as though he was being held together by ever-tightening wires. The night was moonless and without wind; the heat seemed to creep out of the stones of the desert and collect in layers in the air and swim about the body as one walked, as tangible as dust. His uncle Fuad had strung a row of street lights down Salwah's one street, but the main generator was always overtaxed and the bulbs only glowed as yellow as chameleon's eyes, and about as useless.

The doctor in the hospital dispensary was polite and attentive to Abdullah's problem, tested his reflexes, asked how long he usually slept and when, and if his appetite was normal. It was a fairly routine examination but Abdullah was impressed with the way the young doctor went about it. At first he had taken him for a Pakistani or a Palestinian, but the other told him he was a native-born Rahsmani from the south, serving two years at the Salwah hospital as part of his government education contract. His name, he said, was Subah al Yammama, and Abdullah knew from the name that he was part of the Mubarraz tribe that his grandfather and his great-grandfather had spent many years trying to subdue. The Mubarraz were good, tough people. It was interesting to find a traditional enemy of the al Asmaris cropping up like that in a hospital dispensary. And a damned good doctor at that. The country was making progress, after all.

Coming back out into the hot, dark street, Abdullah stopped for a moment to watch the activity around the GAROC lorries that had been drawn up to the garages. The men had been fed and some of their families had come over by automobile from Ras Deir to be with them this last night before their movement into the city. They had found drums, or brought them with them, and the thik-chok of the finger *darboukhas* and the nasal songs of the desert, punctuated by rapid handclapping, filled the night. Several fires had been lit and the new Rahsmani volunteers had given themselves over to a little tribal dancing. Abdullah could see the Bedouin circling around, their robes flapping in the firelight, brandishing the old flintlock rifles that most of them still hoarded and a collection of old swords. Mixed in with them were the workers from the oil fields in their canvas worksuits and white hardhats, clapping and wailing with the rest.

Khaz'al came out of the dark and tugged at Abdullah's shirt. His grandmother wanted to see him before he went to bed. Abdullah followed the Bedouin, turning back to look now and then at some fresh outburst of noise. He supposed most of the men could stay up all night without feeling it; at least the Bedouin, those desert travellers, were used to going without sleep for days. I hope to hell, Abdullah thought, the Saudis stick to their promise to bring in those Hueys in the morning. Otherwise I haven't the faintest idea what to do with these people.

His grandmother was standing in the big room of her tent and there was a teenage boy with her. At least Abdullah took it for a teenage boy. When he looked closer he wasn't so sure.

'O Bibi,' his grandmother said, not bothering with an introduction, 'O Bibi, this is a young girl of good family, Fatma, the daughter of Farid ibn Talal al Asmari who is the son of a cousin of your grandfather's cousin Fuad al Asmari of this camp, and she is now without her father, who has gone to the city to fight with the others, and she wishes to join him.'

'No,' Abdullah said. When his grandmother used that tone of voice she had some complicated scheme up her sleeve and no was always the safest answer.

'Do not rush away, O impatient one, before you have heard me out!' His grandmother pulled off the girl's *kaffiyeh* and Abdullah saw the girl's thick, dark braided hair come tumbling down. 'These clothes of men are only a safeguard. Perhaps they are not becoming, but these are perilous times and women must do the best they can. She wears these pants, observe,' here his grandmother tugged at the girl's clothes, 'only because it is more convenient to do so. But she is a proper, well-brought-up girl: I know her father and her family and if she wishes to go in the lorries I have said that you would give permission.'

'No,' Abdullah said. It was the same girl who had pulled the camel to kneel for him, the *yik, yik, lallah, lallah* female and he had taken a thorough look at her before, and that was enough.

'I just want to ride in the lorries as far as the city,' the girl said. 'I'll stay out of the way.'

It was a flat statement, the same cool manner about her that Abdullah had noted before.

'No you don't. You think you're going to carry a rifle and be a damned heroine,' Abdullah said, annoyed. 'I don't know how you talked my grandmother into this, but you're both nuts if you think I'm going to agree to it.'

'Bibi darling, do not speak English; it is very confusing,' his grandmother said. 'This is her father's only child; he has no other, and he has indulged her, perhaps, but she is used to being with him. She would not be a worry to you as would other girls. She is very self-sufficient.'

'I'll bet. You get out of here,' Abdullah told the girl. 'I wish to discuss this with the Lady Azziza.'

The girl went slowly, tucking her hair back under the *kaffiyeh*. She wasn't too happy, but she didn't exactly look defeated, either. Abdullah glared at her until she was all the way out of the tent.

'Oh lady,' Abdullah burst out, 'what is this you're trying to do to me now? I don't wish to have any women at this time, take my word for it. It is my heart's desire that you do not encourage stray girls to follow me about and try to supply me with that which I do not long for!'

'She is no stray girl!' his grandmother said indignantly. 'This is a well educated girl. She is the pearl of her father's breast – you see how well she speaks English. She is of the sort that I think, now, is best suited to you. The world changes; there are all sorts of women in it these days, and I have no prejudice against girls of good family who are also modern!'

'What the hell has that to do with anything!' Abdullah yelled. The lack of sleep was really beginning to tell in him. 'I'm a busy man! Allah – I have the responsibility of war and my country's destiny upon my soul, so do not harass me with nonsense! If this girl shows up around the lorries at any time I swear I will have her whipped, naked and in public, and you along with her!'

'She has beautiful breasts,' his grandmother said calmly, 'and her aunt assures me she is perfectly formed, even to her garden of private pleasure. Naturally I have not examined her. The girls educated at the Ras Deir school do not allow some of the traditions, but there would be no reason for the family to lie. A nice healthy girl, strong and pretty. She would comfort you.'

Beautiful breasts! That was all he needed to think about.

'I don't need any comforting, Grandmother,' Abdullah said with an effort. 'Let your heart be at peace, I will penetrate thousands of women when I have the time, I promise

318

ou. I am perfectly normal, so do not worry.'

But his grandmother came close to him and for the first time she put her hand up to touch him, a faint look of concern in her eyes. She stroked his cheek.

'What's the matter?' he wanted to know.

'It is always the most beautiful and the most tender,' his grandmother said softly, 'who are the most cruel. Do not be so alone, my darling. I do not wish you to suffer.'

'I'm all right,' Abdullah said, and shook her off. He was still angry. 'I'm just busy, that's all.'

When he came out of the tent she was standing there in the dark, waiting for him, and he didn't even know she was there until she spoke.

'I don't want to sleep with you; I just want to go to the city,' she said. 'I just wanted you to know that.'

'Dammit,' he said, and bent down to pick up a rock and hurl it after her. But she had already disappeared in the dark.

In spite of the Pakistani doctor's warnings in New York and Adam Russell's reminders, he had completely forgotten about the after-effects of being overdosed with LSD, and the heavy charge of phenobarbital he had received from Ameen Said and his friends. He had felt good; there had been no need to remember things like that, and he supposed it had just slipped his mind. The sleeping tablets the Rahsmani doctor at the dispensary had given him put him under into a deep, satisfactory sleep almost at once. But at about two am Abdullah wakened screaming. His body had become glass again and there were all sorts of things around him in the hot, suffocating dark that wanted to grab at him and break him into a thousand pieces.

Don't touch me! Abdullah roared into the night. *Leave me alone!* He was not even sure where he was. Time had betrayed him, New York City and the airport in Kuwait and the smog-bound heights of Beverly Hills were all one and the same. He had to get out of there. Khaz'al and his brother were up in an instant, stumbling about in the dark, also, shrieking to escape the *afreets* and other demons they were sure had come into the tent in the night and were now circling around in the air about them. Abdullah thrashed out of his bed and fell against the cloth walls, making the whole structure shake and tremble as though about to come down on them. It was only when Al-Malih came in and the others had brought kerosene lamps to see what they were doing, that it calmed down at all. Sakir had run off to get the doctor.

'Man, you will raise the whole camp!' Al-Malih panted. They were trying to hold Abdullah down and quiet him. 'In the name of Allah the All-Merciful, cease thy screaming! Consider what it is doing to the others, to hear thy terror in such a manner!'

'The men will run away,' Hussein tried to tell him.

Abdullah heard their voices as if from a great distance, as though the sound came rumbling across the desert from the mountains like the voices of the angels or an earthquake, but he knew what they were talking about. It was terrible; his body was falling around him in pieces every time they touched it. They were breaking him up into little bits, but he clamped shut his mouth, sinking his teeth into his lower lip and tried to stay that way. The sweat broke out on his face.

After a little while the doctor came in, and he could try to speak. 'What did you give me, anyway?' he croaked.

'Chloral hydrate.' The doctor had a small pocket flashlight and was shining it into his eyes. 'What's the matter?'

Abdullah couldn't keep his eyes open. The light was like a knife thrust into his brain. 'Drugs, from New York. My uncles tried to poison me.'

Al-Malih and Hussein, who had been squatting by the low bed, sank back on to their heels in relief. 'He has been drugged,' Hussein said.

'Didn't they tell you not to take anything, even aspirin?' He put the flashlight back into his pocket and reached up and took Abdullah by the hair, sharply, and yanked his head forward on his breast. 'Don't bite your mouth, man,

320

you're bleeding! Fight it! It won't go away, but you can hold it under control if you try. What they're saying is true. If you keep on yelling and screaming the way you did before, they will run away. The men think this of you – that you may be mad like your father.'

'I'm not crazy,' Abdullah said, after a while. The sweat had dripped down into his mouth and he licked at it with his tongue. 'You're a good doctor; I owe my life to doctors. We will need you when we go into the city in the morning. I'm not crazy,' he said again, and closed his eyes. 'There's just so much to think about, that's all. I've got to have a plan; it's got to work out.'

They looked at each other.

'Take slow easy breaths,' the doctor said. He had his fingers on Abdullah's wrist. 'Your pulse is steady, it will go away in a while.'

They sat like that for a long time, Hussein and Al-Malih talking about the lorries in a low voice, the families of the al Asmaris who had come into the camp from the north, the latest news from the city that they had heard on the radio. At last, when they were sleepy again, they took all the lamps but one, leaving the two Bedouin sitting on either side of the bed, to keep watch.

Abdullah looked up at the black folds of the tent billowing over him in the night breeze that had at last come down from the barren hills. It was still very hot. Khaz'al and Sakir had taken off their robes and sat half naked, their bodies gleaming with sweat. Sakir's transistor radio played softly, some girl from Radio Kuwait singing about pomegranates and love.

At dawn they were lucky. Less than a quarter of the men, Al-Malih told them, had left the camp, and these were the ones who probably would have drifted off anyway.

EIGHTEEN

In the morning the sky was overcast, low clouds partly obscuring the empty hills to the west and making it somewhat tricky for the helicopters coming in over them to make their drop but, as Abdullah noted, great for tactical purposes. They couldn't have had better weather if they had ordered it. The cloud cover also helped hold down the heat. As the result of the somewhat cooler weather they were ready and loaded by midafternoon and decided to get started at once in a great noise of clashing gears and shouts and racing engines, eventually forming a line of vehicles that was to travel in three sections, according to Adam Russell's suggestion, with a section boss for each. The plan was to get down the north–south expressway and into the refinery area at abu Deis as fast as possible. From the refinery point the convoys would break away to approach the city from three different directions, coming together finally to join the government forces situated around the Medical Centre. The Saudi helicopters had delivered as promised, but when the weapons were distributed they found that there were not enough M-16 rifles to go around for the number of men on hand, and almost no one knew how to use the grenade launchers. Abdullah sent Al-Malih to pick some of the youngest and brightest among the oil field workers to take all the grenade launchers into one lorry and figure them out as they travelled.

Nothing, they were discovering, was to be done easily. Many of the Bedouin would not give up their tribal flintlocks for the M-16's, and it was eventually decided to let them keep their weapons rather than have them take their families and break camp. A lorry had a flat tyre almost at once as they were moving out, and when the convoys tried to bypass it the men ran out into the road begging to be taken into other lorries rather than stay and fix it. A traffic jam was inevitable. Five miles below Salwah a travelling band of Hammasseh with a hundred sheep blocked the highway. After that, Al-Malih was sent in a jeep to stay ahead and keep the road clear.

In spite of this, everything moved too slowly, and there were a number of accidents. Hussein al Asmari, travelling up and down the first part of the convoy in a small lorry on the shoulders of the expressway, was thrown out when the vehicle hit a pothole, injuring his shoulder. After two hours of mounting confusion Abdullah, riding in the lead lorry, gave orders that the sections were on their own to do the best they could without supervision and the resulting fighting. Almost immediately his lorry was overtaken by a flatbed eight-wheeler used to transport oil pipe, filled with Bedouin singing and brandishing old rifles and swords. They sped off out of sight.

'You can't let them go off without us!' Hussein al Asmari exclaimed. He rode beside Abdullah, his arm in a sling.

Abdullah settled back in the seat of the cab and folded his arms across his chest. The convoys were turning out to be a lousy idea, a disorganized mob on wheels, but there was nothing he could do about it. He supposed they were doing well enough, just to keep moving.

'They're only going to abu Deis,' Abdullah reminded him. 'At least I hope to hell they don't take it into their heads to go straight on into the city.'

It bothered him now that virtually every vehicle had GULF ARABIAN OIL COMPANY plainly marked on the side. It was good it was necessary to come into the city under cover of night. In broad daylight it would look as though the damned oil company was making an invasion, not the new government.

At the abu Deis refinery they finally pulled off the highway and into the asphalt roads that led around the high wire fence and the refinery trucking areas. The main gates were closed and locked, guarded by armed GAROC workers. The abu Deis people weren't taking any chances on a recurrence of what had happened at Ras Deir, when Abdullah had commandeered their lorries and Rahsmani personnel. But there was a small fleet of jeeps and company panel lorries outside the gates to meet them with cans of gasoline and water and a supply of food that they were supposed to add to their own stores. And, encouragingly, a group of volunteers to fight in the city.

Abdullah looked at his wristwatch. There was still a good four hours to wait until dark descended upon them. Some of the lorries still straggled in the north along the highway and would take hours to show up. He sent Hussein off to find Al-Malih and some of Fuad's district government staff with orders to circulate and keep order as much as possible. This was no place to stop and set up bonfires and start the old tribal fighting songs. Abdullah wanted everything quiet.

When the orders had been given Abdullah went down the line of the first section of lorries and found the girl and took her by the arm and dragged her out of the place where she had been riding with some of the Ras Deir oil workers. She half fell coming over the tailgate of the lorry but made no protest, following him along as best she could, stumbling a little in the hard sand and patches of desert grass. They kept going away from the refinery area until Abdullah found a wind-scooped depression big enough so they could slide down into it and be hidden from view. She didn't want to do this. When she balked he gave her a push that sent her pitching forward, coming to rest on her knees. He didn't lose any time; he unbuckled his belt and opened his jeans and slid down beside her.

Eyes wide, she tried to pull away from him.

'What are you doing?' she cried. The thick workman's shirt strained against her breasts. Abdullah held her, and with his free hand began working at the buttons.

'I'm doing what you expected me to do when you came along,' he told her. Since she was an educated girl he knew damned well she understood what he had in mind; certainly she wasn't ignorant as to what came next. And, with any luck, she had had plenty of experience – he had heard the stories about the high school girls at Ras Deir. Besides, besides, she had insisted on coming along when he had ordered her not to.

Now, he found, he was in a hell of a hurry to have her. It had come over him very suddenly. He was angry with her, and that was part of it, but she was also damned pretty. There had been nothing much to do in the last few hours of desert travel but think about her, and in his imagination he had undressed her, peeling off the ugly clothes in his mind and filling in the unknown parts as best he could. He had had several tries at picturing the well-advertised beautiful breasts – small, round and firm, or delicately long and pointed, or even robust and heavy as melons. Any would be perfectly acceptable. He imagined her smooth and naked, with his body upon her and his mouth on her lips. It had been some time since he had last had a woman. Barbra Burchard in Beverly Hills had been the last, and the memory of those encounters did nothing to cool him down.

Only her damned clothes were so hard to get off. She struggled indignantly, rolling from side to side to make it harder, and trying to hit him. He fended off her fists. Also, she wanted to argue.

'Listen, woman,' he snarled, 'do you want me to beat you? Come across and don't give me any crap.'

'You will beat *me*?' she said, amazed. Obviously the thought had never occurred to her. '*Ho* – who do you think you are, *bedu*!'

'What the hell do you mean, *bedu*?' He held on to her, trying to get the shirt out of the way. 'You're just as much a damned *bedu* as I am. Just because your father is a refinery worker you think you're Queen of the World!' He jammed her head back against the sand. 'Your education,' he told her, panting, 'has gone to your head!'

He leaned over her and tried to hold her still long enough to put his mouth on hers, but she jerked her head away. It was as he had thought, she was going to try to make a big deal of it. Well, he was in a hurry, he wanted her like hell, and he was in no frame of mind to stop and argue about it. Nor did he have any intention of returning to the trucks with a woman's scratch marks all over him. He held his forearm across her throat and managed to work the canvas trousers down below the knees. She wore nylon underpants, out of the Indian shops or the GAROC commissary at Ras Deir. Yellow ones, with flowers.

'*Don't!*' she cried. Her voice had changed, all the defiance gone out of it.

Well, she had no reason to get panicky, he told himself. If she'd just stop fighting. He threw himself on her and found her mouth. Her lips were trembling, locked against his.

'Come on,' he told her against her mouth, 'you knew what it was all about or you wouldn't have come. What's the big deal, anyway?'

He heard her draw in a deep, uneven breath. The small face under him was pale, long tapered black eyes wide open and staring up at him as though faced with some terrible vision.

'Don't tear my clothes,' she whispered. 'I haven't got any others.'

She looked as though she were going to weep, but didn't. Wants to chicken out, he thought, watching her. But she was setting him on fire, it was sweeping over him just looking at her. It was hard to explain, even to himself. He told himself that he wasn't going to be rough, no matter what she expected.

'Don't grab at me,' she said in a small voice. She began to unfasten the rest of the buttons on the shirt.

'Leave it on,' he told her. He was in a hell of a hurry. 'Just leave it open down the front.'

Her breasts were very nice after all. Nothing exceptional, not in a class with some of the women he had had in the recent past, but a young girl's breasts, firm and round with overblown pink nipples that glistened. He put his mouth on her and he could feel her shrinking back. He dug his face

326

into her skin, pushing her hands away, savouring it. He could smell a sweet familiar smell of gardens and flowers, mingled with perspiration. It was very lovely. She was as smooth and delicate to the touch as silk.

'God I want you!' he said. He was surprised at the strength of his feeling. 'Don't put on some kind of act, will you? Just cooperate.'

He pushed her knees apart and went into her slowly, something of an achievement considering his hurry. She arched her body up at him and gripped his shoulders with her fingers, hard, but no sound came from her. For a moment it was as difficult as hell, she was very tight and he considered pulling back, but decided to go ahead, not really able to stop, anyway. A long shudder went down her thighs and finally her mouth opened a little under his lips, responding. He kept on, not so slowly now, lifting her a little with his hands under her hips until he felt her give way completely.

'Ow!' she cried, getting her elbow under his chest in her excitement, and then her knee up, awkwardly. She didn't seem to know what to do with herself, all surprise and consternation, growing wilder until he felt the clasp of her flesh fluttering and the heat passing into him. He didn't let himself finish until she dropped her head back, eyes half closed, gasping a little.

It was very nice, very sweet, and he hadn't thought she would get into it so fast. It was plain she was a very passionate girl, if pretty clumsy. He put his head down against her shoulder, his hair brushing the sand, and tried to catch his breath. It was as though he couldn't get enough of her.

'One more time,' he muttered, because he still wasn't satisfied. He put his hand down between their bodies and brought it up and held it to his eyes, frowning. There was a small amount of red. He stared at it. For a moment he couldn't believe what he was seeing. 'Allah, what a disaster!' he cried. 'What have you done to me?'

He had been tricked.

'It's not your responsibility,' she said in the same small voice. 'I did it myself.'

'What the hell do you mean, *you did it yourself?* Dammit, you know how these things go as well as I do!' He thought of his grandmother. He thought of her father. 'We're practically married!' He started to let her go, to push her away from him completely, then thought better of it.

'It hurts,' she said, closing her eyes.

'It always hurts,' he told her savagely. 'Nevertheless, you had your satisfaction. I felt it.'

He didn't know what to do. He wasn't the type who took any pleasure in deflowering virgins. Usually he avoided it at all costs. Now this!

'Oh don't,' she whispered, as he moved. 'I can't.'

'Yes you can. It won't make any difference one more time, you'll be just as sore afterward.' And he really wanted her; it was driving him crazy. He was amazed that she could have such an effect on him. He remembered her supercilious look, the way she defied him. She cried out as he moved more deeply into her and struggled, but even then she tried to give something back, if only to keep from being overwhelmed. But she was no match for him.

It was the last time, for it was growing late and he had to be back with the others, yet it was as though he couldn't stop. He had her completely and thoroughly and it was as though he was in touch once more with the vast earth and the things that flow from it, the things that madden and drive one and yet comfort, too. And deep down inside he was pleased that she had been a virgin and, in spite of her big talk, had known no other man but himself. That was the way it should be, he told himself. And, belatedly, he realized he hadn't been very good to her at all.

'Dammit, I'm sorry,' Abdullah said, finally. 'It takes time; it will be better. I'll make it better for you. At least you're passionate, that's a good beginning. You'll be so again for me, in a little while.'

But she set her chin stubbornly. It was hard for her to speak, her mouth was somewhat swollen and her hair had come partly loose, a strand at the corner of her lips.

'You're hurting my ribs,' was all she said.

He looked down at her. 'I'm going to move away. It will hurt a little.'

'I wish you'd stop instructing me.' She shut her eyes. 'I'm not a child.'

He could see that it would be very easy to become infuriated with her. Nothing seemed to make any impression at all.

When she sat up and began buttoning up her shirt she said, 'Now I want a gun.'

It took him completely off guard. He could only stare. Then, slowly, he began to redden.

'You can't say that to me,' he told her, 'You can't say that to me. I'll put you on your back again and screw you senseless if you think you're going to pull anything like that!'

The dark oval-shaped eyes looked up at him and the resistance was like the shock of a blow. 'I did this with you,' she said, 'because it was my own decision. But now I wish to have a gun like the others, because I deserve it.'

'What do you mean, BECAUSE YOU DESERVE IT?' He tried to keep from shouting because he didn't want the others to hear him. But he couldn't control his hands. They reached up and seized her around the throat. He wanted to shake her as one shakes something infuriating and unbearable. 'Is this some new kind of whoring, for *guns*? What the hell have you picked up at this American school, anyway?'

Even then she did nothing; she couldn't speak, but the black eyes never wavered. He let her go, pushed her away from him. She put her hands up immediately and rubbed her throat.

'Nevertheless,' she said huskily, 'I have loved you. From the moment I saw you come out of the desert, thus —' She couldn't finish it. A strange look came over her face. 'And the camel wouldn't kneel. I will not kneel, either. That is not the kind of woman you need.'

He was amazed to see what was going on, and baffled. A

329

large tear dropped from her lashes and rolled down her cheek. A perfect tear, crystal and sparkling, like a gem.

'Oh crap,' he muttered. It was taking some time to digest all this, it really made him deeply uneasy. But he put out his hand and touched her hair. What a strange girl, he told himself. There was something stirring in him, too, a sort of deep satisfaction that she wasn't what she tried so hard to be, after all. 'Well, don't cry, for God's sake,' he said.

She drew herself up proudly. 'My family were warriors,' she said. The tear dripped off her chin and fell into the shirt. 'The Burada al Asmari, perhaps you have heard of them. We do not weep.'

'I'm sick of hearing about your family,' he told her. But he put his arms around her, tentatively. She was such a small girl. He could feel the softness of her body against him and the stiff, unyielding way she held her back, her legs braced against his thighs. Not giving an inch. After a time he put his hands at the back of her head and moved her face toward him and kissed her. It was a very long kiss and she finally rested against him, warm and uncertain. He discovered this made him almost absurdly happy and satisfied.

'Nevertheless,' he told her, 'if I give you a gun it will only be a pistol, and don't try anything smart with it. You stay with Hussein and don't get in my hair.'

They got up and he helped her out of the sandy depression where they had made love and he brushed her off, his hands moving across the back of her shirt and her small backside, lingering, feeling how pleasant it was to have someone to do this to. 'Smile,' he told her.

And she suddenly smiled at him. It was growing dark but he could see her face fairly well and the smile for him was funny and crooked, but it moved right up to the corners of her eyes, making them wrinkle, a true smile. He threw his arms around her.

'Do you love me?' he said into her hair. The moment the words were out of his mouth he was appalled. It was the last thing in the world he had intended to say, ever. And the words seemed to hang in the air, echoing, not wanting to go away.

'Yes,' she said.

She didn't press him for anything else, and he was relieved. She was a very discerning sort of person, he thought; nothing would have turned him off more at that moment than demands that he love her back, or anything else that he really wasn't ready for. When there was time, he told himself, he wanted to be with her a lot, so that she could talk to him. He imagined she was a very interesting person.

He took her by the hand. When they turned in the dusk they almost ran into someone standing there. They both gave a start, stepped back a pace.

'Abdullah?' the figure said, peering at them.

The voice was James Brooke-Cullingham's. But if it was Brooke-Cullingham, Abdullah thought, he was wearing a damned incredible outfit, a pair of old British army walking shorts ending just above regulation wool knee socks, and with a battered army solar topee pushed back from his forehead. For a moment, Abdullah could hardly keep from laughing. He supposed the Englishman had had the clothes in a trunk somewhere.

Brooke-Cullingham was not sure who it was, either. The apparition had seemed to spring from the earth at his feet, a tall slender young man with longish hair and a wild look, carrying an M-16 rifle in one hand and leading a fairly dishevelled young girl by the other. It was obvious what had been going on.

'Abdullah,' Brooke-Cullingham said with more certainty. 'They said you were somewhere about.'

'Ya, Jim!' It was so good to see the Englishman, like someone catapulted from heaven into that improbable place, that Abdullah was almost overcome. He threw his arms around the Englishman, almost taking him off balance, and hugged him. Then they embraced, kissing first on one cheek and then the other, wrapping their arms around each other and staying that way, affectionately, for a few moments. It was like seeing one's friend and father, both.

'Where the hell did you come from?' Abdullah wanted to know.

'Followed the rumours; wasn't terribly hard. In the city they say you're marching down from the north with an army of thousands. We came up to warn you you'd better get off the main road.'

'It's not an army.' Abdullah stepped back, now, to take a good look at the Englishman. Brooke-Cullingham was as cool as ever, but the strain of the past weeks had dug great pits of fatigue under his eyes. 'We have only enough automatic rifles for five hundred men, so we're short, and some walkie-talkies and grenade launchers that we haven't figured out how to operate. Plus the lorries.'

'That's a damned good show. Congratulations.' Brooke-Cullingham had been studying him just as intently. Now he turned to the girl, eyebrows raised.

'Miss Fatma bint Farid al Asmari,' Abdullah said.

'How do you do?' the girl said to Brooke-Cullingham. She had nice manners; she shook hands in a very direct manner. Abdullah could see Brooke-Cullingham turn very politely correct. It made him very pleased to see Brooke-Cullingham act this way. It confirmed his own feelings.

'Now tell me what the hell's going on,' Abdullah said. 'How did you get here? How did you hear about us? We haven't had a damned bit of information. Radio Rahsmani's off the air half the time and only plays music the other half; Radio Kuwait's news says almost nothing. The people who came with me from Salwah don't know much more, either.'

They were walking toward the lorries.

'Things could be better,' Brooke-Cullingham said. 'If we drag on much longer some of the neighbours are going to step in; that's the big worry. A bit of "protective action". The Libyans have announced they're going to start aiding the rebels.

'The hell you say! Your forces –'

'Don't misunderstand,' Brooke-Cullingham said quickly. 'I'm not in command of anything.'

Ahead of them a small group had detached themselves

rom the line of jeeps and had started toward them. Five men, all wearing the red and black Rahsmani *kaffiyeh* and n nondescript clothes or military castoffs.

'Quick, I want a word with you,' Brooke-Cullingham said in a low voice. 'This is damned near all that's left of any organization on our side – the Rahsmani Emergency Government Council they call themselves. They're mostly your cousins. You'll recognize them when they get here. Of the older ones, only Fuad is still around. He's had the worst of t, the fighting down at the docks. But the rest are hiding but or trying to get their money and their families out of the country. Now listen.' Brooke-Cullingham said hurriedly. 'Of this group about half want a parliamentary government now. They think it's the only thing that will work. With an elected president, naturally. Watch your step.'

Abdullah had only a few seconds to absorb what the Englishman had said before the group was upon them. Then it was the same thing all over again: they had difficulty recognizing him as he had with them; they had all changed so much.

His cousin Mansur was there. Abdullah couldn't believe his eyes. His elegant relative of the manicured hands and expensive appetites was now some tough-looking unwashed acquaintance with a bushy untrimmed moustache, wearing a .38 revolver in his belt and an old tennis sweater with holes in it. Mansur had lost a lot of weight. The bones of his face showed through the flesh, making him appear almost middle-aged. They stared at each other. God knows what Mansur was thinking of him in return, Abdullah told himself. You could think it was funny, at first.

With Mansur was Talal ibn Habib al Asmari, one of the directors of his uncle Fuad's Office of Information. He remembered this cousin. He was one of Mansur's old social set, those al Asmaris who had jobs somewhere but rarely ever went to them. There was another cousin two or three times removed whose name Abdullah couldn't remember; he thought this one had been away at some university in London until recently. Two others, Karim and Sa'ab al

Musheit, were not of the Asmari tribes but a related family in the southern desert. They all spent moments peering at each other, wordlessly. Abdullah was beginning to think that he had changed the most; no one seemed to recognize him at all at first.

Now it was suddenly Mansur who came forward and seized Abdullah's hand and bent and kissed it, the old acknowledgment that was usually given to the Emir.

There was a moment of silence. *So that's how it goes,* Abdullah thought. He took his cousin Mansur by the arm and pulled him up quickly.

'Forget it,' Abdullah told him. He took his cousin by the shoulders and embraced him on both cheeks as he had done with Brooke-Cullingham, and then gave him an extended hug. The greeting of friends, nothing more. Then, deliberately, Abdullah passed on to the two al Musheit brothers and did the same. Except for a moment of hesitation there, they returned it heartily. The cousins, Talal ibn Habib and the one whose name he couldn't remember, were next, and Abdullah took his time about it. He stepped back with each one, afterward, to look and see how they had taken it, this gesture that said there was no need for the old submission to the ruler.

'The change is remarkable. I wouldn't have known you,' Talal ibn Habib said.

'We have all changed,' Abdullah said easily. 'Years have passed in these last few days.'

There was a murmur of assent, nothing more.

'Now let's get down to business,' Abdullah said. He had decided there was no better time for it, right where they stood. It was better to get it thrashed out right on the spot. 'I have brought guns and men and transportation. The government of Rahsmani has not ceased, it is but going through a time of difficulty. But I am not going to let these damned immigrants, whom we have taken in with the best of intentions, grab our land and our oil wells and get away with it. And take it away from us is what they intend to do – in spite of all this shit about Third World and people's

334

rights and the rest of that crap. They are fools if they think we're going to give up what is ours!'

It was the right sort of appeal and yet there seemed to be no clear reaction to it. No one said anything for a moment or two.

'There has been much blood spilled,' one of the al Musheit said cautiously. 'It is our wish to avenge it. Our father was killed. He went to the mosque to pray with many of the old ones and a hand grenade was thrown in among them. In the mosque.'

'They have no respect for anything,' the other one said. Karl Marx is what they pray to.'

'It's not as simple as that.' This was the cousin Talal. There are those who agree with what they say. Ameen Said, the Emir's son by the concubine, is one of their leaders.'

There was a long silence, and Abdullah bided his time, letting them think it over. Then he said, suddenly, 'Have we lost fathers? My grandfather is dead. He was an old man, also; they shot him as he got out of bed. Have we lost mothers, sisters? My wife is dead, and my son, too, cut in pieces by their bullets. They are murderers. They wish to exterminate us. Also, they will exterminate Hakim al Asmari and Ameen Said al Asmari when they have done with them; this is their way. So we will not survive unless we stamp them out. Then we will talk of changes and people's rights and all that. That is, for those who are left.'

The two al Musheit gave a murmur of approval. Mansur nodded. It's the other two, then, Abdullah told himself, and made a note of it and filed it away. But you had to remember that they were, as Brooke-Cullingham had said, all that was left.

Maybe it's enough. Abdullah thought, looking around. Talal will have to be cut out. I don't want him in on anything important. Mansur I can trust, but then you always have to be careful with relatives. Espcially those who have talked about electing a president. That leaves the al Musheit. I can work with those two.

'What's up?' he said. He could tell there was something else going on, too.

'They have cut the pipelines,' Mansur said in a low voice. 'At about four o'clock this afternoon.'

Abdullah shut his eyes for a moment. That was bad. Without the natural gas from the oil fields the city had no fuel, no electricity in a place almost run exclusively by electricity, and no water. The desalinization plant would shut down immediately.

'How bad is it now?' he wanted to know.

'Bad. There was some rioting at first and looting, but now most people merely want to get out. The city is dying. Two days without power and water and it will be finished.'

'They cut their own throats,' Abdullah observed. 'This is a desperate measure. Or just plain stupidity. My uncles will gain nothing but their own destruction.'

'They do not think so. But they have broken up into factions, anyway, and quarrel among themselves. They say a band of Palestinian terrorists, Habash's PFLP, is acting as advisers to the Children of the Fire. Anarchy is all they desire, then the strongest will seize power.'

Abdullah looked from face to face. They still couldn't bring themselves to consider him as any sort of leader, that was plain, although the al Musheit were wavering, and so was Mansur. They waited, sceptically, hoping for something, as they did not know what to do themselves.

'If you set up a provisional democratic government it hasn't got a chance,' he said flatly. 'These makeshifts always fail. We have only one government. We'll have to reestablish its power.'

'Whose government is that?' The voice challenged him. It was fairly dark; Abdullah couldn't see who it was.

'Mine.' He thrust the M-16 before them suddenly, arm extended, so that they couldn't miss it. 'This says so! For my family and the men I have brought with me. For my father and my grandfather and his father before him. The same blood is in me!'

They stood there, thoughtfully, and still could not make up their minds.

'How are we to believe this?' The voice was Talal ibn Habib's, Abdullah was beginning to know it.

'Cut the crap,' Abdullah said in English. 'I want this stopped because we've got other things to do. If you want to argue, here's the argument, right here in my hand. Try me and see.'

'Abdullah –' Brooke-Cullingham broke in.

'You shut up, Englishman – this is our affair! And this is what I say,' Abdullah said to the others, 'that we are now going to do what Abdullah Mubarrak did.'

There was another silence. Some of them did not recognize the name of the former Kuwaiti Chief of Secret Police.

'Who was that?' one of the al Musheit asked, finally.

They had all been to English schools or had had English tutors; they had all read the same English schoolbooks. He would have to pick something all of them knew and recognized and could react to. Abdullah smiled grimly.

'Remember the Red Queen? "Off with their heads!"'

NINETEEN

It was no exaggeration to say that the city was dying. A mile out of the refinery at abu Deis they began to see the first of the refugees struggling along the shoulder of the expressway, the majority of them families pushing their household goods in prams or makeshift carts. These were mostly the poor immigrants from the shanty-towns, the Pakistanis and Egyptians mixed with a few Iranians and even fewer Palestinians. The Rahsmani citizens streamed past in late-model automobiles, speeding northward to safety, and food and water. At the slight rise at the exit to the airport they could see the city before them as a black pool without lights, punctuated only by random fires that stained the night sky with red, and reflected in the sea like spilled blood. A stink of burning, heavy with oil and rubber, hung in the air.

'Get off the road now,' Brooke-Cullingham told one of the al Musheit, who was driving. They had just passed several lorries running with their lights off. The lorries did not stop to look them over but did as they did, speeding away in the opposite direction.

Mansur was sitting beside Abdullah in the back seat of the jeep, the grenade launcher in his lap.

'The idea,' Abdullah said for the third time that hour, 'is to get in and get out fast. Any other way, they're going to pick us off.' But he was thinking about Brooke-Cullingham and the order to turn off the road. He supposed it was all right for the Englishman to give orders, he had had more military experience than the rest of them, but the feeling was growing in him that they did not need Brooke-Cullingham now. He was not one of them. And besides, they

338

didn't need a witness, and a foreigner at that, to what they were about to do.

'Jim,' Abdullah said suddenly, 'I'm going to drop you off at al Zeitouna. That's near enough to the Medical Centre; you ought to get back all right.'

The Englishman said nothing. He's getting used to it, Abdullah thought. Everything's changing, now. And it's just as well.

They left Brooke-Cullingham by the side of the road. As they drove away, Abdullah turned back to look. Brooke-Cullingham appeared very solitary there in the old British army uniform and, from a distance, suddenly very old. They're dropping away, Abdullah thought. Brooke-Cullingham's not part of it anymore, even as little as he wants to be. Crossland is gone; the days of the oil company advisers are just about over. My grandfather, Fawzia, Karim my son, all dead. Wadiyeh, Ramzi Alam have betrayed me. Ali Hassan got tangled up in the pitfalls of friendship and eliminated himself. I'm beginning to think there isn't anybody going to be left but me. And that's damned lonely.

A cloud of smoke was drifting in the streets. In the outer part of town the new apartment houses for government office workers looked abandoned. If there were any people left in them, they were holed up in the last stages of despair, waiting for the fighting to burn itself out or for somebody to come along and do something, anything. The ghostly quality of the empty city, here away from the fighting, was unnerving. But his grandfather's beloved trees, the small park they passed, still smelled of water and greenery and there was the odour of flowers. Something in this haunted Abdullah and made him curiously restless.

The world changes and we are left alone in it, he reminded himself. It can't be the same place, this city, where I once floated along on the surface of things, bored and shut away in that vacuum I made for myself, wanting only to be free of it. Now here it is again, and I'm looking at it, at the destruction and ruin and I want to kill somebody for what's been done to it. It's my whole damned life they're wrecking. I didn't realize it before, but it is.

'We've got to get the damned power turned back on,' was all he said to Mansur beside him.

'To the left,' Mansur directed the al Musheit. 'Up among the big houses at the end of the street. Some of the telephones are still working,' he said to Abdullah. 'You've got to watch out for the bastards. Just when you think the lines are down they get them hooked up to another revolutionary cell and can call for backups.'

All he hoped was that the insurgents hadn't evacuated their families yet. He was counting on their not being able to find a safe place in the countryside, dominated by Rahsmanis, to send them. 'Whatever you do, keep going,' he told them. He was quoting Adam Russell, now. 'Don't stop to help anybody. Each one of us is expendable, even me.'

The other jeep had not showed up as planned; they seemed to have lost it somewhere behind in the city. But they knew it was no time to sit in the dark street and wait for them to show up. They parked at the corner, left the motor running, and began to race for the entrance to the apartment house. There was no one at the outer door or in the lobby; the place was dark as a cave and as silent. They ran into the stairwell, groped their way up the stairs and on to the third-floor landing. When they opened the door to the hall there was a burst of gunfire in the dark. One of the al Musheit opened the fire door, raked the hallway with loud bursts from his M-16 and then stepped back in again. There was no answering fire.

They stepped out into the hallway carefully. Then they went down the hall, half running, blasting each metal apartment door with gunfire, kicking the doors open when the hinges broke. A deep carpet sucked at their feet. The hall was lined with mirrors, their passing like shadows reflected in them. It was an expensive place to live. A fancy table with artificial flowers fell under their feet and they stumbled over it. At the middle of the hallway gunfire suddenly roared out at them.

'Okay, take this one!' Mansur shouted.

The al Musheit came out of an open doorway, cursing.

'What happened?'

'Ah, shit! A bunch of women and kids. I think I got all of them.' He made a gagging noise in his throat.

They lay against the wall at the baseboard, listening to the bullets tear through the metal door out at them. There was more than one AK-47 from the sound of the bursts. Mansur edged along the carpet until he could find a spot on the far side and then squatted and aimed the grenade launcher. There was only a dull *poop!* as it fired and then a tremendous explosion that seemed to scoop them up from the floor and propel them backward, piling them up a few feet farther on. Small fragments were in their clothes and in their flesh. The door had been blown inward. It was dark beyond.

Abdullah scrambled up. 'Fire again, stupid!' he yelled. 'Inside!'

Mansur rolled over, his face bleeding, and put the grenade launcher to his shoulder. The second charge went through the door and into the apartment. Then it became quiet.

They were all bleeding somewhat. Fortunately, they had been low, against the floor, escaping most of the shrapnel that sprayed the hallway when the grenade hit the metal door. Mansur was the worst, he was bleeding profusely. Dust and smoke had settled over them.

'Hurry up, keep moving!' Abdullah shouted.

There was no longer a door and what was beyond was no longer much of a room, walls standing on rubble, a tangle of wood and smoke and blood. The al Musheit and his brother had gone inside one of the bedrooms. One of them came out, dragging something after him. It was still breathing, but not for long.

'What'd we get?' Abdullah wanted to know.

'The Children of the Fire. Some of them are in pieces, about five. What a weapon!' the al Musheit brother marvelled.

'Shit!' Abdullah yelled. 'What are we doing assing around with the Children of the Fire?' Rage spilled over him, he kicked at the broken stuff under his feet. 'I want the god-damned National Police, or Hakim al Asmari or that fart Ameen Said! Not these chicken-shit kid groups! Who's got the damned address list?'

'Come on,' Mansur said, taking him by the arm and dragging him. Mansur was bleeding in rivulets down his face. 'We don't want to get trapped in here. Hit and run was what you said.'

When they came out into the street the other jeep was pulling up behind them.

'We got lost. We can't find any of these damned streets without any lights.' The driver of the second jeep was one of the Ras Deir workers in coveralls and the white hardhat that said GAROC across the front. 'How did you make out?'

Another oil worker with a walkie-talkie said, 'Al-Malih's in trouble. He says he's pinned down at King Qabus and the Sheraton Hotel.'

'He's not supposed to be down there,' Abdullah said. He got into the jeep and sat down beside Mansur, who was wiping his bleeding face. 'God, everybody's getting lost! Okay,' he said to the others, 'they know we're around by now, so keep sharp.'

'I don't think they have any grenade launchers,' Mansur said. 'They would have shot us up if they had. Allah!' he said, looking down at the blood on his hands. 'The first thing to know is not to fire it in a hallway. I'm full of little metal pieces.'

As Abdullah had said, the idea was to strike fast, chop off all their heads, eliminate all the leaders of the insurgent groups they knew of, including the Palestinian factions, the Children of the Fire terrorists, the People's Liberation Army – which was said to be his uncles' outfit – taking them one by one and from the top, families and other hangers-on included. This is what Mubarrak had done in 1956 when the Kuwaitis had had their troubles with the same sort of immigrant groups. It was bloody, but it worked. Al-Malih

342

had been sent to check out the addresses, the People's Liberation Army in particular, and especially wherever Hakim al Asmari might be located. They kept in touch by walkie-talkie after a fashion but had their problems. The transmitters were still something of a mystery. Once, coming around in a circle by the Medical Centre, they caught a conversation with the first line of GAROC lorries entering the city from the west but couldn't get on their frequency. Yet, they told themselves, it was good to know the lorries had made it.

At the corner of King Qabus Street they saw a jeep and they approached it at full speed, thinking it was Al-Malih and his party. But they caught a burst of fire from AK-47's and ran up on the pavement, made a U-turn back into the street and got out of there as fast as they could. At two am they made their scheduled rendezvous in the driveway of Mansur's house. Al-Malih's group was there, waiting. In the dark as they drove up they could see some of Al-Malih's men had fallen out on the deep grass among the oleander bushes, dog-weary.

'Have you got any water?' Al-Malih wanted to know. He came up on the side of the jeep and took the water can from one of the al-Musheit. 'Jesus, what a night!' He was sweating, he had unbuttoned the front of his shirt and it flapped open. 'How are you doing?'

Abdullah shook his head. 'Not much luck. But we've shot up a lot of women and children.' He took the water can himself and had a drink. They had been dying of thirst all night, and he had drunk so much water himself he was feeling bloated. 'Killing women and babies in the dark, it's great work. You can't tell until the last minute who's there, and then it's too late.'

'Yes, I know,' Al-Malih said.

They could hear the dull bumping of dynamite charges to the west, in the shantytowns on the other side of the highway. It had been going on for some time as the Bedouin prepared the fire breaks.

343

'That's where they are,' Mansur said. 'Over in Third World heaven, holed up. That's where we'll get most of them.'

'We raised Hussein on the walkie-talkies a little while ago,' Al-Malih said. 'He's says the big concentration, the tough ones, are pulling out of the docks and coming up to meet us.'

'Fuad should try to hold them. Has anybody heard?' There had been no contact; they didn't even know what the old sheik's position was.

'Try the rest of the places on the list,' Abdullah said. 'Finish up if you can. They're goddamned well somewhere in the city; they've got to be. I want my uncles, Hakim and Ameen Said – when they're dead the plug's pulled out as far as the rest are concerned. But if I can't get both, I'll take one of them.'

He looked around at the group, wet with sweat and rough-edged with fatigue. That which none of them could speak of hung in the air. They had all lost relatives, their homes, some of them, seen their lives nearly wrecked by this damned insurrection, and one would think, Abdullah told himself, that the desire for vengeance would be like a frenzy now, driving them on at any cost. But that was not the way they were finding it. Going about in the night in the deserted streets, ferreting out those who were hiding, shooting up anything that moved, was curiously unrewarding. They needed to meet the enemy face on. Slaughtering the families was not so great. It was as he had told Al-Malih: in the last second before firing one could only guess what was there in the dark, and then it was too late. One of the children had been his own son's age, not quite dead. The second burst, at close quarters, had nearly blown the body apart.

'Let's get going,' Abdullah said. He was finding he didn't know every street in the city, either. They had spent a good bit of time going around in circles like everyone else. And there were still the big houses out on the beach on the road

344

to the airport. They had been abandoned by their owners, but they were said to be occupied by the People's Liberation groups.

Some time later, it must have been three-thirty or so, they came upon a bakery delivery van at one of the ramps to the expressway. The van was full of people with AK-47's and they staged a pitched battle right where they were. But the delivery van sped away when they opened up with grenade launchers.

'I told you so!' Mansur shouted. 'They haven't got these things! Allah be merciful – let them start spreading the word! My arms are so tired I can't lift this damned thing, I swear.'

The fire had been started in the west of the city. They could see the warm, strangely cosy glow of it in the sky, larger than the other fires, a band of yellow at the horizon then turning to orange, deepening to red as it mixed with the night sky. The stink of smoke was already beginning to choke them. Even as far away as the fire was, they could see the black drifts begin to flow down through the city streets.

They had found nothing for hours. There were several abandoned houses on the beach road with doors and windows left wide open and the marks of heavy vehicles in the driveways, but little else. At the last, they had gone up very cautiously, poking around and hoping not to find more women and children left squatting in the dark, hiding from the nightmare outside.

The whole area west of the expressway was slowly filling with rolling clouds of black smoke like a noxious fog. A soft wind seeped from the west, carrying it over the city. The lorries and the Bedouin had been positioned to the north and south of the shantytown and upwind as much as possible, but the M-16's had done their work. The bodies lay like a line of demarcation just this side of the sandy roads that led into the workers' town.

345

Brooke-Cullingham had been standing in the back of a GAROC lorry using his field glasses; now he jumped down and ran toward them. He was at the side of Abdullah's jeep before it had stopped moving.

'Abdullah, for Christ's sake!' he shouted. 'There are whole families in there, thousands of people! The place is saturated with oil; it's going up like a torch!'

Abdullah only looked at him, unmoved.

'Nobody comes out,' he said. 'Not until the men come out. I want the rest turned back to carry the message.'

Brooke-Cullingham stared at Abdullah. The Englishman was deathly pale, his face grimed with smoke.

'Those goddamned Bedouin —' he choked. He stopped, made an effort to recover himself. 'It's insane to set fire to an area like this, in a city without any water! The whole damned place will go up. Use your head, man!'

Abdullah said nothing. What the hell did Brooke-Cullingham expect? He asked himself. The Bedouin were the only people for this sort of work, they were doing what he had told them to do. He hadn't expected anybody to think it was a damned picnic.

'Abdullah, listen.' Brooke-Cullingham put his hand on the frame of the jeep and leaned on it, heavily. 'They're burning alive in there. Bedouin keep turning people back. They sent a boy back in there. His clothes were on fire. They shoot them if they try to come out!'

Abdullah sat in the jeep and regarded Brooke-Cullingham without expression. Now, he thought, I suppose this takes care of the speculation about my strength of leadership. None of them will admit it, but what they've been doing these past few weeks is going around looking for the one who has the stomach for the real dirty work. And now they've found him. In the end I suppose my fame will be right up there for all of them to remember, along with the deeds of my esteemed ancestors. I've burned whole populations alive. I've made my mark shooting up innocent women and children. You can't top that.

It was just too goddamned bad about James Brooke-Cullingham.

'War is hell,' Abdullah said flatly.

Brooke-Cullingham stared at him for a long moment, his eyes gone suddenly tired and cold.

'I'd like to have your permission to leave,' the Englishman said, curiously formal. 'I'd like to go back to the Medical Centre.'

'Go right ahead.'

Mansur said, 'Are you going to get out?' Even he looked somewhat shaken.

The two al Musheit brothers had got out of the jeep and were standing there watching the glowing red towers of flame shoot up into the night. The wind carried the sound of screaming and gunfire from somewhere on the right where the Hammasseh tribesmen were stationed.

Abdullah climbed over the side of the jeep and came down in the sandy road. Even here the earth was greasy with oil, the cheap crude used in the shantytowns for lighting and cooking. As Brooke-Cullingham had pointed out, the whole place was like a torch.

Someone touched Abdullah on the shoulder. It was Al-Malih. Even he couldn't keep his eyes from the flames, following the great fountains of fire building.

'Come over here. I want to show you something,' he said.

Al-Malih's jeeps were parked down the road. There was a tangle of lorries around them; the Bedouin were coming and going to get cans of water. They had all been racked with thirst during the night. Now the smoke was making it worse.

Khaz'al lounged in the back of Al-Malih's jeep, his arm thrown across the seat, partly supporting a figure dressed in a dusty black business suit, the shirt open at the throat.

'Take a good look,' Al-Malih said. 'He's a little messed up, but I think we got the right one this time.' He grasped the hair with one hand and pulled the head back so that the light from the fire could catch the face.

347

It seemed that he was asleep, a somewhat disordered sleep, for the mouth turned down bitterly at the corners as if considering the dream and finding it distasteful. You could see the beautiful Egyptian concubine in him, the long oval eyes, the incredible deep eyelashes a woman would have longed to have for her own. And yet, Abdullah thought, as he bent over Ameen Said, for the love of Allah, truly – he has made us like brothers! There is so much of the old man in both of us, now. It's as though I'm looking at my own death! It was so senseless. They had been raised strangers and enemies, to kill each other. When it might have been otherwise.

'It's him,' Abdullah said. And then, because he knew it was expected of him he said, 'It is good, he was the killer of my grandfather and my son, and the murderer of others. It is right he should be dead.'

Al-Malih turned to look in the direction of the fire. The screaming had grown louder, a great pitch of agony mixed with bursts of fire from the M-16's.

'Do we have to hang around here?' Al-Malih wanted to know.

Abdullah shrugged. It was time, he supposed, to pull back a little and consider letting some of them out. What he had already done had assured his fame for all time – for whatever that was worth. 'Go and tell the Hammasseh to fall back to the outer road where there's some space, and start letting the women and kids that are alive come out. The men won't show until the last minute, and then they'll probably try to rush us. There's no need to shit around – shoot them down, even the ones with their hands up. Most of them will be carrying grenades, anyway. If I find one live male I'll set the *bedus*' clothes on fire, personally. You tell them that.'

Khaz'al was grinning from the back of the jeep. 'What do you want me to do with this one?' he cried.

Abdullah did not bother to turn.

'Pick him up and take him over to the fire, to a spot that is burning well, and throw him into it. In this way no one will seek to find the body, either to abuse or honour it.'

I'm glad he's dead, he repeated to himself. When you come right down to it, there's no other way. And eventually I'll find Hakim al Asmari and kill him, too, and take care of that. Then I suppose I just sit and wait until the next one comes along. There's always another, that's what they tell me.

Later, when it was dawn and he had searched among the lorries of Hussein's section near the Medical Centre for the best part of half an hour, he found the girl curled up in the back of an oil-pipe transport, a blanket thrown over her. He crawled in beside her.

'How are you making out?' he said, pulling the blanket away. Then, 'What the hell's happened to your face?' He turned her face with both his hands so that it could catch the light and he could see. There were spots red as insect bites across her forehead and cheekbones.

'Glass,' she said. 'It will come out. It is from the door of the hotel down the street, when they shot the grenade launchers. It was a big battle, the others fighting against the old sheik. We killed most of them.'

He drew her close to him. 'I hope to hell you're satisfied,' he told her. It was hardly his own voice, almost burned out with smoke and weariness. 'I hope to hell you never lift a gun again. I'm damned sick and tired of people who want to kill. I don't want any woman like that around me.' He slid down and buried his face against her shirt, smelling the warm comforting scent of her skin, feeling the softness of her body. 'Women shouldn't want to kill anything, they should want to have babies and make things grow, and love things.'

She gave a great sigh. 'That is true.' Her fingers stroked his face and pulled back his hair from his forehead and tried to smooth it.

You don't know what I've done, he thought, but you'll hear about it. And I don't wish to speak of it to you or try to explain it, I wish there only to be a great silence between

349

us on this one thing, forever. I wish you only to love me. I am going to be in great need of someone to love me from now on.

'I can't stay very long,' he told her. 'I've got to get up and go around and let everybody know where I am.'

TWENTY

The sun on the sea was very brilliant, the shifting surface of the water reflecting spears of light like a moving mirror on to the stucco walls of the terrace and the ceiling of the room beyond where Abdullah was dressing. A beautiful day, heavy with the heat of morning, sent small white clouds across a crystal sky, broken now and then with ominous trails of thick black smoke like the forerunners of a storm. Abdullah came out on the terrace to look, craning his head out and up to see toward the city.

'What's burning now?' he called to Adam Russell.

The Englishman came out on the terrace. 'It may be the Medical Centre again. That's the direction.'

'Hell, I thought the Medical Centre was gone.'

Russell shrugged. 'There's still plenty left to burn. The surgical wing's still standing.'

Abdullah frowned as a heavy billow of black appeared from the west, passed over a broken abutment of the fort above him and wafted out to sea. 'Well, go and find out about it. Something's burning like hell.'

The sight offended him. And the smell of burning, which he had grown to hate, was starting all over again. Russell turned back to use the bedroom telephone. His wife had followed Abdullah out on to the terrace, the folds of the ceremonial *disdasha* over her arm, to see what he was talking about. Bisharah was not far behind her, his face set unhappily, holding the embroidered slippers in one hand.

Abdullah stood in his underwear, hands on hips, watching them as they leaned out to see the smoke. Bisharah followed her everywhere. I was bad enough, he thought, that the Bedouin was jealous of Khaz'al and Sakir but now, it appeared, he was going to be jealous of Fatma, too.

'Hey, baby,' he said to his wife in English, 'why don't you let Bisharah dress me? That's what he wants. He hasn't got much to do, and you're giving him a nervous breakdown taking over some of his jobs.'

Fatma only leaned farther out over the terrace wall to watch a particularly large plume of smoke go past. 'Why don't you tell him to go stand in the corridor and guard the doors?' she said, unconcerned. 'He gets in the way, here. Every time I turn around I bump into him.'

Abdullah took the slippers from Bisharah. 'Go guard the door and do not come back in until I tell you. I wish to beat my wife; she is impertinent.'

A small smile of satisfaction lit Bisharah's face, and he left.

'You wouldn't really beat me, would you?' Fatma said, turning away from the edge of the terrace.

Abdullah put his arms around her and pulled her close. 'Maybe just a little,' he said, 'and only because it's sexy.'

He was kissing her when Russell walked back out on the terrace. 'Damn, what do you want now?' he said to Russell.

'You wanted to know about the burning.' Russell sat down in one of the terrace wicker chairs and put his feet up on a small table. 'It's the hospital right enough but they've got the pumps going, they say it ought to be under control shortly. Evidently it wasn't put out right in the first place. By the way,' Russell said, 'Charlie Averbach is here in the first city, came in this morning. He wants to make an appointment with you to discuss a number of things. Top priority, I gather, is getting some of his firefighting equipment back.'

'I'll think about it.' Abdullah's words were muffled, he was getting the ceremonial *disdasha* over his head. 'GAROC can sit on their asses and wait a while like everybody else. Averbach's come down to argue about the takeover. That's his problem. Well I can't take time to do it, not with half the city still on fire.' Abdullah looked down at the robe, which only reached just above the ankles. 'Jesus, what happened?' he said.

His wife stared at it, too. 'I think you're taller than your grandfather now,' she ventured.

He couldn't believe it. His grandfather was a tall man, he always towered over him. 'That's impossible. It must have shrunk.' He turned to Russell. 'Did you see Brooke-Cullingham?' The Englishman had left that morning.

'Yes, looked a bit fagged out. This has been hard on him, you know. I gather he wasn't too sorry to get away.'

'That's what he told me. Make a note – in addition to the money and all that I think we ought to give him a medal. Meritorious service, bravery under fire, something like that.' Abdullah stood for a moment, examining the bottom of the *disdasha*. There wasn't even any way to make it longer that he could see. 'And how about you, Adam?' he said suddenly. 'Will you be happy to leave when the time comes?'

'Not me,' Russell said imperviously. 'There's nothing in Twickenham for me. I'm a career man.'

'That's good.' He saw Russell wasn't going to respond to the needling. 'We need the English now, good, neutral people; they help to keep the Americans out of our hair. Listen,' he said, 'you need to get married, settle down here. Assures loyalty. My wife's got a few hundred female cousins you can look over, if you want to.'

'Hmmm,' was the only response. Then, 'When do you want to meet with Averbach?' Russell had his notebook out.

'Hell, I don't know. Haven't we got some UN mission coming in now, and the Mitsumi people? We're booked tight for months. Listen, do something about the hotel situation – get that damned Hotel Board off their butts. Right now we don't have enough hotels to go around, not in good shape, anyway. Find out how soon they plan to rebuild. Let's fix up Mansur's house for the time being. How about a couple of Hakim's palaces?'

There was a stir at the outer doors to the apartment and his grandmother swept through the bedroom, looked around, and then came out to the terrace where they were. She gave Russell, his feet on the small table, a glittering look. Russell took his feet down quickly and stood up. Fatma she did not look at, at all. She threw her arms around Abdullah, pressed him to her bosom passionately.

'Bibi, my darling, my little leopard,' she crooned. 'How beautiful you look!'

'As do you, O lady,' he responded politely. 'Your beauty and brilliance put the moon and stars to shame.' Actually, he told himself, his grandmother was looking really great. Now that she was installed once more in the fort with her supply of creams and beauty machines, she was completely restored to her former glory. The new, paler shade of her hair, a muted cinnamon, was very becoming, and she wore a voluminous chiffon red and orange cocktail dress embroidered in glass beads and pearls. The sun caught the dress and went mad in a shower of sparks.

'Bibi,' she cried, 'the Sudanese is in the *hareem*! O tell me, my beloved, why is the evil presence still remaining here, to breathe the very air of your house and poison it? Tell me, sweetheart, did you know that this was so?'

'She has always been here, lady,' he told her, 'even during the fighting.' He took his grandmother's hands down from his shoulders and held them between his own, comfortingly. 'She has no other place to go. Remember, she is not a full wife, only a concubine, disgrace is upon her because of the treachery of her son Ameen Said, and she has no friends. There are those who would wish to kill her and gain merit by so doing. I tried to give her a house, but she refused it. So I told her that she could stay.'

'No!' His grandmother drew back from him and flung her arms wide, dramatically. 'You are too innocent, my lamb! I know this despicable one from long ago – the street spawn of Cairo, sold by her family, the garbage of Egyptian *souks*! Believe me, she was the whore of thousands before he brought her to his bed! She will defame your house, poison your wife – attend me, I am serious – murder your children!'

354

'Grandmother, calm down a minute, will you? I can't toss her out on the street; it wouldn't look good. If it upsets you, I'll think of something else. God knows I don't want any more women hanging around the damned *hareem*, I want to close the thing down. Listen,' he said persuasively, 'how about lunch tomorrow? We'll have it together in the old dining room, vast as a thousand tents, just you and I.' Over her shoulder he saw his wife make a face. That blows tomorrow, he thought, but I have to do something. Nobody's paid any attention to my grandmother lately, and she's been through hell. 'Go now,' he said, giving her a gentle push. 'The hour grows late, and I have to make this damned meeting.'

'Bibi, there is much I have to tell you!'

'Tomorrow,' he promised. After she had gone he turned back to Russell and said, 'Now, where were we?'

'You were going to take that off, I think,' Russell said. 'It doesn't quite cover your legs.'

'Fatma, for the love of Allah, bring me a plain one, will you?' he called to her. 'Let's get off to a whole new start. A plain white robe and an ordinary red and black Rahsmani *kaffiyeh*, that's more my style. You can't tell me apart from the Bedouin. Man of the common people and all.' The idea appealed to him. 'Besides, you can't say I haven't sweated out my time with my subjects – I've fought in the streets with them, I've crossed the goddamned desert on a camel, I married an oil worker's daughter out of the Ras Deir high school. As images go, you can't beat it.'

'That reminds me,' Russell said. 'You have a request from *Newsweek* for an interview. They want to do a cover story on oil government rulers, especially enlightened types like yourself. And can you let them know as soon as possible.'

'I just gave a damned press conference.' He remembered that was yesterday. *Enlightened types?* he thought, and paused to think it over. He wondered just how enlightened they would think he was, anyway. He hadn't even considered it. 'You figure out if we need all this publicity, and for what,' he said, cautiously. He had been burned in that

355

fire once before. Fatma had returned with a white *disdasha* that she shook out now, waiting for him to put it on over his head.

'Forget the dagger,' Abdullah told her. 'I haven't got room for it.' He pushed the ceremonial weapon away. He carried a Smith and Wesson .38 now, stuck in his belt. These days he practically slept with it. 'Give me the agenda,' he told Russell.

His grandfather used to go into the small council meetings with everything in his head and rarely forgot the order of business. But, Abdullah told himself, he wasn't ready for that yet. It was safer to have everything written down. The list Russell had given him of topics to be taken up was long; he doubted they would get through half of it.

'Take out two-thirds of this,' he told him, handing him the paper. 'Pick out the most urgent things for today.'

Russell frowned. 'It's all urgent. If I take out half, it means you'll have to call another council meeting in two or three days.'

'Call one every damned day until we get it all taken care of,' Abdullah told him. 'The city's on an emergency basis; there's no need to screw around. Get everybody up here at six am if necessary.'

He went into the bedroom where his wife had laid out the red-and-black-checkered *kaffiyeh* on the bed, the black silk headrope curled beside it. She had learned to let him do this last thing himself. He had grown fussy about the way he wore his *kaffiyeh* now and preferred to fold and drape it just so, the rope tilted at a rakish angle over one side of his head. It had become his trademark.

Russell lounged against the door jamb, watching him. 'Brooke-Cullingham said to keep your eye on the south. You're going to have full-fledged war down there. The People's Republic of Yemen is helping the rebels. That means Chinese-made arms, and a lot of them.'

'Poison the wells,' Abdullah said, turning. He saw Russell's startled expression. 'I mean it. Send some of Fuad's Hammasseh tribesmen down there to do it. It's the

356

old-fashioned way of getting things back in line in a hurry. They can put something in the wells that's bio-degradable and that will wear out in a couple of months, I don't want the water wrecked permanently. But it's all desert down there; the wells are vital. After a few hundred of those bare-foot bastards have been exterminated they'll get the hint.'

'Perhaps we should take this up later,' Russell said hastily. He looked at his watch. 'We're running half an hour late, as it is.'

Abdullah bent to look in his grandfather's old pier glass, his image framed in Venetian gilt work of cupids and ribbons and doves with gold olive branches held in their beaks. A sun-darkened young man, rather older than he had expected, looked back, a stranger with a hard gleam in his eyes. He regarded his reflection thoughtfully. His grandfather used to say that a man was shaped by his deeds. Obviously, there had been some changes.

Bisharah had come in now and stood behind him. 'The two Salwah Hammasseh wish to enter,' Bisharah told him. 'I said that I would ask.'

'They have permission,' Abdullah said. He thought he had made that clear, that they had permission to come and go, too. But it looked as though Bisharah would make an issue of it. Each and every time.

Khaz'al and his brother came into the bedroom, dressed for the council meeting, their white tribal robes rustling as they moved. Carefully, they found a cleared space between the bed and the wardrobe and then lowered themselves to the floor, flat on their stomachs, their hands out above their heads and nearly touching a pile of discarded clothes. When they began to recite the long formal greeting with the blessings of God invoked, Abdullah cut them short.

'Get up, dammit; you're getting dirty. What is it now?' Something was going on. He could tell by the way they looked at him, nervous as she-camels and nearly trembling.

'O lord, our father is here. He wishes to speak to you,' Sakir said.

Behind him, Russell pointed to his wristwatch and shook

357

his head. It would have to wait. They were running late.

'Bring him in,' Abdullah said.

He turned to Russell and Fatma, who had started to come in from the terrace. His wife was all right; there was only time for a word of warning to the Englishman. 'Show nothing,' he said quickly. 'The father is here.' He saw Fatma's lips tighten. She went back out on the terrace at once.

The old man came in now with his two sons, dressed in an old robe of fine white wool that was virtually a museum piece. He was as weathered and dry as the trees one finds at the last edge of the desert and as tenacious of life, the small eyes like onyx, glistening. He did not prostrate himself. Instead, he gave the salutation of hand to mouth and forehead, slowly.

'The debt is paid, O lord Emir,' the old Bedouin announced.

'Allah is merciful,' Abdullah responded.

'Forgiveness is yours to bestow.'

'It is only God's to give, truly.'

'Yes, it is written,' the old man said with some satisfaction. He paused now to look Abdullah over thoroughly, the eyes like a lizard's. 'I see thy grandfather in thee, Abdullah ibn Tewfik ibn Ibrahim.'

'Thanks be to God, then,' Abdullah said cautiously. He could see Russell following all this out of the corner of his eye, impatiently.

'For my sons,' the old man cried, 'who have known your mercy, and for myself, to wipe out the dishonour. It is done!' The old man knelt suddenly and laid a bundle of red silk at Abdullah's feet. A loose knot held it at the top. The fingers worked the knot open. What was inside was wrapped in the plastic wrap that could be bought in the government commissary at Salwah and that the *bedu* used now as ground cloths and all-purpose coverings when on the move. The old man peeled the plastic away, carefully, as one would the wrapper around a sandwich.

'He came to me, honour giving him no other place to go,

and knowing this would be done. And I told him that I would do it by my own hand, as is the custom. Allah is merciful and compassionate. Surely for the God-fearing there is a place of forgiveness.'

'Paradise will be his refuge,' Abdullah said. 'For it is true, he loved only God.'

The plastic wrap had held in the heat and the gases and the head was not in good shape, but it didn't take much to recognize Wadiyeh al Qasim. The Hammasseh were still fine swordsmen and the head was severed as neatly as though a surgeon had done it. It was hard, Abdullah thought, to kill your son with a single sword blow and see that it was done well, too.

Now the old man rose to his feet, seized Abdullah's hand, and looked deep into his eyes. Finally he bent and kissed the back of his fingers.

'God is good,' he said judiciously. 'He has favoured you. This I have heard, that you are young and wilful, but with the strong mark of the ruler on thy brow. Now I see it. In time, you will achieve wisdom. May God be good.'

Abdullah took the old man by the shoulders and drew him close and kissed him deliberately on each cheek, going very slowly. 'Travel with God,' Abdullah said. 'May your day be well, the hours untroubled. We meet in Paradise.'

When the two Hammasseh had taken their father out Adam Russell looked down at the bundle at Abdullah's feet and said, 'Good lord! What will we do with it?'

'I can't worry about it now,' Abdullah told him. He looked at his watch. 'Let's get on with this damned meeting. How late are we now?'

They picked their way down the corridors of the fort carefully, for the walls that had been damaged with gunfire were being repaired and there was rubble underfoot and pans of fresh mortar left laying about. When they entered the council hall the members were in their assigned places, sitting on the several layers of Persian carpets, close under the banks of bright fluorescent lights. Before each council member was a serving of Turkish coffee on a low wooden tambour. The dates and hard candy had already been passed around.

On the far right in his accustomed place Abdullah's uncle Fuad al Asmari rose up like a grizzled mountain, his white robes billowing about him, his left arm in a cast where it had been broken by a bullet from an AK-47 in the recent fighting. Next to Sheik Fuad sat Abdullah's cousin Mansur al Asmari, newly appointed head of the Ministry of Education and Public Works. And next to him and the only one of the al Asmari family not in traditional clothes was Al-Malih al Asmari, new director of the Rahsmani Overseas Investment Corporation. Adam Russell slid quietly into James Brooke-Cullingham's old seat. Sam Crossland had retired. There was to be no oil adviser to the government now, as the government was in the process of organizing the Rahsmani Oil Company Limited. The new member of the Council, Ahmed Sullakh al Husseini, represented the People's Socialist Democratic party. He was a Rahsmani but not one of the al Asmari family, a graduate of Oxford and Harvard, the editor of the former underground newspaper *Free People* and associated, at least politically, with the insurgent movement. The selecion of al Husseini as a council member had been a fairly agonizing process; Abdullah had finally got his name proposed by the new Constitutional Committee, which had been formed by young Rahsmanis and representatives of the noncitizen groups. It had taken time to bring one of the radicals out into the open, even to sit on the council, and al Husseini was the only one willing to do it.

Abdullah sat down in his grandfather's gilt-trimmed, red velvet armchair with the special Reclino-rest construction his grandfather had been so fond of when he was alive, custom built so that he could elevate his legs during attacks of the gout. In the first few moments, trying to get used to the thing, Abdullah knew he should have come into the council hall earlier to try it out and see how he could fit his body into it. He didn't want it to suddenly swing into RE-

360

CLINE when he was least expecting it. Bisharah stood behind him, in his place as the traditional Bedouin bodyguard, and behind Bisharah were Khaz'al and Sakil.

'Well, here we are,' Abdullah said, and repeated it in Arabic with all the formal embellishments for the sake of his uncle Fuad. 'Now let's get down to business. I want a report of this new fire and the condition of the damned hospital complex, which seems just about to have had it. How do we get the names of the best architects we used before? There must be a copy of it somewhere.' One of the buildings that housed the records of the Department of Public Works had been a casualty of the fire.

Adam Russell hadn't been able to locate the list of architects but he had some other figures in hand. It was suggested they bypass the usual bids on construction of new buildings and merely contract directly with the firms that had proven themselves in the past. Construction had been somewhat of a sore spot anyway; too many foreign firms had thrown up buildings that fell apart almost before they were opened. The West Germans had a good reputation. The voice of Fuad al Asmari interrupted part way through. His arm was hurting him and he wanted to know when they would get to the business of allotting bonuses to his fighters who had carried the action so successfully in the city dock areas.

Abdullah listened, pausing now and then to feel for the Smith and Wesson police special tucked in his belt. He was not yet accustomed to wearing it. Now and then a nervous thought nagged at him that some sudden movement, such as bending forward too abruptly, might send a bullet through his crotch. It was something to think about.

'Let us have a public accounting of the government incomes!' a voice cried out. 'Let us publish the amounts of oil royalties and see how much of this money is truly allotted for public works! And a committee should be formed, to plan for a new hospital complex that suits the needs of all people!'

For a moment there had been a visible start, then the

heads turned in the direction of the new member. Abdullah squinted against the fluorescent lights to see the face of al Husseini, a young man already growing a little bald, burning eyes behind horn-rimmed glasses. Damn, Abdullah told himself, that's getting off to a fast start.

'We haven't got time for a people's committee,' he said mildly. 'When we get the buildings up, we'll take the matter under consideration.'

'Also,' the voice went right on, 'the people of this country should have a public statement from the government on how it plans to produce and sell its oil on the world market, and at what pegged price. And what agreements we will have with the Organization of Petroleum Exporting Countries about this.'

'The Gulf Arabian Oil Company,' Abdullah said, 'will continue to market Rahsmani oil under the present agreement. The production and refining remains with the Rahsmani government, under the new Rahsmani Oil Company Limited.'

'The oil belongs to the people!' al Husseini shouted. He swept off his eyeglasses. 'To be used as a political weapon against Western imperialist aggressors! It cannot do this if the capitalist exploiters control any part of it!'

'Yeah, well, the capitalist exploiters have got to hold up their end of it for the time being,' Abdullah said dryly. 'As no one around here is exactly a world oil marketing expert as yet.'

Abdullah had gestured with one hand. Now, he found to his surprise that Bisharah was trying to put something into it. A piece of paper. Abdullah took it and opened it up. The message said: 'Take note, O my beloved, his father's half brother was of the Halaby family of Jaffa, my father knew them well. These Halabys were very active in the Palestinian movement and the Arab League, and also in Jordan, later.'

Abdullah stared at the paper in his hand. The message, written with a ball-point pen, was in his grandmother's cramped handwriting. For a moment he told himself not to look, then curiosity got the best of him. Very carefully, he leaned his elbow on the arm of the chair and inclined his head so that he could look out of the corner of his eye. The wooden screen stood in its usual place, slightly to the back of where he sat. From it wafted the strong scent of Joy, advertised as the world's most expensive perfume. Abdullah balled up the piece of paper with the message on it and looked around. The old brass tray on its wooden stand stood at his side. He tossed the paper on to it.

'The money!' Sheik Fuad was bawling, trying to override the voice of the Third World. 'Pay my fighters what is due them without delay — it requires only this cheque business from the Accounting Department! The money building still stands; there are still people working in it — do we return to this execrable paperwork that has so entangled us in the past, or do we make short work of it? Pay your armies!'

'The armies have been paid,' Abdullah said. 'Russell took care of it. We will get into the matter of the bonuses shortly.'

'Some sort of planning commission should be set up,' Russell was trying to say. A municipal planning commission had been one of Brooke-Cullingham's pet projects. 'Not only for the construction of an expanded Medical Centre but for the rest of the city, also. To begin with a survey, I have a preliminary report on the buildings lost to the fire. One hundred per cent damage —'

Bisharah was back again. Abdullah took the note from him. This one said: 'Fuad al Asmari grows old. Always he talked too much, now it is worse. He has a promising son, the one who works for Hussein al Asmari in the northern district government offices, Sa'ab ibn Fuad al Asmari. This one could take the old man's place.'

Abdullah balled up the piece of paper and threw it beside the other on the brass tray.

At moments like these, he remembered, when the talk all moved at once and at cross purposes, his grandfather used to draw into one of his instant meditations, wandering among the *surahs* of the Qur'an he loved so much, like a man indulging in some private, endlessly comforting world of his own. Unfortunately, Abdullah told himself, he didn't have one damned quotation that he could recall of anything. Not one scrap of poetry, nothing at all of that rote learning in classical Arabic that sustained the older generation. All he could do was sit and watch and try to pay attention to what would become, he was sure of it, years of endless jabber with damned little work of real value stuck in between.

When they got the parliamentary system going it would be simpler. Then all the different factions could talk themselves to death for the benefit of the newspapers and the constituents. While he kept a firm grip on the stuff that mattered.

It was going to take a hell of a lot of patience, he told himself. He wondered what in the hell his wife was doing right then. And his grandmother, that wily old lady peeping through the filigree screen and making notes. It had been smart of her to gather the information about the Third World member's Palestinian connections. It was useful, but he couldn't let the Lady Azziza sit behind the throne, literally and figuratively, for too damned long. After a minute he told himself, I'm going to shut them up. Fuad is right, we ought to get the bonus cheques issued and keep the loyal ones happy; they're our strength. Deciding how much is the only thing. No need to load them down with money when they already have more than they can spend. And then, idly, he remembered that in the garage on the ground level of the fort, he had found his Harley-Davidson, covered with a dirty tarpaulin behind the last row of the Emir's Cadillacs. He thought about it for quite a few long moments as the voices went on around him.

'All right,' Abdullah said abruptly. 'The subject under discussion is the construction for the new Medical Centre complex, and a survey of buildings lost to the fire in recent weeks. I see by my notes,' he said, consulting the typewritten sheet Adam Russell had given him, 'the new member, Mr Ahmed Sullakh al Husseini of the People's Socialist Democratic party, wishes to make a few remarks.' He lifted his arm and took a long, deliberate look at his wristwatch. 'That will be the last order of business. We'll adjourn at eleven o'clock, sharp.'